MIDDLE SCHOOL MISADVENTURES

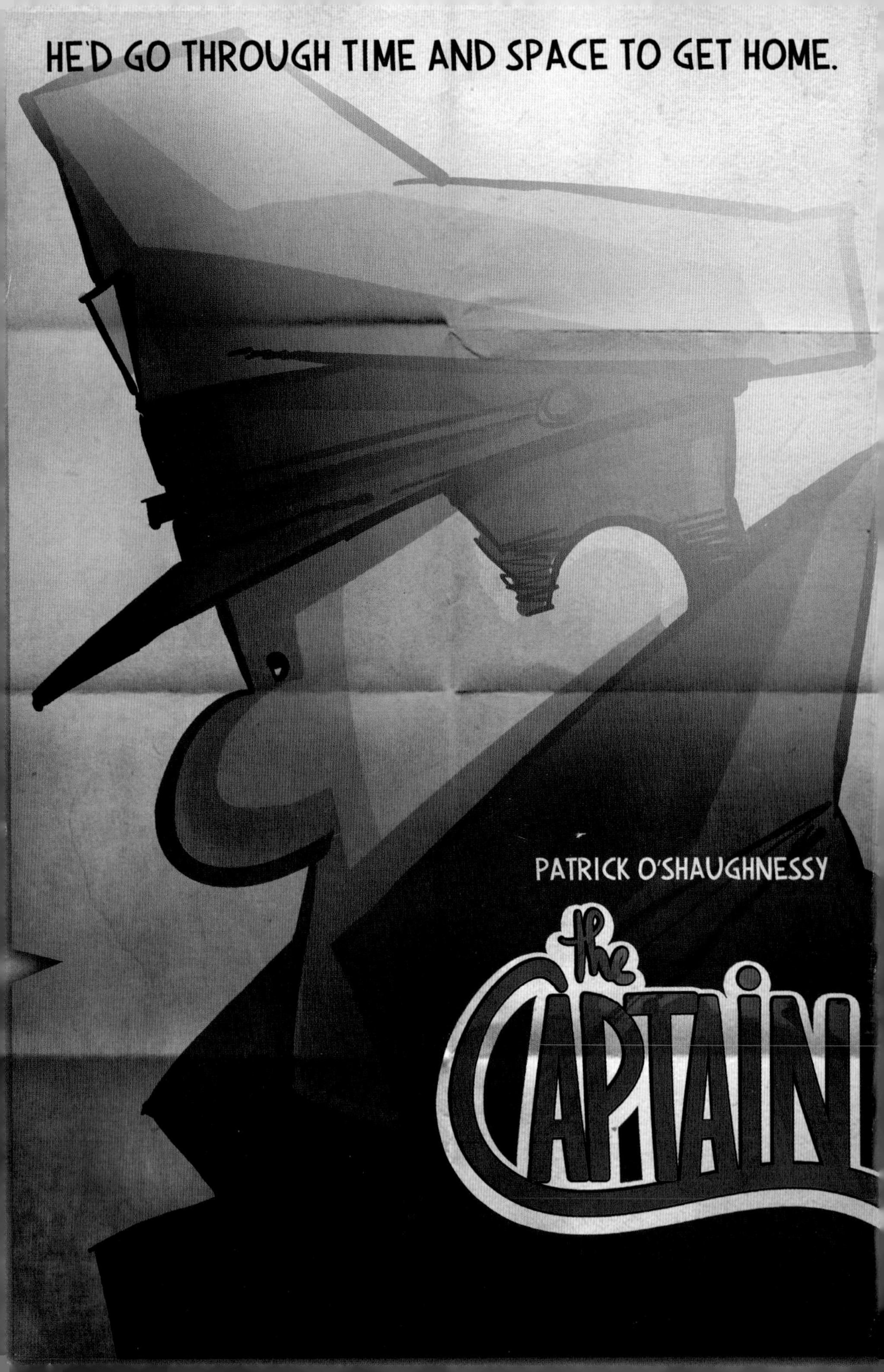
HE'D GO THROUGH TIME AND SPACE TO GET HOME.
PATRICK O'SHAUGHNESSY
the CAPTAIN

MIDDLE SCHOOL MISADVENTURES

OPERATION: HAT HEIST!

JASON PLATT

LB

LITTLE, BROWN AND COMPANY
NEW YORK BOSTON

ABOUT THIS BOOK

The illustrations of this book were done in Corel Painter on the Wacom Cintiq companion and colored in Adobe Photoshop. This book was edited by Rachel Poloski and designed by Christina Quintero. The production was supervised by Virginia Lawther, and the production editor was Lindsay Walter-Greaney. The text was set in MisterAndMeBook, and the display type is MisterAndMe.

Little, Brown and Company
Hachette Book Group
1290 Avenue of the Americas, New York, NY 10104
Visit us at LBYR.com

First Edition: April 2020

Little, Brown and Company is a division of Hachette Book Group, Inc.
The Little, Brown name and logo are trademarks of Hachette Book Group, Inc.

The publisher is not responsible for websites (or their content) that are not owned by the publisher.

Library of Congress Cataloging-in-Publication Data
Names: Platt, Jason, author, illustrator.
Title: Operation: hat heist! / Jason Platt.
Description: First edition. | New York ; Boston : Little Brown and Company, 2020. | Series: Middle school misadventures | Summary: When Newell's very special hat is taken away at school, he and his most talented friends concoct the perfect plan to get it back.
Identifiers: LCCN 2019022189 | ISBN 9780316416900 (hardcover) | ISBN 9780316416894 (pbk.) | ISBN 9780316416917 (ebk.) | ISBN 9780316537148 (library edition ebook)
Subjects: LCSH: Graphic novels. | CYAC: Graphic novels. | Stealing—Fiction. | Middle schools—Fiction. | Schools—Fiction. | Friendship—Fiction. | Fathers and sons—Fiction.
Classification: LCC PZ7.7.P55 Ope 2020 | DDC 741.5/973—dc23
LC record available at https://lccn.loc.gov/2019022189

ISBNs: 978-0-316-41690-0 (hardcover), 978-0-316-41689-4 (paperback), 978-0-316-41691-7 (ebook), 978-0-316-53717-9 (ebook), 978-0-316-53716-2 (ebook)

Printed in China

1010

Hardcover: 10 9 8 7 6 5 4 3 2 1
Paperback: 10 9 8 7 6 5 4 3 2 1

TO MY CHILDHOOD HEROES

* * *

REAL OR FICTITIOUS, YOU HAVE INSPIRED ME.
THANK YOU FOR ALL THE ADVENTURES.

CHAPTER ONE
I SWEAR THAT THIS IS A TRUE STORY

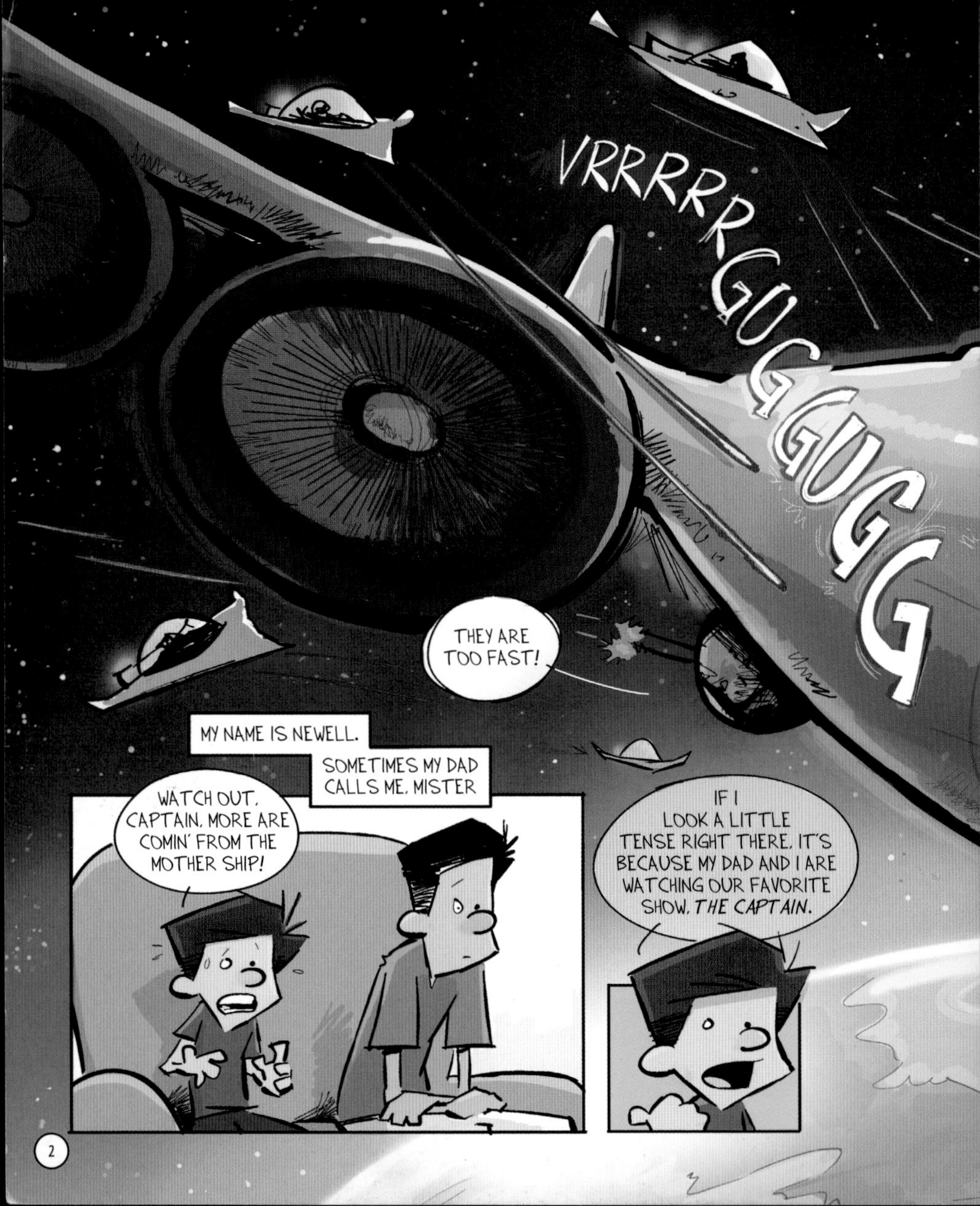

VRRRRRGUGGUGG
THEY ARE TOO FAST!
MY NAME IS NEWELL.
SOMETIMES MY DAD CALLS ME, MISTER
WATCH OUT, CAPTAIN, MORE ARE COMIN' FROM THE MOTHER SHIP!
IF I LOOK A LITTLE TENSE RIGHT THERE, IT'S BECAUSE MY DAD AND I ARE WATCHING OUR FAVORITE SHOW, *THE CAPTAIN*.

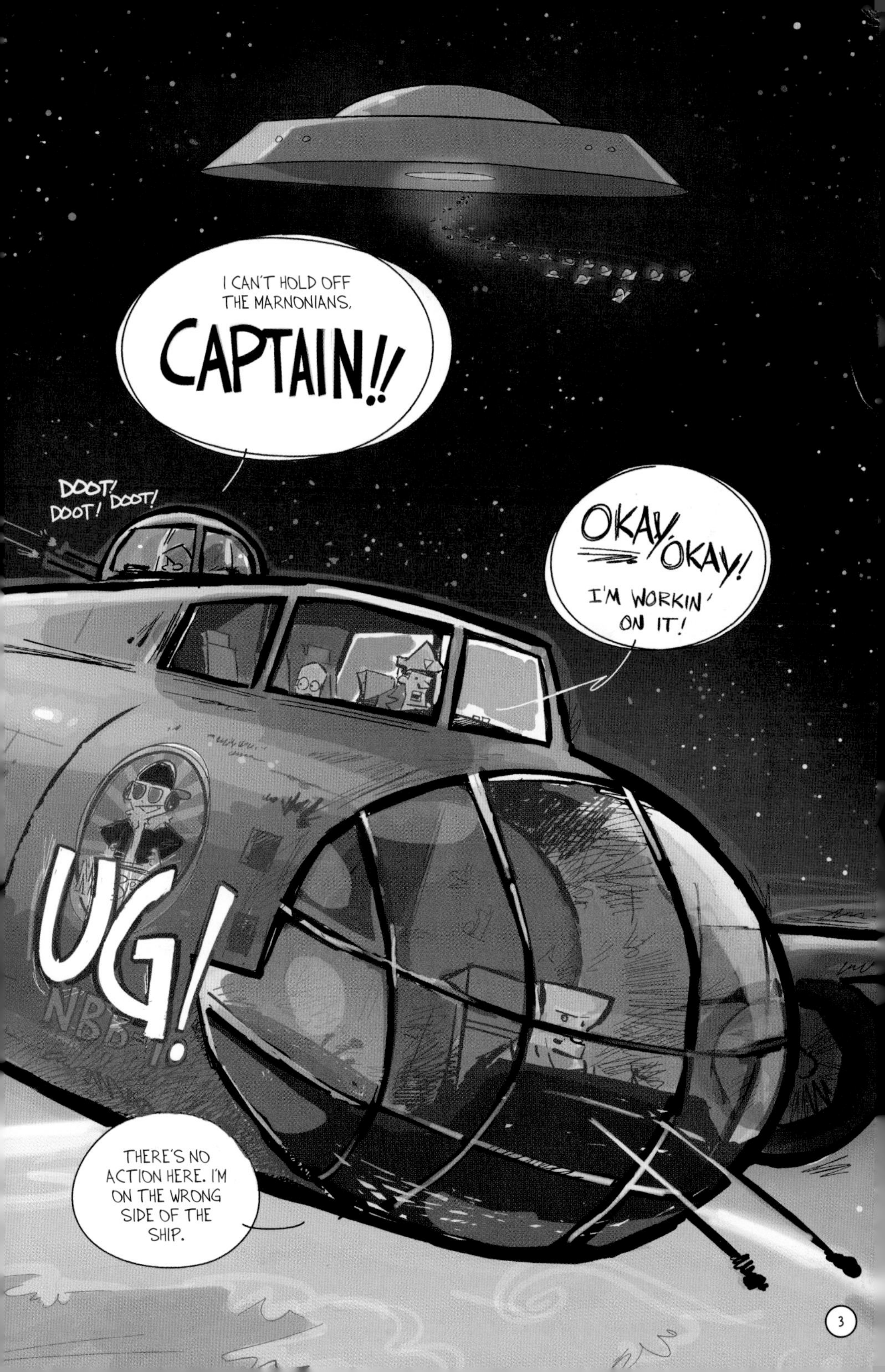
I CAN'T HOLD OFF THE MARNONIANS, CAPTAIN!!
DOOT! DOOT! DOOT!
OKAY, OKAY! I'M WORKIN' ON IT!
UG!
NBB-1
THERE'S NO ACTION HERE. I'M ON THE WRONG SIDE OF THE SHIP.

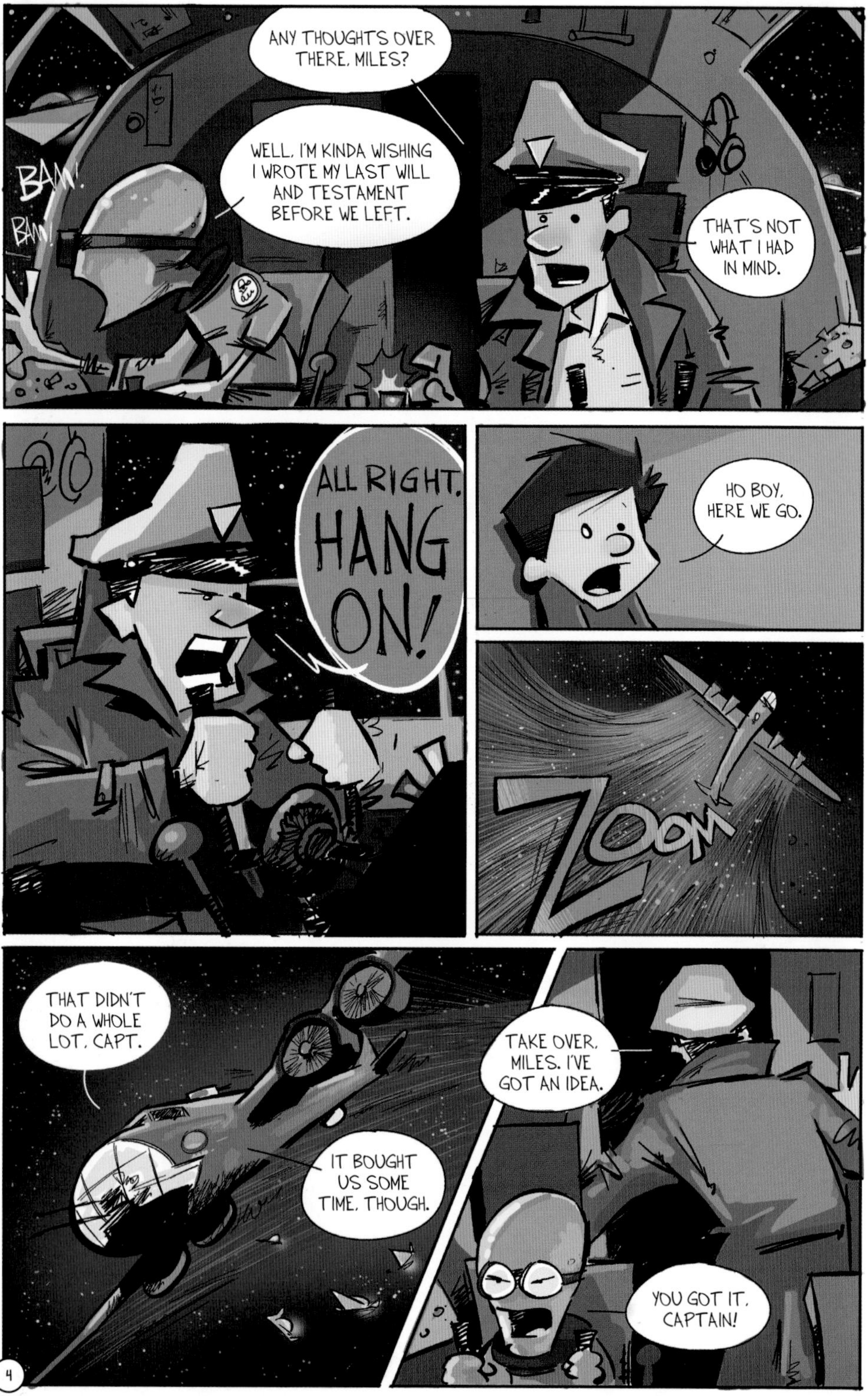
ANY THOUGHTS OVER THERE, MILES?
BAM!
BAM!
WELL, I'M KINDA WISHING I WROTE MY LAST WILL AND TESTAMENT BEFORE WE LEFT.
THAT'S NOT WHAT I HAD IN MIND.
ALL RIGHT. HANG ON!
HO BOY, HERE WE GO.
ZOOM
THAT DIDN'T DO A WHOLE LOT, CAPT.
IT BOUGHT US SOME TIME, THOUGH.
TAKE OVER, MILES. I'VE GOT AN IDEA.
YOU GOT IT, CAPTAIN!

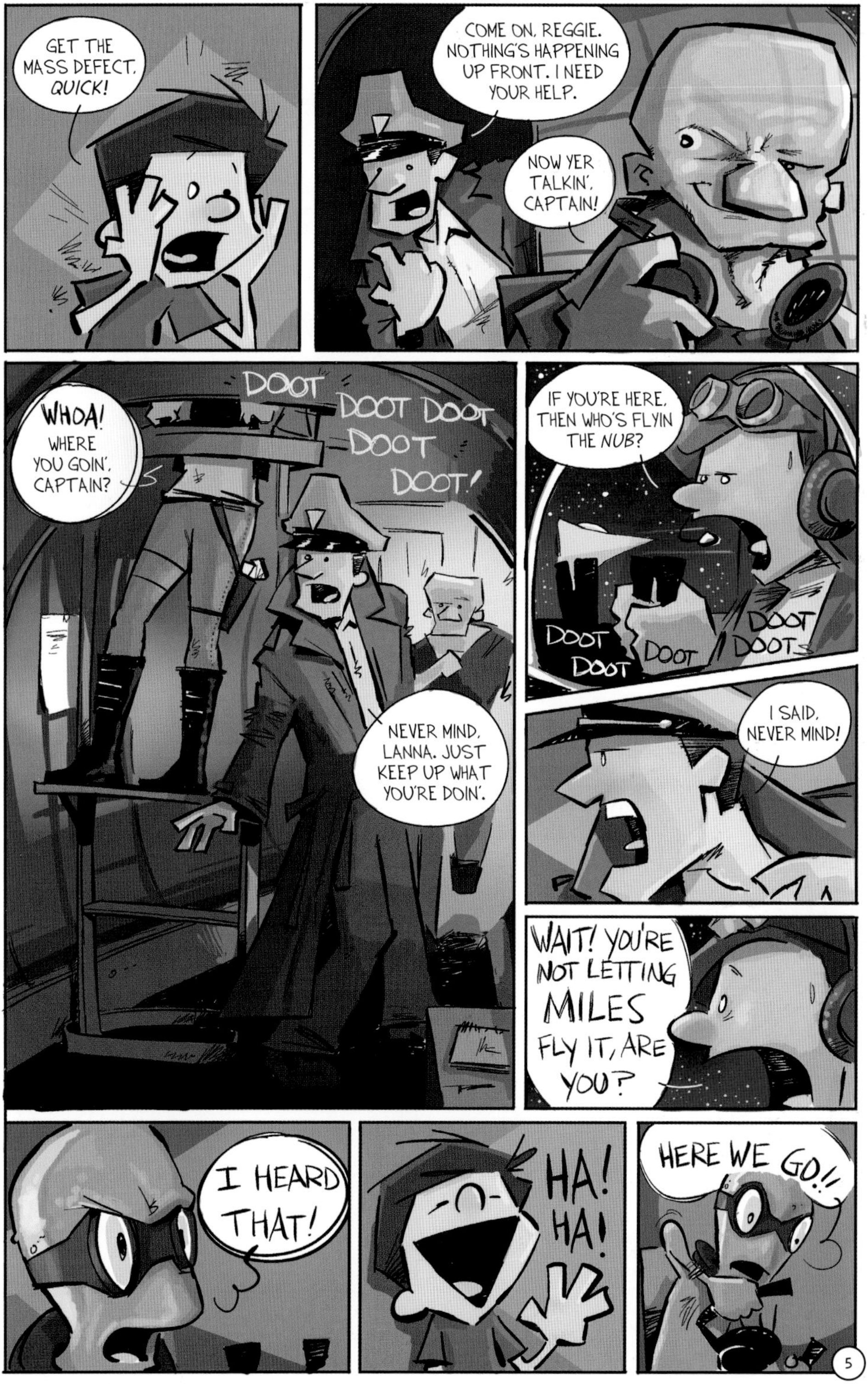
GET THE MASS DEFECT, QUICK!
COME ON, REGGIE. NOTHING'S HAPPENING UP FRONT. I NEED YOUR HELP.
NOW YER TALKIN', CAPTAIN!
DOOT DOOT DOOT DOOT DOOT!
WHOA! WHERE YOU GOIN', CAPTAIN?
NEVER MIND, LANNA. JUST KEEP UP WHAT YOU'RE DOIN'.
IF YOU'RE HERE, THEN WHO'S FLYIN THE NUB?
DOOT DOOT DOOT DOOT DOOTS
I SAID, NEVER MIND!
WAIT! YOU'RE NOT LETTING MILES FLY IT, ARE YOU?
I HEARD THAT!
HA! HA!
HERE WE GO!!

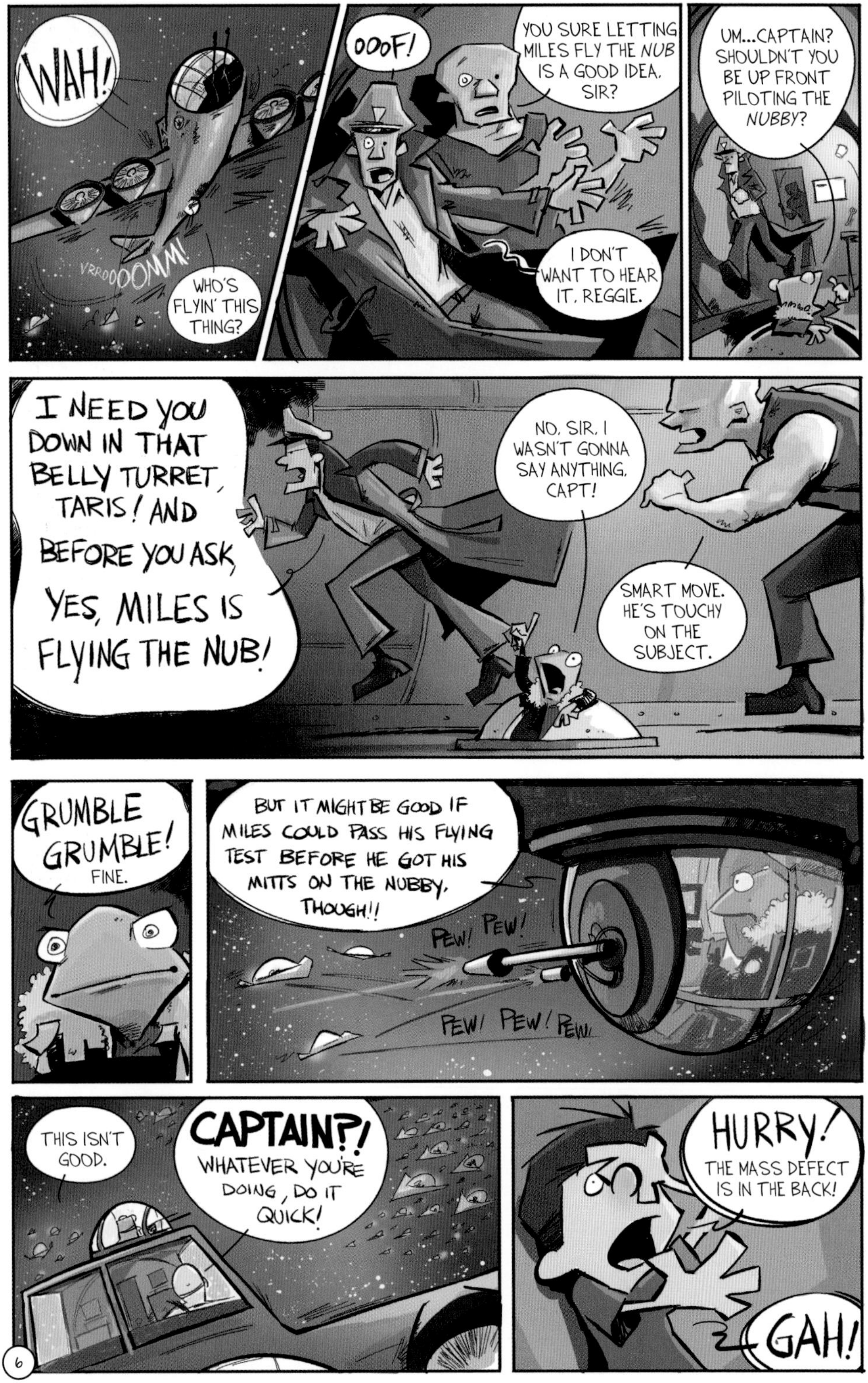
WAH!
VRROOOOOMM!
WHO'S FLYIN' THIS THING?
OOOF!
YOU SURE LETTING MILES FLY THE NUB IS A GOOD IDEA, SIR?
I DON'T WANT TO HEAR IT, REGGIE.
UM...CAPTAIN? SHOULDN'T YOU BE UP FRONT PILOTING THE NUBBY?
I NEED YOU DOWN IN THAT BELLY TURRET, TARIS! AND BEFORE YOU ASK, YES, MILES IS FLYING THE NUB!
NO, SIR, I WASN'T GONNA SAY ANYTHING, CAPT!
SMART MOVE. HE'S TOUCHY ON THE SUBJECT.
GRUMBLE GRUMBLE! FINE.
BUT IT MIGHT BE GOOD IF MILES COULD PASS HIS FLYING TEST BEFORE HE GOT HIS MITTS ON THE NUBBY, THOUGH!!
PEW! PEW!
PEW! PEW! PEW
THIS ISN'T GOOD.
CAPTAIN?! WHATEVER YOU'RE DOING, DO IT QUICK!
HURRY! THE MASS DEFECT IS IN THE BACK!
GAH!

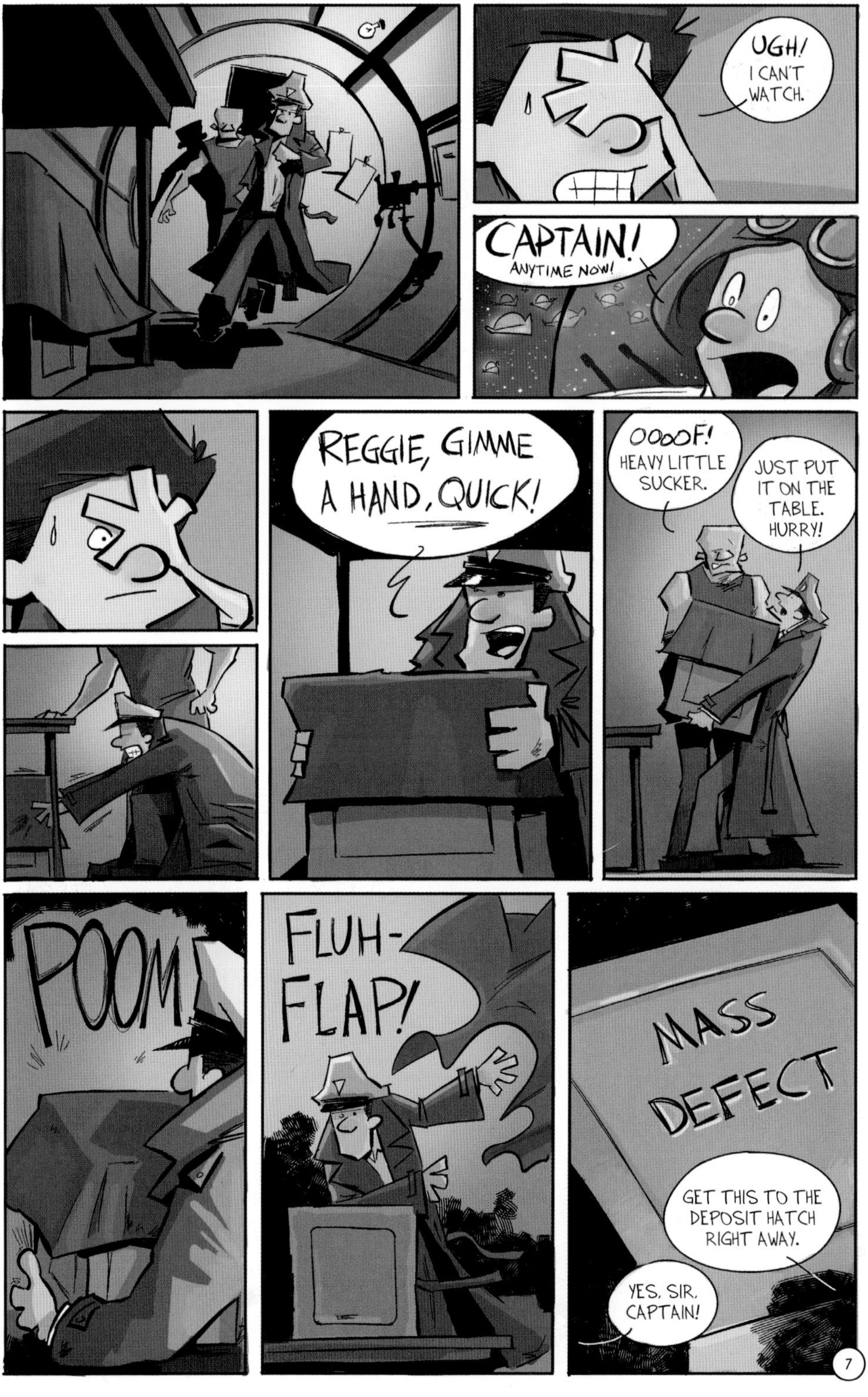
UGH! I CAN'T WATCH.
CAPTAIN! ANYTIME NOW!
REGGIE, GIMME A HAND, QUICK!
OOOOF! HEAVY LITTLE SUCKER.
JUST PUT IT ON THE TABLE. HURRY!
POOM!
FLUH-FLAP!
MASS DEFECT
GET THIS TO THE DEPOSIT HATCH RIGHT AWAY.
YES, SIR, CAPTAIN!

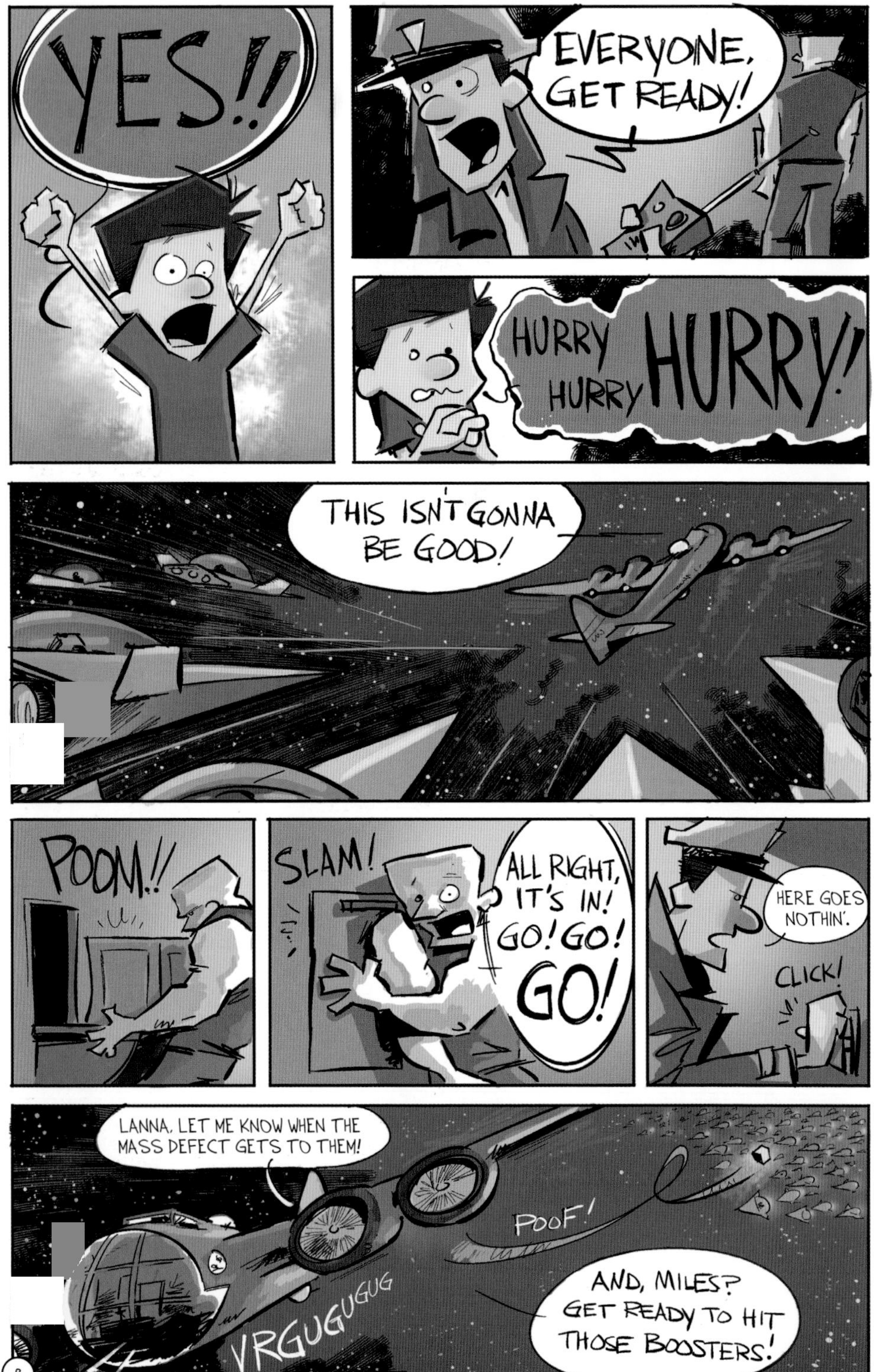
YES!!
EVERYONE, GET READY!
HURRY HURRY HURRY!
THIS ISN'T GONNA BE GOOD!
POOM!!
SLAM!
ALL RIGHT, IT'S IN! GO! GO! GO!
HERE GOES NOTHIN'.
CLICK!
LANNA, LET ME KNOW WHEN THE MASS DEFECT GETS TO THEM!
POOF!
VRGUGUGUG
AND, MILES? GET READY TO HIT THOSE BOOSTERS!

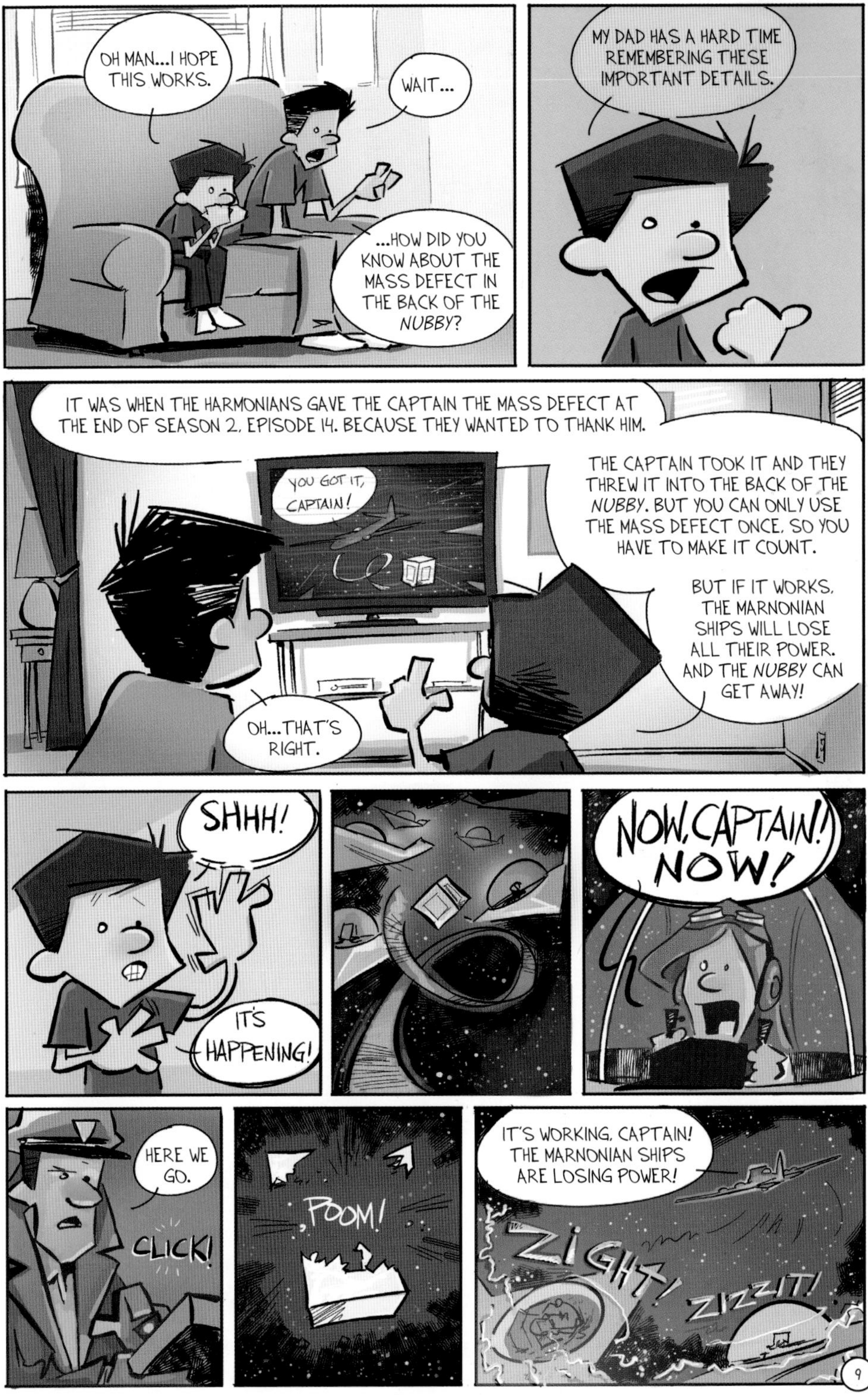
OH MAN...I HOPE THIS WORKS.
WAIT...
...HOW DID YOU KNOW ABOUT THE MASS DEFECT IN THE BACK OF THE *NUBBY*?
MY DAD HAS A HARD TIME REMEMBERING THESE IMPORTANT DETAILS.
IT WAS WHEN THE HARMONIANS GAVE THE CAPTAIN THE MASS DEFECT AT THE END OF SEASON 2, EPISODE 14. BECAUSE THEY WANTED TO THANK HIM.
YOU GOT IT, CAPTAIN!
THE CAPTAIN TOOK IT AND THEY THREW IT INTO THE BACK OF THE *NUBBY*. BUT YOU CAN ONLY USE THE MASS DEFECT ONCE, SO YOU HAVE TO MAKE IT COUNT.
BUT IF IT WORKS, THE MARNONIAN SHIPS WILL LOSE ALL THEIR POWER. AND THE *NUBBY* CAN GET AWAY!
OH...THAT'S RIGHT.
SHHH!
IT'S HAPPENING!
NOW, CAPTAIN! NOW!
HERE WE GO.
CLICK!
POOM!
IT'S WORKING, CAPTAIN! THE MARNONIAN SHIPS ARE LOSING POWER!
ZIGHT!
ZIZZIT!

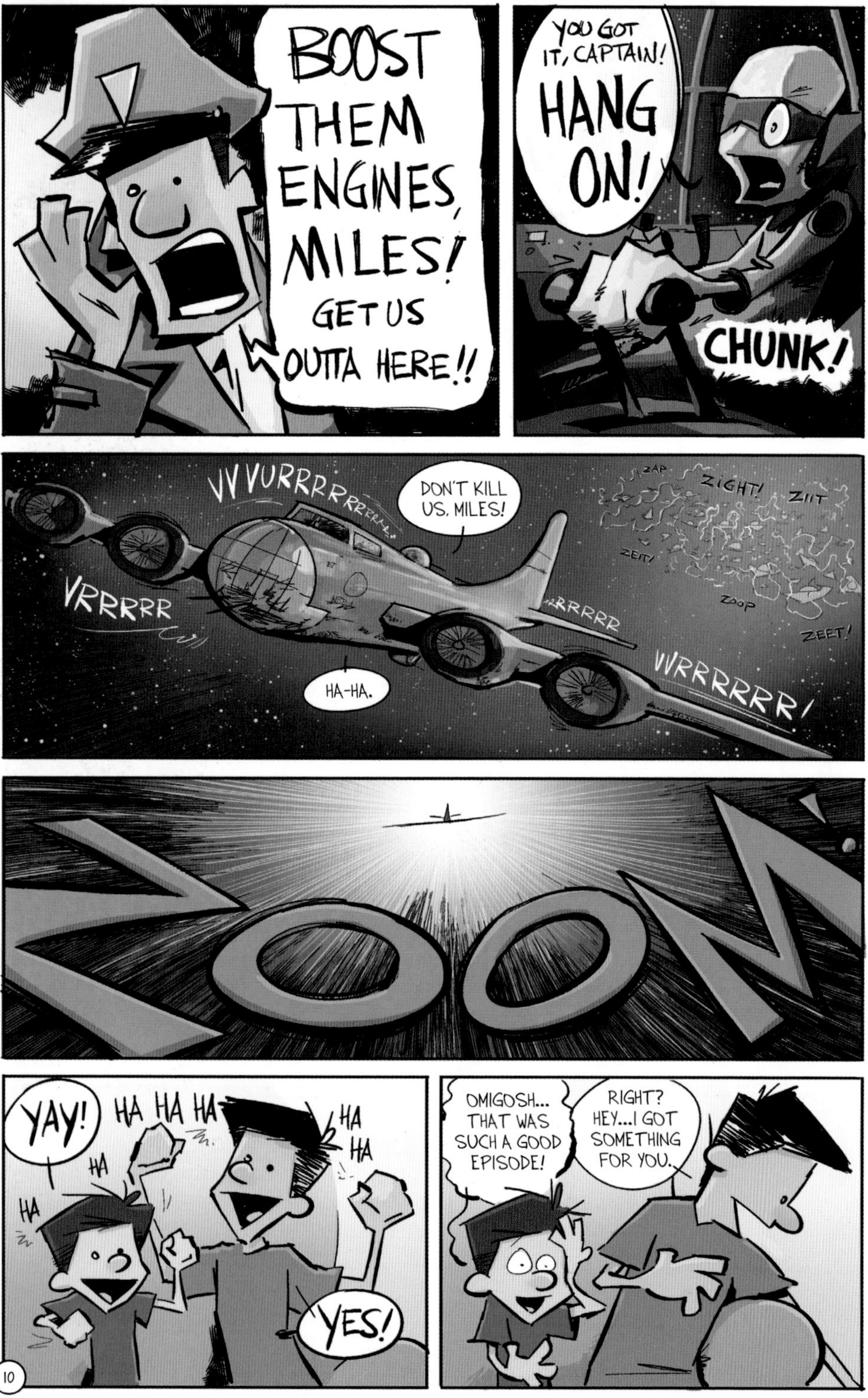
BOOST THEM ENGINES, MILES! GET US OUTTA HERE!!
YOU GOT IT, CAPTAIN! HANG ON!
CHUNK!
VVVURRRRRRRRRR
DON'T KILL US, MILES!
ZAP
ZIGHT!
ZIIT
ZEIT!
VRRRRR
RRRRR
ZOOP
ZEET!
VVRRRRRR!
HA-HA.
ZOOM
YAY!
HA HA HA
HA HA
HA
HA
YES!
OMIGOSH... THAT WAS SUCH A GOOD EPISODE!
RIGHT? HEY...I GOT SOMETHING FOR YOU.

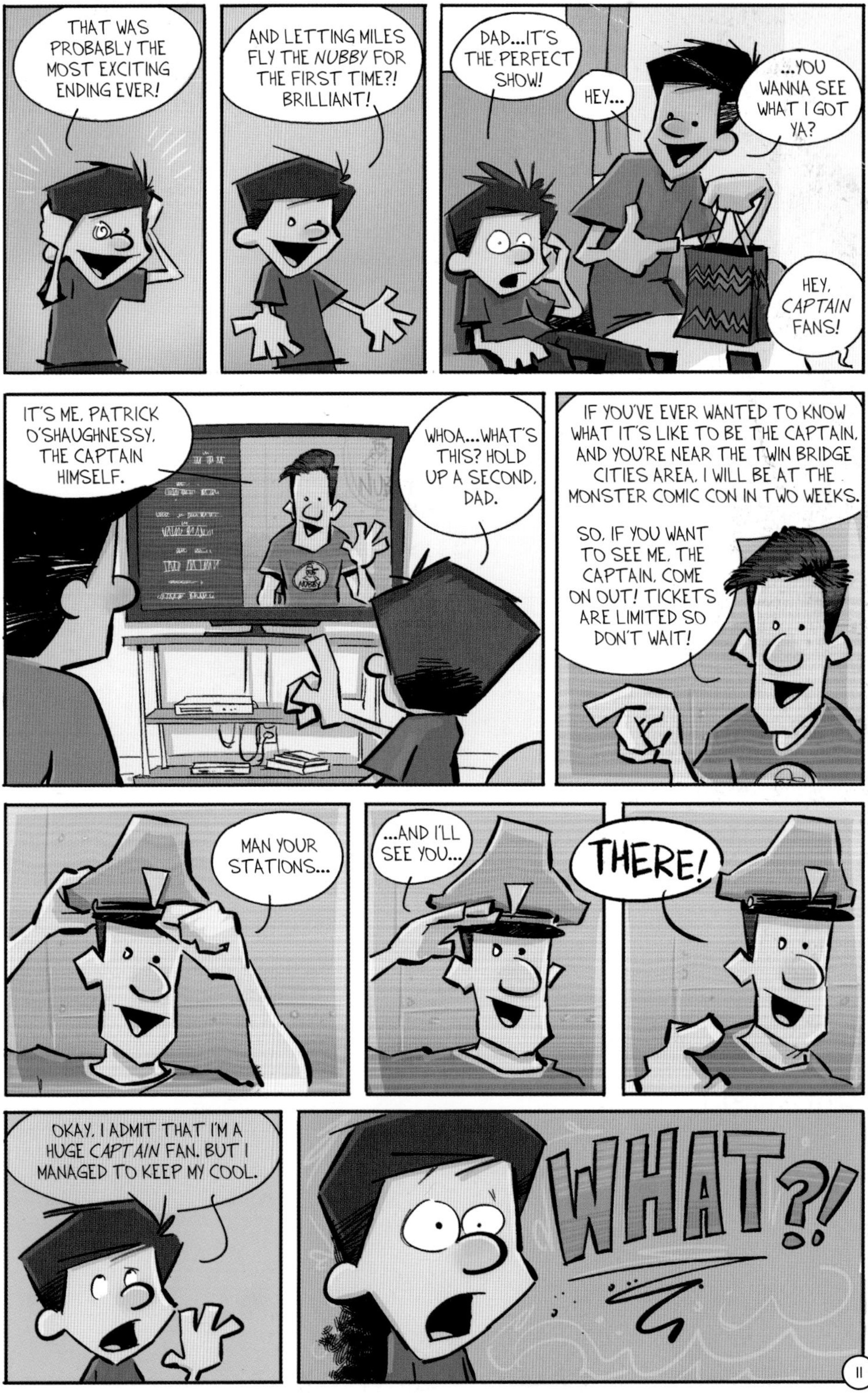
THAT WAS PROBABLY THE MOST EXCITING ENDING EVER!
AND LETTING MILES FLY THE *NUBBY* FOR THE FIRST TIME?! BRILLIANT!
DAD...IT'S THE PERFECT SHOW!
HEY...
...YOU WANNA SEE WHAT I GOT YA?
HEY, *CAPTAIN* FANS!
IT'S ME, PATRICK O'SHAUGHNESSY, THE CAPTAIN HIMSELF.
WHOA...WHAT'S THIS? HOLD UP A SECOND, DAD.
IF YOU'VE EVER WANTED TO KNOW WHAT IT'S LIKE TO BE THE CAPTAIN, AND YOU'RE NEAR THE TWIN BRIDGE CITIES AREA, I WILL BE AT THE MONSTER COMIC CON IN TWO WEEKS.
SO, IF YOU WANT TO SEE ME, THE CAPTAIN, COME ON OUT! TICKETS ARE LIMITED SO DON'T WAIT!
MAN YOUR STATIONS...
...AND I'LL SEE YOU...
THERE!
OKAY, I ADMIT THAT I'M A HUGE *CAPTAIN* FAN. BUT I MANAGED TO KEEP MY COOL.
WHAT?!

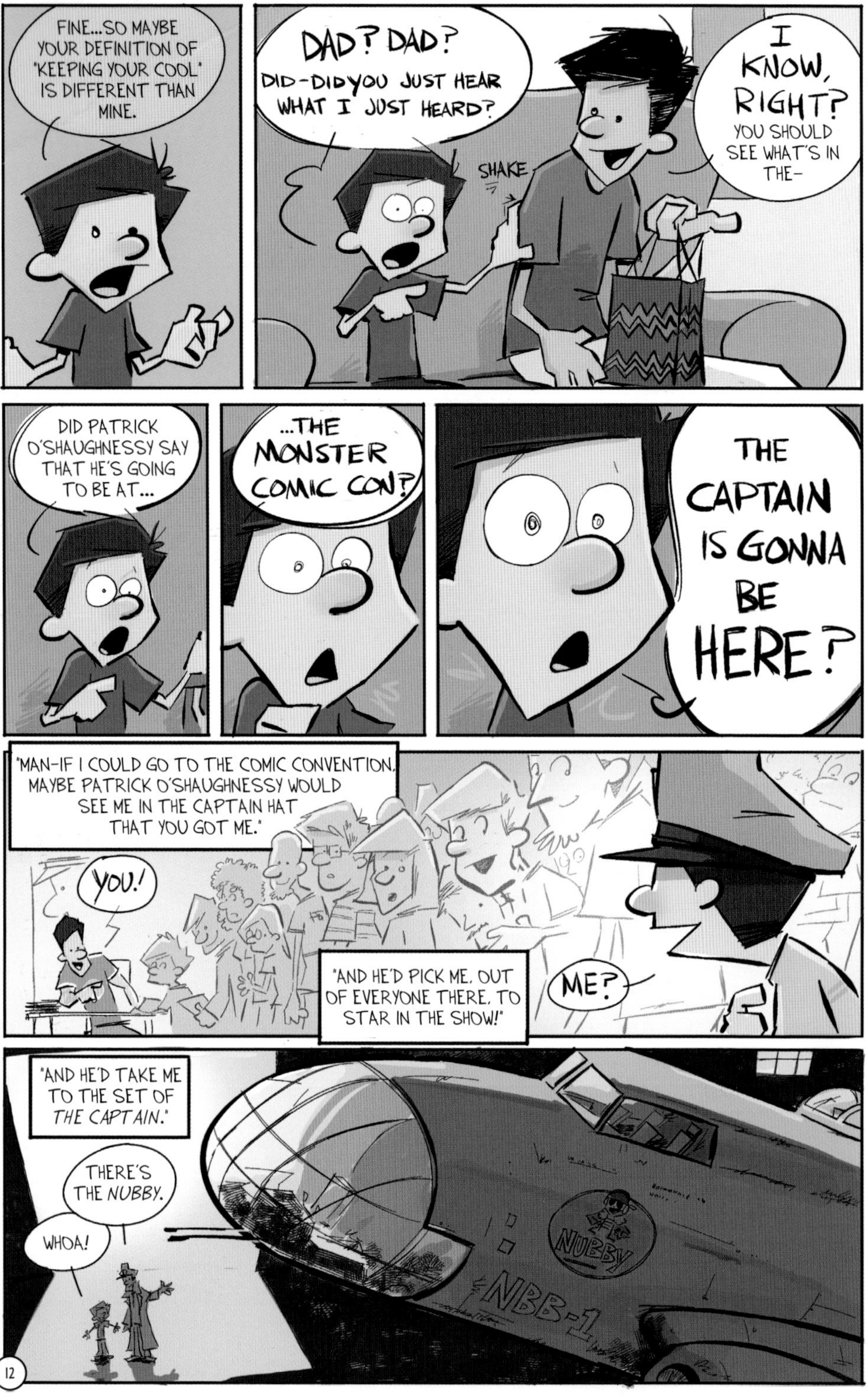
FINE...SO MAYBE YOUR DEFINITION OF "KEEPING YOUR COOL" IS DIFFERENT THAN MINE.
DAD? DAD? DID-DID YOU JUST HEAR WHAT I JUST HEARD?
SHAKE
I KNOW, RIGHT? YOU SHOULD SEE WHAT'S IN THE–
DID PATRICK O'SHAUGHNESSY SAY THAT HE'S GOING TO BE AT...
...THE MONSTER COMIC CON?
THE CAPTAIN IS GONNA BE HERE?
"MAN–IF I COULD GO TO THE COMIC CONVENTION, MAYBE PATRICK O'SHAUGHNESSY WOULD SEE ME IN THE CAPTAIN HAT THAT YOU GOT ME."
YOU!
"AND HE'D PICK ME, OUT OF EVERYONE THERE, TO STAR IN THE SHOW!"
ME?
"AND HE'D TAKE ME TO THE SET OF *THE CAPTAIN*."
THERE'S THE *NUBBY*.
WHOA!
NUBBY
NBB-1

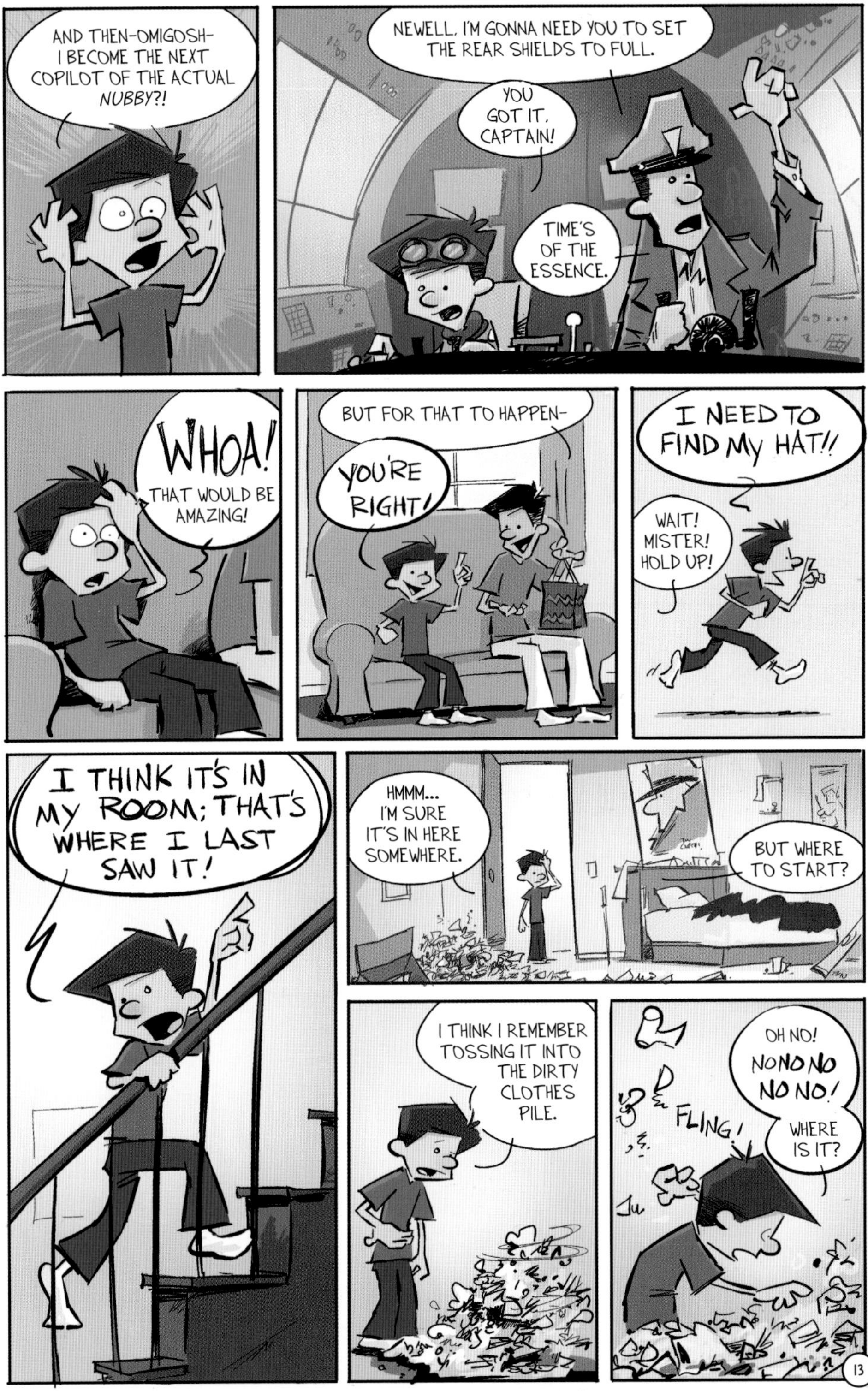
AND THEN—OMIGOSH—
I BECOME THE NEXT
COPILOT OF THE ACTUAL
NUBBY?!
NEWELL, I'M GONNA NEED YOU TO SET THE REAR SHIELDS TO FULL.
YOU GOT IT, CAPTAIN!
TIME'S OF THE ESSENCE.
WHOA! THAT WOULD BE AMAZING!
BUT FOR THAT TO HAPPEN—
YOU'RE RIGHT!
I NEED TO FIND MY HAT!!
WAIT! MISTER! HOLD UP!
I THINK IT'S IN MY ROOM; THAT'S WHERE I LAST SAW IT!
HMMM... I'M SURE IT'S IN HERE SOMEWHERE.
BUT WHERE TO START?
I THINK I REMEMBER TOSSING IT INTO THE DIRTY CLOTHES PILE.
OH NO! NONO NO NO NO!
FLING!
WHERE IS IT?

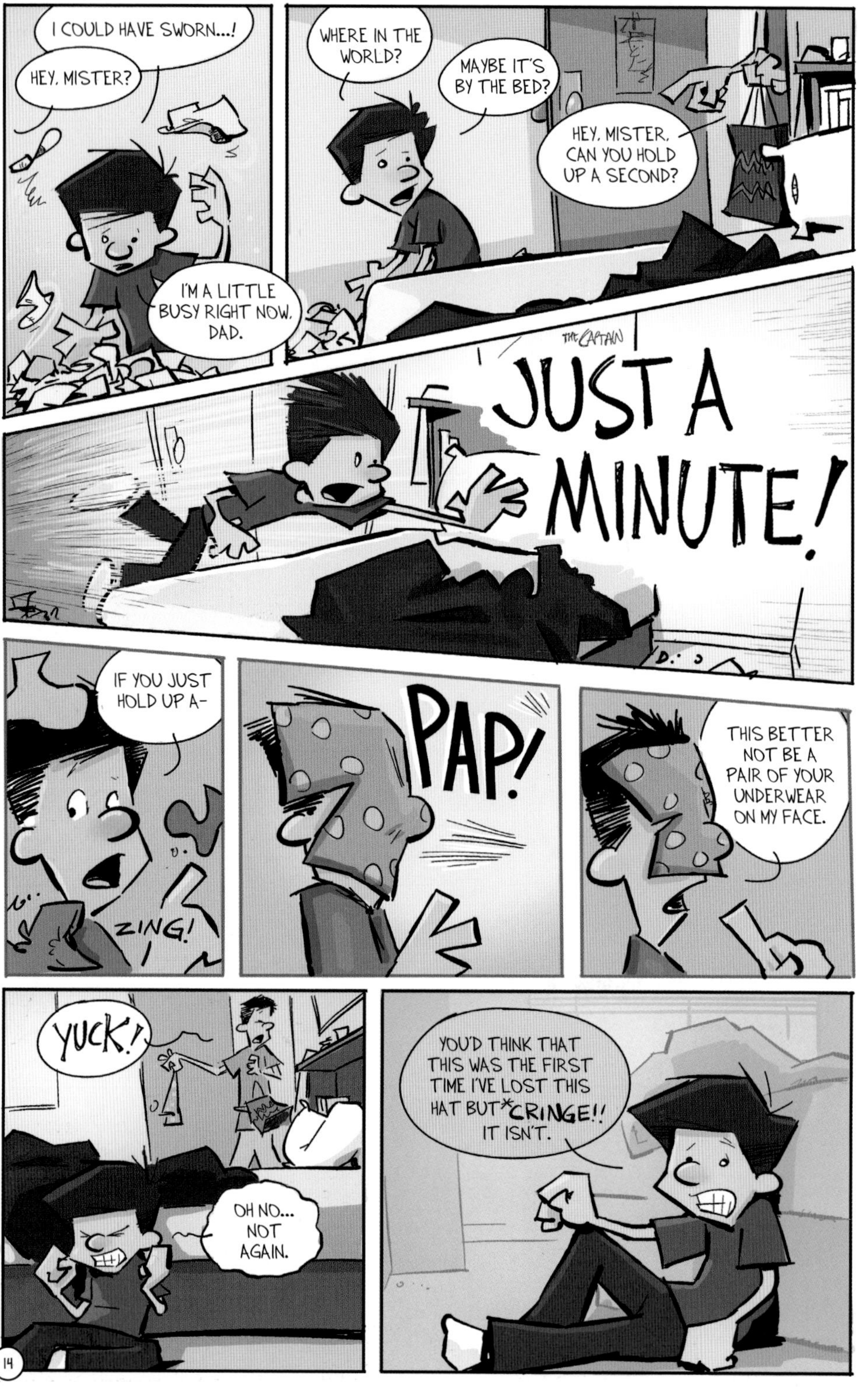
I COULD HAVE SWORN...!
HEY, MISTER?
I'M A LITTLE BUSY RIGHT NOW, DAD.
WHERE IN THE WORLD?
MAYBE IT'S BY THE BED?
HEY, MISTER, CAN YOU HOLD UP A SECOND?
THE CAPTAIN
JUST A MINUTE!
IF YOU JUST HOLD UP A-
ZING!
PAP!
THIS BETTER NOT BE A PAIR OF YOUR UNDERWEAR ON MY FACE.
YUCK!
OH NO... NOT AGAIN.
YOU'D THINK THAT THIS WAS THE FIRST TIME I'VE LOST THIS HAT BUT *CRINGE!* IT ISN'T.

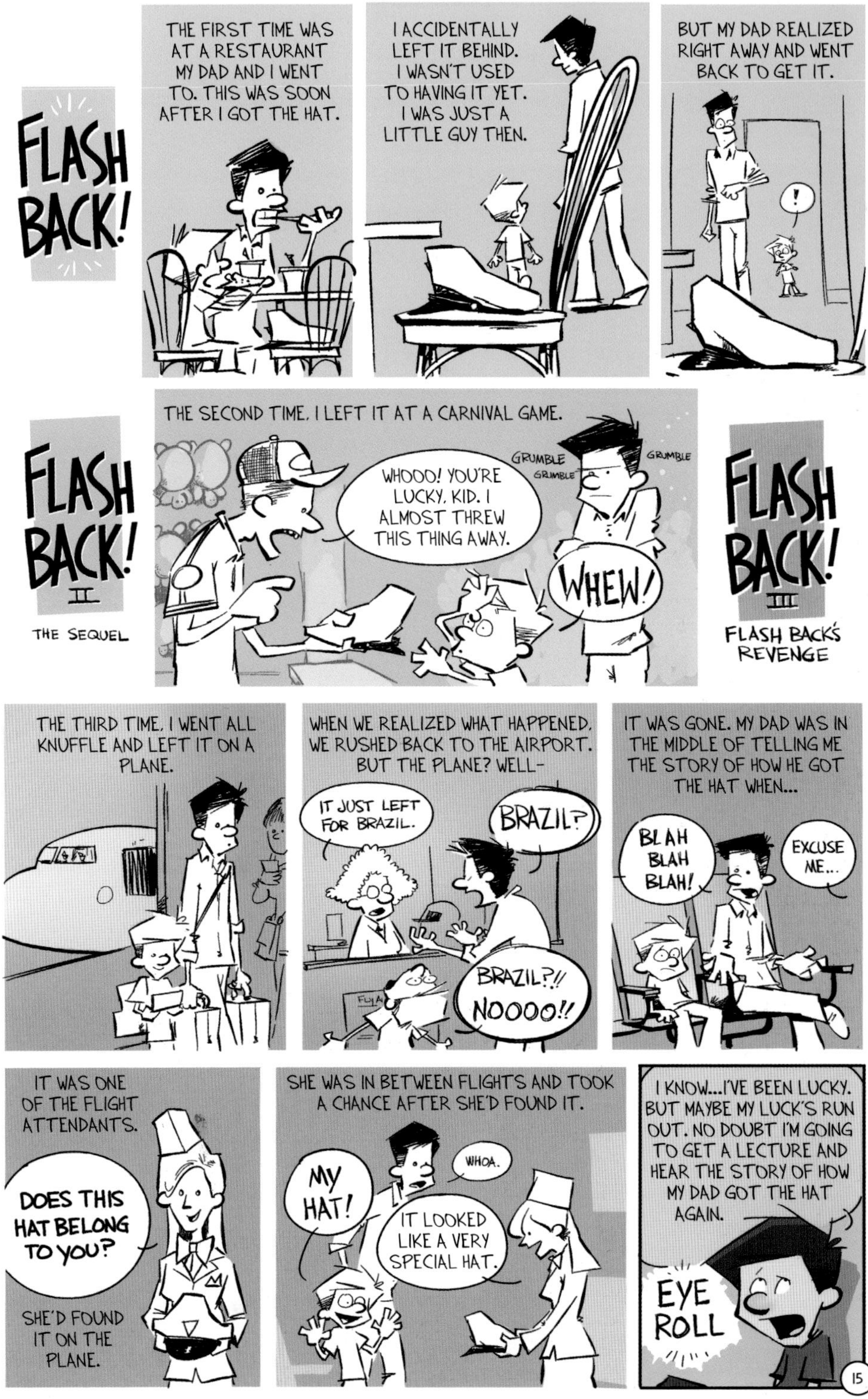
FLASH BACK!
THE FIRST TIME WAS AT A RESTAURANT MY DAD AND I WENT TO. THIS WAS SOON AFTER I GOT THE HAT.
I ACCIDENTALLY LEFT IT BEHIND. I WASN'T USED TO HAVING IT YET. I WAS JUST A LITTLE GUY THEN.
BUT MY DAD REALIZED RIGHT AWAY AND WENT BACK TO GET IT.
!
FLASH BACK! II THE SEQUEL
THE SECOND TIME, I LEFT IT AT A CARNIVAL GAME.
GRUMBLE GRUMBLE GRUMBLE
WHOOO! YOU'RE LUCKY, KID. I ALMOST THREW THIS THING AWAY.
WHEW!
FLASH BACK! III FLASH BACK'S REVENGE
THE THIRD TIME, I WENT ALL KNUFFLE AND LEFT IT ON A PLANE.
WHEN WE REALIZED WHAT HAPPENED, WE RUSHED BACK TO THE AIRPORT. BUT THE PLANE? WELL-
IT JUST LEFT FOR BRAZIL.
BRAZIL?
BRAZIL?!! NOOOO!!
IT WAS GONE. MY DAD WAS IN THE MIDDLE OF TELLING ME THE STORY OF HOW HE GOT THE HAT WHEN...
BLAH BLAH BLAH!
EXCUSE ME...
IT WAS ONE OF THE FLIGHT ATTENDANTS.
DOES THIS HAT BELONG TO YOU?
SHE'D FOUND IT ON THE PLANE.
SHE WAS IN BETWEEN FLIGHTS AND TOOK A CHANCE AFTER SHE'D FOUND IT.
MY HAT!
WHOA.
IT LOOKED LIKE A VERY SPECIAL HAT.
I KNOW...I'VE BEEN LUCKY. BUT MAYBE MY LUCK'S RUN OUT. NO DOUBT I'M GOING TO GET A LECTURE AND HEAR THE STORY OF HOW MY DAD GOT THE HAT AGAIN.
EYE ROLL

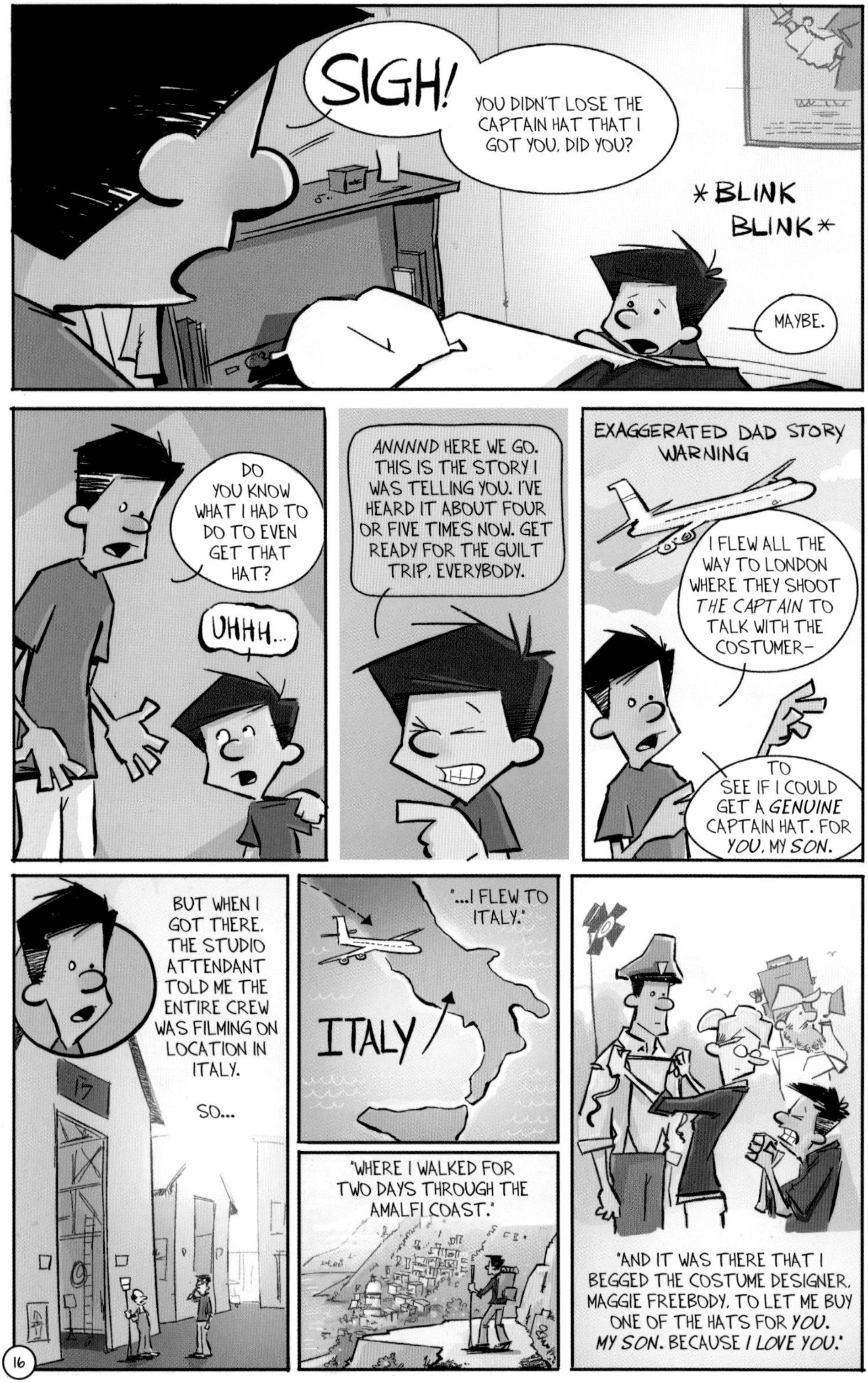
SIGH!
YOU DIDN'T LOSE THE CAPTAIN HAT THAT I GOT YOU, DID YOU?
BLINK BLINK
MAYBE.
DO YOU KNOW WHAT I HAD TO DO TO EVEN GET THAT HAT?
UHHH...
ANNNND HERE WE GO. THIS IS THE STORY I WAS TELLING YOU. I'VE HEARD IT ABOUT FOUR OR FIVE TIMES NOW. GET READY FOR THE GUILT TRIP, EVERYBODY.
EXAGGERATED DAD STORY WARNING
I FLEW ALL THE WAY TO LONDON WHERE THEY SHOOT THE CAPTAIN TO TALK WITH THE COSTUMER–
TO SEE IF I COULD GET A GENUINE CAPTAIN HAT. FOR YOU, MY SON.
BUT WHEN I GOT THERE, THE STUDIO ATTENDANT TOLD ME THE ENTIRE CREW WAS FILMING ON LOCATION IN ITALY.
SO...
17
"...I FLEW TO ITALY."
ITALY
"WHERE I WALKED FOR TWO DAYS THROUGH THE AMALFI COAST."
"AND IT WAS THERE THAT I BEGGED THE COSTUME DESIGNER, MAGGIE FREEBODY, TO LET ME BUY ONE OF THE HATS FOR YOU. MY SON. BECAUSE I LOVE YOU."

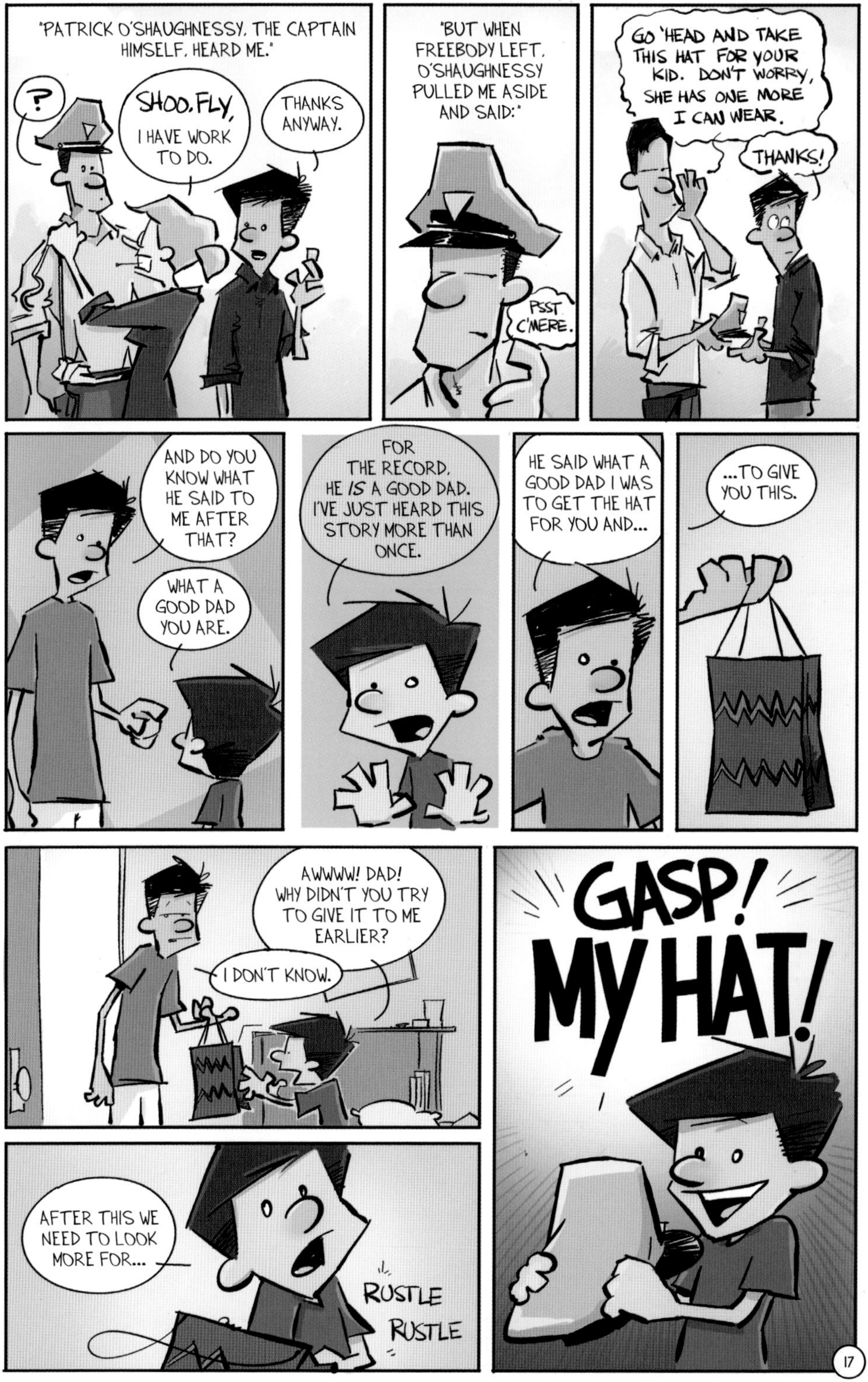
"PATRICK O'SHAUGHNESSY, THE CAPTAIN HIMSELF, HEARD ME."
?
SHOO, FLY, I HAVE WORK TO DO.
THANKS ANYWAY.
"BUT WHEN FREEBODY LEFT, O'SHAUGHNESSY PULLED ME ASIDE AND SAID:"
PSST. C'MERE.
GO 'HEAD AND TAKE THIS HAT FOR YOUR KID. DON'T WORRY, SHE HAS ONE MORE I CAN WEAR.
THANKS!
AND DO YOU KNOW WHAT HE SAID TO ME AFTER THAT?
WHAT A GOOD DAD YOU ARE.
FOR THE RECORD, HE IS A GOOD DAD. I'VE JUST HEARD THIS STORY MORE THAN ONCE.
HE SAID WHAT A GOOD DAD I WAS TO GET THE HAT FOR YOU AND...
...TO GIVE YOU THIS.
AWWWW! DAD! WHY DIDN'T YOU TRY TO GIVE IT TO ME EARLIER?
I DON'T KNOW.
AFTER THIS WE NEED TO LOOK MORE FOR...
RUSTLE
RUSTLE
GASP! MY HAT!

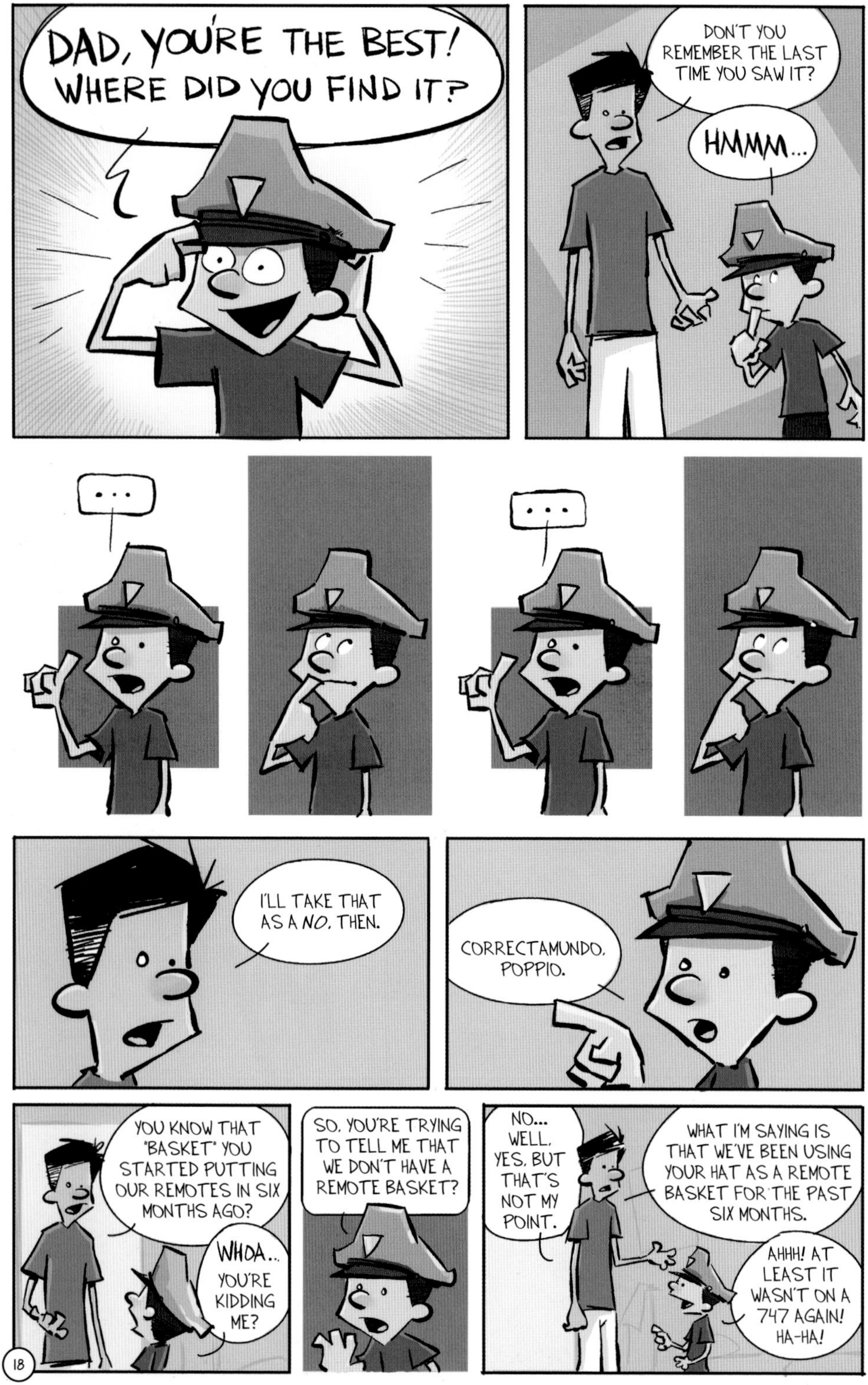
DAD, YOU'RE THE BEST! WHERE DID YOU FIND IT?
DON'T YOU REMEMBER THE LAST TIME YOU SAW IT?
HMMM...
...
...
I'LL TAKE THAT AS A NO, THEN.
CORRECTAMUNDO, POPPIO.
YOU KNOW THAT "BASKET" YOU STARTED PUTTING OUR REMOTES IN SIX MONTHS AGO?
WHOA... YOU'RE KIDDING ME?
SO, YOU'RE TRYING TO TELL ME THAT WE DON'T HAVE A REMOTE BASKET?
NO... WELL, YES, BUT THAT'S NOT MY POINT.
WHAT I'M SAYING IS THAT WE'VE BEEN USING YOUR HAT AS A REMOTE BASKET FOR THE PAST SIX MONTHS.
AHHH! AT LEAST IT WASN'T ON A 747 AGAIN! HA-HA!

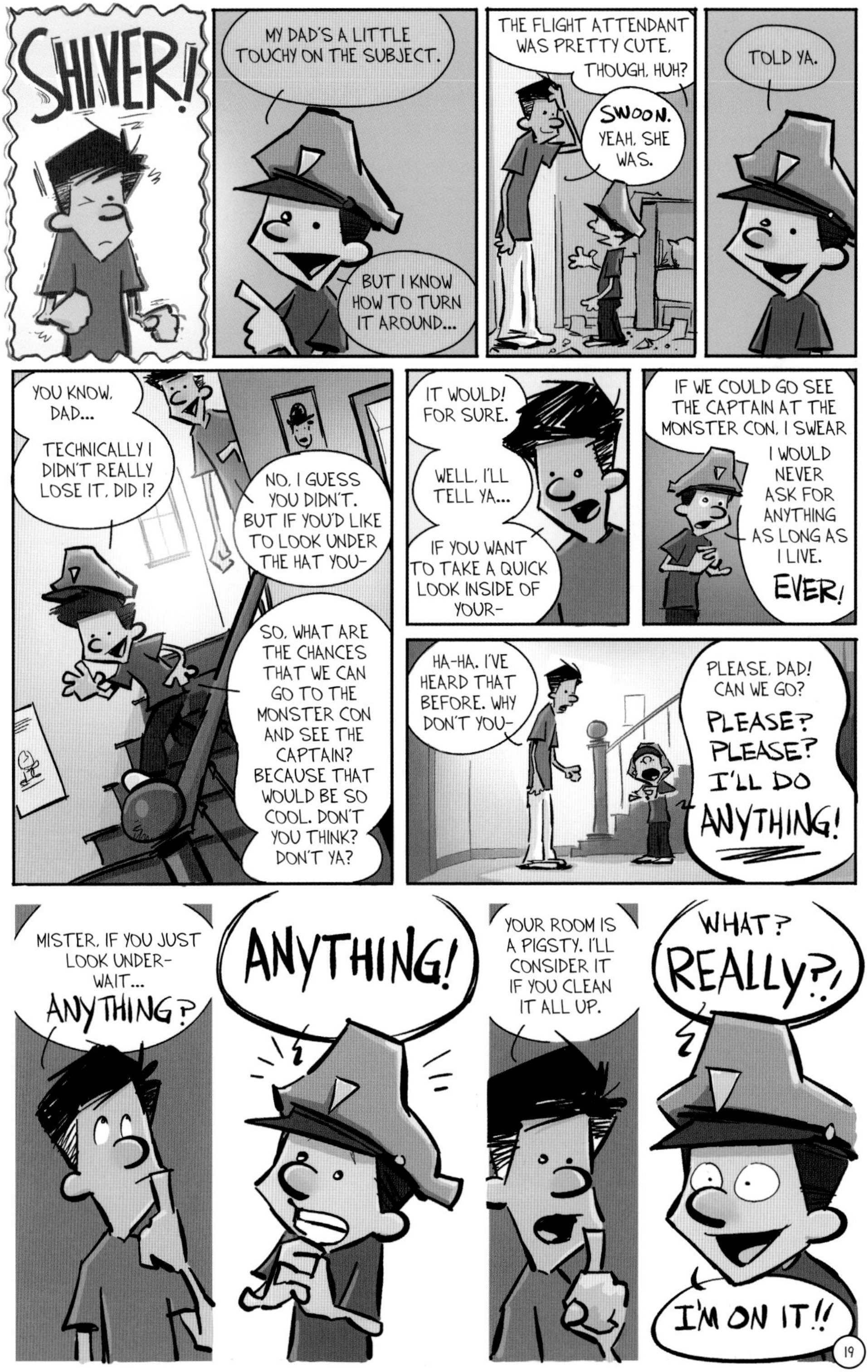
SHIVER!
MY DAD'S A LITTLE TOUCHY ON THE SUBJECT.
BUT I KNOW HOW TO TURN IT AROUND...
THE FLIGHT ATTENDANT WAS PRETTY CUTE, THOUGH, HUH?
SWOON. YEAH, SHE WAS.
TOLD YA.
YOU KNOW, DAD...
TECHNICALLY I DIDN'T REALLY LOSE IT, DID I?
NO, I GUESS YOU DIDN'T. BUT IF YOU'D LIKE TO LOOK UNDER THE HAT YOU-
SO, WHAT ARE THE CHANCES THAT WE CAN GO TO THE MONSTER CON AND SEE THE CAPTAIN? BECAUSE THAT WOULD BE SO COOL. DON'T YOU THINK? DON'T YA?
IT WOULD! FOR SURE.
WELL, I'LL TELL YA...
IF YOU WANT TO TAKE A QUICK LOOK INSIDE OF YOUR-
IF WE COULD GO SEE THE CAPTAIN AT THE MONSTER CON, I SWEAR I WOULD NEVER ASK FOR ANYTHING AS LONG AS I LIVE. EVER!
HA-HA. I'VE HEARD THAT BEFORE. WHY DON'T YOU-
PLEASE, DAD! CAN WE GO? PLEASE? PLEASE? I'LL DO ANYTHING!
MISTER, IF YOU JUST LOOK UNDER- WAIT... ANYTHING?
ANYTHING!
YOUR ROOM IS A PIGSTY. I'LL CONSIDER IT IF YOU CLEAN IT ALL UP.
WHAT? REALLY?!
I'M ON IT!!

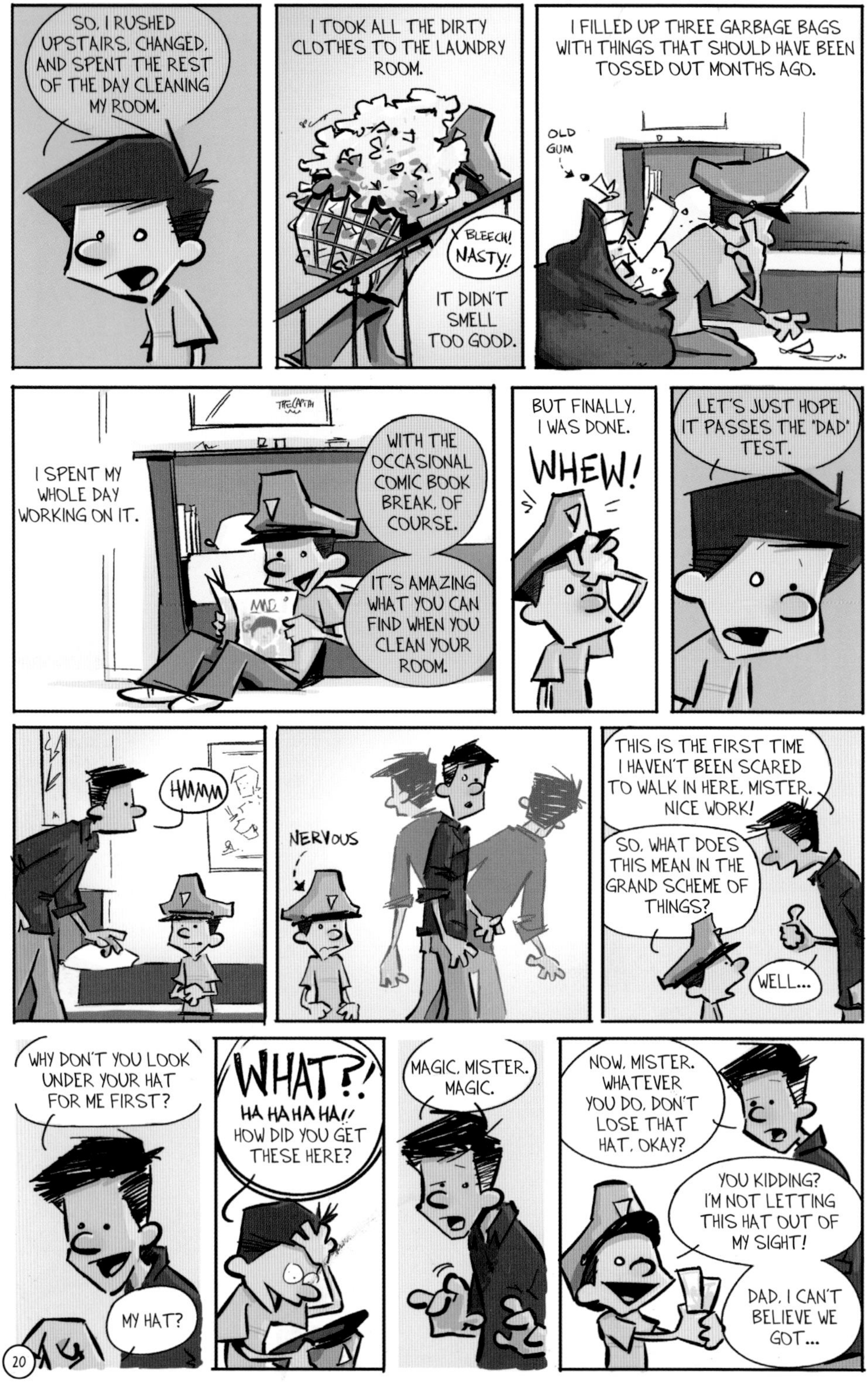
SO, I RUSHED UPSTAIRS, CHANGED, AND SPENT THE REST OF THE DAY CLEANING MY ROOM.
I TOOK ALL THE DIRTY CLOTHES TO THE LAUNDRY ROOM.
BLEECH! NASTY!
IT DIDN'T SMELL TOO GOOD.
I FILLED UP THREE GARBAGE BAGS WITH THINGS THAT SHOULD HAVE BEEN TOSSED OUT MONTHS AGO.
OLD GUM
I SPENT MY WHOLE DAY WORKING ON IT.
WITH THE OCCASIONAL COMIC BOOK BREAK, OF COURSE.
IT'S AMAZING WHAT YOU CAN FIND WHEN YOU CLEAN YOUR ROOM.
BUT FINALLY, I WAS DONE.
WHEW!
LET'S JUST HOPE IT PASSES THE "DAD" TEST.
HMMM
NERVOUS
THIS IS THE FIRST TIME I HAVEN'T BEEN SCARED TO WALK IN HERE, MISTER. NICE WORK!
SO, WHAT DOES THIS MEAN IN THE GRAND SCHEME OF THINGS?
WELL...
WHY DON'T YOU LOOK UNDER YOUR HAT FOR ME FIRST?
MY HAT?
WHAT?!
HA HA HA HA!!
HOW DID YOU GET THESE HERE?
MAGIC, MISTER. MAGIC.
NOW, MISTER. WHATEVER YOU DO, DON'T LOSE THAT HAT, OKAY?
YOU KIDDING? I'M NOT LETTING THIS HAT OUT OF MY SIGHT!
DAD, I CAN'T BELIEVE WE GOT...

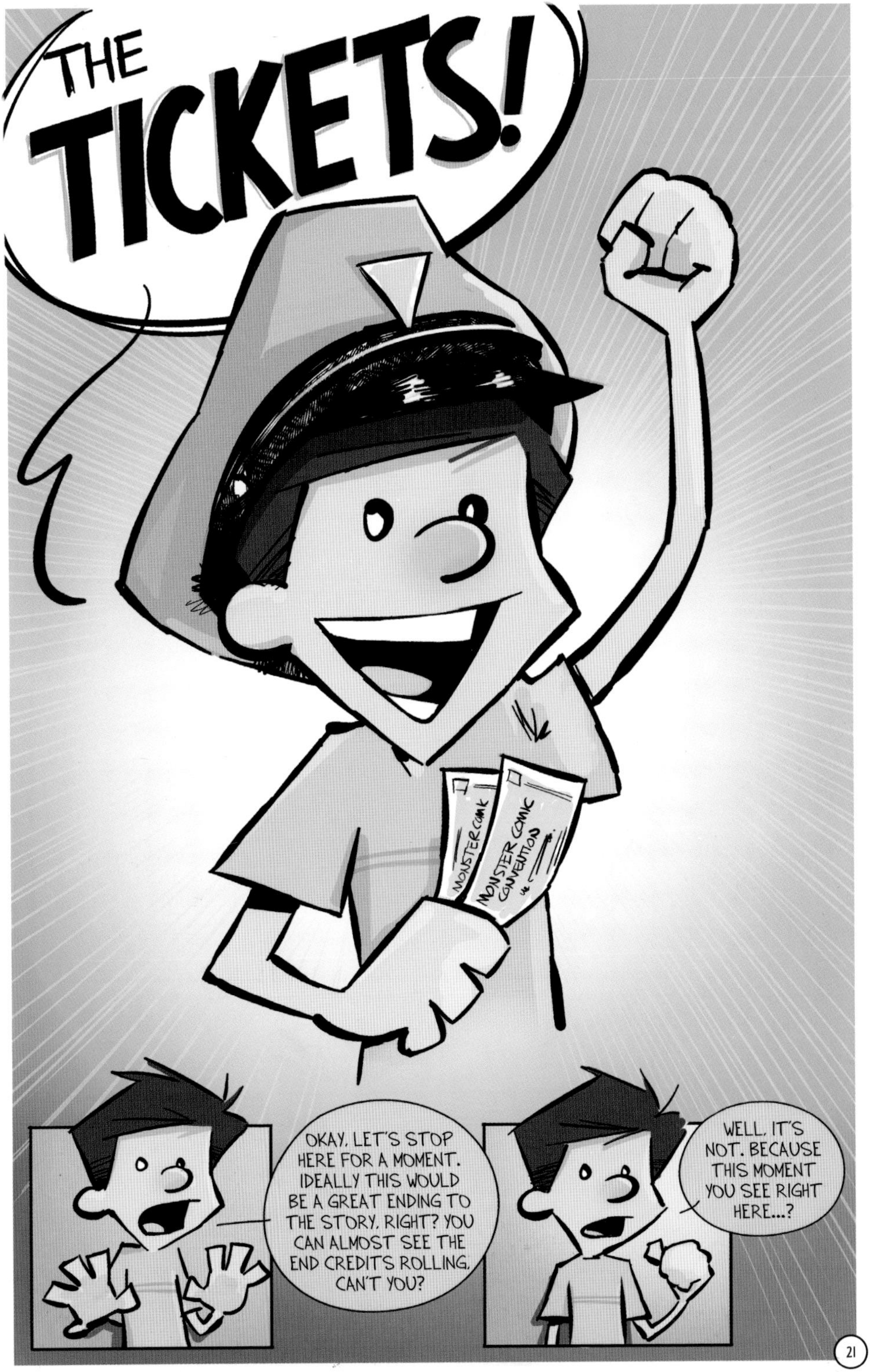
THE TICKETS!
MONSTER COMIC
MONSTER COMIC CONVENTION
OKAY, LET'S STOP HERE FOR A MOMENT. IDEALLY THIS WOULD BE A GREAT ENDING TO THE STORY, RIGHT? YOU CAN ALMOST SEE THE END CREDITS ROLLING, CAN'T YOU?
WELL, IT'S NOT. BECAUSE THIS MOMENT YOU SEE RIGHT HERE...?

CHAPTER TWO
THIS IS ONLY THE BEGINNING

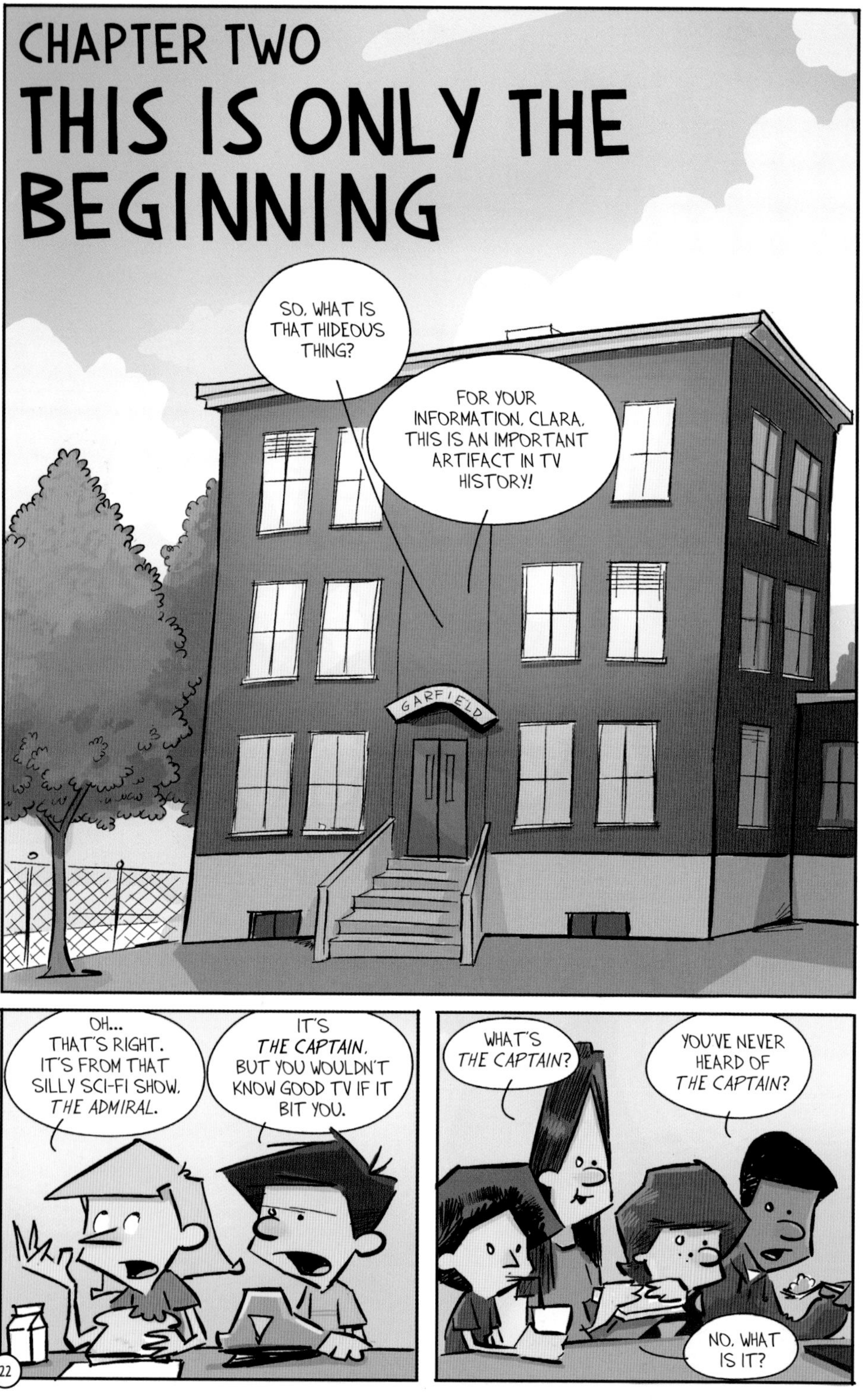

SO, WHAT IS THAT HIDEOUS THING?
FOR YOUR INFORMATION, CLARA, THIS IS AN IMPORTANT ARTIFACT IN TV HISTORY!
GARFIELD
OH... THAT'S RIGHT. IT'S FROM THAT SILLY SCI-FI SHOW, *THE ADMIRAL*.
IT'S *THE CAPTAIN*, BUT YOU WOULDN'T KNOW GOOD TV IF IT BIT YOU.
WHAT'S *THE CAPTAIN*?
YOU'VE NEVER HEARD OF *THE CAPTAIN*?
NO, WHAT IS IT?

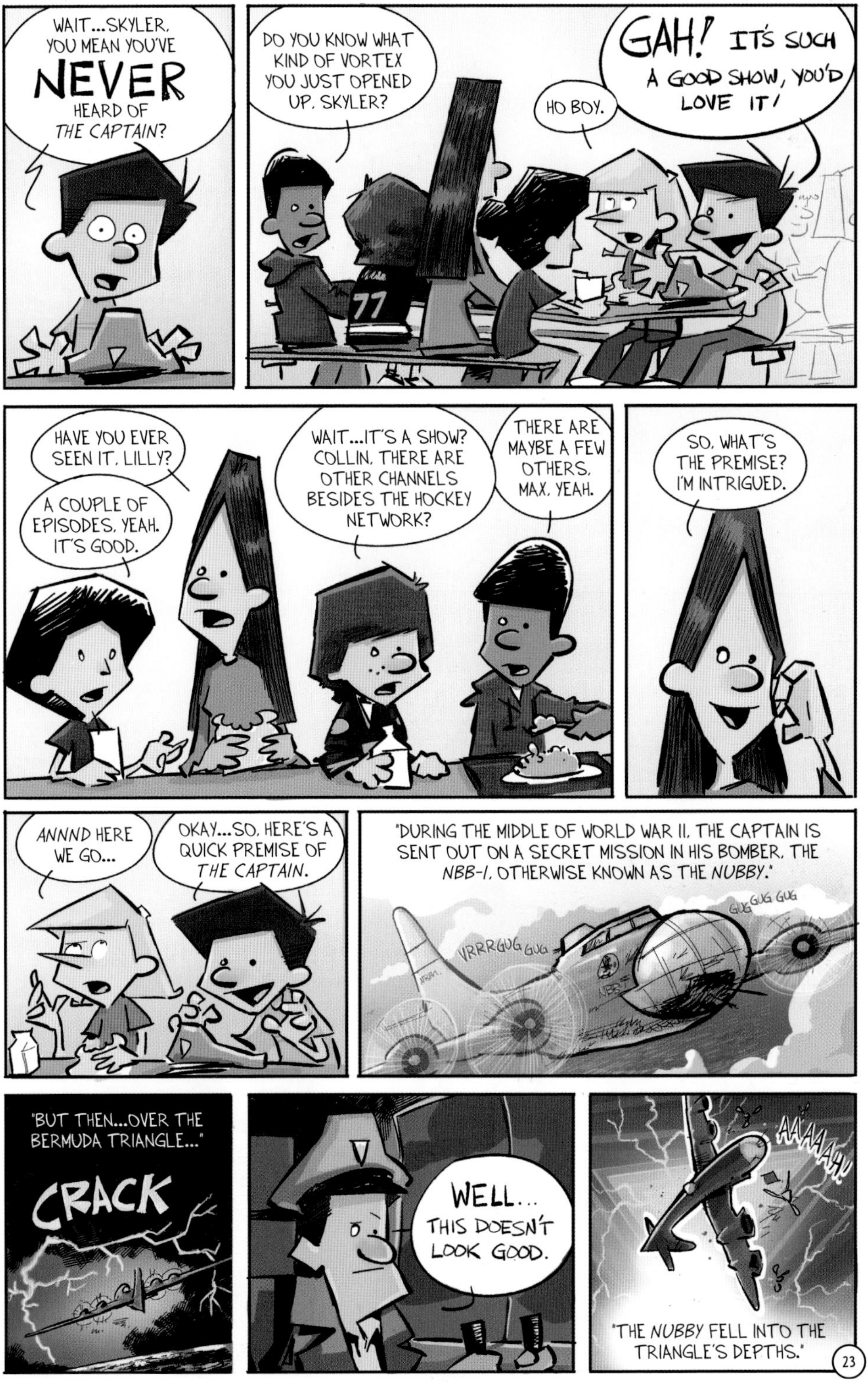

WAIT...SKYLER, YOU MEAN YOU'VE NEVER HEARD OF THE CAPTAIN?
DO YOU KNOW WHAT KIND OF VORTEX YOU JUST OPENED UP, SKYLER?
HO BOY.
GAH! IT'S SUCH A GOOD SHOW, YOU'D LOVE IT!
HAVE YOU EVER SEEN IT, LILLY?
A COUPLE OF EPISODES, YEAH. IT'S GOOD.
WAIT...IT'S A SHOW? COLLIN, THERE ARE OTHER CHANNELS BESIDES THE HOCKEY NETWORK?
THERE ARE MAYBE A FEW OTHERS, MAX, YEAH.
SO, WHAT'S THE PREMISE? I'M INTRIGUED.
ANNND HERE WE GO...
OKAY...SO, HERE'S A QUICK PREMISE OF THE CAPTAIN.
"DURING THE MIDDLE OF WORLD WAR II, THE CAPTAIN IS SENT OUT ON A SECRET MISSION IN HIS BOMBER, THE NBB-1, OTHERWISE KNOWN AS THE NUBBY."
VRRRGUG GUG
GUG GUG GUG
"BUT THEN...OVER THE BERMUDA TRIANGLE..."
CRACK
WELL... THIS DOESN'T LOOK GOOD.
AAAAAAH!
"THE NUBBY FELL INTO THE TRIANGLE'S DEPTHS."

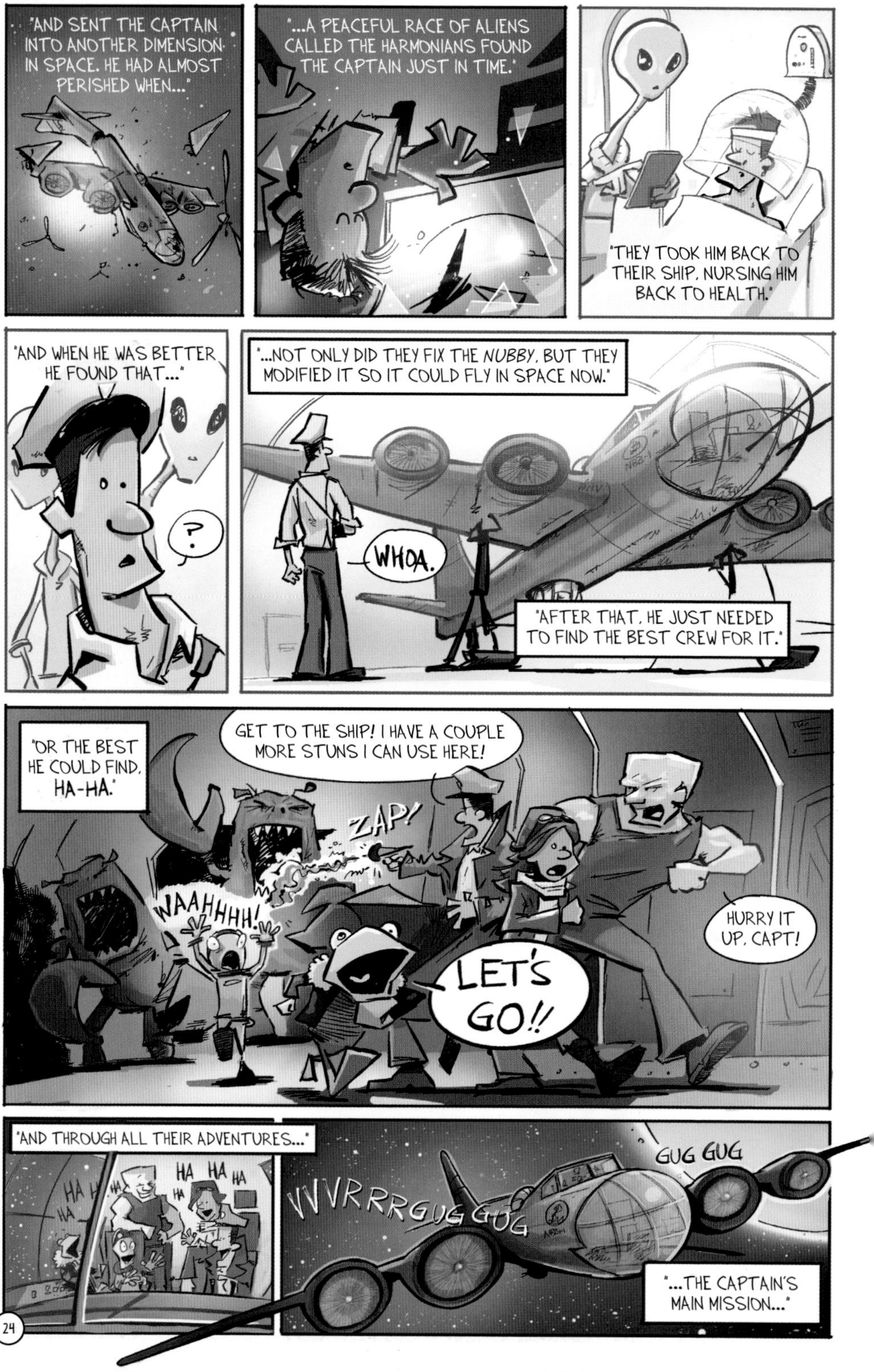
"AND SENT THE CAPTAIN INTO ANOTHER DIMENSION IN SPACE. HE HAD ALMOST PERISHED WHEN..."
"...A PEACEFUL RACE OF ALIENS CALLED THE HARMONIANS FOUND THE CAPTAIN JUST IN TIME."
"THEY TOOK HIM BACK TO THEIR SHIP, NURSING HIM BACK TO HEALTH."
"AND WHEN HE WAS BETTER HE FOUND THAT..."
?
"...NOT ONLY DID THEY FIX THE *NUBBY*, BUT THEY MODIFIED IT SO IT COULD FLY IN SPACE NOW."
WHOA.
"AFTER THAT, HE JUST NEEDED TO FIND THE BEST CREW FOR IT."
"OR THE BEST HE COULD FIND, HA-HA."
GET TO THE SHIP! I HAVE A COUPLE MORE STUNS I CAN USE HERE!
ZAP!
WAAHHHH!
HURRY IT UP, CAPT!
LET'S GO!!
"AND THROUGH ALL THEIR ADVENTURES..."
HA HA HA HA HA HA HA
VVVRRRRGUG GUG
GUG GUG
"...THE CAPTAIN'S MAIN MISSION..."

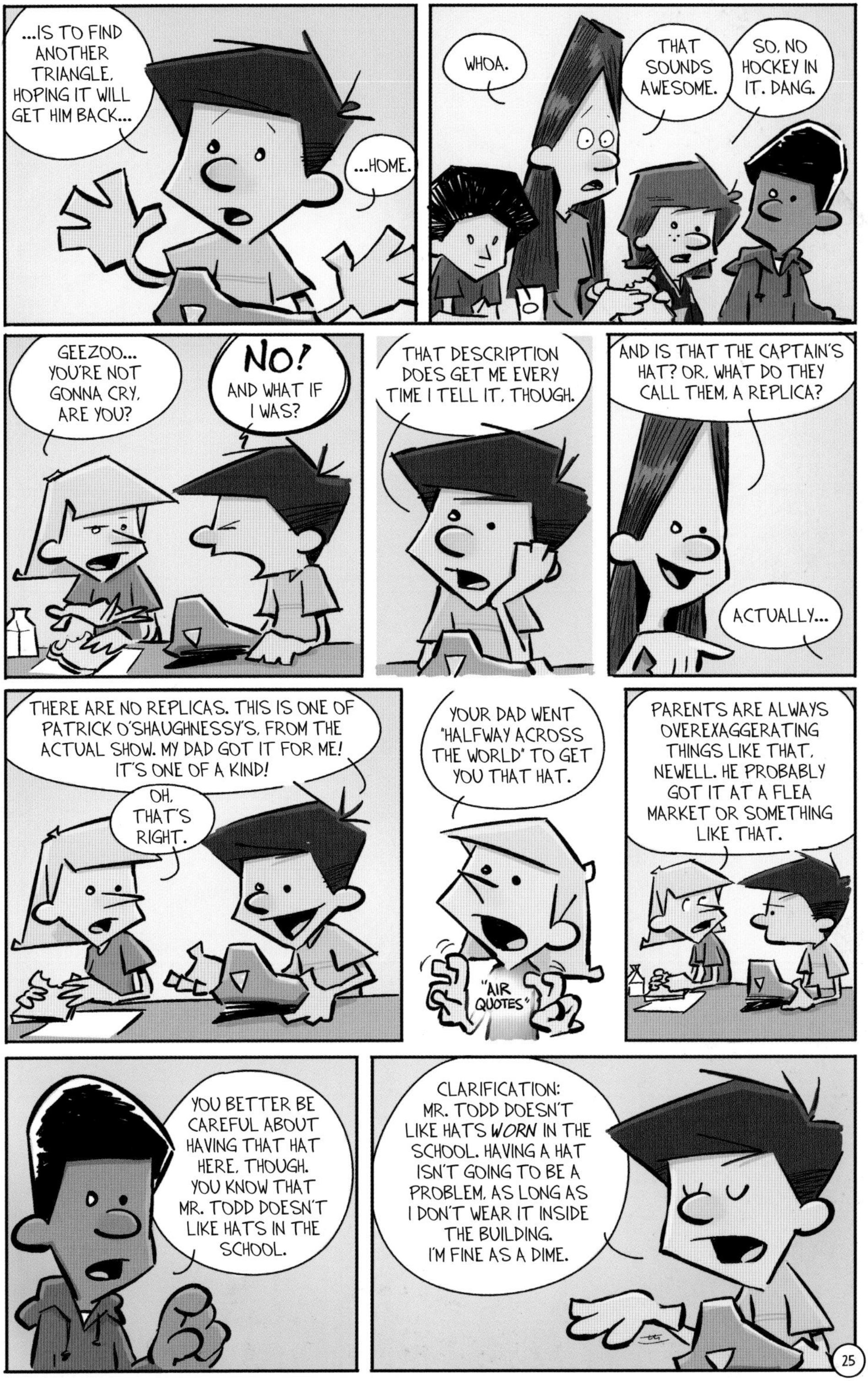

...IS TO FIND ANOTHER TRIANGLE, HOPING IT WILL GET HIM BACK...
...HOME.
WHOA.
THAT SOUNDS AWESOME.
SO, NO HOCKEY IN IT. DANG.
GEEZOO... YOU'RE NOT GONNA CRY, ARE YOU?
NO! AND WHAT IF I WAS?
THAT DESCRIPTION DOES GET ME EVERY TIME I TELL IT, THOUGH.
AND IS THAT THE CAPTAIN'S HAT? OR, WHAT DO THEY CALL THEM, A REPLICA?
ACTUALLY...
THERE ARE NO REPLICAS. THIS IS ONE OF PATRICK O'SHAUGHNESSY'S, FROM THE ACTUAL SHOW. MY DAD GOT IT FOR ME! IT'S ONE OF A KIND!
OH, THAT'S RIGHT.
YOUR DAD WENT "HALFWAY ACROSS THE WORLD" TO GET YOU THAT HAT.
"AIR QUOTES"
PARENTS ARE ALWAYS OVEREXAGGERATING THINGS LIKE THAT, NEWELL. HE PROBABLY GOT IT AT A FLEA MARKET OR SOMETHING LIKE THAT.
YOU BETTER BE CAREFUL ABOUT HAVING THAT HAT HERE, THOUGH. YOU KNOW THAT MR. TODD DOESN'T LIKE HATS IN THE SCHOOL.
CLARIFICATION: MR. TODD DOESN'T LIKE HATS WORN IN THE SCHOOL. HAVING A HAT ISN'T GOING TO BE A PROBLEM, AS LONG AS I DON'T WEAR IT INSIDE THE BUILDING. I'M FINE AS A DIME.

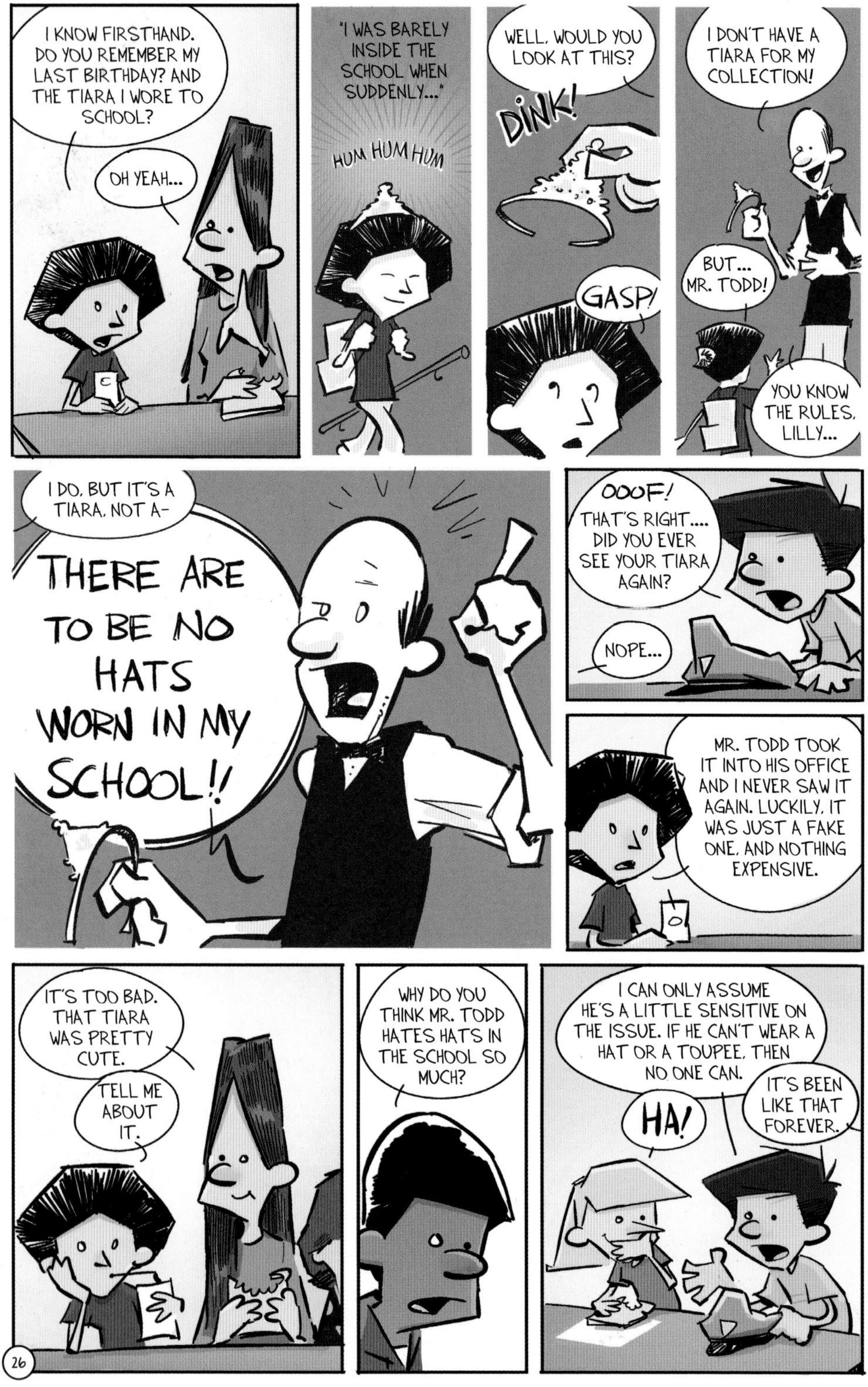
I KNOW FIRSTHAND. DO YOU REMEMBER MY LAST BIRTHDAY? AND THE TIARA I WORE TO SCHOOL?
OH YEAH...
"I WAS BARELY INSIDE THE SCHOOL WHEN SUDDENLY..."
HUM HUM HUM
WELL, WOULD YOU LOOK AT THIS?
DINK!
GASP!
I DON'T HAVE A TIARA FOR MY COLLECTION!
BUT... MR. TODD!
YOU KNOW THE RULES, LILLY...
I DO, BUT IT'S A TIARA, NOT A-
THERE ARE TO BE NO HATS WORN IN MY SCHOOL!!
OOOF!
THAT'S RIGHT.... DID YOU EVER SEE YOUR TIARA AGAIN?
NOPE...
MR. TODD TOOK IT INTO HIS OFFICE AND I NEVER SAW IT AGAIN. LUCKILY, IT WAS JUST A FAKE ONE, AND NOTHING EXPENSIVE.
IT'S TOO BAD. THAT TIARA WAS PRETTY CUTE.
TELL ME ABOUT IT.
WHY DO YOU THINK MR. TODD HATES HATS IN THE SCHOOL SO MUCH?
I CAN ONLY ASSUME HE'S A LITTLE SENSITIVE ON THE ISSUE. IF HE CAN'T WEAR A HAT OR A TOUPEE, THEN NO ONE CAN.
HA!
IT'S BEEN LIKE THAT FOREVER.

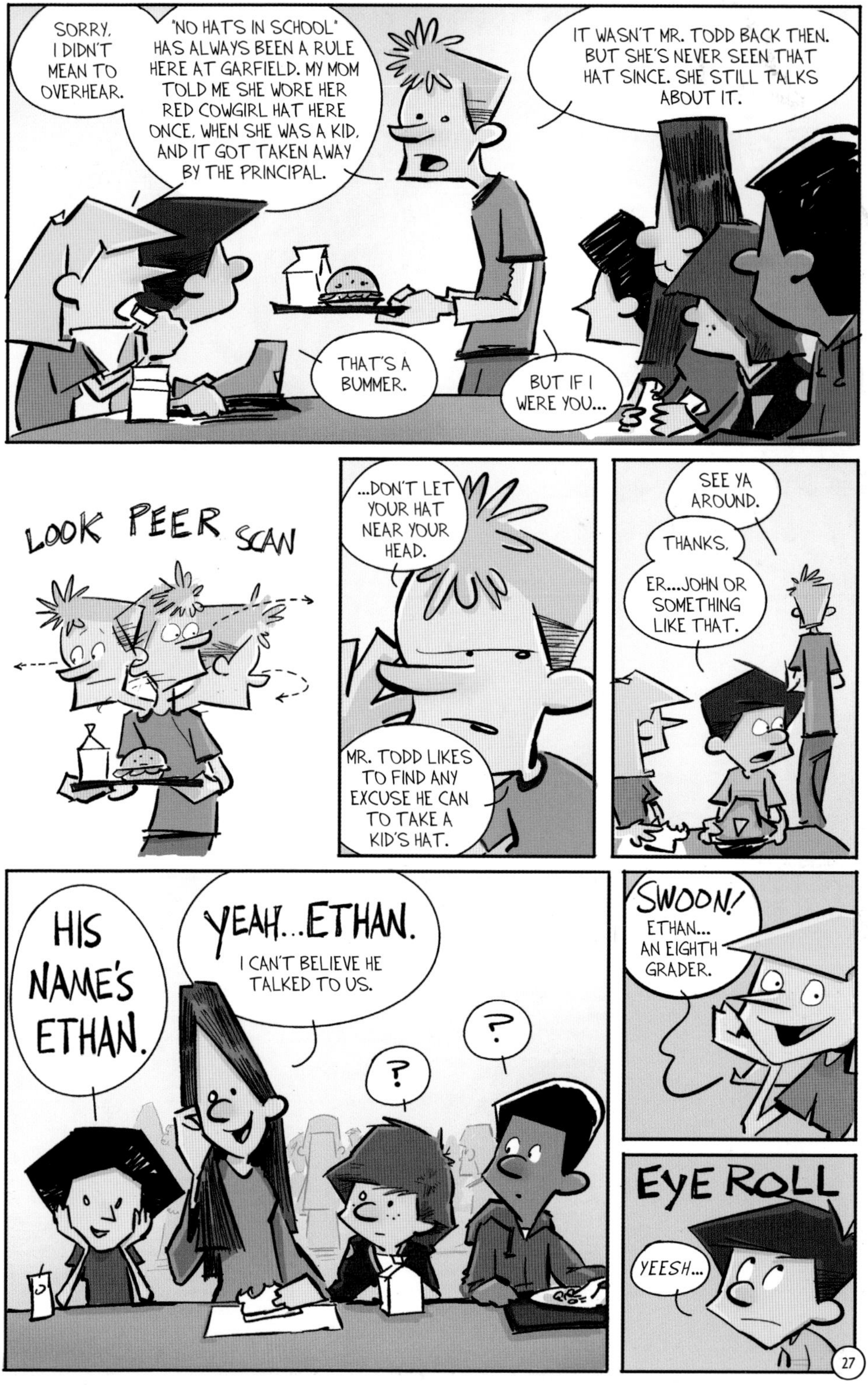
SORRY, I DIDN'T MEAN TO OVERHEAR.
"NO HATS IN SCHOOL" HAS ALWAYS BEEN A RULE HERE AT GARFIELD. MY MOM TOLD ME SHE WORE HER RED COWGIRL HAT HERE ONCE, WHEN SHE WAS A KID, AND IT GOT TAKEN AWAY BY THE PRINCIPAL.
IT WASN'T MR. TODD BACK THEN. BUT SHE'S NEVER SEEN THAT HAT SINCE. SHE STILL TALKS ABOUT IT.
THAT'S A BUMMER.
BUT IF I WERE YOU...
LOOK PEER SCAN
...DON'T LET YOUR HAT NEAR YOUR HEAD.
MR. TODD LIKES TO FIND ANY EXCUSE HE CAN TO TAKE A KID'S HAT.
SEE YA AROUND.
THANKS,
ER...JOHN OR SOMETHING LIKE THAT.
HIS NAME'S ETHAN.
YEAH...ETHAN.
I CAN'T BELIEVE HE TALKED TO US.
?
?
SWOON!
ETHAN... AN EIGHTH GRADER.
EYE ROLL
YEESH...

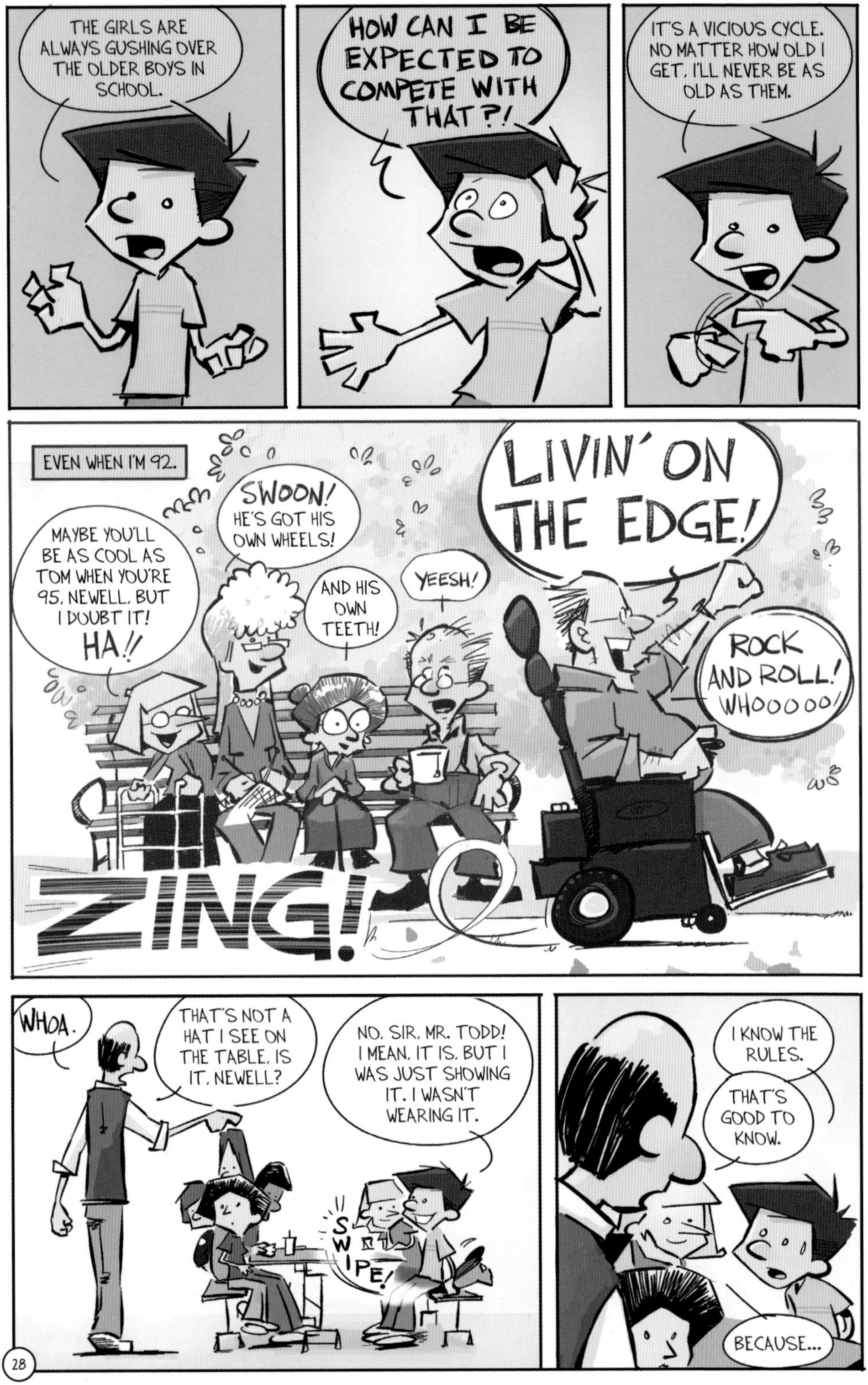
THE GIRLS ARE ALWAYS GUSHING OVER THE OLDER BOYS IN SCHOOL.
HOW CAN I BE EXPECTED TO COMPETE WITH THAT?!
IT'S A VICIOUS CYCLE. NO MATTER HOW OLD I GET, I'LL NEVER BE AS OLD AS THEM.
EVEN WHEN I'M 92.
MAYBE YOU'LL BE AS COOL AS TOM WHEN YOU'RE 95, NEWELL, BUT I DOUBT IT! HA!!
SWOON! HE'S GOT HIS OWN WHEELS!
AND HIS OWN TEETH!
YEESH!
LIVIN' ON THE EDGE!
ROCK AND ROLL! WHOOOOO!
ZING!
WHOA.
THAT'S NOT A HAT I SEE ON THE TABLE, IS IT, NEWELL?
NO, SIR, MR. TODD! I MEAN, IT IS, BUT I WAS JUST SHOWING IT. I WASN'T WEARING IT.
SWIPE!
I KNOW THE RULES.
THAT'S GOOD TO KNOW.
BECAUSE...

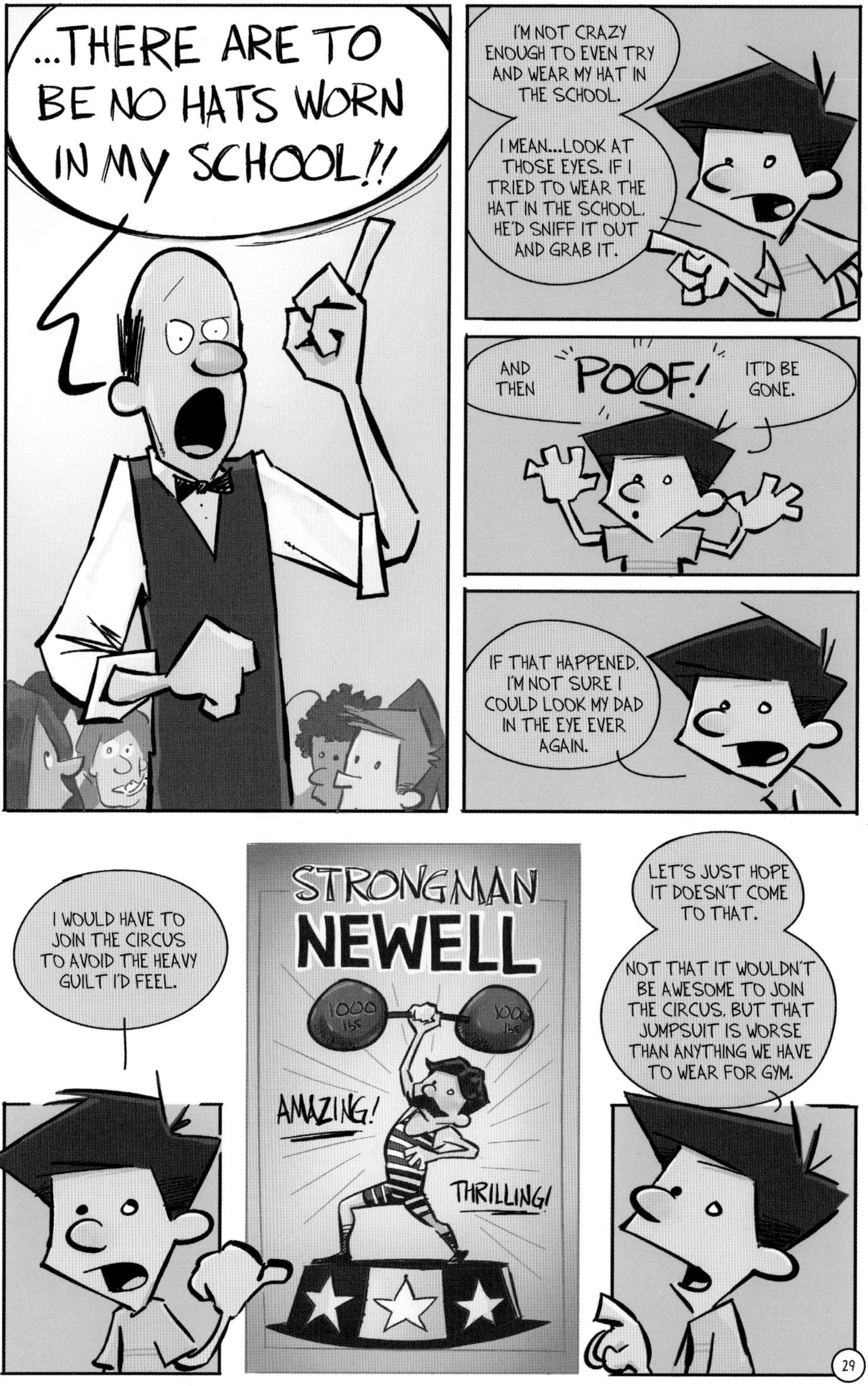
...THERE ARE TO BE NO HATS WORN IN MY SCHOOL!!
I'M NOT CRAZY ENOUGH TO EVEN TRY AND WEAR MY HAT IN THE SCHOOL.
I MEAN...LOOK AT THOSE EYES. IF I TRIED TO WEAR THE HAT IN THE SCHOOL, HE'D SNIFF IT OUT AND GRAB IT.
AND THEN
POOF!
IT'D BE GONE.
IF THAT HAPPENED, I'M NOT SURE I COULD LOOK MY DAD IN THE EYE EVER AGAIN.
I WOULD HAVE TO JOIN THE CIRCUS TO AVOID THE HEAVY GUILT I'D FEEL.
STRONGMAN
NEWELL
1000 lbs
1000 lbs
AMAZING!
THRILLING!
LET'S JUST HOPE IT DOESN'T COME TO THAT.
NOT THAT IT WOULDN'T BE AWESOME TO JOIN THE CIRCUS, BUT THAT JUMPSUIT IS WORSE THAN ANYTHING WE HAVE TO WEAR FOR GYM.

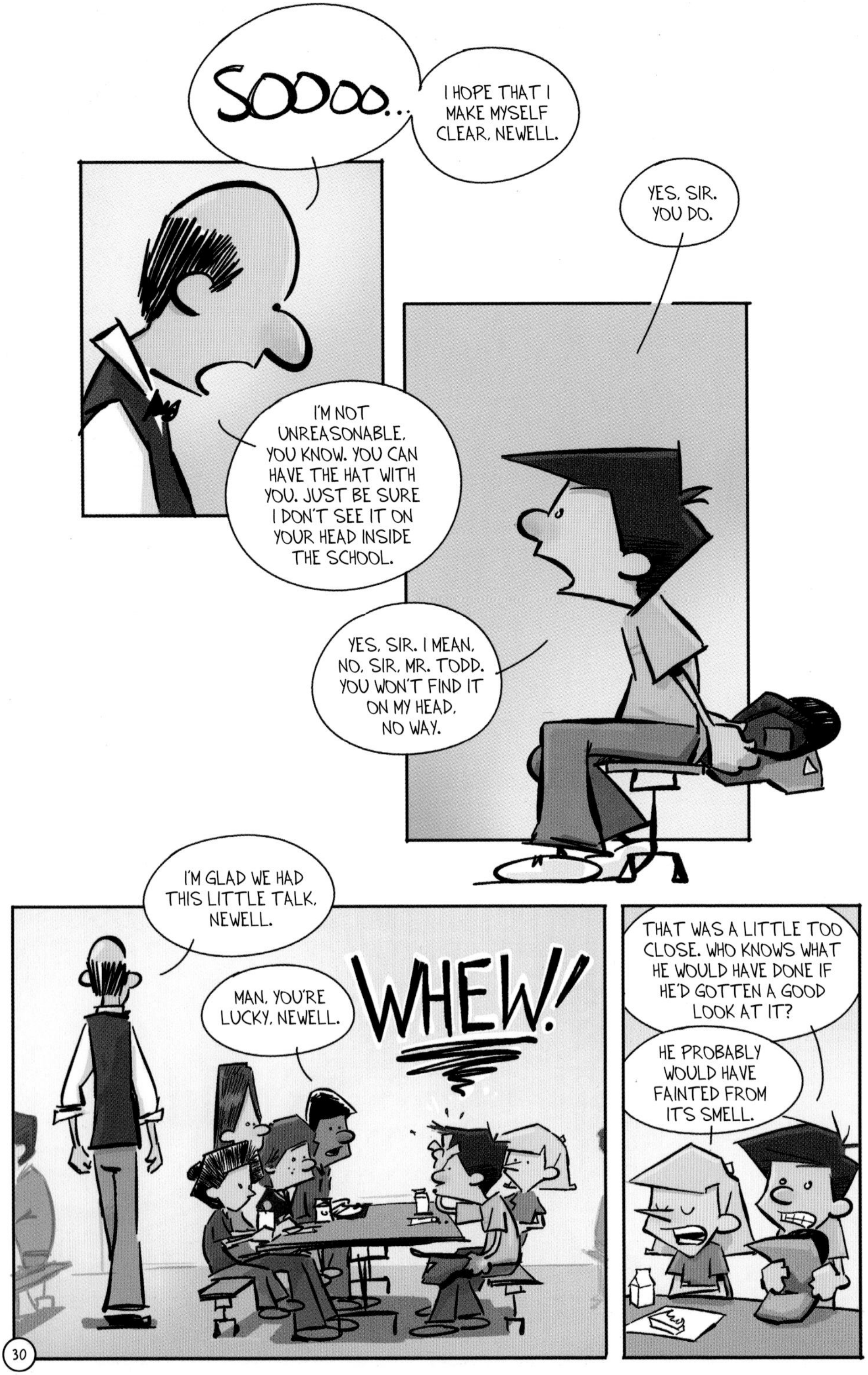
SOOOO...
I HOPE THAT I MAKE MYSELF CLEAR, NEWELL.
YES, SIR. YOU DO.
I'M NOT UNREASONABLE, YOU KNOW. YOU CAN HAVE THE HAT WITH YOU. JUST BE SURE I DON'T SEE IT ON YOUR HEAD INSIDE THE SCHOOL.
YES, SIR. I MEAN, NO, SIR, MR. TODD. YOU WON'T FIND IT ON MY HEAD, NO WAY.
I'M GLAD WE HAD THIS LITTLE TALK, NEWELL.
MAN, YOU'RE LUCKY, NEWELL.
WHEW!
THAT WAS A LITTLE TOO CLOSE. WHO KNOWS WHAT HE WOULD HAVE DONE IF HE'D GOTTEN A GOOD LOOK AT IT?
HE PROBABLY WOULD HAVE FAINTED FROM ITS SMELL.

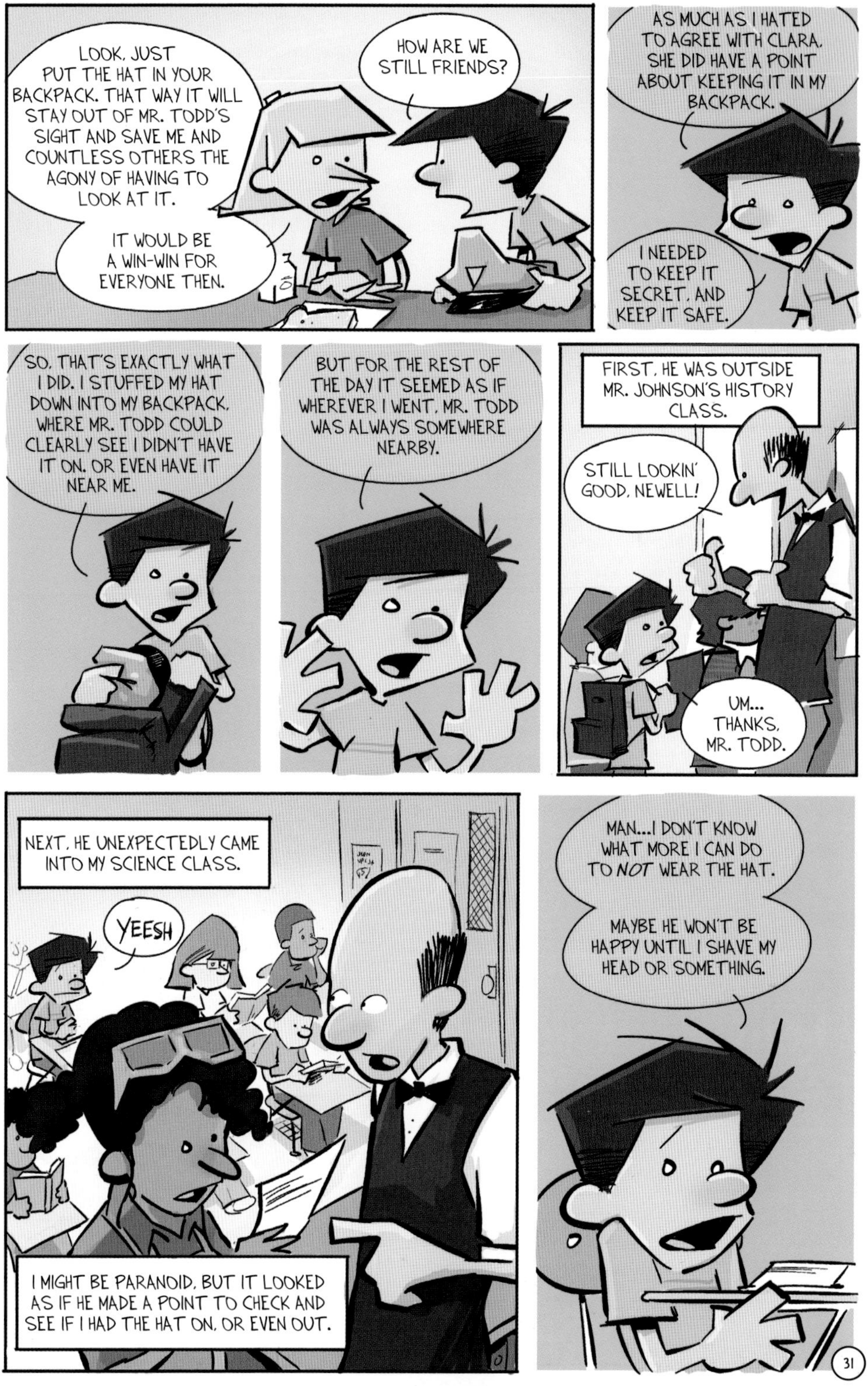
LOOK, JUST PUT THE HAT IN YOUR BACKPACK. THAT WAY IT WILL STAY OUT OF MR. TODD'S SIGHT AND SAVE ME AND COUNTLESS OTHERS THE AGONY OF HAVING TO LOOK AT IT.
IT WOULD BE A WIN-WIN FOR EVERYONE THEN.
HOW ARE WE STILL FRIENDS?
AS MUCH AS I HATED TO AGREE WITH CLARA, SHE DID HAVE A POINT ABOUT KEEPING IT IN MY BACKPACK.
I NEEDED TO KEEP IT SECRET, AND KEEP IT SAFE.
SO, THAT'S EXACTLY WHAT I DID. I STUFFED MY HAT DOWN INTO MY BACKPACK, WHERE MR. TODD COULD CLEARLY SEE I DIDN'T HAVE IT ON, OR EVEN HAVE IT NEAR ME.
BUT FOR THE REST OF THE DAY IT SEEMED AS IF WHEREVER I WENT, MR. TODD WAS ALWAYS SOMEWHERE NEARBY.
FIRST, HE WAS OUTSIDE MR. JOHNSON'S HISTORY CLASS.
STILL LOOKIN' GOOD, NEWELL!
UM... THANKS, MR. TODD.
NEXT, HE UNEXPECTEDLY CAME INTO MY SCIENCE CLASS.
YEESH
I MIGHT BE PARANOID, BUT IT LOOKED AS IF HE MADE A POINT TO CHECK AND SEE IF I HAD THE HAT ON, OR EVEN OUT.
MAN...I DON'T KNOW WHAT MORE I CAN DO TO *NOT* WEAR THE HAT.
MAYBE HE WON'T BE HAPPY UNTIL I SHAVE MY HEAD OR SOMETHING.

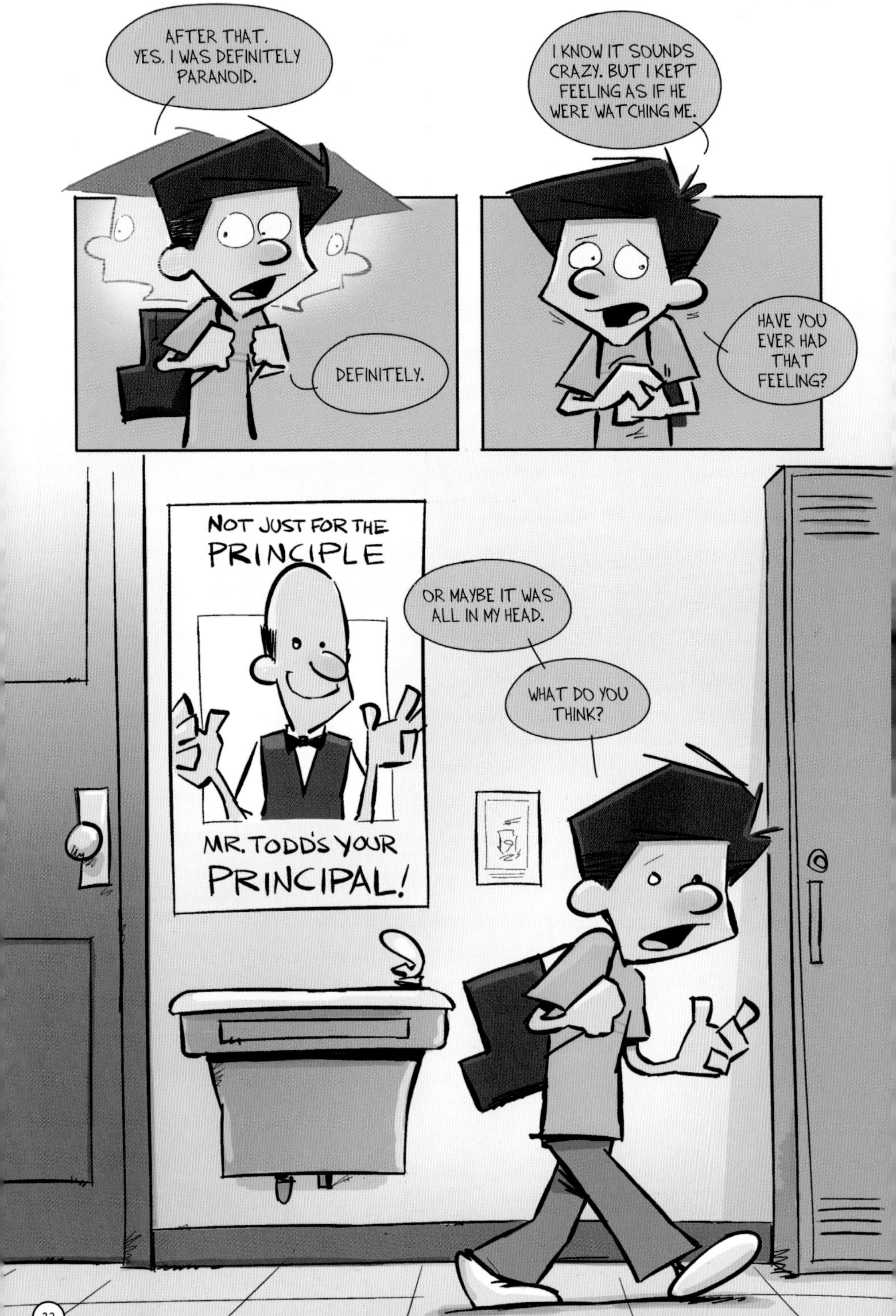
AFTER THAT, YES, I WAS DEFINITELY PARANOID.
DEFINITELY.
I KNOW IT SOUNDS CRAZY, BUT I KEPT FEELING AS IF HE WERE WATCHING ME.
HAVE YOU EVER HAD THAT FEELING?
NOT JUST FOR THE PRINCIPLE
MR. TODD'S YOUR PRINCIPAL!
OR MAYBE IT WAS ALL IN MY HEAD.
WHAT DO YOU THINK?

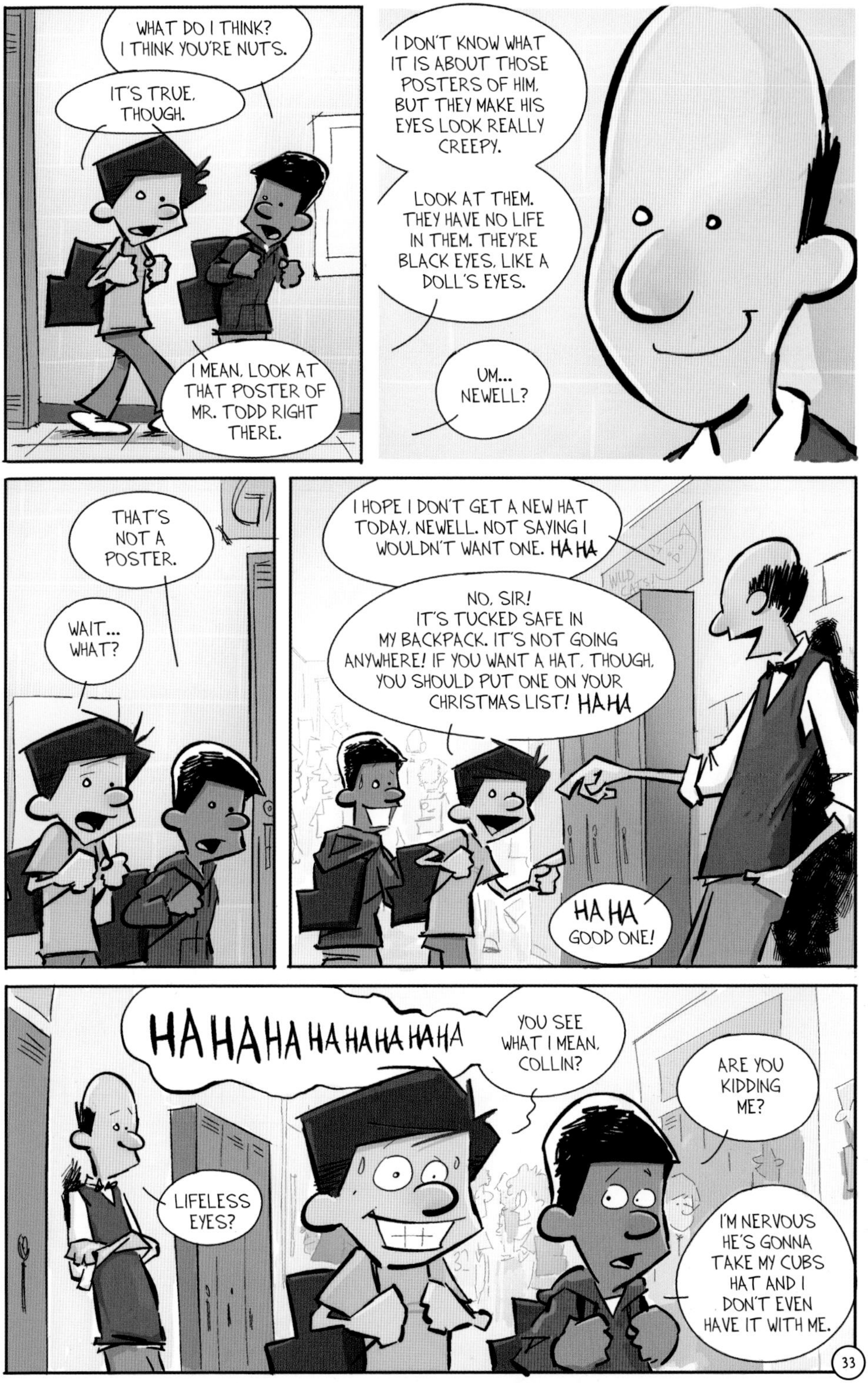
WHAT DO I THINK? I THINK YOU'RE NUTS.
IT'S TRUE, THOUGH.
I MEAN, LOOK AT THAT POSTER OF MR. TODD RIGHT THERE.
I DON'T KNOW WHAT IT IS ABOUT THOSE POSTERS OF HIM, BUT THEY MAKE HIS EYES LOOK REALLY CREEPY.
LOOK AT THEM. THEY HAVE NO LIFE IN THEM. THEY'RE BLACK EYES, LIKE A DOLL'S EYES.
UM... NEWELL?
THAT'S NOT A POSTER.
WAIT... WHAT?
I HOPE I DON'T GET A NEW HAT TODAY, NEWELL. NOT SAYING I WOULDN'T WANT ONE. HA HA
NO, SIR! IT'S TUCKED SAFE IN MY BACKPACK. IT'S NOT GOING ANYWHERE! IF YOU WANT A HAT, THOUGH, YOU SHOULD PUT ONE ON YOUR CHRISTMAS LIST! HA HA
HA HA GOOD ONE!
HA HA HA HA HA HA HA HA HA
YOU SEE WHAT I MEAN, COLLIN?
ARE YOU KIDDING ME?
LIFELESS EYES?
I'M NERVOUS HE'S GONNA TAKE MY CUBS HAT AND I DON'T EVEN HAVE IT WITH ME.

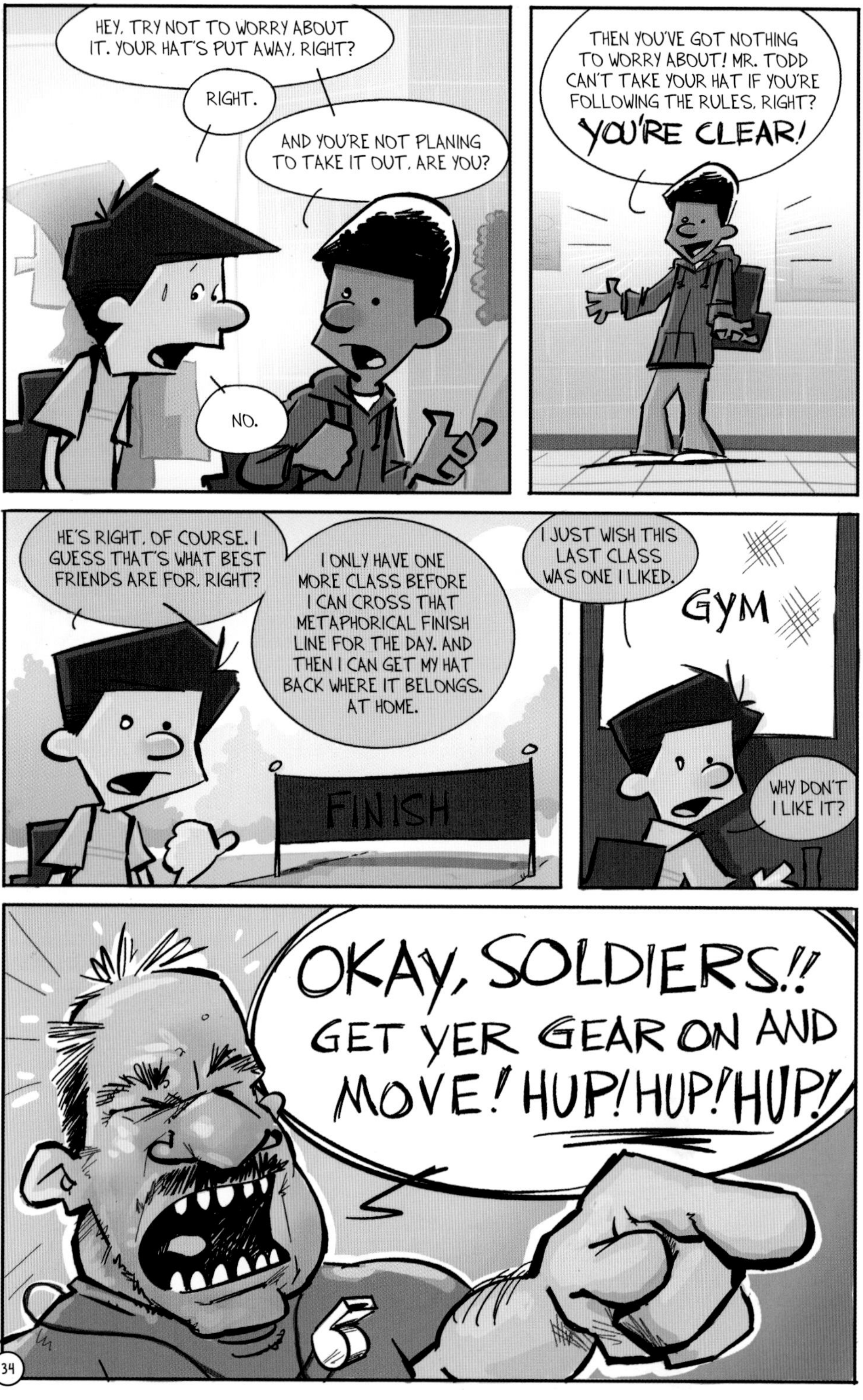
HEY, TRY NOT TO WORRY ABOUT IT. YOUR HAT'S PUT AWAY, RIGHT?
RIGHT.
AND YOU'RE NOT PLANING TO TAKE IT OUT, ARE YOU?
NO.
THEN YOU'VE GOT NOTHING TO WORRY ABOUT! MR. TODD CAN'T TAKE YOUR HAT IF YOU'RE FOLLOWING THE RULES, RIGHT? YOU'RE CLEAR!
HE'S RIGHT, OF COURSE. I GUESS THAT'S WHAT BEST FRIENDS ARE FOR, RIGHT?
I ONLY HAVE ONE MORE CLASS BEFORE I CAN CROSS THAT METAPHORICAL FINISH LINE FOR THE DAY. AND THEN I CAN GET MY HAT BACK WHERE IT BELONGS. AT HOME.
FINISH
I JUST WISH THIS LAST CLASS WAS ONE I LIKED.
GYM
WHY DON'T I LIKE IT?
OKAY, SOLDIERS!! GET YER GEAR ON AND MOVE! HUP! HUP! HUP!

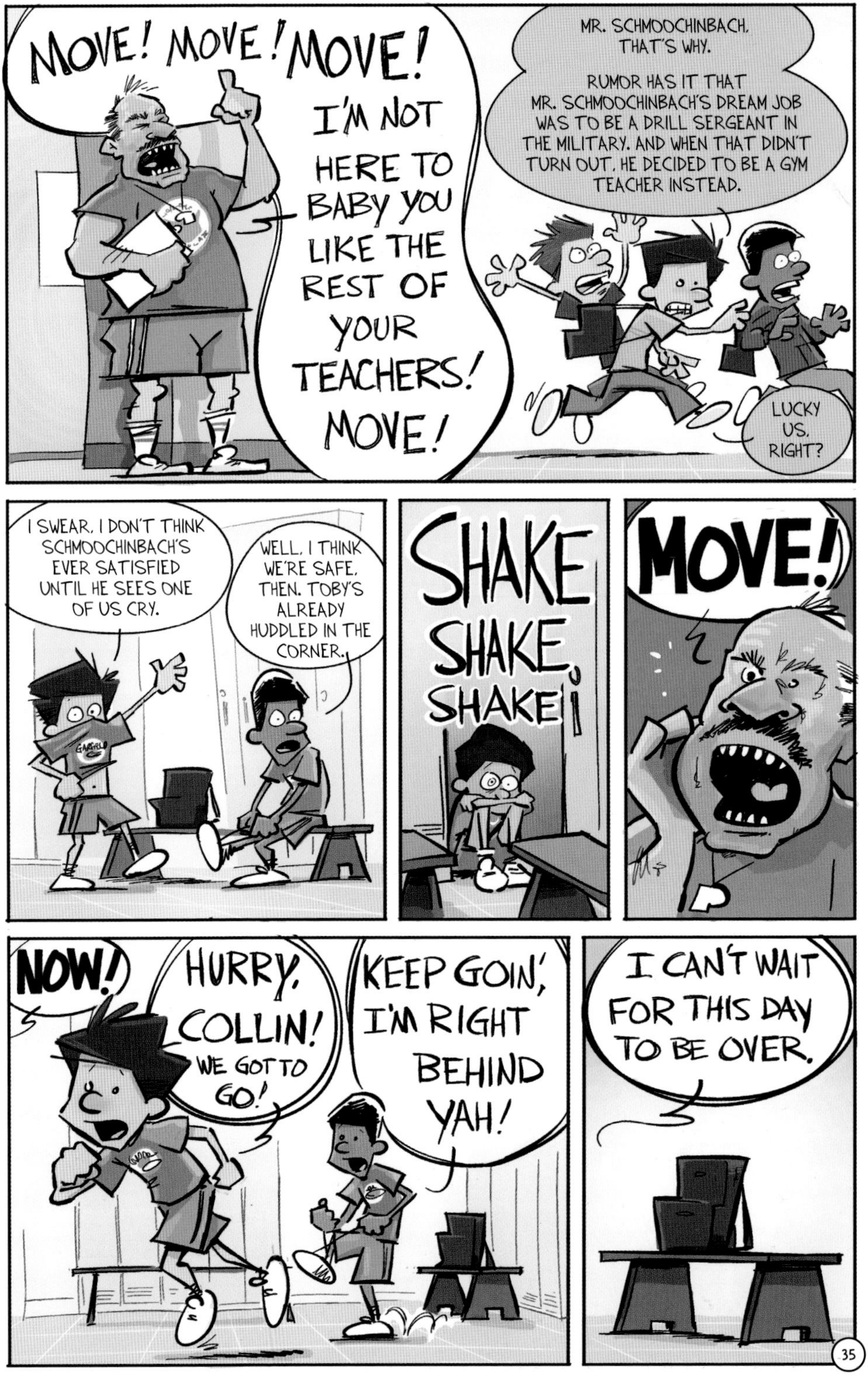
MOVE! MOVE! MOVE!
I'M NOT HERE TO BABY YOU LIKE THE REST OF YOUR TEACHERS! MOVE!
MR. SCHMOOCHINBACH, THAT'S WHY.
RUMOR HAS IT THAT MR. SCHMOOCHINBACH'S DREAM JOB WAS TO BE A DRILL SERGEANT IN THE MILITARY. AND WHEN THAT DIDN'T TURN OUT, HE DECIDED TO BE A GYM TEACHER INSTEAD.
LUCKY US, RIGHT?
I SWEAR, I DON'T THINK SCHMOOCHINBACH'S EVER SATISFIED UNTIL HE SEES ONE OF US CRY.
WELL, I THINK WE'RE SAFE, THEN. TOBY'S ALREADY HUDDLED IN THE CORNER.
SHAKE
SHAKE,
SHAKE
MOVE!
NOW!
HURRY, COLLIN! WE GOTTO GO!
KEEP GOIN', I'M RIGHT BEHIND YAH!
I CAN'T WAIT FOR THIS DAY TO BE OVER.

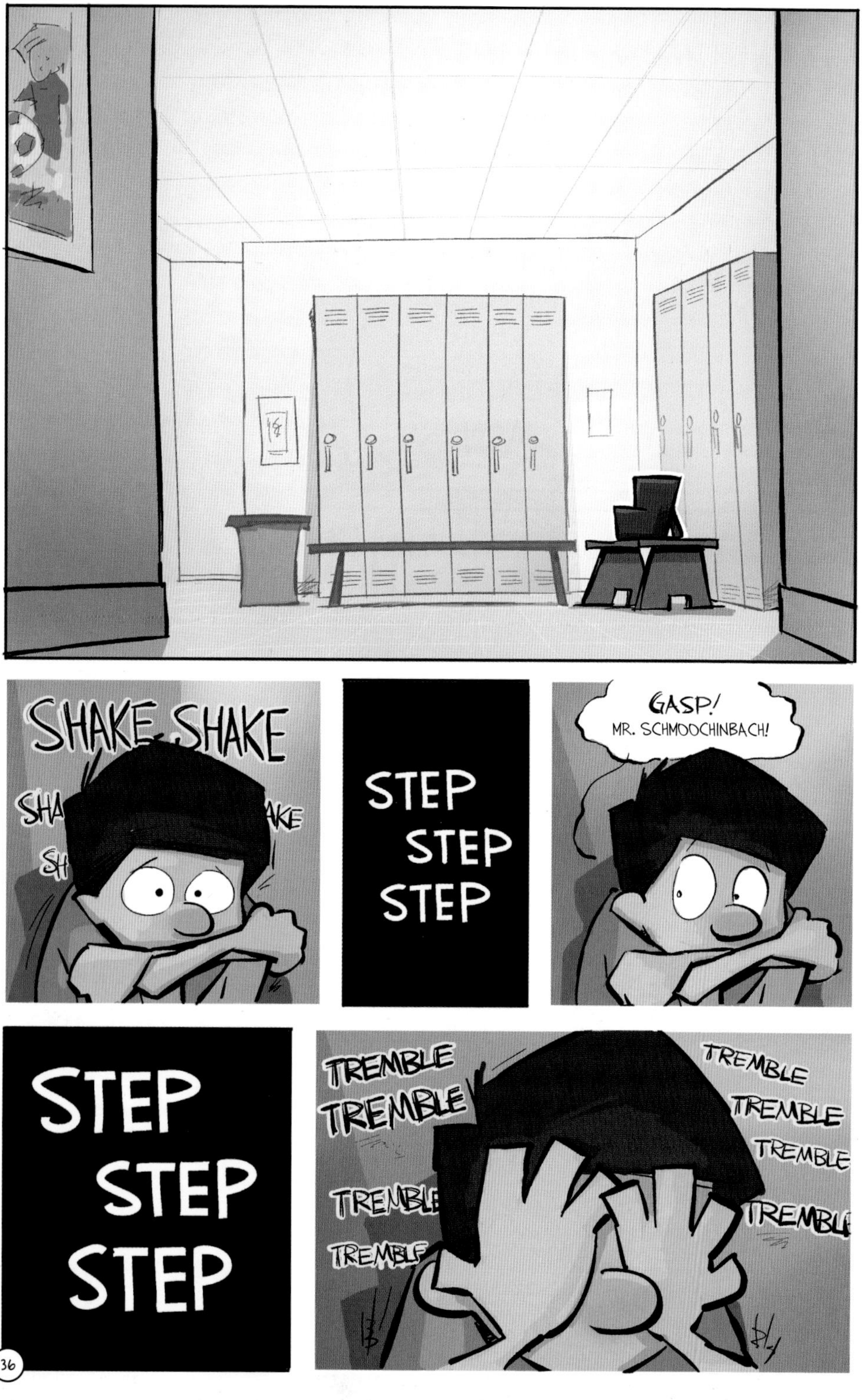
SHAKE SHAKE
STEP
STEP
STEP
GASP!
MR. SCHMOOCHINBACH!
STEP
STEP
STEP
TREMBLE
TREMBLE
TREMBLE
TREMBLE
TREMBLE
TREMBLE
TREMBLE
TREMBLE

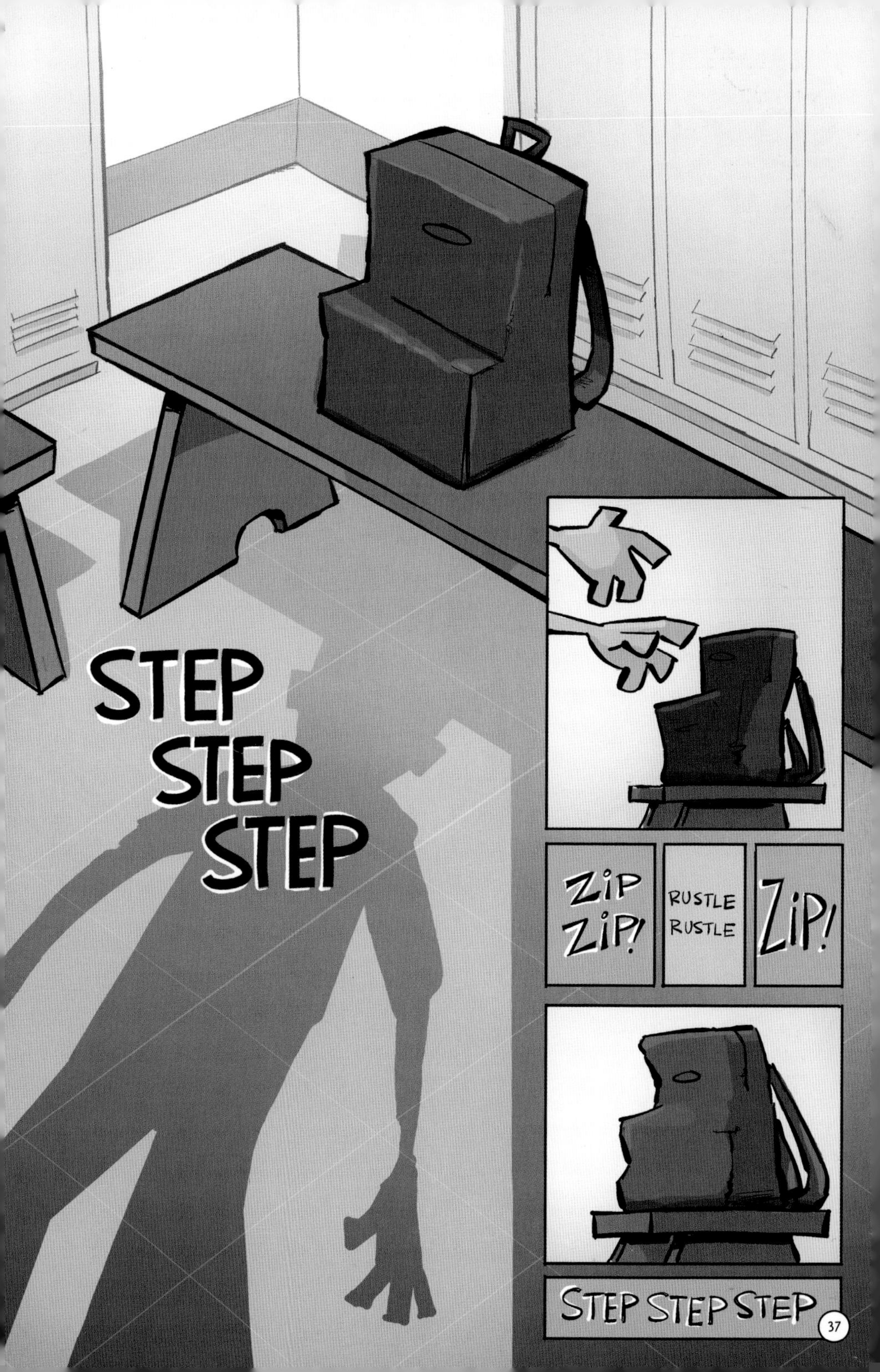
STEP
STEP
STEP
ZIP
ZIP!
RUSTLE
RUSTLE
ZIP!
STEP STEP STEP

CHAPTER THREE
SO CLOSE, AND YET SO FAR

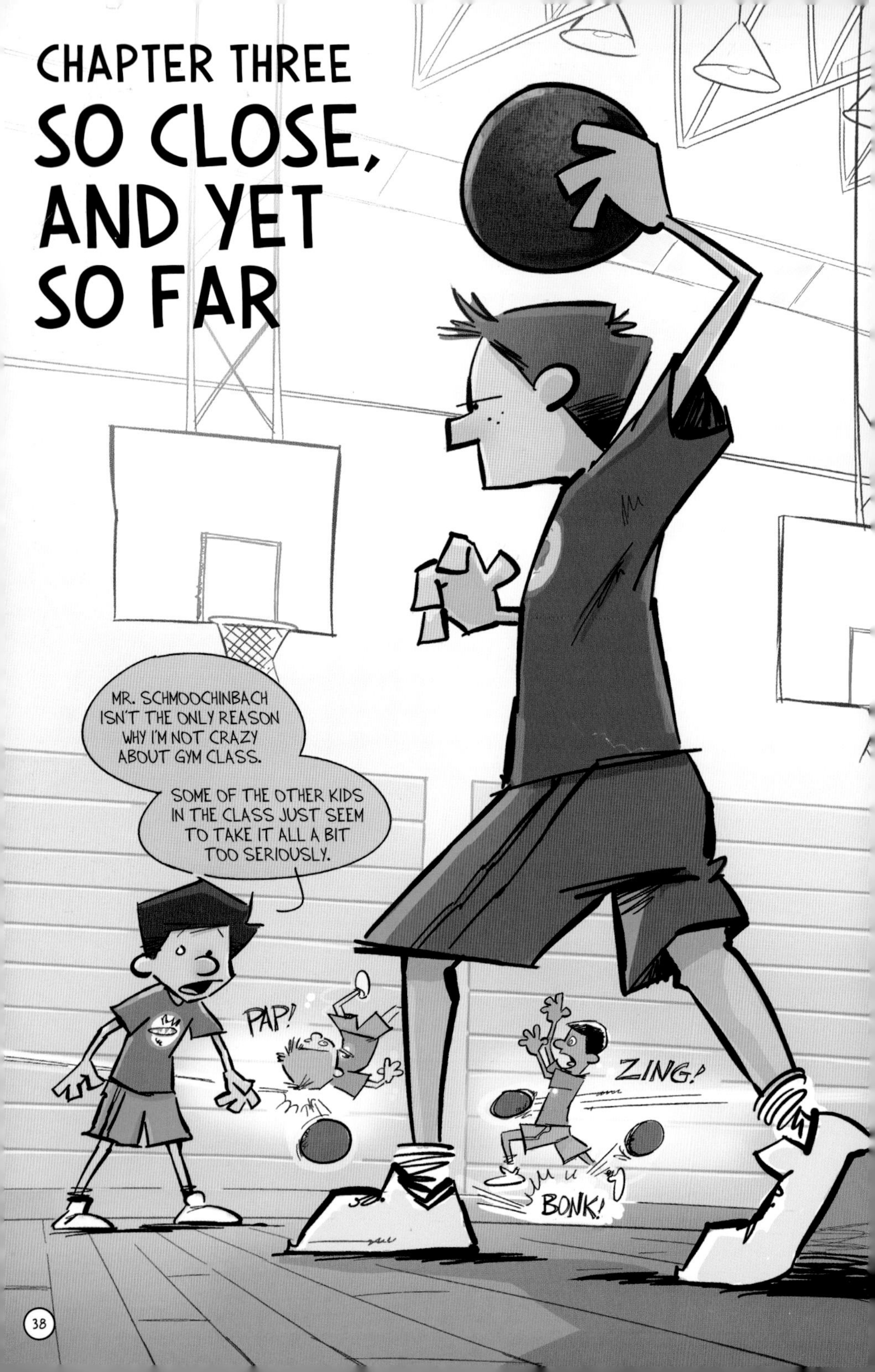
MR. SCHMOOCHINBACH ISN'T THE ONLY REASON WHY I'M NOT CRAZY ABOUT GYM CLASS.
SOME OF THE OTHER KIDS IN THE CLASS JUST SEEM TO TAKE IT ALL A BIT TOO SERIOUSLY.
PAP!
ZING!
BONK!

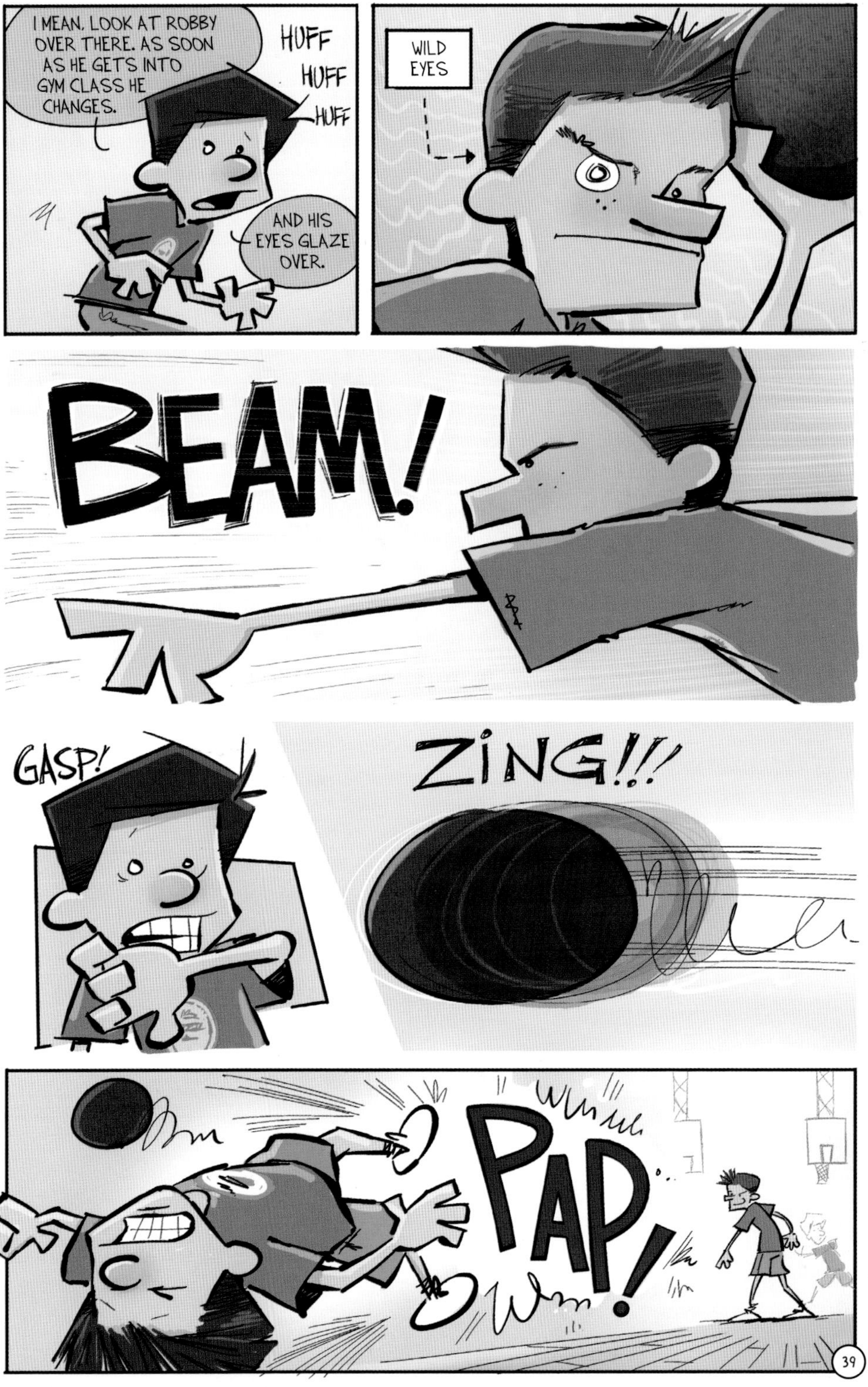
I MEAN, LOOK AT ROBBY OVER THERE. AS SOON AS HE GETS INTO GYM CLASS HE CHANGES.
HUFF
HUFF
HUFF
AND HIS EYES GLAZE OVER.
WILD EYES
BEAM!
GASP!
ZING!!!
PAP!

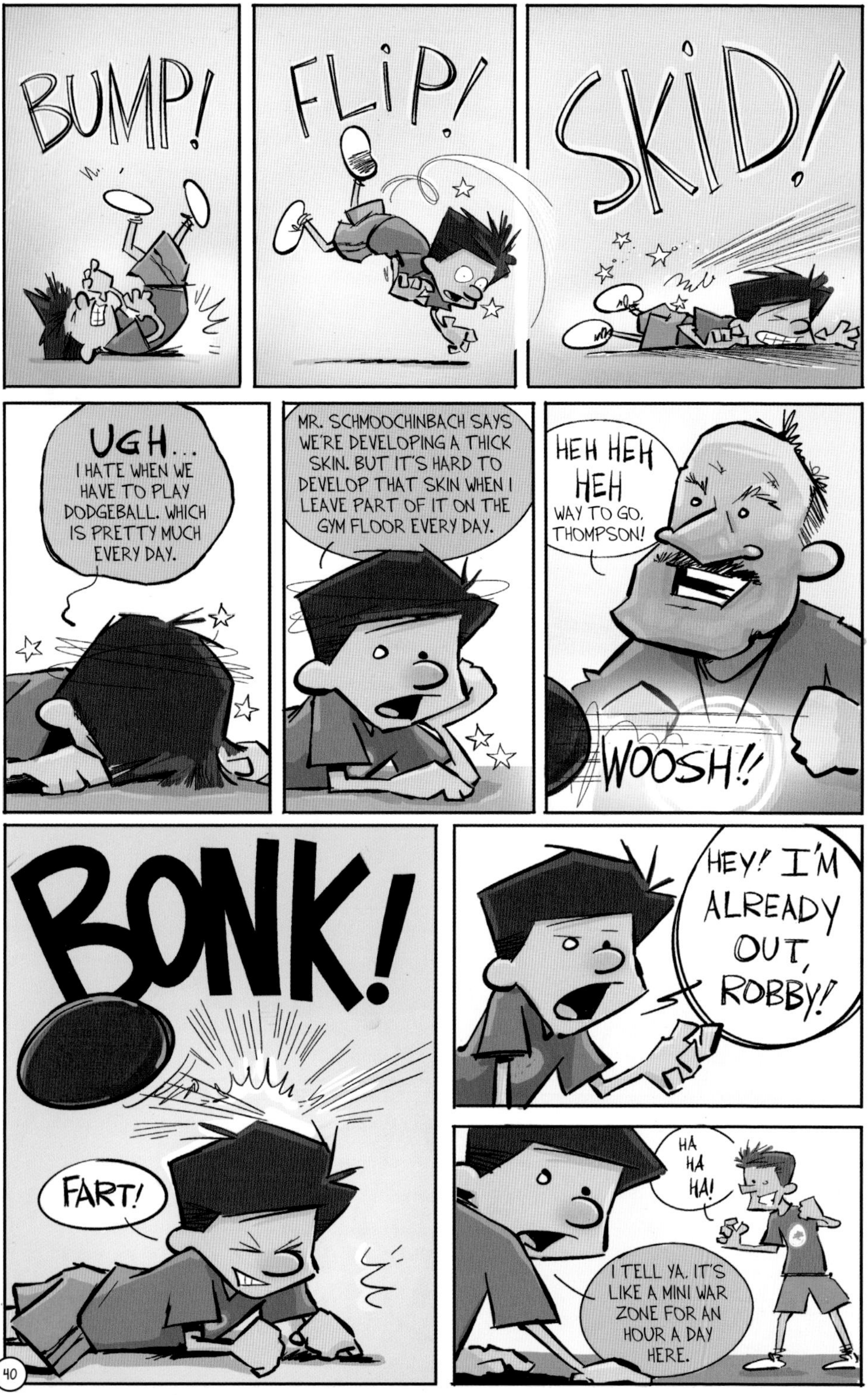
BUMP!
FLIP!
SKID!
UGH... I HATE WHEN WE HAVE TO PLAY DODGEBALL. WHICH IS PRETTY MUCH EVERY DAY.
MR. SCHMOOCHINBACH SAYS WE'RE DEVELOPING A THICK SKIN. BUT IT'S HARD TO DEVELOP THAT SKIN WHEN I LEAVE PART OF IT ON THE GYM FLOOR EVERY DAY.
HEH HEH HEH WAY TO GO, THOMPSON!
WOOSH!!
BONK!
FART!
HEY! I'M ALREADY OUT, ROBBY!
HA HA HA!
I TELL YA, IT'S LIKE A MINI WAR ZONE FOR AN HOUR A DAY HERE.

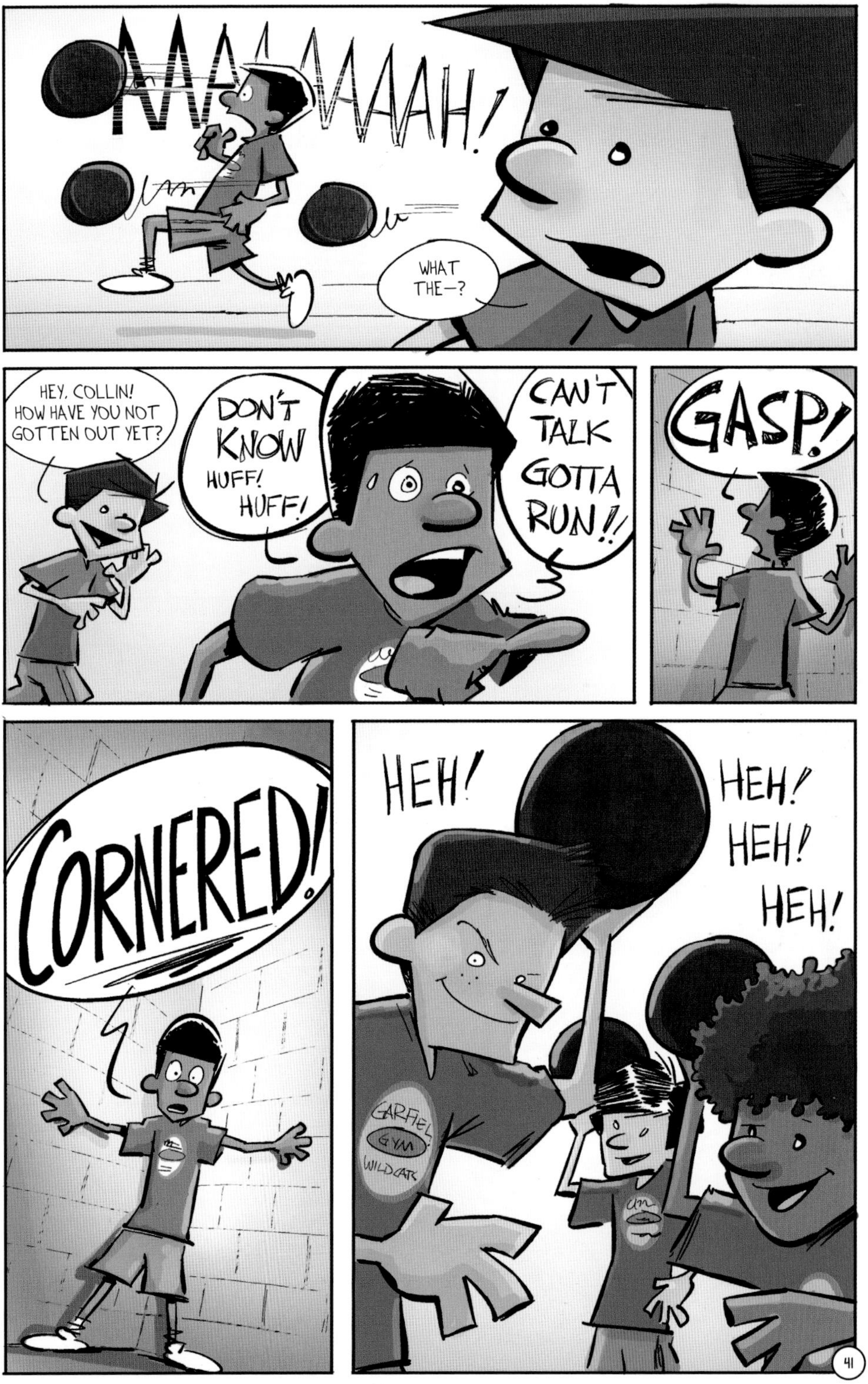
AAAAAAAAH!
WHAT THE—?
HEY, COLLIN! HOW HAVE YOU NOT GOTTEN OUT YET?
DON'T KNOW HUFF! HUFF!
CAN'T TALK GOTTA RUN!!
GASP!
CORNERED!
HEH!
HEH! HEH! HEH!
GARFIEL GYM WILDCATS

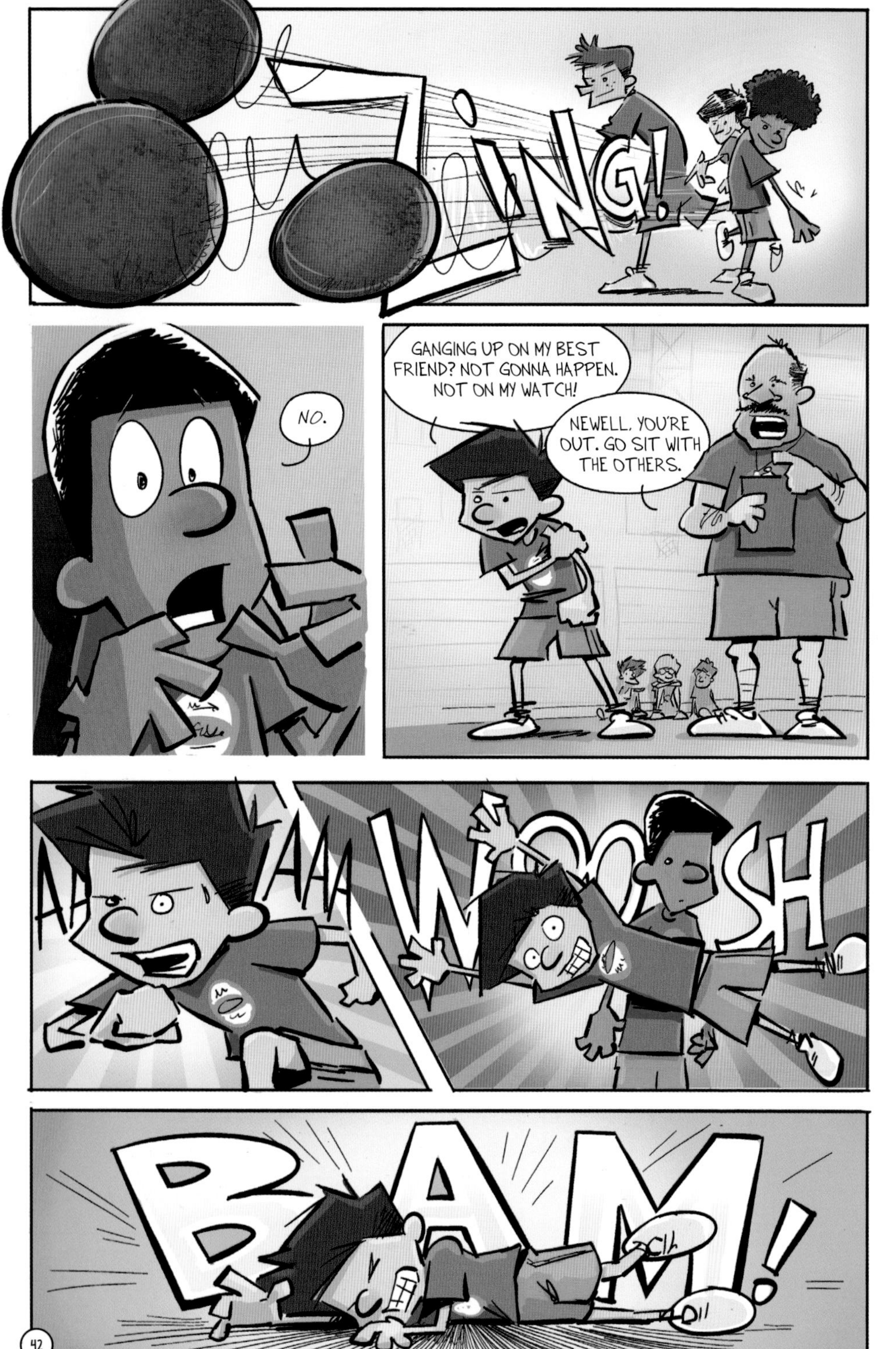
ZING!
NO.
GANGING UP ON MY BEST FRIEND? NOT GONNA HAPPEN. NOT ON MY WATCH!
NEWELL, YOU'RE OUT. GO SIT WITH THE OTHERS.
AAAA
WOOOSH
BAM!

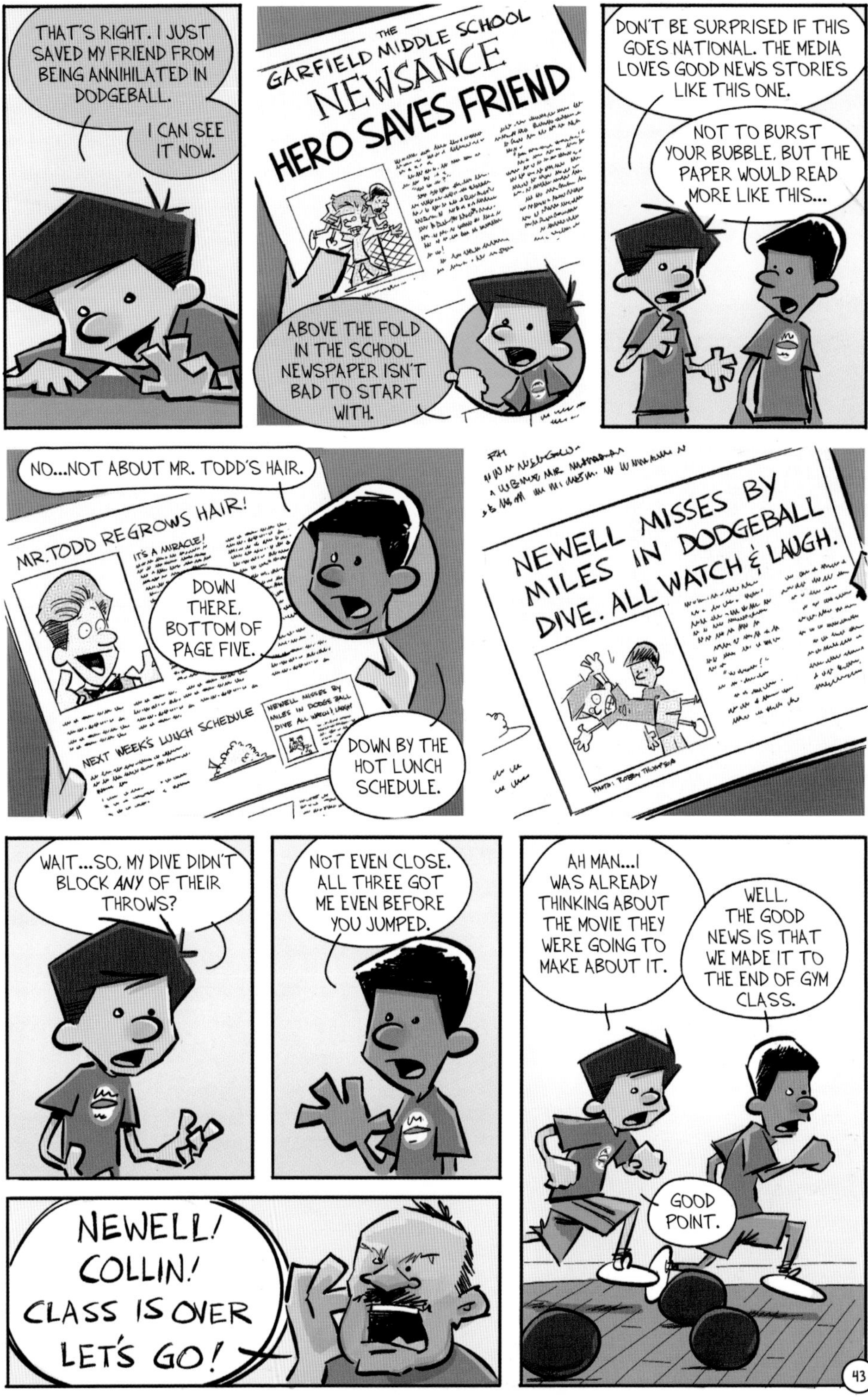
THAT'S RIGHT. I JUST SAVED MY FRIEND FROM BEING ANNIHILATED IN DODGEBALL.
I CAN SEE IT NOW.
THE GARFIELD MIDDLE SCHOOL NEWSANCE
HERO SAVES FRIEND
ABOVE THE FOLD IN THE SCHOOL NEWSPAPER ISN'T BAD TO START WITH.
DON'T BE SURPRISED IF THIS GOES NATIONAL. THE MEDIA LOVES GOOD NEWS STORIES LIKE THIS ONE.
NOT TO BURST YOUR BUBBLE, BUT THE PAPER WOULD READ MORE LIKE THIS...
NO...NOT ABOUT MR. TODD'S HAIR.
MR. TODD REGROWS HAIR!
IT'S A MIRACLE!
DOWN THERE, BOTTOM OF PAGE FIVE.
NEXT WEEK'S LUNCH SCHEDULE
NEWELL MISSES BY MILES IN DODGE BALL DIVE. ALL WATCH & LAUGH
DOWN BY THE HOT LUNCH SCHEDULE.
NEWELL MISSES BY MILES IN DODGEBALL DIVE. ALL WATCH & LAUGH.
WAIT...SO, MY DIVE DIDN'T BLOCK *ANY* OF THEIR THROWS?
NOT EVEN CLOSE. ALL THREE GOT ME EVEN BEFORE YOU JUMPED.
AH MAN...I WAS ALREADY THINKING ABOUT THE MOVIE THEY WERE GOING TO MAKE ABOUT IT.
WELL, THE GOOD NEWS IS THAT WE MADE IT TO THE END OF GYM CLASS.
GOOD POINT.
NEWELL! COLLIN! CLASS IS OVER LET'S GO!

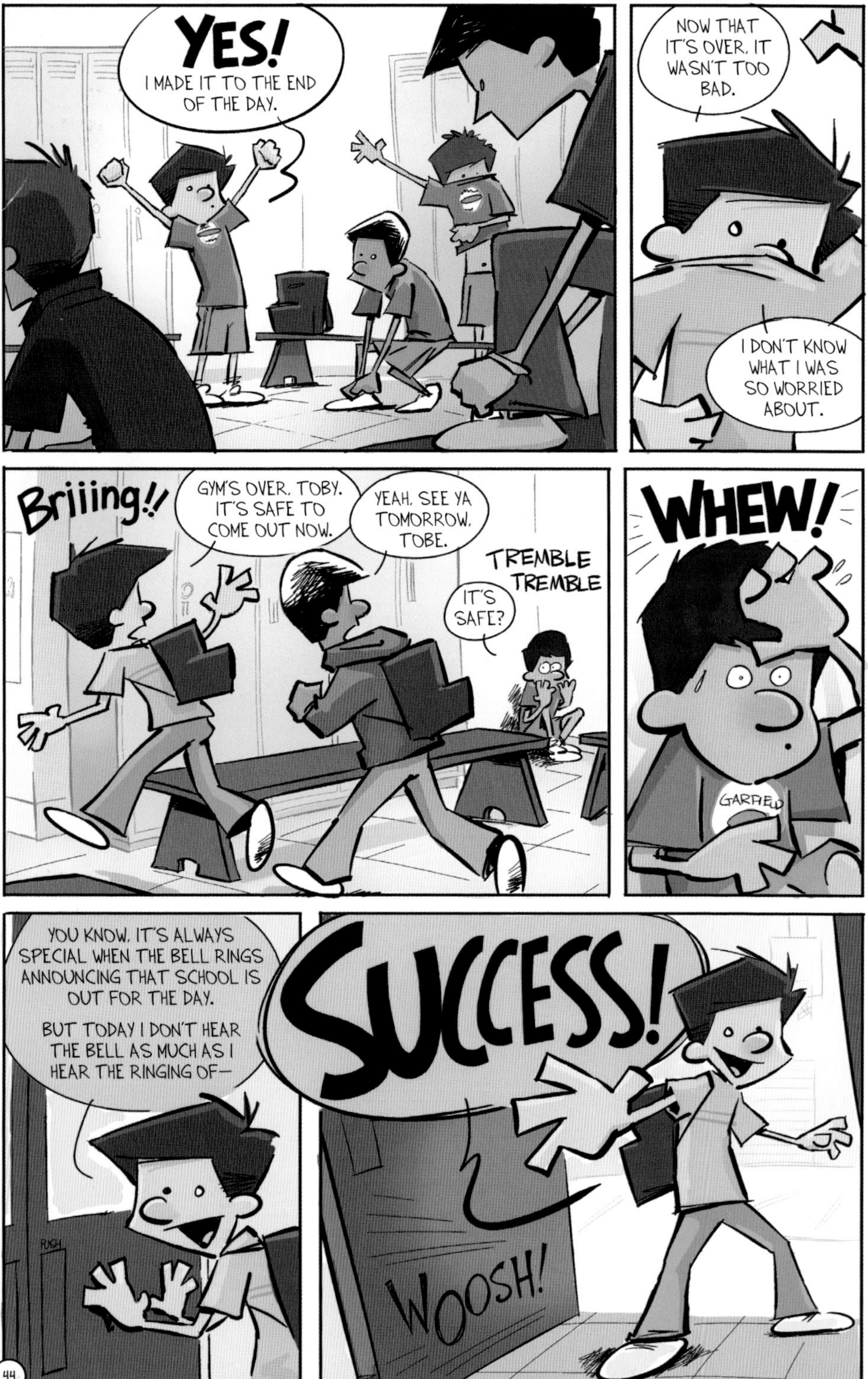

YES! I MADE IT TO THE END OF THE DAY.
NOW THAT IT'S OVER, IT WASN'T TOO BAD.
I DON'T KNOW WHAT I WAS SO WORRIED ABOUT.
Briiing!!
GYM'S OVER, TOBY. IT'S SAFE TO COME OUT NOW.
YEAH, SEE YA TOMORROW, TOBE.
TREMBLE TREMBLE
IT'S SAFE?
WHEW!
GARFIELD
YOU KNOW, IT'S ALWAYS SPECIAL WHEN THE BELL RINGS ANNOUNCING THAT SCHOOL IS OUT FOR THE DAY.
BUT TODAY I DON'T HEAR THE BELL AS MUCH AS I HEAR THE RINGING OF—
SUCCESS!
WOOSH!

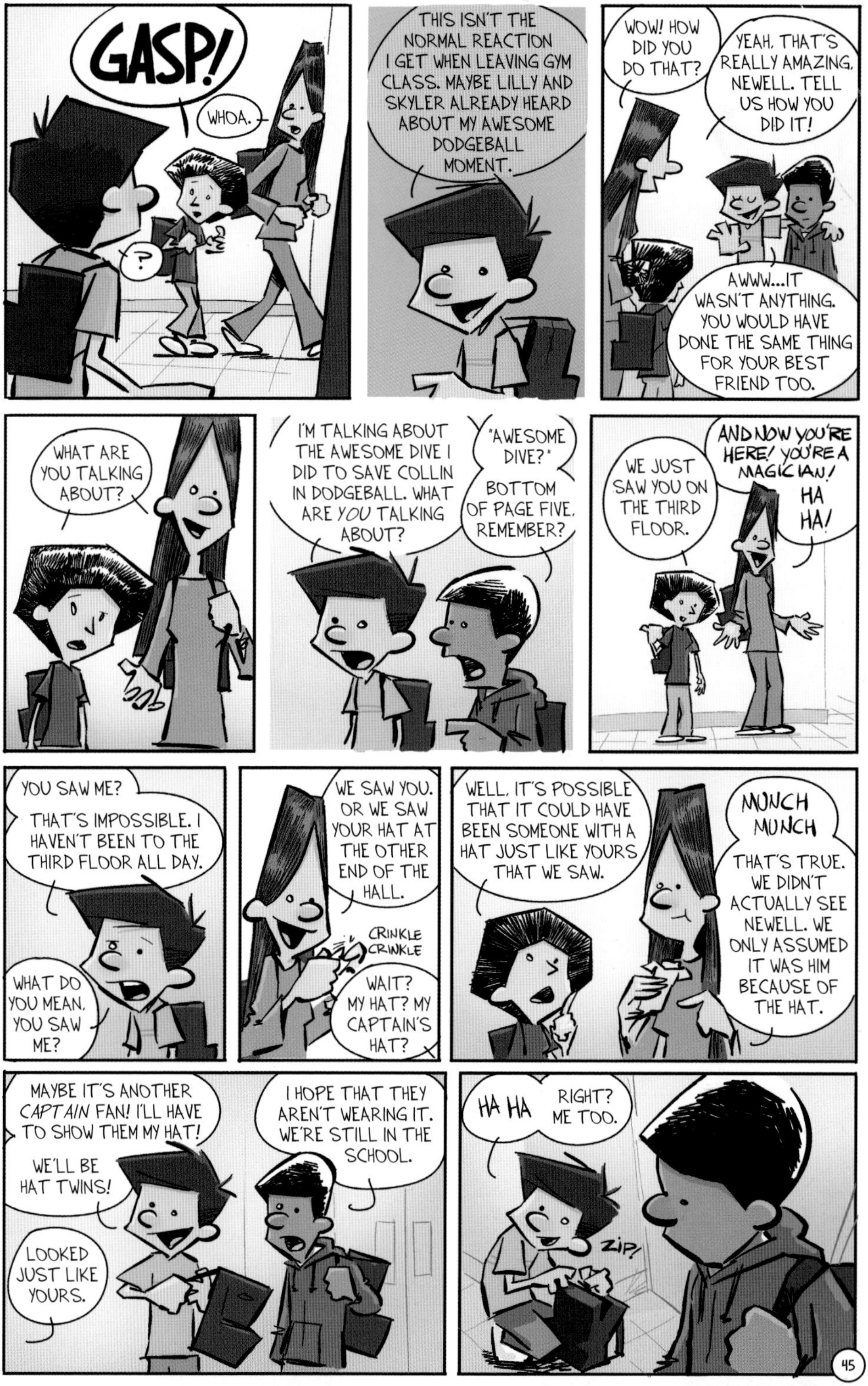
GASP!
WHOA.
?
THIS ISN'T THE NORMAL REACTION I GET WHEN LEAVING GYM CLASS. MAYBE LILLY AND SKYLER ALREADY HEARD ABOUT MY AWESOME DODGEBALL MOMENT.
WOW! HOW DID YOU DO THAT?
YEAH, THAT'S REALLY AMAZING, NEWELL. TELL US HOW YOU DID IT!
AWWW...IT WASN'T ANYTHING. YOU WOULD HAVE DONE THE SAME THING FOR YOUR BEST FRIEND TOO.
WHAT ARE YOU TALKING ABOUT?
I'M TALKING ABOUT THE AWESOME DIVE I DID TO SAVE COLLIN IN DODGEBALL. WHAT ARE *YOU* TALKING ABOUT?
"AWESOME DIVE?"
BOTTOM OF PAGE FIVE, REMEMBER?
WE JUST SAW YOU ON THE THIRD FLOOR.
AND NOW YOU'RE HERE! YOU'RE A MAGICIAN!
HA HA!
YOU SAW ME?
THAT'S IMPOSSIBLE. I HAVEN'T BEEN TO THE THIRD FLOOR ALL DAY.
WHAT DO YOU MEAN, YOU SAW ME?
WE SAW YOU. OR WE SAW YOUR HAT AT THE OTHER END OF THE HALL.
CRINKLE CRINKLE
WAIT? MY HAT? MY CAPTAIN'S HAT?
WELL, IT'S POSSIBLE THAT IT COULD HAVE BEEN SOMEONE WITH A HAT JUST LIKE YOURS THAT WE SAW.
MUNCH MUNCH
THAT'S TRUE. WE DIDN'T ACTUALLY SEE NEWELL. WE ONLY ASSUMED IT WAS HIM BECAUSE OF THE HAT.
MAYBE IT'S ANOTHER *CAPTAIN* FAN! I'LL HAVE TO SHOW THEM MY HAT!
WE'LL BE HAT TWINS!
LOOKED JUST LIKE YOURS.
I HOPE THAT THEY AREN'T WEARING IT. WE'RE STILL IN THE SCHOOL.
HA HA
RIGHT? ME TOO.
ZIP!

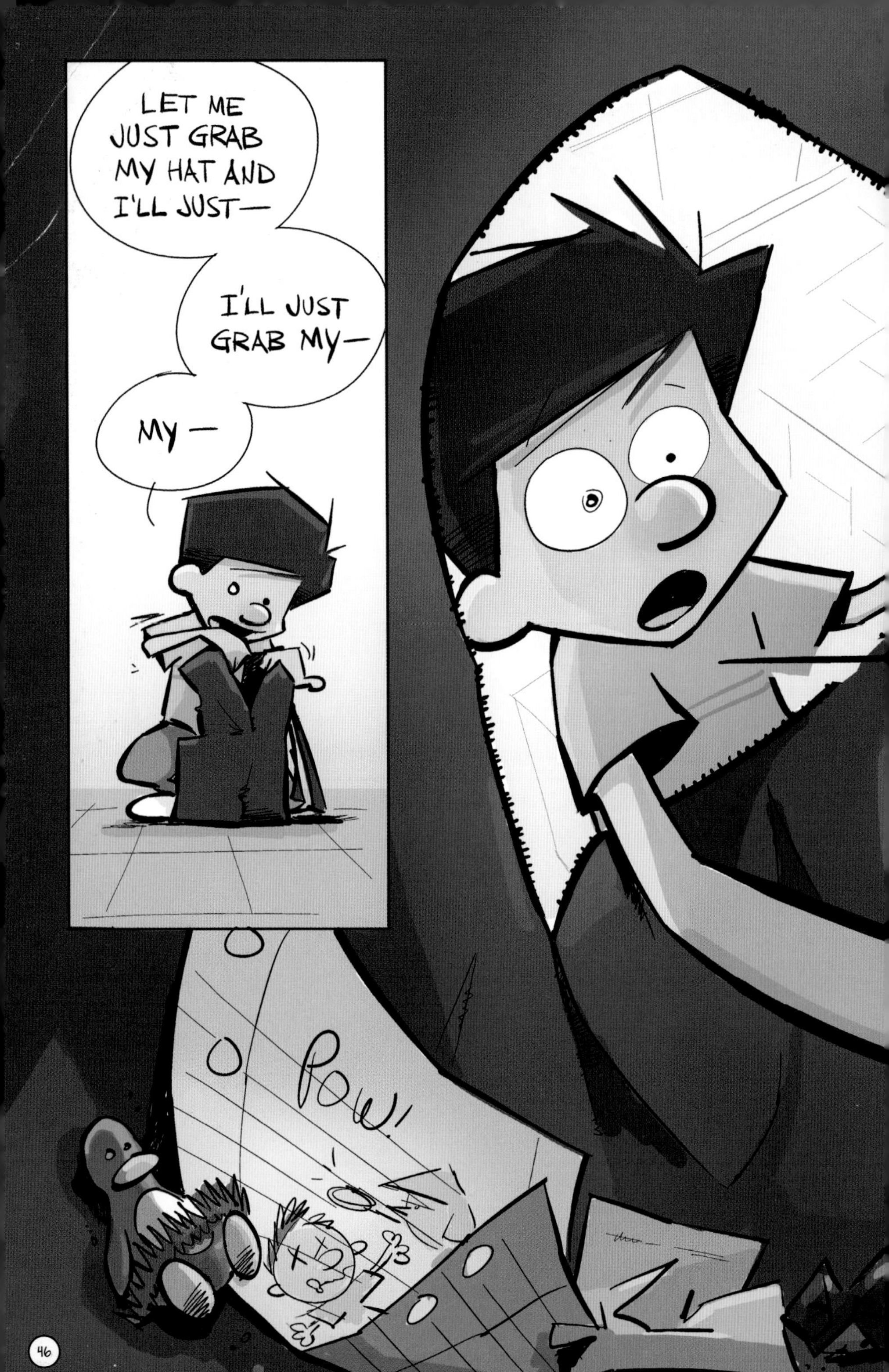
LET ME JUST GRAB MY HAT AND I'LL JUST—
I'LL JUST GRAB MY—
MY—
POW!

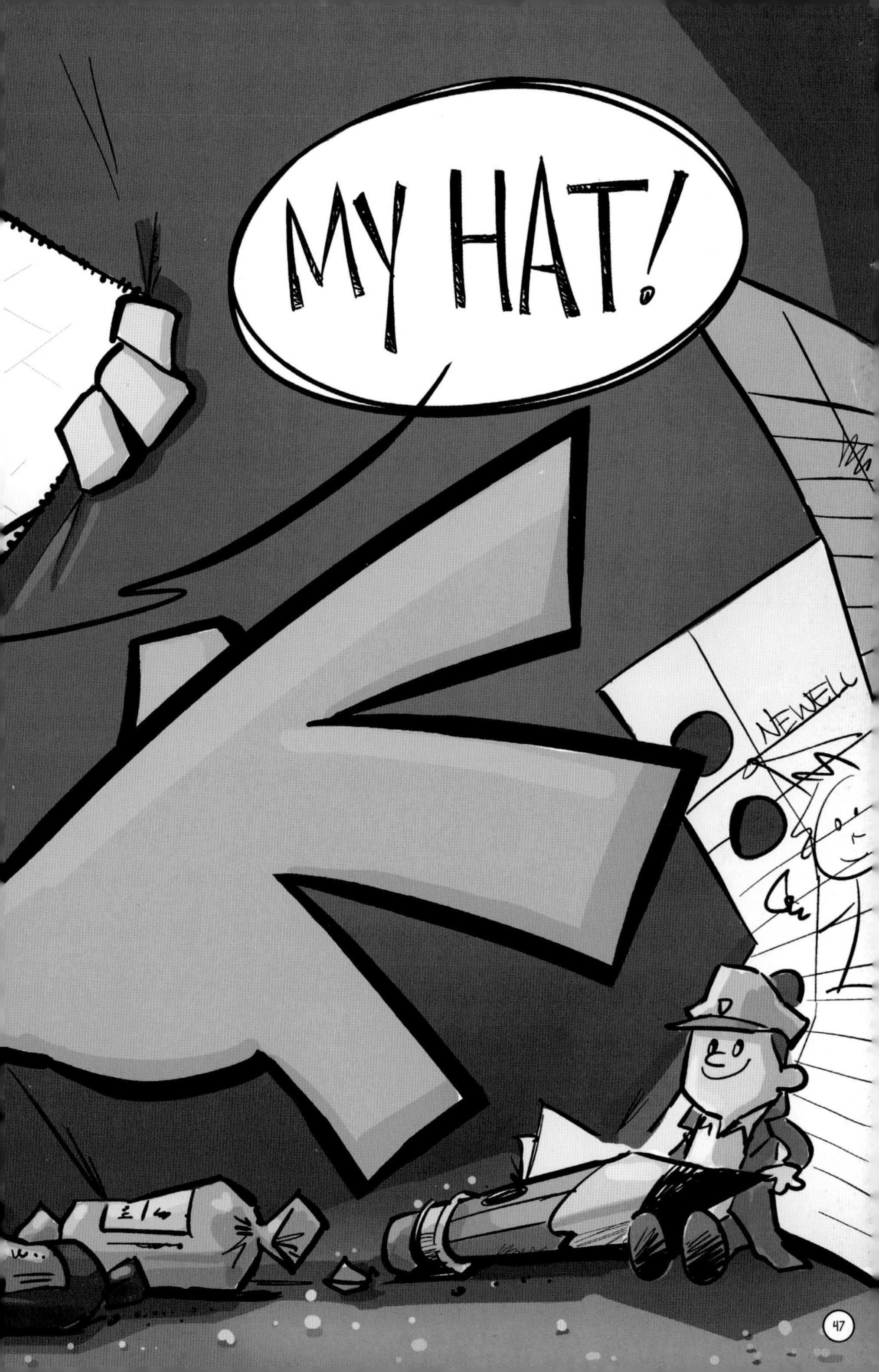
MY HAT!
NEWELL

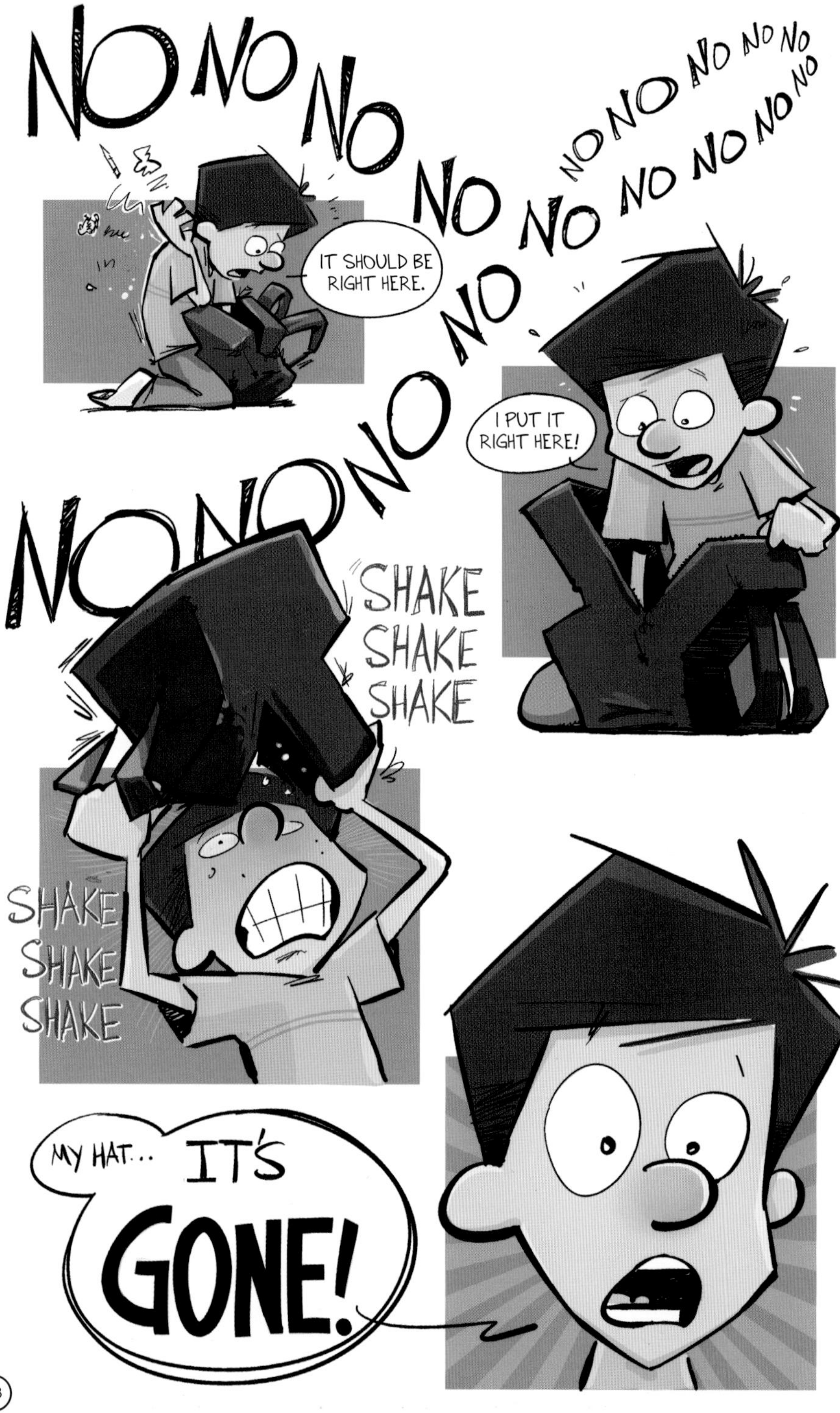
NO NO NO NO NO NO NO NO NO NO
IT SHOULD BE RIGHT HERE.
NO NO NO NO NO NO NO NO
I PUT IT RIGHT HERE!
NO NO NO NO
SHAKE SHAKE SHAKE
SHAKE SHAKE SHAKE
MY HAT... IT'S GONE!

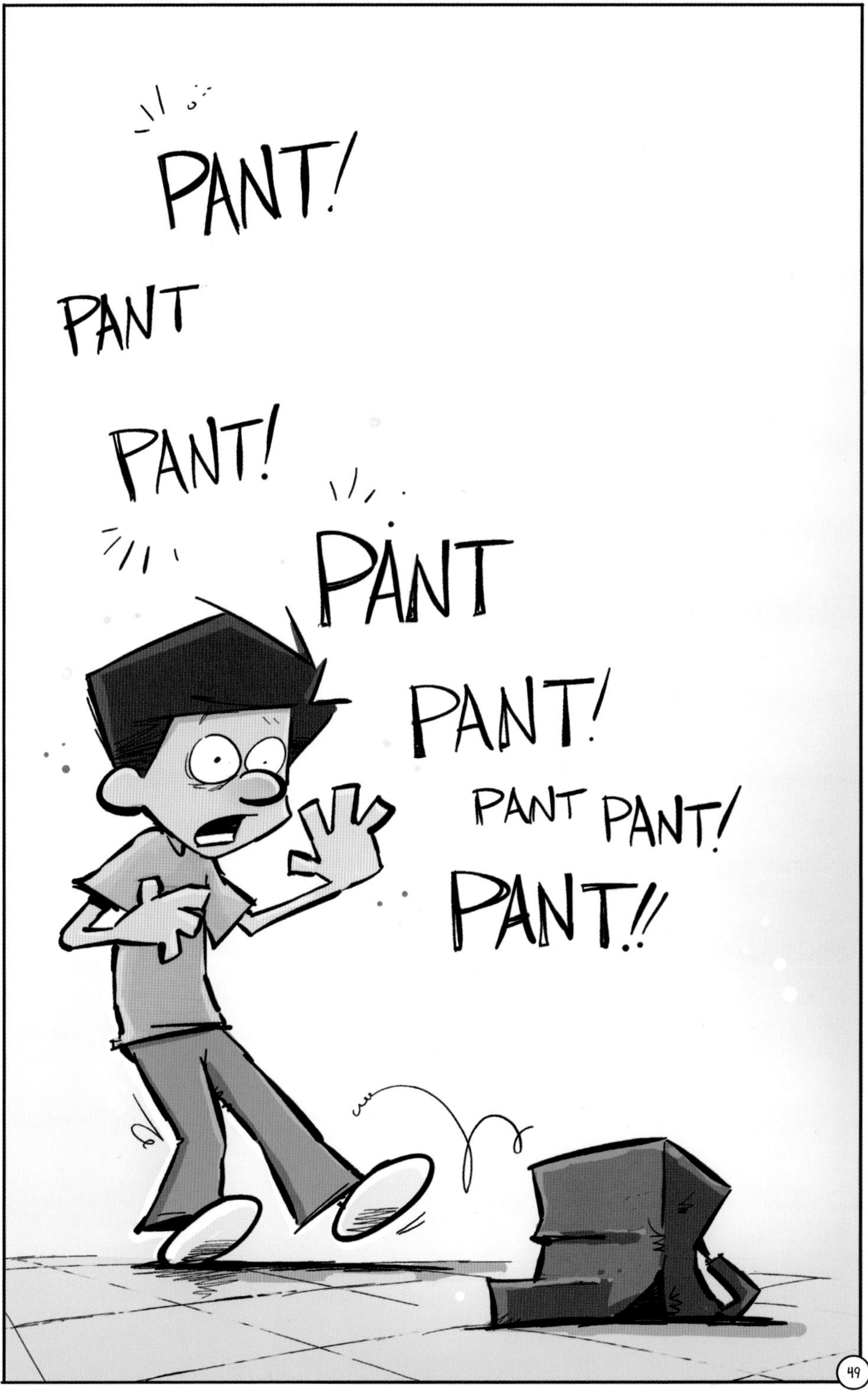
PANT!
PANT
PANT!
PANT
PANT!
PANT PANT!
PANT!!

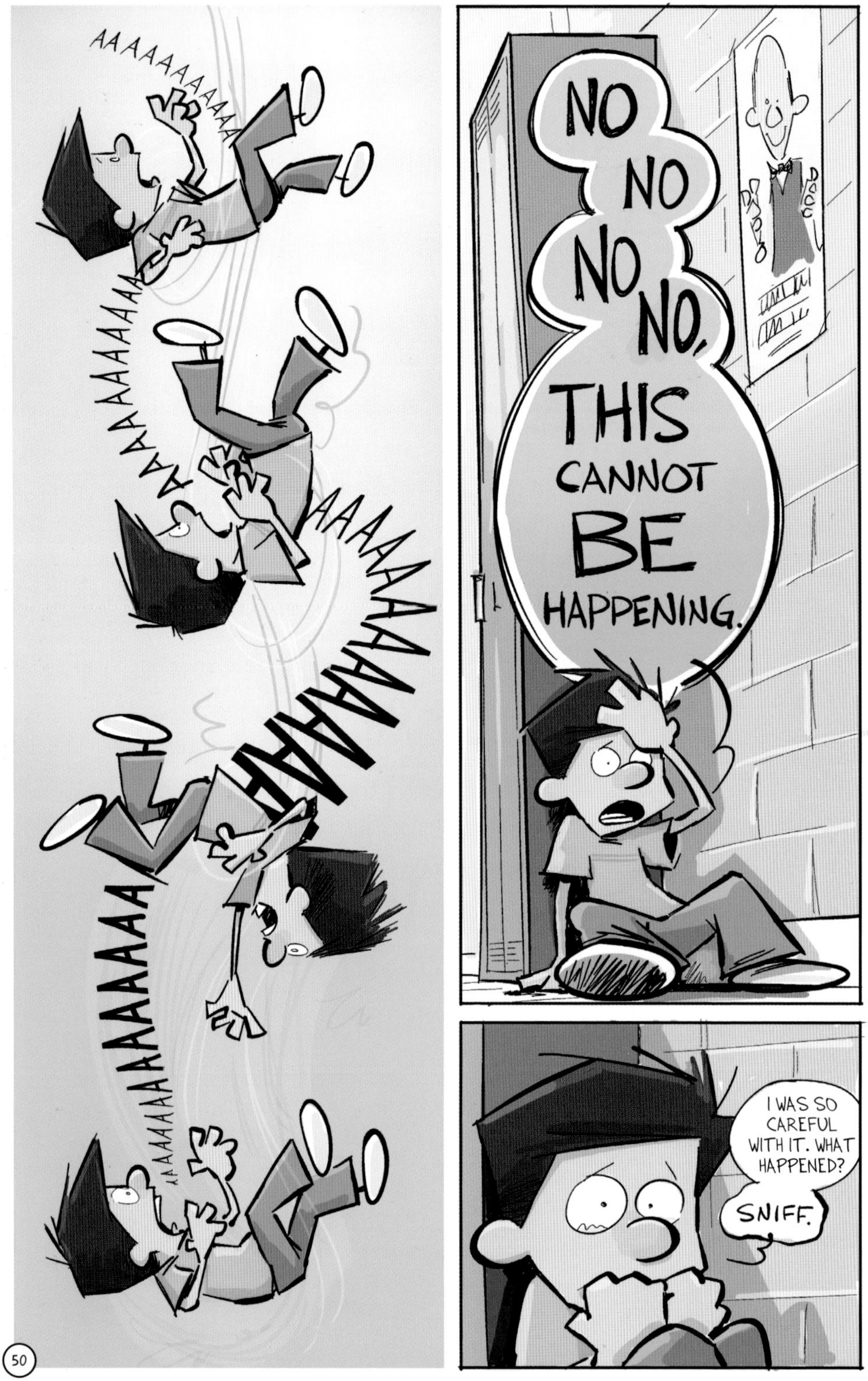

AAAAAAAAAAAAAAAAAAAAAAAAAAAAAAAAAAAAAHHH
AAAAAAAAAAAAAAAAAAAAAAAAAAAAAAAAAAAA
NO NO NO NO NO, THIS CANNOT BE HAPPENING.
I WAS SO CAREFUL WITH IT. WHAT HAPPENED?
SNIFF.

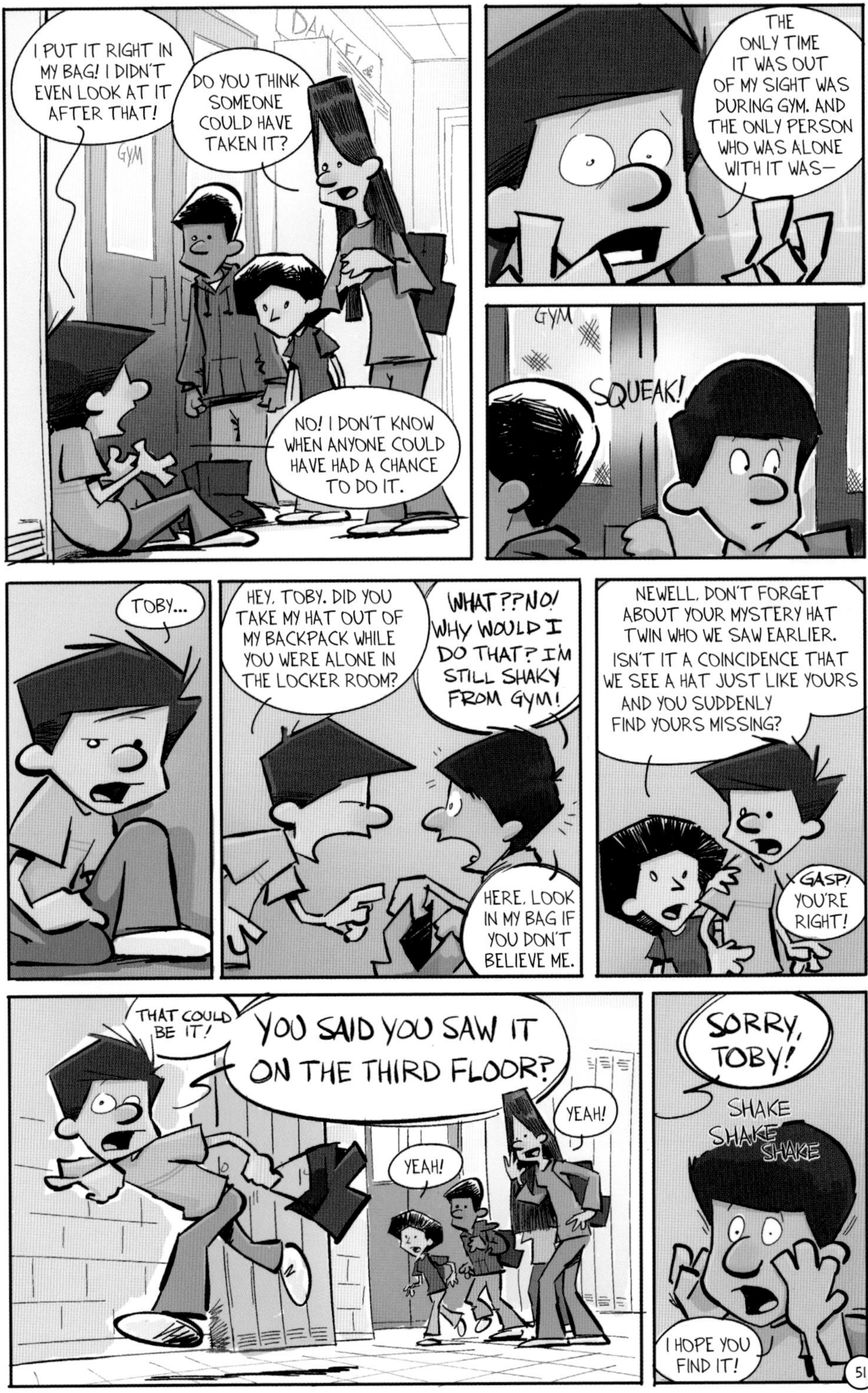
DANCE!
GYM
I PUT IT RIGHT IN MY BAG! I DIDN'T EVEN LOOK AT IT AFTER THAT!
DO YOU THINK SOMEONE COULD HAVE TAKEN IT?
NO! I DON'T KNOW WHEN ANYONE COULD HAVE HAD A CHANCE TO DO IT.
THE ONLY TIME IT WAS OUT OF MY SIGHT WAS DURING GYM. AND THE ONLY PERSON WHO WAS ALONE WITH IT WAS—
GYM
SQUEAK!
TOBY...
HEY, TOBY. DID YOU TAKE MY HAT OUT OF MY BACKPACK WHILE YOU WERE ALONE IN THE LOCKER ROOM?
WHAT??NO! WHY WOULD I DO THAT? I'M STILL SHAKY FROM GYM!
HERE. LOOK IN MY BAG IF YOU DON'T BELIEVE ME.
NEWELL, DON'T FORGET ABOUT YOUR MYSTERY HAT TWIN WHO WE SAW EARLIER.
ISN'T IT A COINCIDENCE THAT WE SEE A HAT JUST LIKE YOURS AND YOU SUDDENLY FIND YOURS MISSING?
GASP! YOU'RE RIGHT!
THAT COULD BE IT!
YOU SAID YOU SAW IT ON THE THIRD FLOOR?
YEAH!
YEAH!
SORRY, TOBY!
SHAKE SHAKE SHAKE
I HOPE YOU FIND IT!

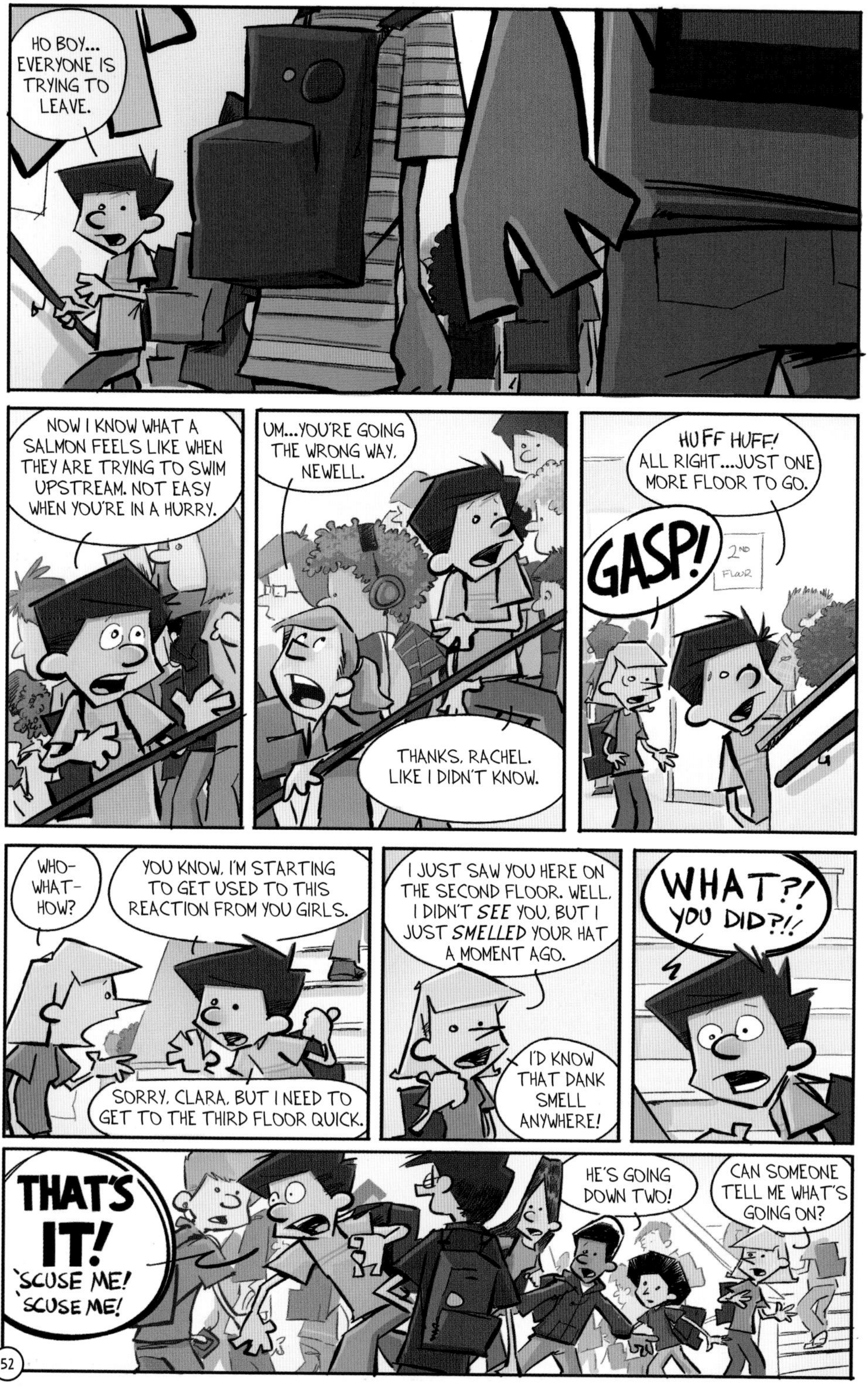
HO BOY... EVERYONE IS TRYING TO LEAVE.
NOW I KNOW WHAT A SALMON FEELS LIKE WHEN THEY ARE TRYING TO SWIM UPSTREAM. NOT EASY WHEN YOU'RE IN A HURRY.
UM...YOU'RE GOING THE WRONG WAY, NEWELL.
THANKS, RACHEL. LIKE I DIDN'T KNOW.
HUFF HUFF! ALL RIGHT...JUST ONE MORE FLOOR TO GO.
GASP!
2ND FLOOR
WHO- WHAT- HOW?
YOU KNOW, I'M STARTING TO GET USED TO THIS REACTION FROM YOU GIRLS.
SORRY, CLARA, BUT I NEED TO GET TO THE THIRD FLOOR QUICK.
I JUST SAW YOU HERE ON THE SECOND FLOOR. WELL, I DIDN'T *SEE* YOU, BUT I JUST *SMELLED* YOUR HAT A MOMENT AGO.
I'D KNOW THAT DANK SMELL ANYWHERE!
WHAT?! YOU DID?!!
THAT'S IT! 'SCUSE ME! 'SCUSE ME!
HE'S GOING DOWN TWO!
CAN SOMEONE TELL ME WHAT'S GOING ON?

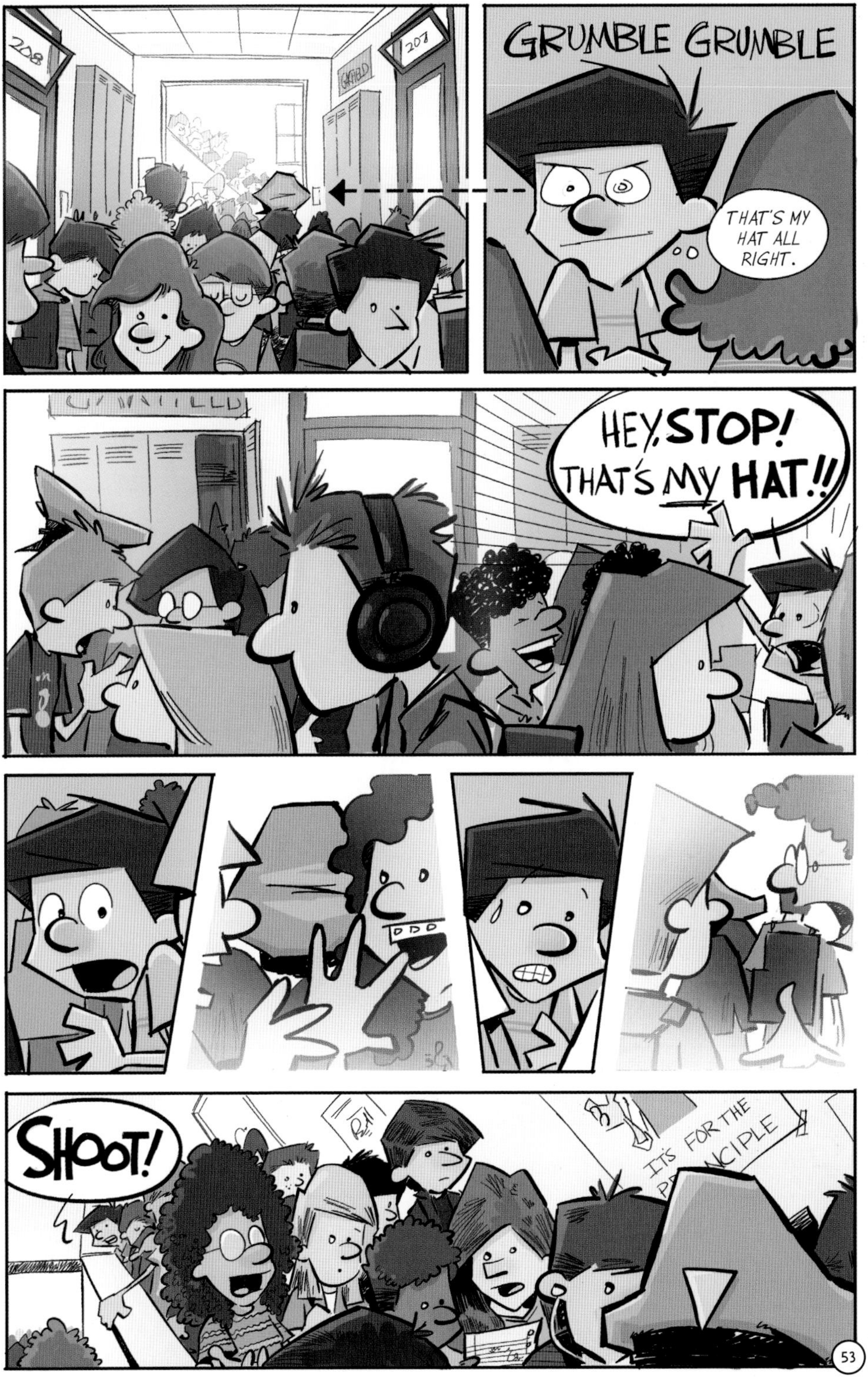
208
207
GARFIELD
GRUMBLE GRUMBLE
THAT'S MY HAT ALL RIGHT.
HEY, STOP! THAT'S MY HAT!!
SHOOT!
IT'S FOR THE PRINCIPLE

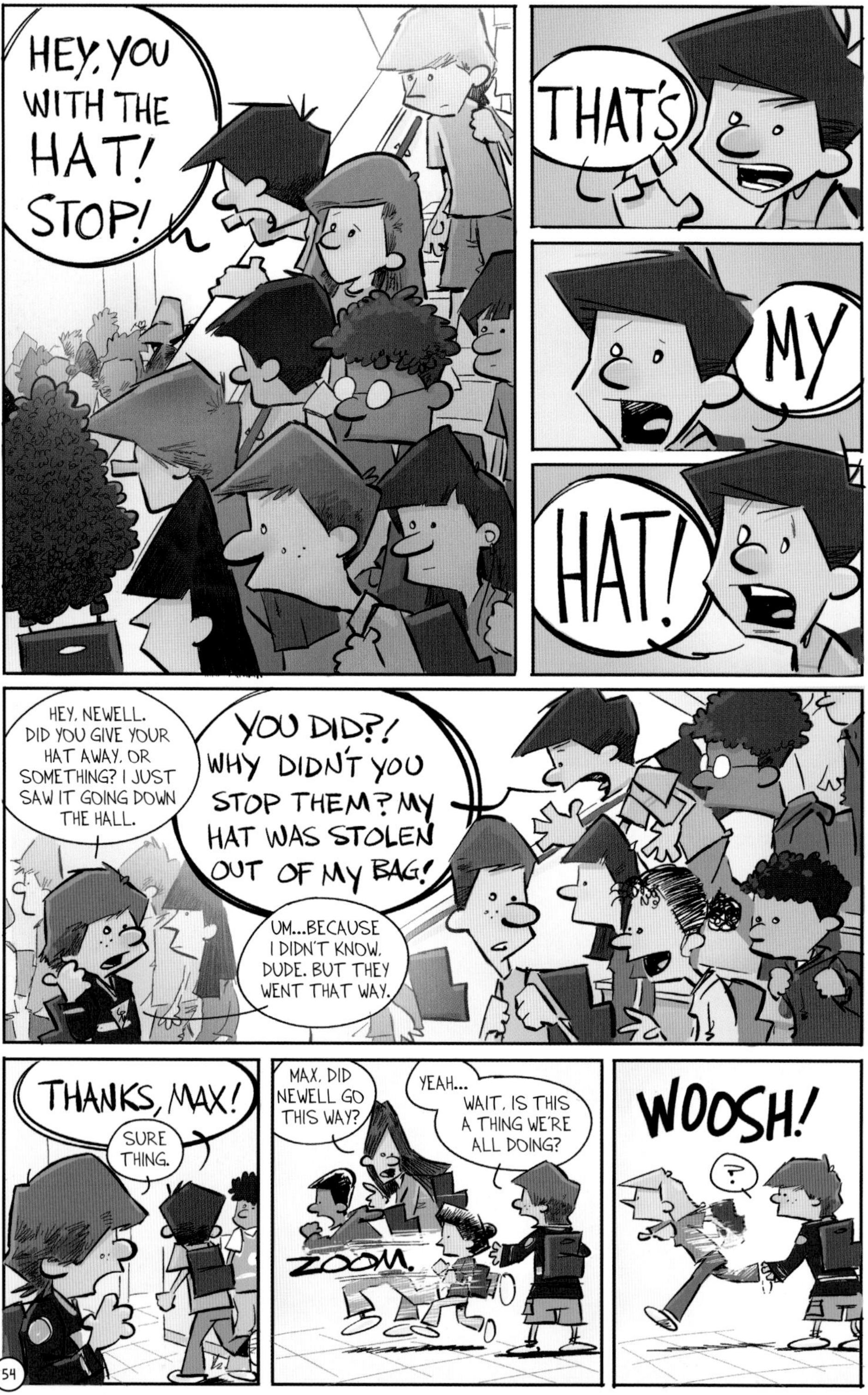
HEY, YOU WITH THE HAT! STOP!
THAT'S
MY
HAT!
HEY, NEWELL. DID YOU GIVE YOUR HAT AWAY, OR SOMETHING? I JUST SAW IT GOING DOWN THE HALL.
YOU DID?! WHY DIDN'T YOU STOP THEM? MY HAT WAS STOLEN OUT OF MY BAG!
UM...BECAUSE I DIDN'T KNOW, DUDE. BUT THEY WENT THAT WAY.
THANKS, MAX!
SURE THING.
MAX, DID NEWELL GO THIS WAY?
YEAH...
WAIT, IS THIS A THING WE'RE ALL DOING?
ZOOM.
WOOSH!
?

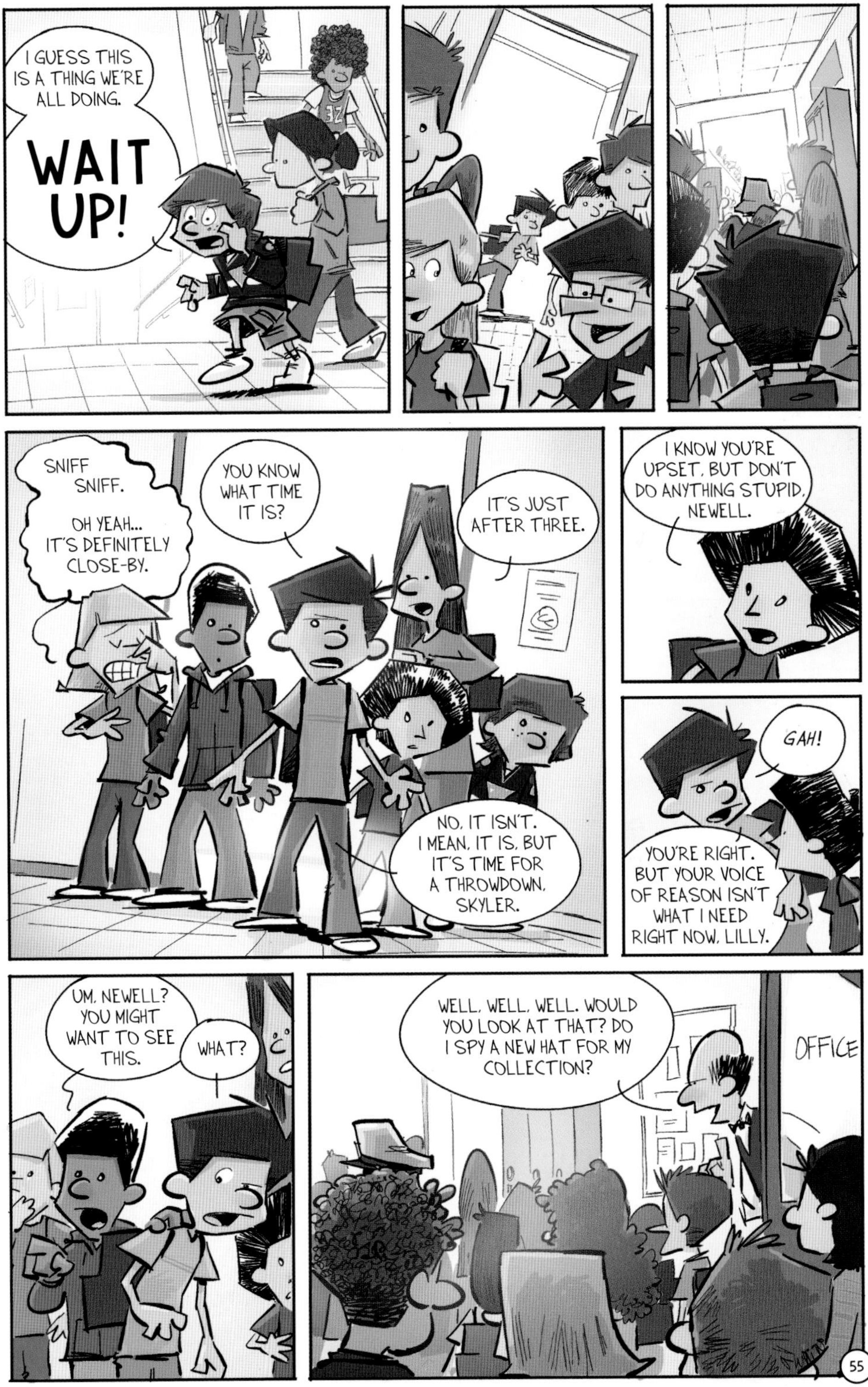
I GUESS THIS IS A THING WE'RE ALL DOING.
WAIT UP!
SNIFF SNIFF.
OH YEAH... IT'S DEFINITELY CLOSE-BY.
YOU KNOW WHAT TIME IT IS?
IT'S JUST AFTER THREE.
NO, IT ISN'T. I MEAN, IT IS, BUT IT'S TIME FOR A THROWDOWN, SKYLER.
I KNOW YOU'RE UPSET, BUT DON'T DO ANYTHING STUPID, NEWELL.
GAH!
YOU'RE RIGHT. BUT YOUR VOICE OF REASON ISN'T WHAT I NEED RIGHT NOW, LILLY.
UM, NEWELL? YOU MIGHT WANT TO SEE THIS.
WHAT?
WELL, WELL, WELL. WOULD YOU LOOK AT THAT? DO I SPY A NEW HAT FOR MY COLLECTION?
OFFICE

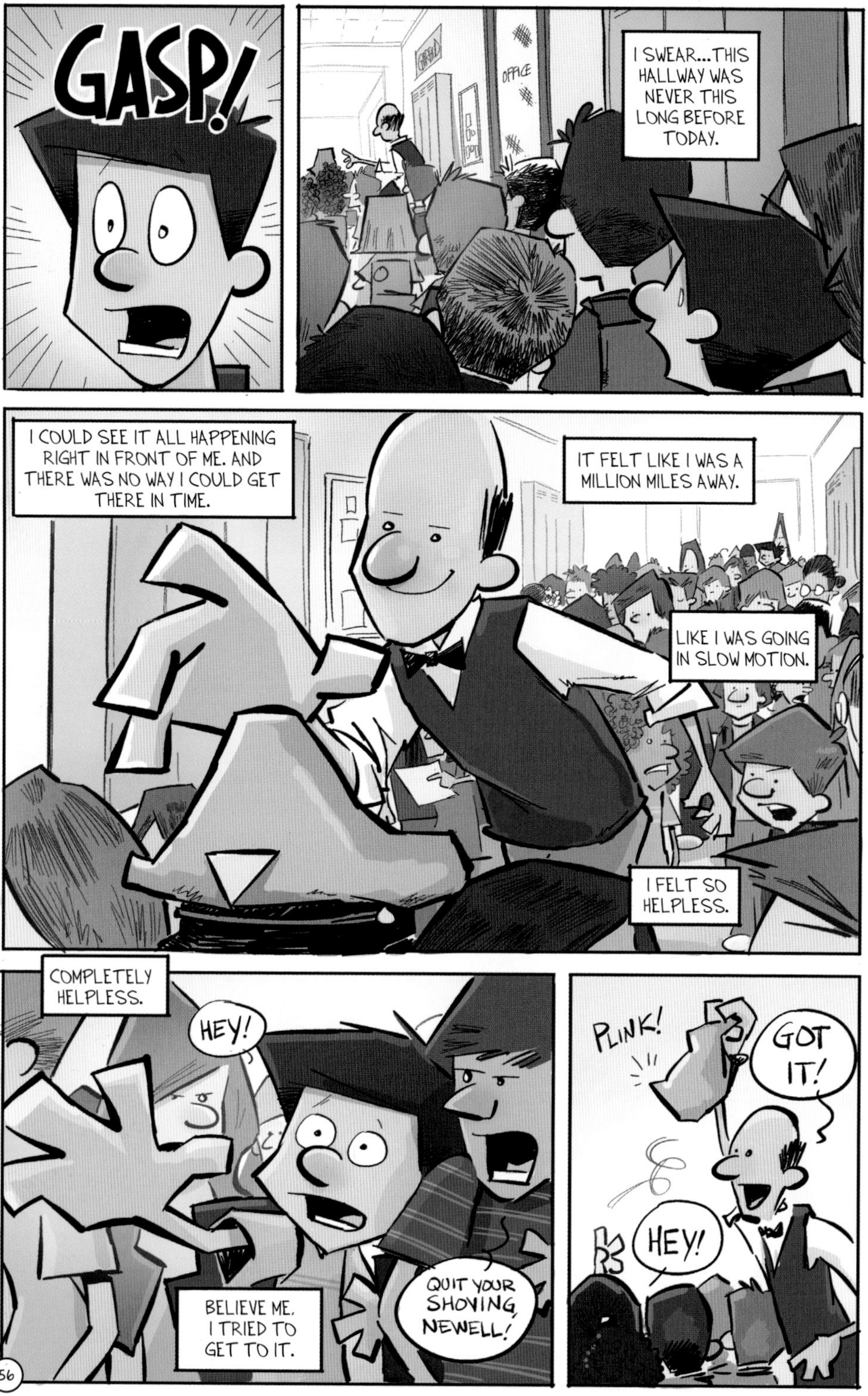
GASP!
OFFICE
I SWEAR...THIS HALLWAY WAS NEVER THIS LONG BEFORE TODAY.
I COULD SEE IT ALL HAPPENING RIGHT IN FRONT OF ME. AND THERE WAS NO WAY I COULD GET THERE IN TIME.
IT FELT LIKE I WAS A MILLION MILES AWAY.
LIKE I WAS GOING IN SLOW MOTION.
I FELT SO HELPLESS.
COMPLETELY HELPLESS.
HEY!
BELIEVE ME, I TRIED TO GET TO IT.
QUIT YOUR SHOVING, NEWELL!
PLINK!
GOT IT!
HEY!

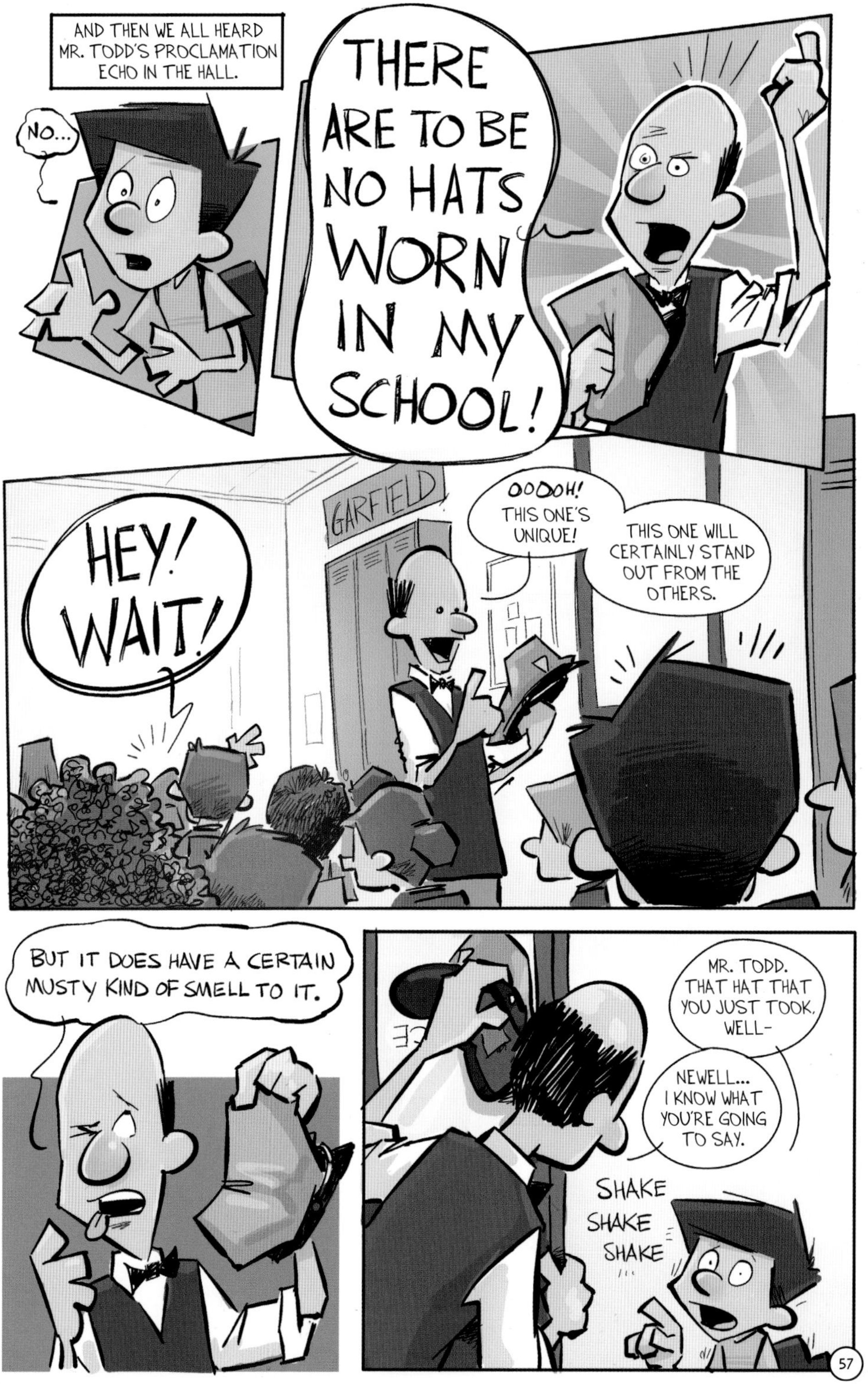

AND THEN WE ALL HEARD MR. TODD'S PROCLAMATION ECHO IN THE HALL.
NO...
THERE ARE TO BE NO HATS WORN IN MY SCHOOL!
HEY! WAIT!
GARFIELD
OOOOH! THIS ONE'S UNIQUE!
THIS ONE WILL CERTAINLY STAND OUT FROM THE OTHERS.
BUT IT DOES HAVE A CERTAIN MUSTY KIND OF SMELL TO IT.
MR. TODD. THAT HAT THAT YOU JUST TOOK, WELL-
NEWELL... I KNOW WHAT YOU'RE GOING TO SAY.
SHAKE
SHAKE
SHAKE

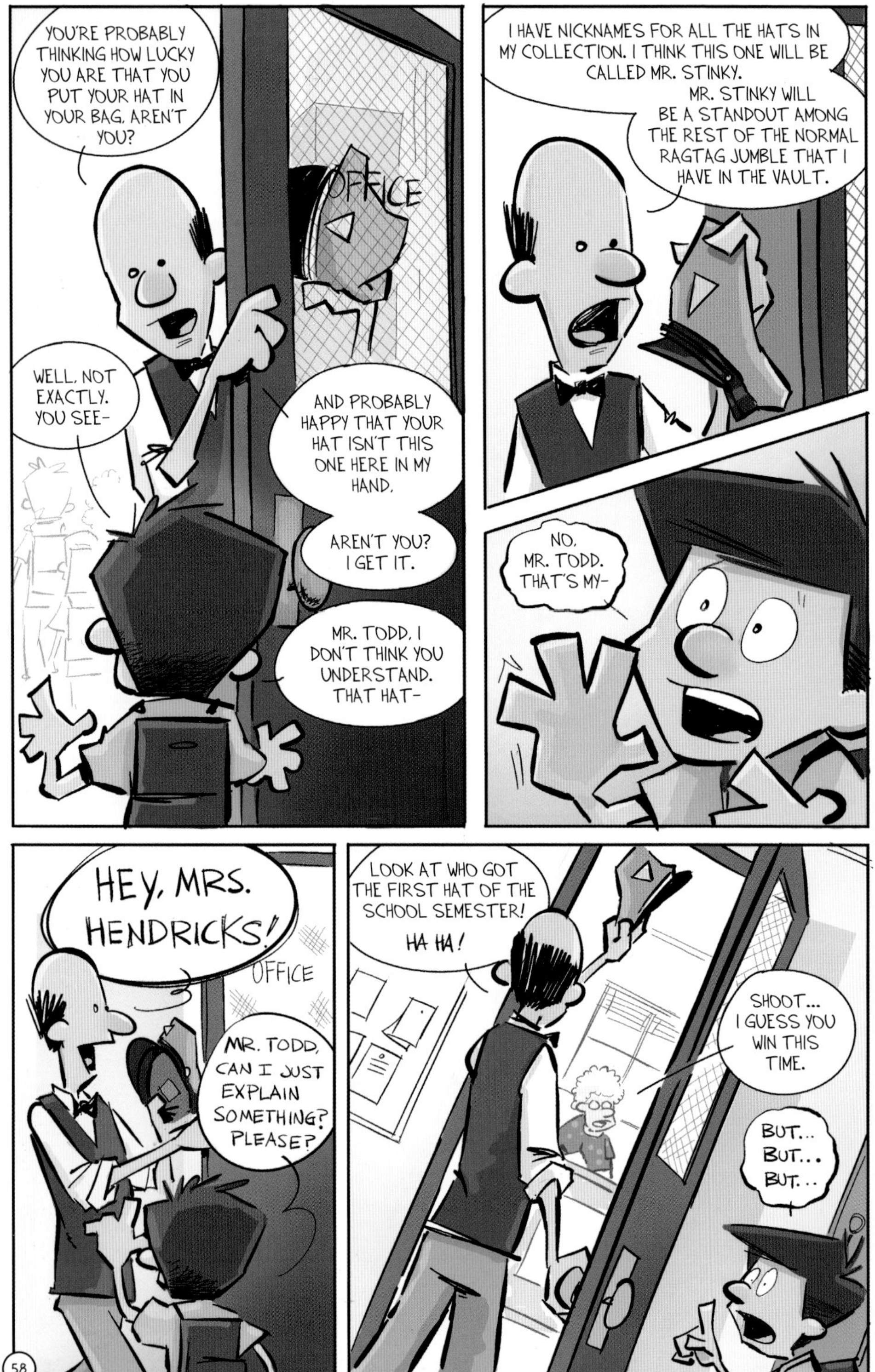
YOU'RE PROBABLY THINKING HOW LUCKY YOU ARE THAT YOU PUT YOUR HAT IN YOUR BAG, AREN'T YOU?
OFFICE
WELL, NOT EXACTLY. YOU SEE-
AND PROBABLY HAPPY THAT YOUR HAT ISN'T THIS ONE HERE IN MY HAND.
AREN'T YOU? I GET IT.
MR. TODD, I DON'T THINK YOU UNDERSTAND. THAT HAT-
I HAVE NICKNAMES FOR ALL THE HATS IN MY COLLECTION. I THINK THIS ONE WILL BE CALLED MR. STINKY.
MR. STINKY WILL BE A STANDOUT AMONG THE REST OF THE NORMAL RAGTAG JUMBLE THAT I HAVE IN THE VAULT.
NO, MR. TODD. THAT'S MY-
HEY, MRS. HENDRICKS!
OFFICE
MR. TODD, CAN I JUST EXPLAIN SOMETHING? PLEASE?
LOOK AT WHO GOT THE FIRST HAT OF THE SCHOOL SEMESTER!
HA HA!
SHOOT... I GUESS YOU WIN THIS TIME.
BUT... BUT... BUT...

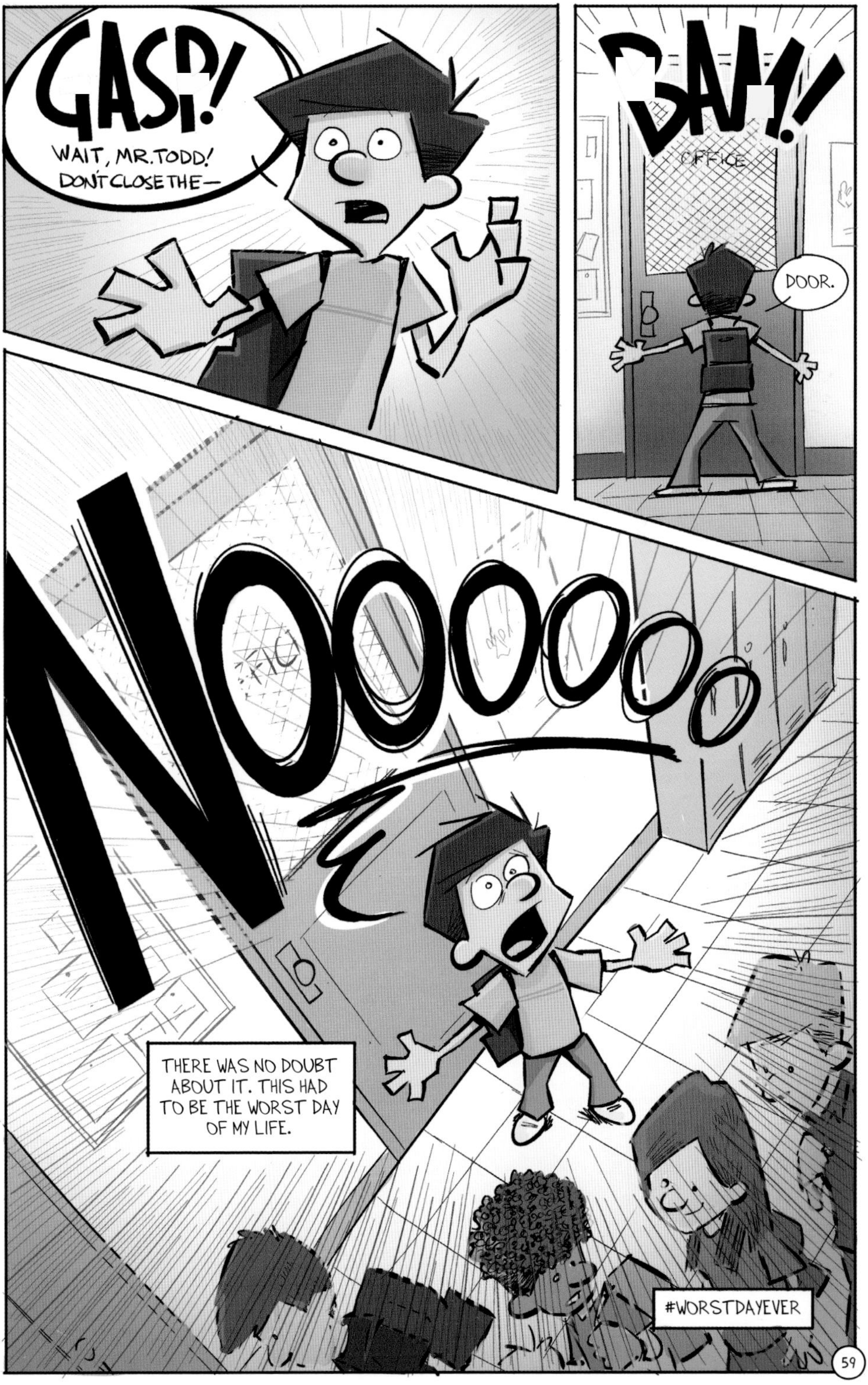
GASP!
WAIT, MR. TODD! DON'T CLOSE THE—
BAM!!
OFFICE
DOOR.
NOOOOOOOO
THERE WAS NO DOUBT ABOUT IT. THIS HAD TO BE THE WORST DAY OF MY LIFE.
#WORSTDAYEVER

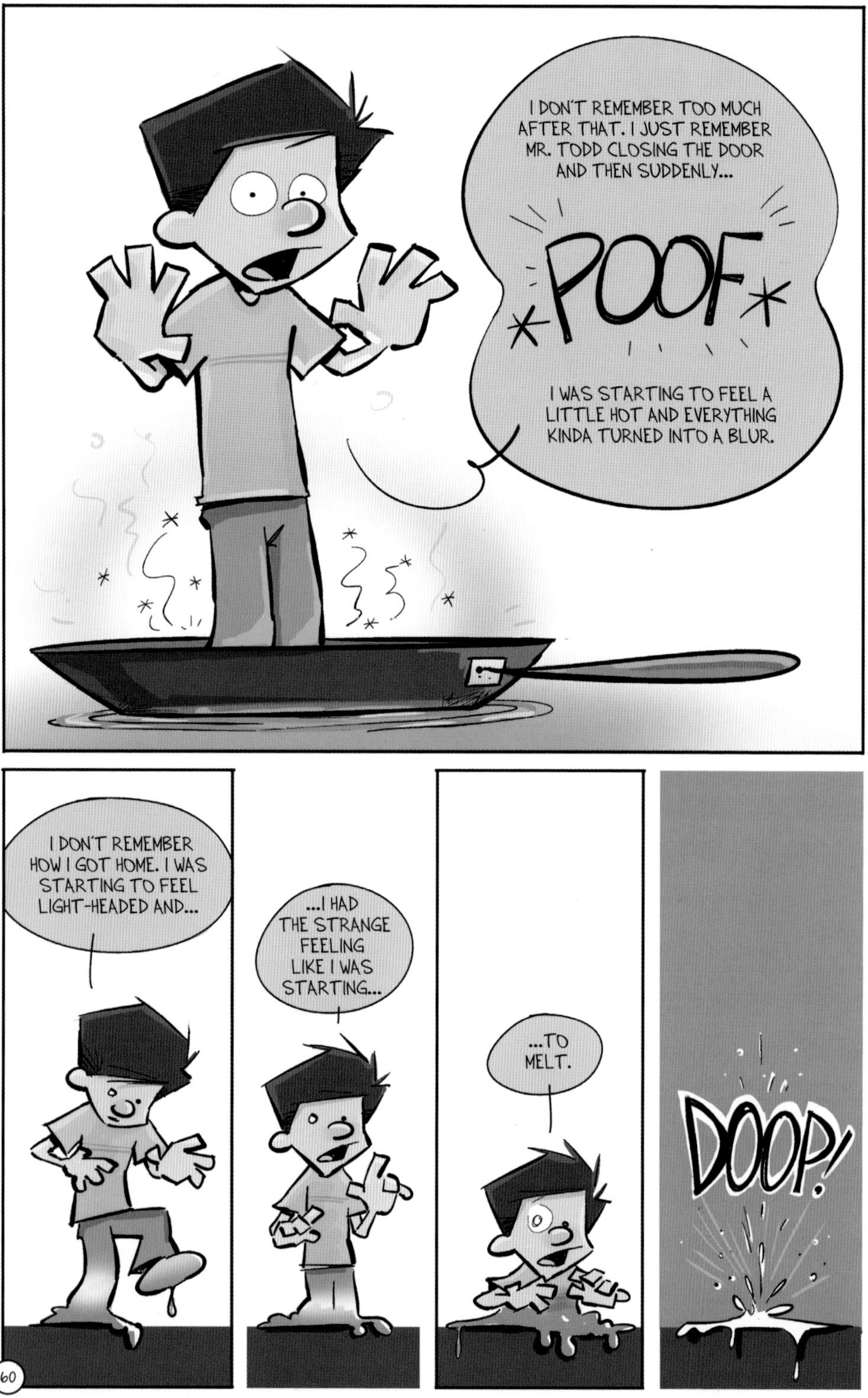

I DON'T REMEMBER TOO MUCH AFTER THAT. I JUST REMEMBER MR. TODD CLOSING THE DOOR AND THEN SUDDENLY...
POOF
I WAS STARTING TO FEEL A LITTLE HOT AND EVERYTHING KINDA TURNED INTO A BLUR.
I DON'T REMEMBER HOW I GOT HOME. I WAS STARTING TO FEEL LIGHT-HEADED AND...
...I HAD THE STRANGE FEELING LIKE I WAS STARTING...
...TO MELT.
DOOP!

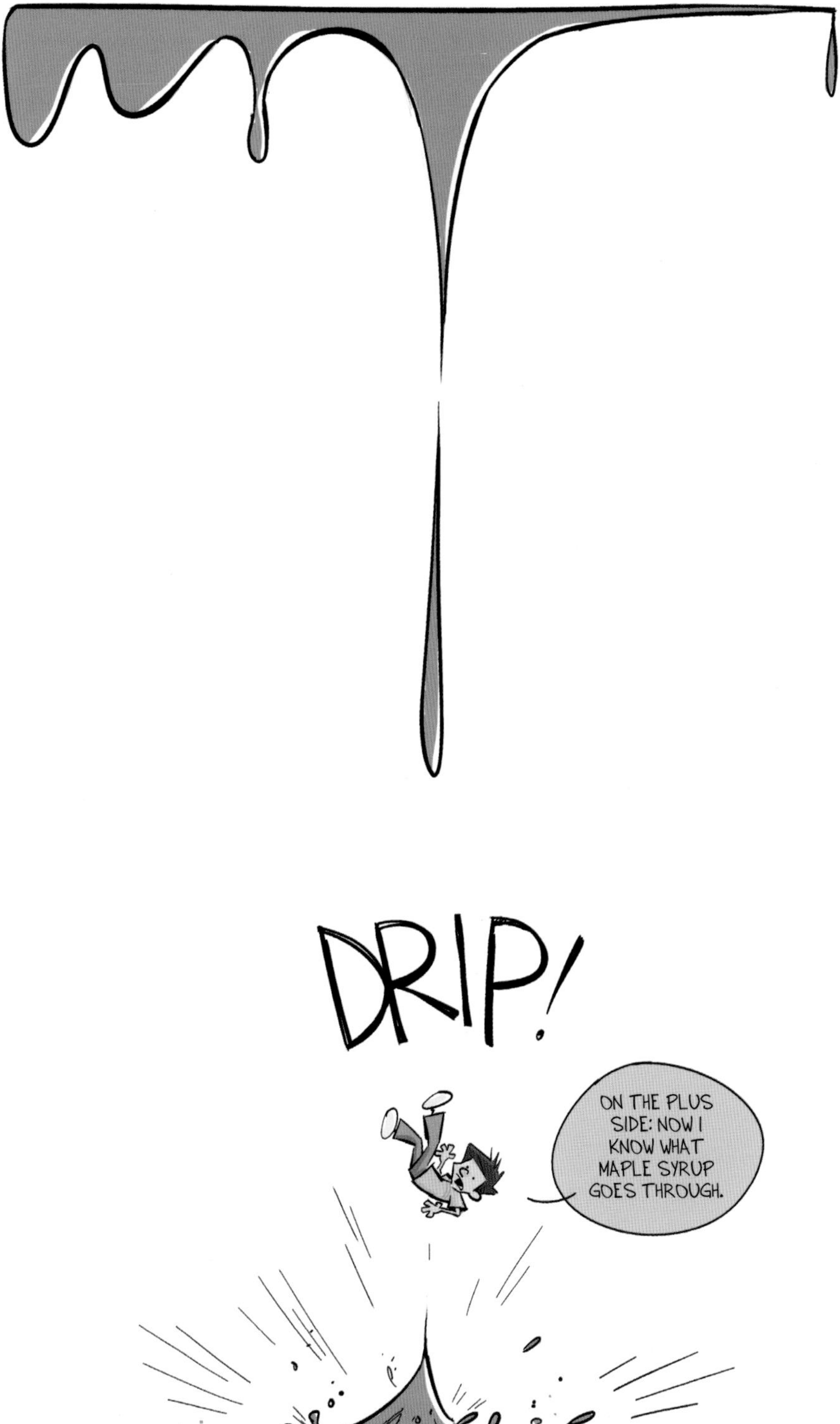
DRIP!
ON THE PLUS SIDE: NOW I KNOW WHAT MAPLE SYRUP GOES THROUGH.

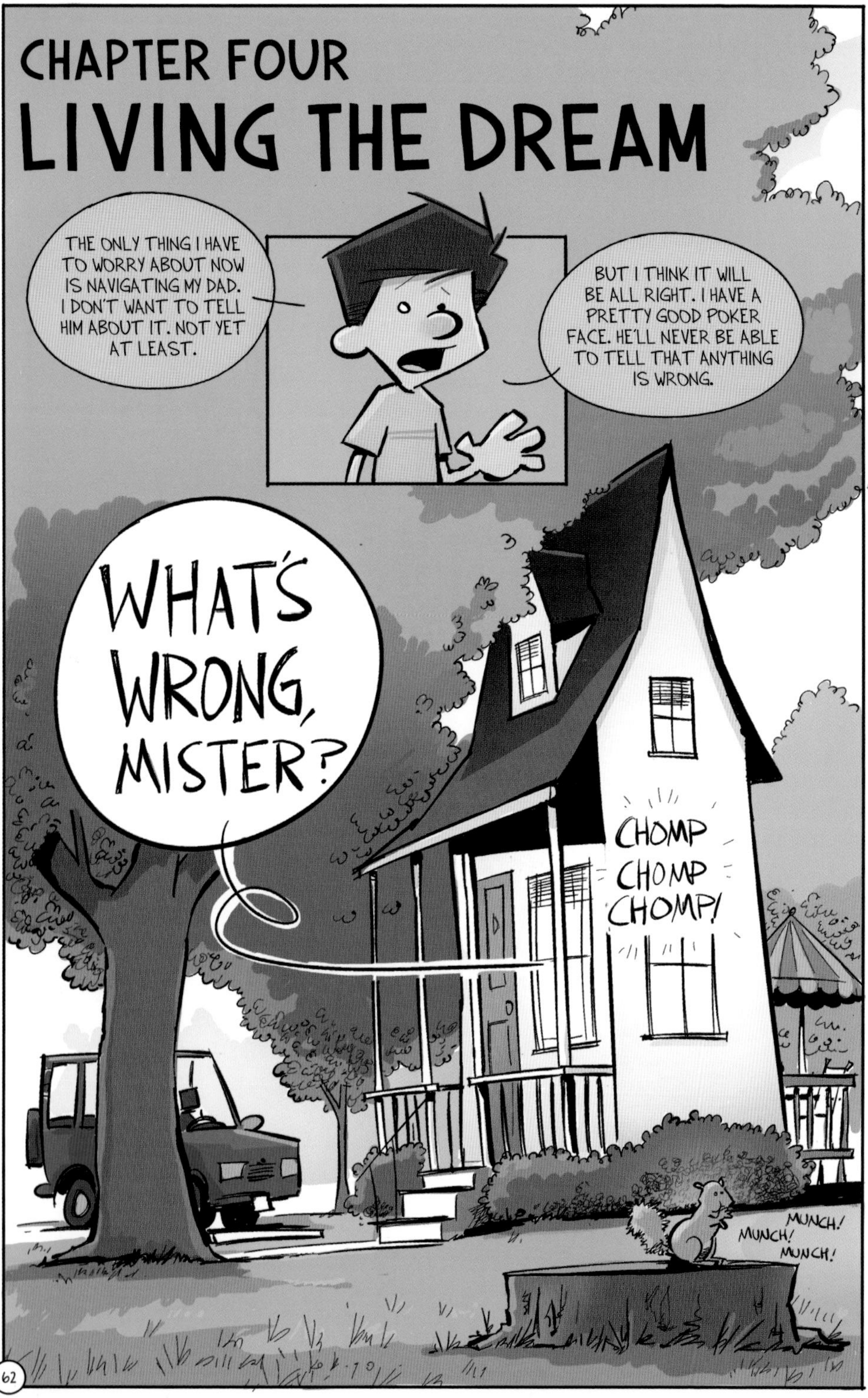
CHAPTER FOUR
LIVING THE DREAM
THE ONLY THING I HAVE TO WORRY ABOUT NOW IS NAVIGATING MY DAD. I DON'T WANT TO TELL HIM ABOUT IT. NOT YET AT LEAST.
BUT I THINK IT WILL BE ALL RIGHT. I HAVE A PRETTY GOOD POKER FACE. HE'LL NEVER BE ABLE TO TELL THAT ANYTHING IS WRONG.
WHAT'S WRONG, MISTER?
CHOMP CHOMP CHOMP!
MUNCH! MUNCH! MUNCH!

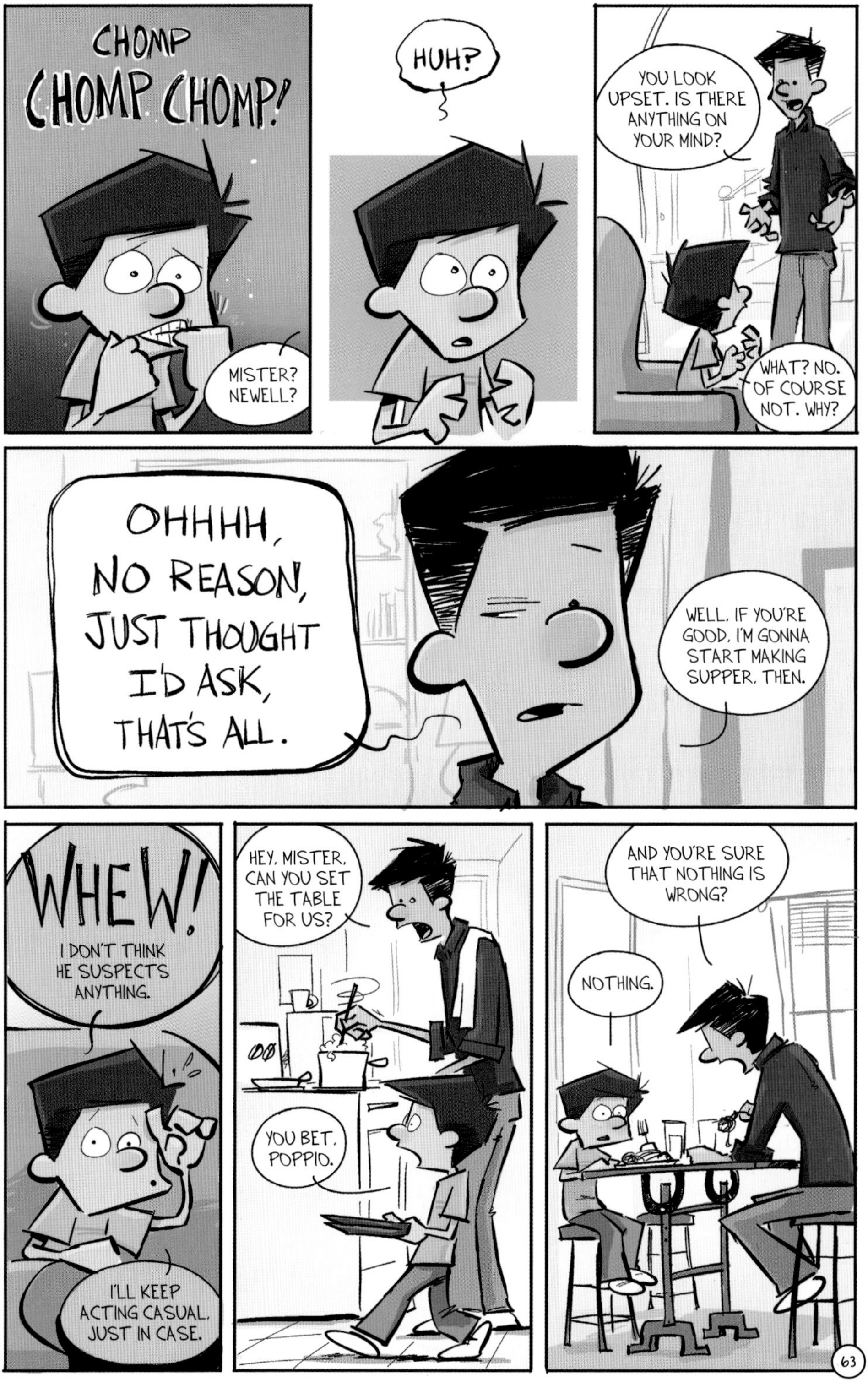
CHOMP
CHOMP CHOMP!
MISTER? NEWELL?
HUH?
YOU LOOK UPSET. IS THERE ANYTHING ON YOUR MIND?
WHAT? NO. OF COURSE NOT. WHY?
OHHHH, NO REASON, JUST THOUGHT I'D ASK, THAT'S ALL.
WELL, IF YOU'RE GOOD, I'M GONNA START MAKING SUPPER, THEN.
WHEW!
I DON'T THINK HE SUSPECTS ANYTHING.
I'LL KEEP ACTING CASUAL, JUST IN CASE.
HEY, MISTER, CAN YOU SET THE TABLE FOR US?
YOU BET, POPPIO.
AND YOU'RE SURE THAT NOTHING IS WRONG?
NOTHING.

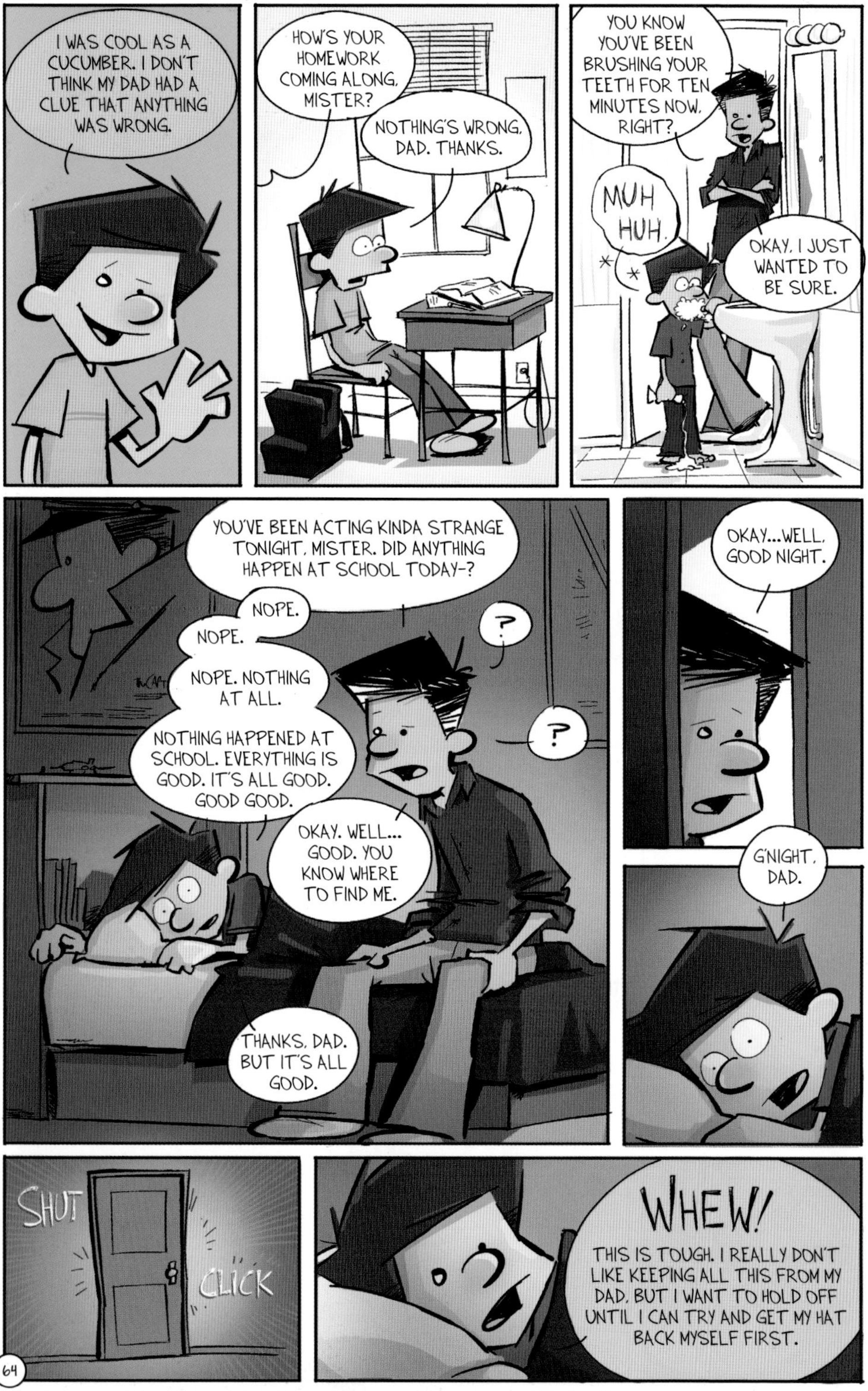
I WAS COOL AS A CUCUMBER. I DON'T THINK MY DAD HAD A CLUE THAT ANYTHING WAS WRONG.
HOW'S YOUR HOMEWORK COMING ALONG, MISTER?
NOTHING'S WRONG, DAD. THANKS.
YOU KNOW YOU'VE BEEN BRUSHING YOUR TEETH FOR TEN MINUTES NOW, RIGHT?
MUH HUH.
OKAY, I JUST WANTED TO BE SURE.
YOU'VE BEEN ACTING KINDA STRANGE TONIGHT, MISTER. DID ANYTHING HAPPEN AT SCHOOL TODAY-?
NOPE.
NOPE.
NOPE. NOTHING AT ALL.
NOTHING HAPPENED AT SCHOOL. EVERYTHING IS GOOD. IT'S ALL GOOD. GOOD GOOD.
?
?
OKAY. WELL... GOOD. YOU KNOW WHERE TO FIND ME.
THANKS, DAD. BUT IT'S ALL GOOD.
OKAY...WELL, GOOD NIGHT.
G'NIGHT, DAD.
SHUT
CLICK
WHEW!
THIS IS TOUGH. I REALLY DON'T LIKE KEEPING ALL THIS FROM MY DAD, BUT I WANT TO HOLD OFF UNTIL I CAN TRY AND GET MY HAT BACK MYSELF FIRST.

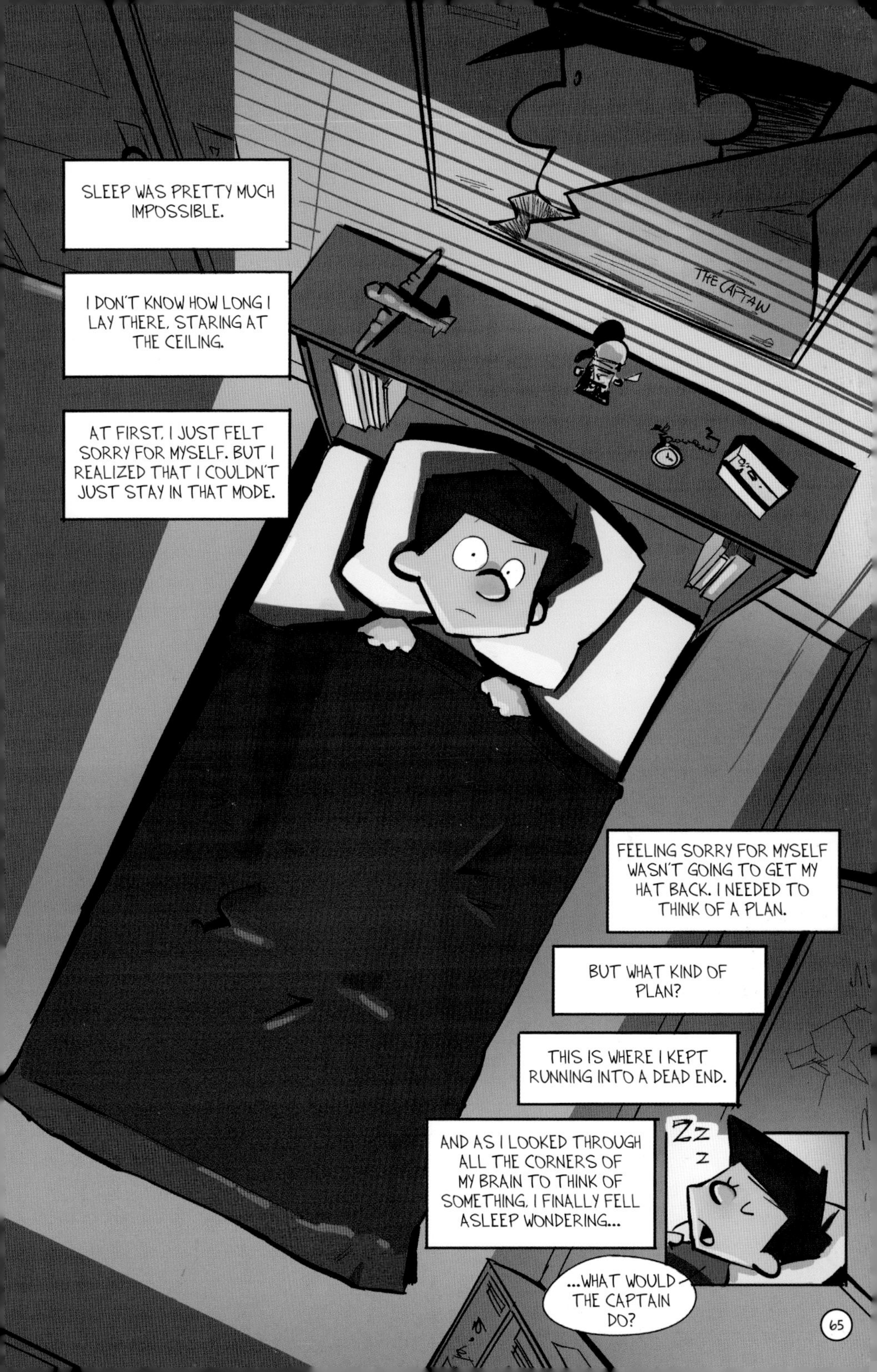
SLEEP WAS PRETTY MUCH IMPOSSIBLE.
I DON'T KNOW HOW LONG I LAY THERE, STARING AT THE CEILING.
AT FIRST, I JUST FELT SORRY FOR MYSELF. BUT I REALIZED THAT I COULDN'T JUST STAY IN THAT MODE.
THE CAPTAIN
FEELING SORRY FOR MYSELF WASN'T GOING TO GET MY HAT BACK. I NEEDED TO THINK OF A PLAN.
BUT WHAT KIND OF PLAN?
THIS IS WHERE I KEPT RUNNING INTO A DEAD END.
AND AS I LOOKED THROUGH ALL THE CORNERS OF MY BRAIN TO THINK OF SOMETHING, I FINALLY FELL ASLEEP WONDERING...
ZZ Z
...WHAT WOULD THE CAPTAIN DO?

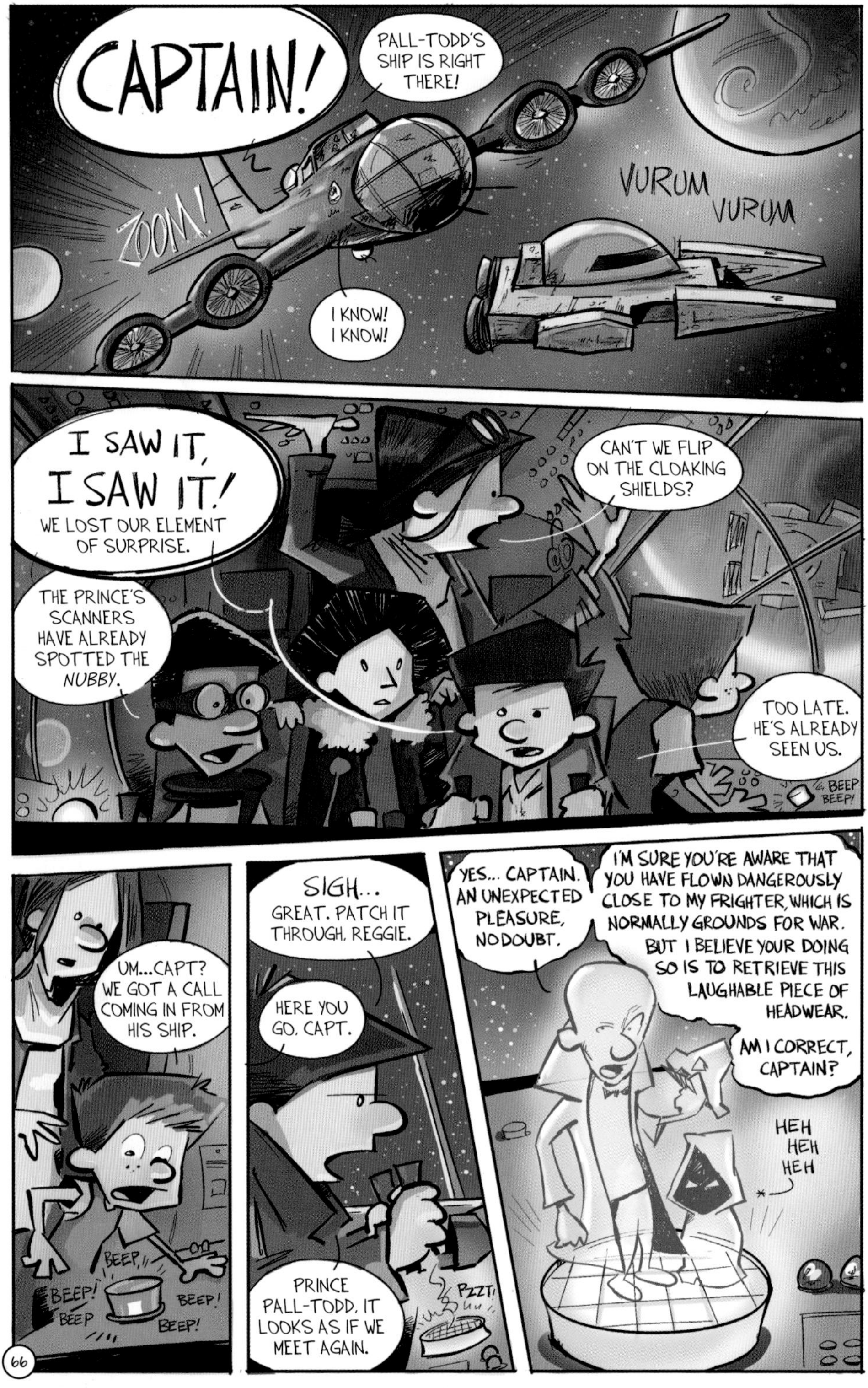

CAPTAIN!
PALL-TODD'S SHIP IS RIGHT THERE!
ZOOM!
VURUM VURUM
I KNOW! I KNOW!
I SAW IT, I SAW IT! WE LOST OUR ELEMENT OF SURPRISE.
CAN'T WE FLIP ON THE CLOAKING SHIELDS?
THE PRINCE'S SCANNERS HAVE ALREADY SPOTTED THE *NUBBY*.
TOO LATE. HE'S ALREADY SEEN US.
BEEP BEEP!
UM...CAPT? WE GOT A CALL COMING IN FROM HIS SHIP.
BEEP, BEEP! BEEP BEEP! BEEP!
SIGH... GREAT. PATCH IT THROUGH, REGGIE.
HERE YOU GO, CAPT.
PRINCE PALL-TODD, IT LOOKS AS IF WE MEET AGAIN.
PZZT!
YES... CAPTAIN. AN UNEXPECTED PLEASURE, NO DOUBT.
I'M SURE YOU'RE AWARE THAT YOU HAVE FLOWN DANGEROUSLY CLOSE TO MY FRIGHTER, WHICH IS NORMALLY GROUNDS FOR WAR.
BUT I BELIEVE YOUR DOING SO IS TO RETRIEVE THIS LAUGHABLE PIECE OF HEADWEAR.
AM I CORRECT, CAPTAIN?
HEH HEH HEH

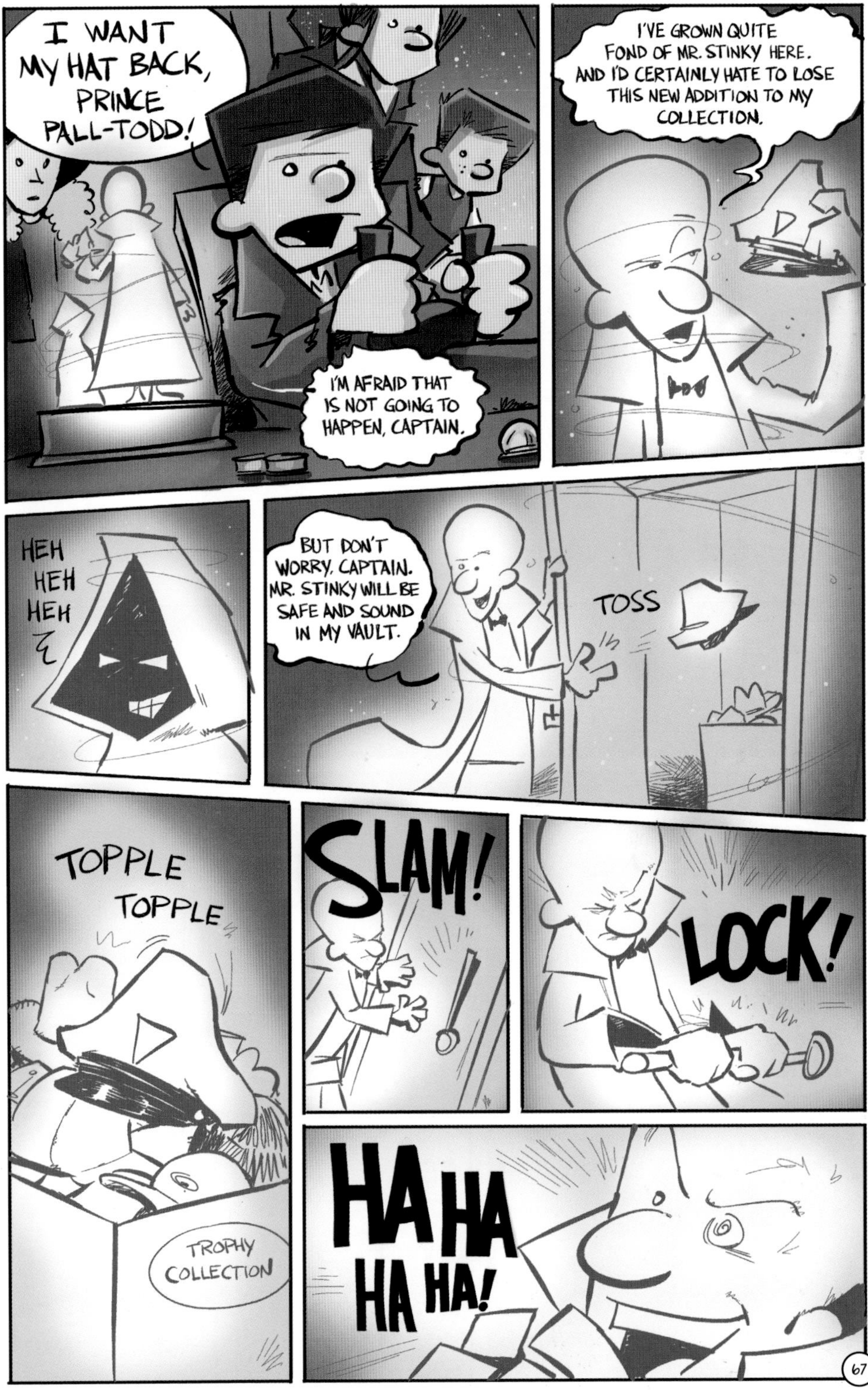
I WANT MY HAT BACK, PRINCE PALL-TODD!
I'M AFRAID THAT IS NOT GOING TO HAPPEN, CAPTAIN.
I'VE GROWN QUITE FOND OF MR. STINKY HERE. AND I'D CERTAINLY HATE TO LOSE THIS NEW ADDITION TO MY COLLECTION.
HEH HEH HEH
BUT DON'T WORRY, CAPTAIN. MR. STINKY WILL BE SAFE AND SOUND IN MY VAULT.
TOSS
TOPPLE TOPPLE
TROPHY COLLECTION
SLAM!
LOCK!
HA HA HA HA!

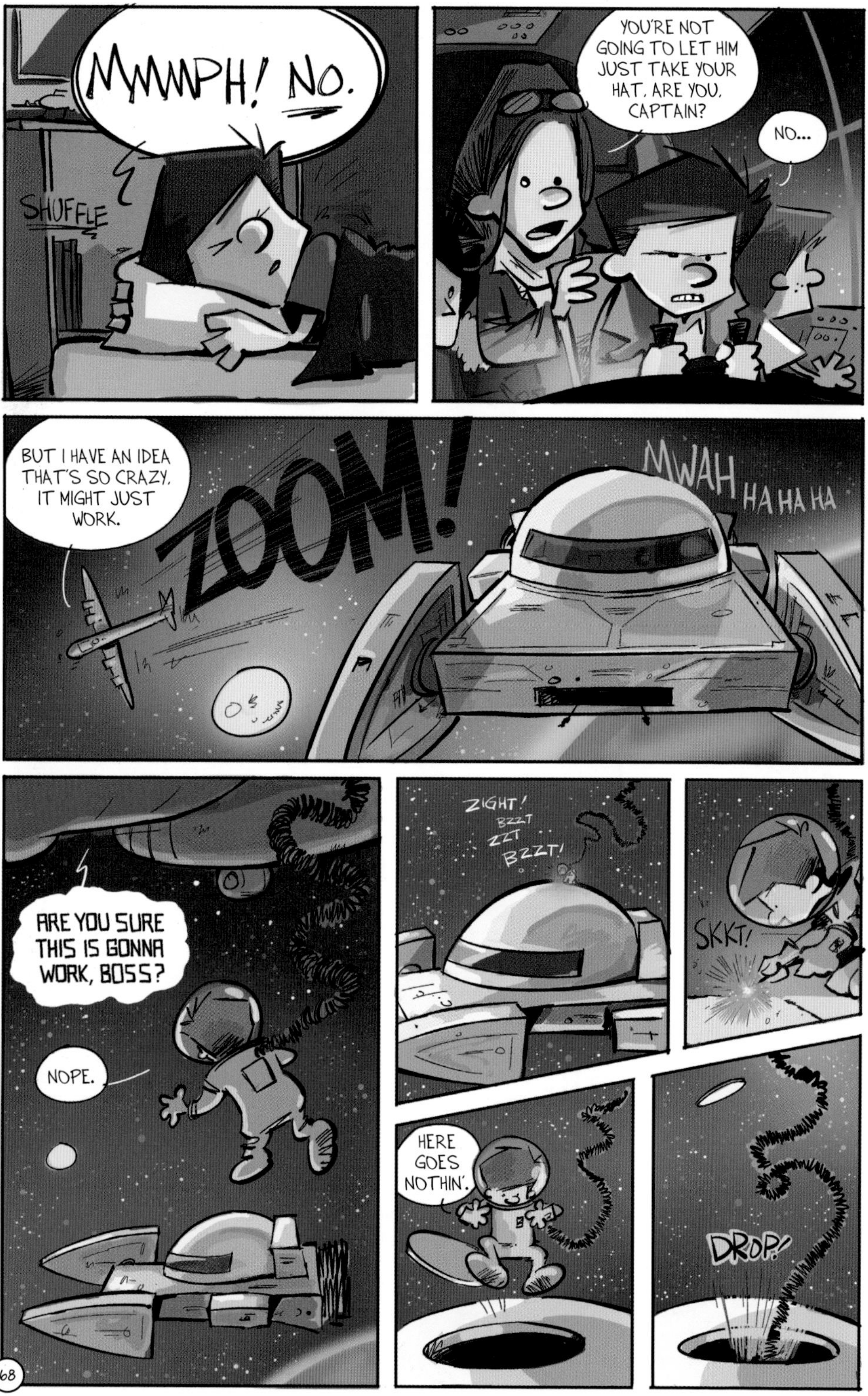
MMMPH! NO.
SHUFFLE
YOU'RE NOT GOING TO LET HIM JUST TAKE YOUR HAT, ARE YOU, CAPTAIN?
NO...
BUT I HAVE AN IDEA THAT'S SO CRAZY, IT MIGHT JUST WORK.
ZOOM!
MWAH HA HA HA
ARE YOU SURE THIS IS GONNA WORK, BOSS?
NOPE.
ZIGHT! BZZT ZZT BZZT!
SKKT!
HERE GOES NOTHIN'.
DROP!

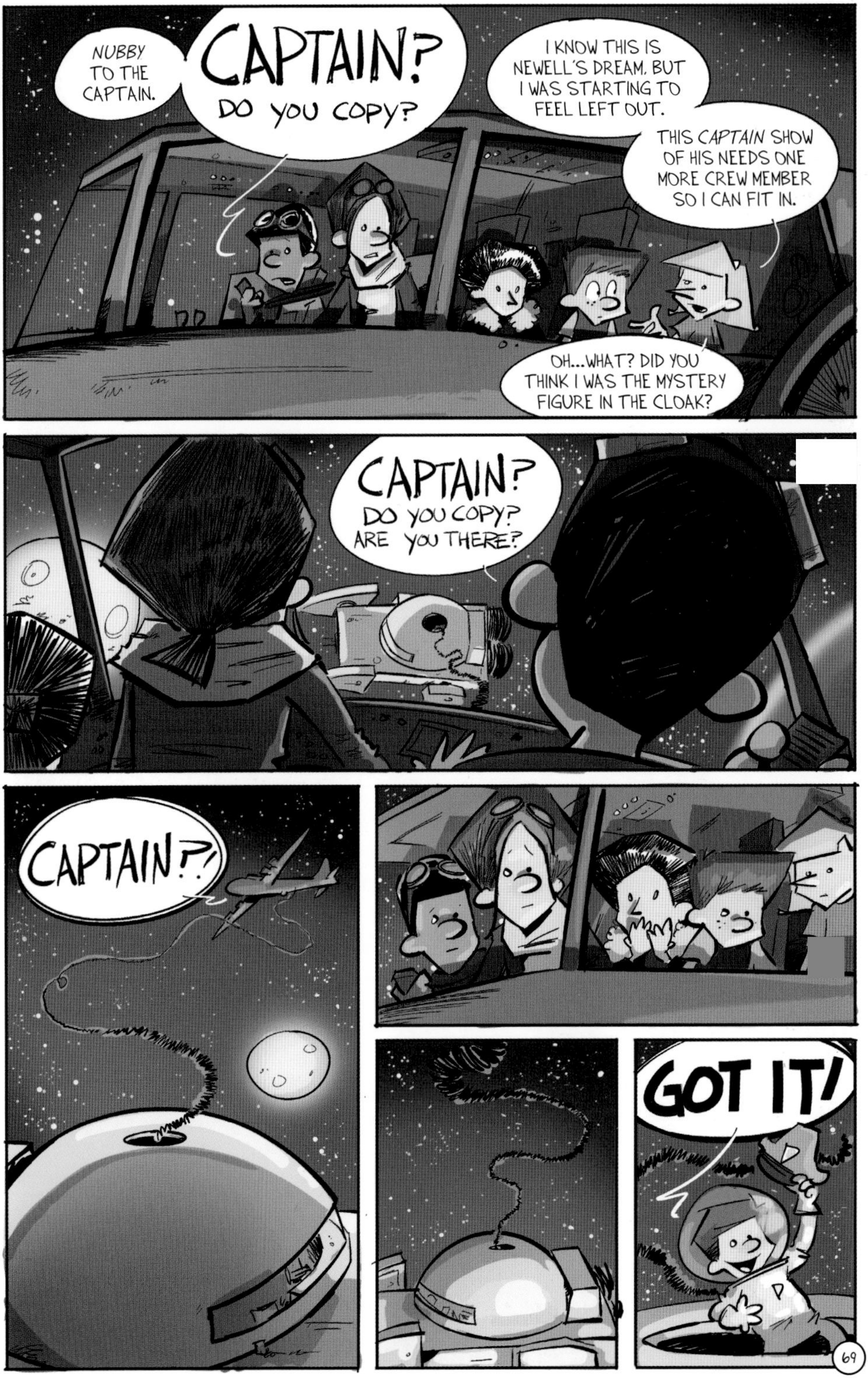
NUBBY TO THE CAPTAIN.
CAPTAIN? DO YOU COPY?
I KNOW THIS IS NEWELL'S DREAM, BUT I WAS STARTING TO FEEL LEFT OUT.
THIS CAPTAIN SHOW OF HIS NEEDS ONE MORE CREW MEMBER SO I CAN FIT IN.
OH...WHAT? DID YOU THINK I WAS THE MYSTERY FIGURE IN THE CLOAK?
CAPTAIN? DO YOU COPY? ARE YOU THERE?
CAPTAIN?!
GOT IT!

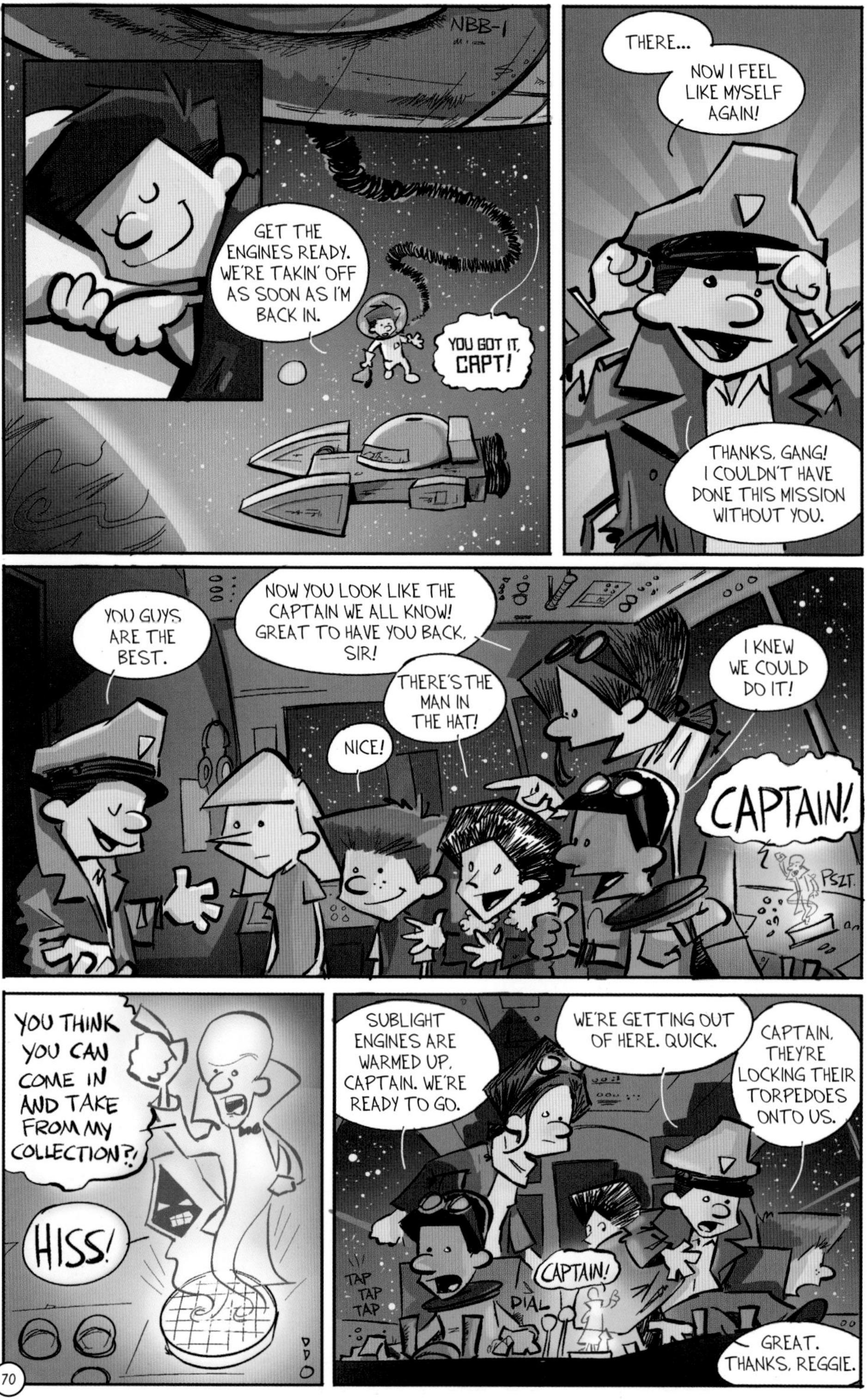
NBB-1
GET THE ENGINES READY. WE'RE TAKIN' OFF AS SOON AS I'M BACK IN.
YOU GOT IT, CAPT!
THERE...
NOW I FEEL LIKE MYSELF AGAIN!
THANKS, GANG! I COULDN'T HAVE DONE THIS MISSION WITHOUT YOU.
YOU GUYS ARE THE BEST.
NOW YOU LOOK LIKE THE CAPTAIN WE ALL KNOW! GREAT TO HAVE YOU BACK, SIR!
NICE!
THERE'S THE MAN IN THE HAT!
I KNEW WE COULD DO IT!
CAPTAIN!
PSZT.
YOU THINK YOU CAN COME IN AND TAKE FROM MY COLLECTION?!
HISS!
SUBLIGHT ENGINES ARE WARMED UP, CAPTAIN. WE'RE READY TO GO.
WE'RE GETTING OUT OF HERE. QUICK.
CAPTAIN, THEY'RE LOCKING THEIR TORPEDOES ONTO US.
TAP TAP TAP
CAPTAIN!
DIAL
GREAT. THANKS, REGGIE.

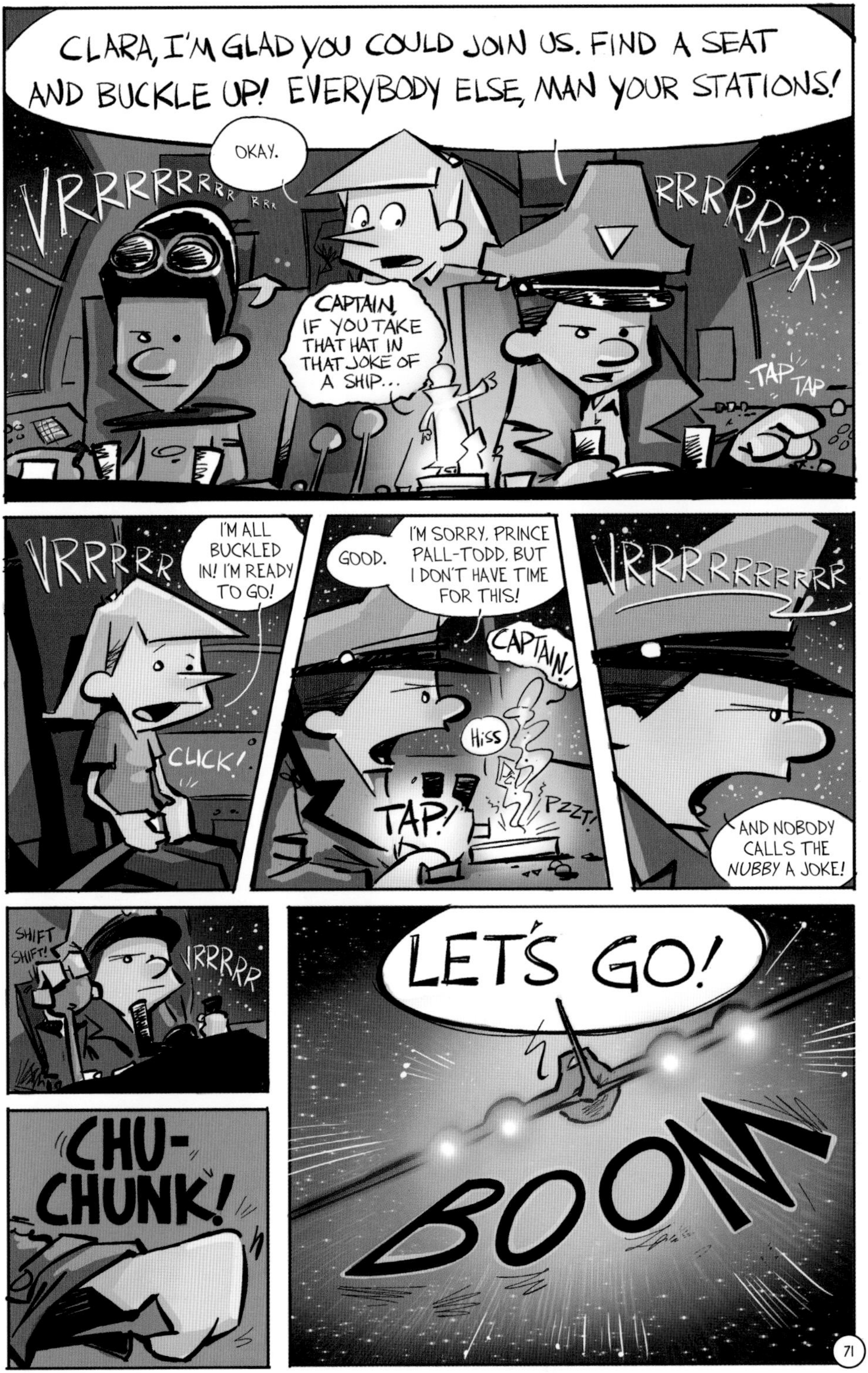
CLARA, I'M GLAD YOU COULD JOIN US. FIND A SEAT AND BUCKLE UP! EVERYBODY ELSE, MAN YOUR STATIONS!
OKAY.
VRRRRRRRR RRR
RRRRRRRR
CAPTAIN, IF YOU TAKE THAT HAT IN THAT JOKE OF A SHIP...
TAP TAP
VRRRRR
I'M ALL BUCKLED IN! I'M READY TO GO!
CLICK!
GOOD.
I'M SORRY, PRINCE PALL-TODD, BUT I DON'T HAVE TIME FOR THIS!
CAPTAIN!
HISS
TAP!
PZZT!
VRRRRRRRRRRR
AND NOBODY CALLS THE NUBBY A JOKE!
SHIFT SHIFT!
VRRRRR
CHU-CHUNK!
LET'S GO!
BOOM

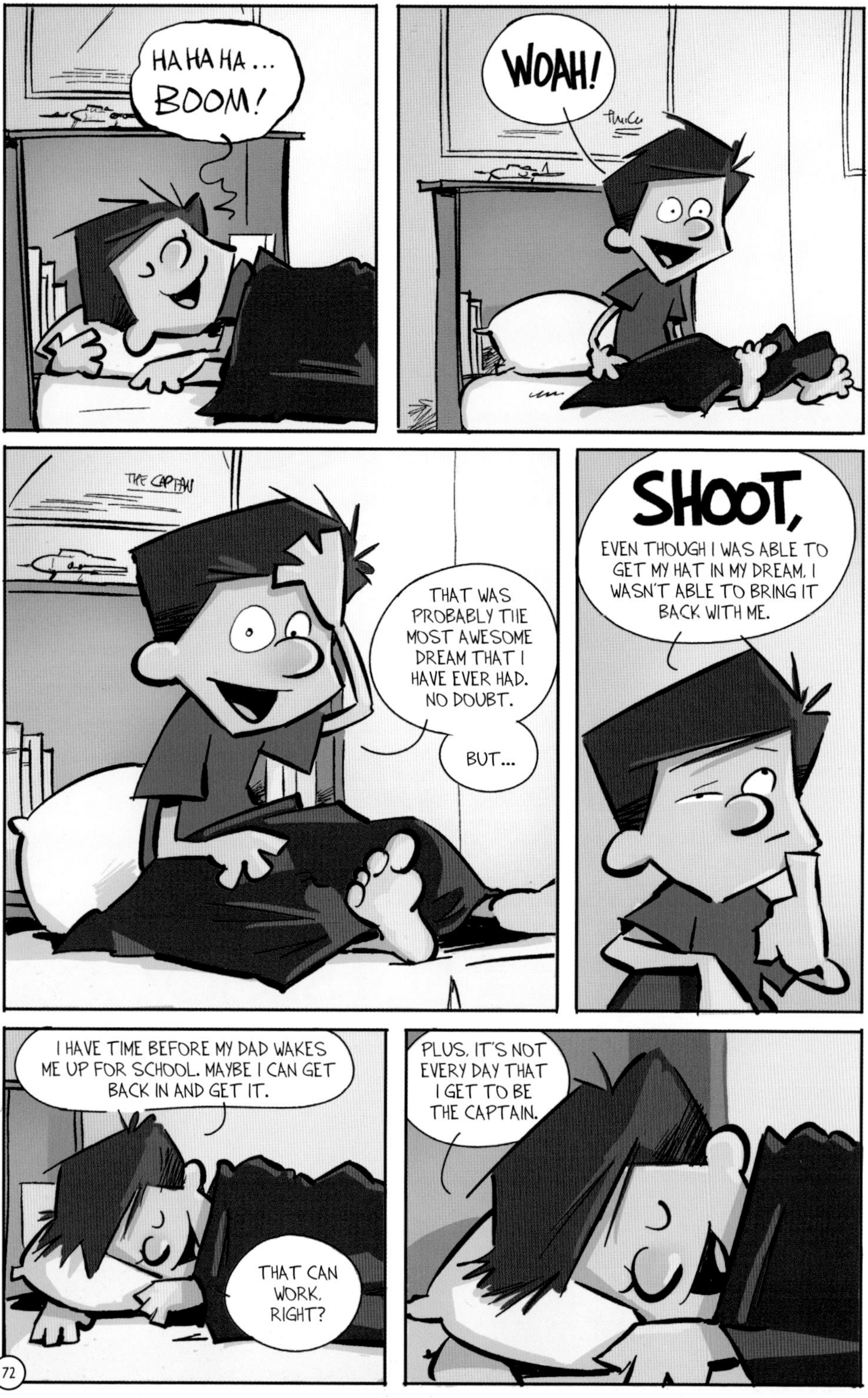
HA HA HA... BOOM!
WOAH!
THE CAPTAIN
THAT WAS PROBABLY THE MOST AWESOME DREAM THAT I HAVE EVER HAD. NO DOUBT.
BUT...
SHOOT,
EVEN THOUGH I WAS ABLE TO GET MY HAT IN MY DREAM, I WASN'T ABLE TO BRING IT BACK WITH ME.
I HAVE TIME BEFORE MY DAD WAKES ME UP FOR SCHOOL. MAYBE I CAN GET BACK IN AND GET IT.
THAT CAN WORK, RIGHT?
PLUS, IT'S NOT EVERY DAY THAT I GET TO BE THE CAPTAIN.

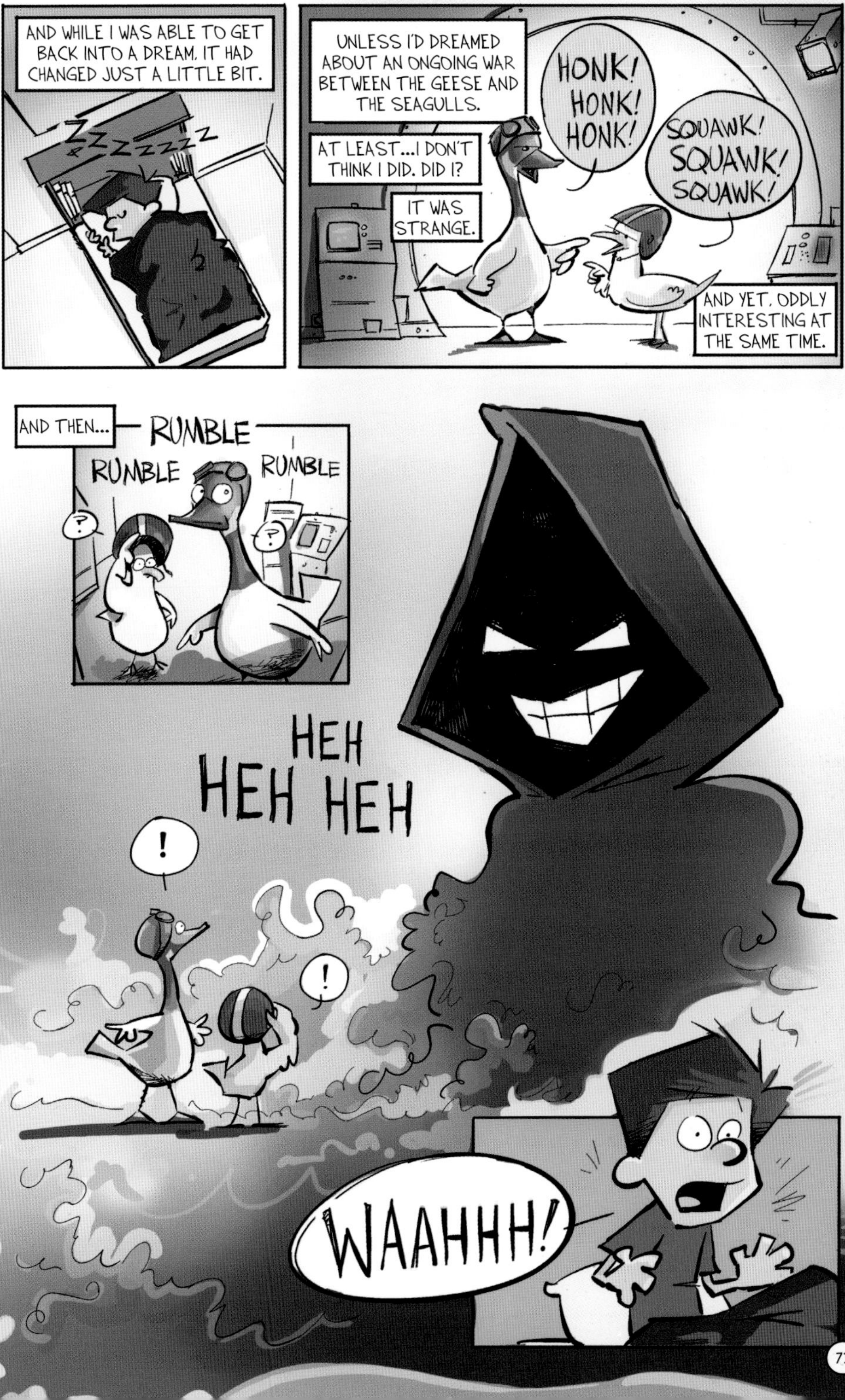
AND WHILE I WAS ABLE TO GET BACK INTO A DREAM, IT HAD CHANGED JUST A LITTLE BIT.
ZZZZZZZZ
UNLESS I'D DREAMED ABOUT AN ONGOING WAR BETWEEN THE GEESE AND THE SEAGULLS.
AT LEAST...I DON'T THINK I DID. DID I?
IT WAS STRANGE.
HONK! HONK! HONK!
SQUAWK! SQUAWK! SQUAWK!
AND YET, ODDLY INTERESTING AT THE SAME TIME.
AND THEN...
RUMBLE
RUMBLE
RUMBLE
?
?
HEH HEH HEH
!
!
WAAHHH!

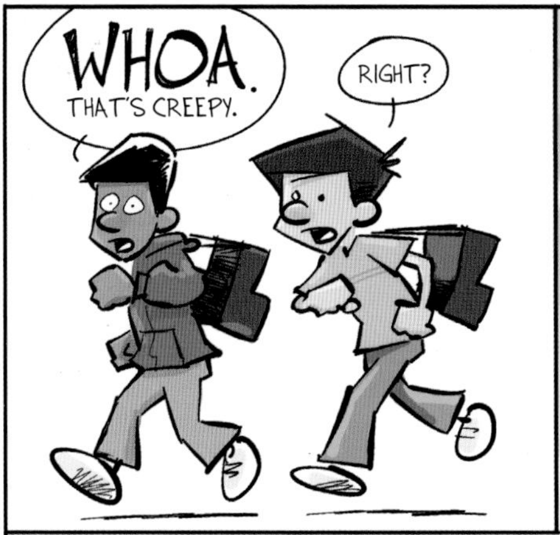
WHOA. THAT'S CREEPY.
RIGHT?

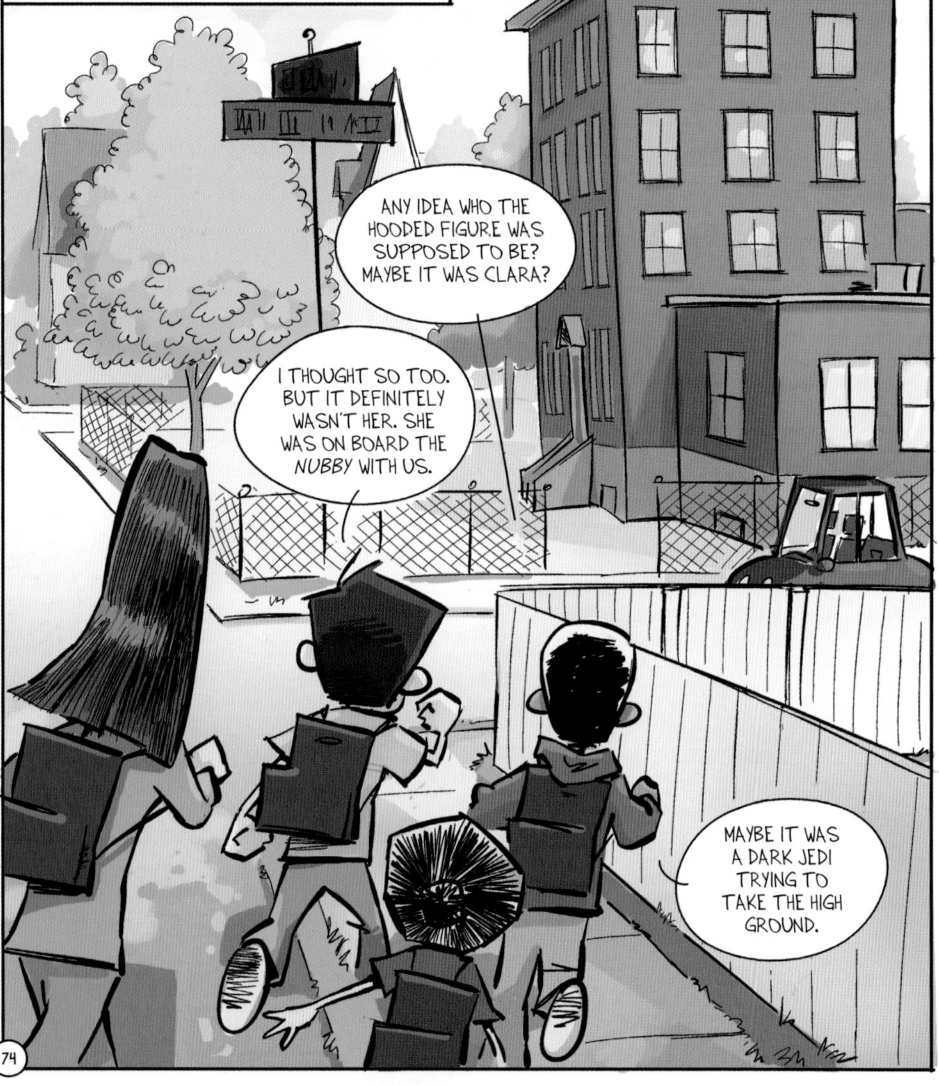
ANY IDEA WHO THE HOODED FIGURE WAS SUPPOSED TO BE? MAYBE IT WAS CLARA?
I THOUGHT SO TOO. BUT IT DEFINITELY WASN'T HER. SHE WAS ON BOARD THE *NUBBY* WITH US.
MAYBE IT WAS A DARK JEDI TRYING TO TAKE THE HIGH GROUND.

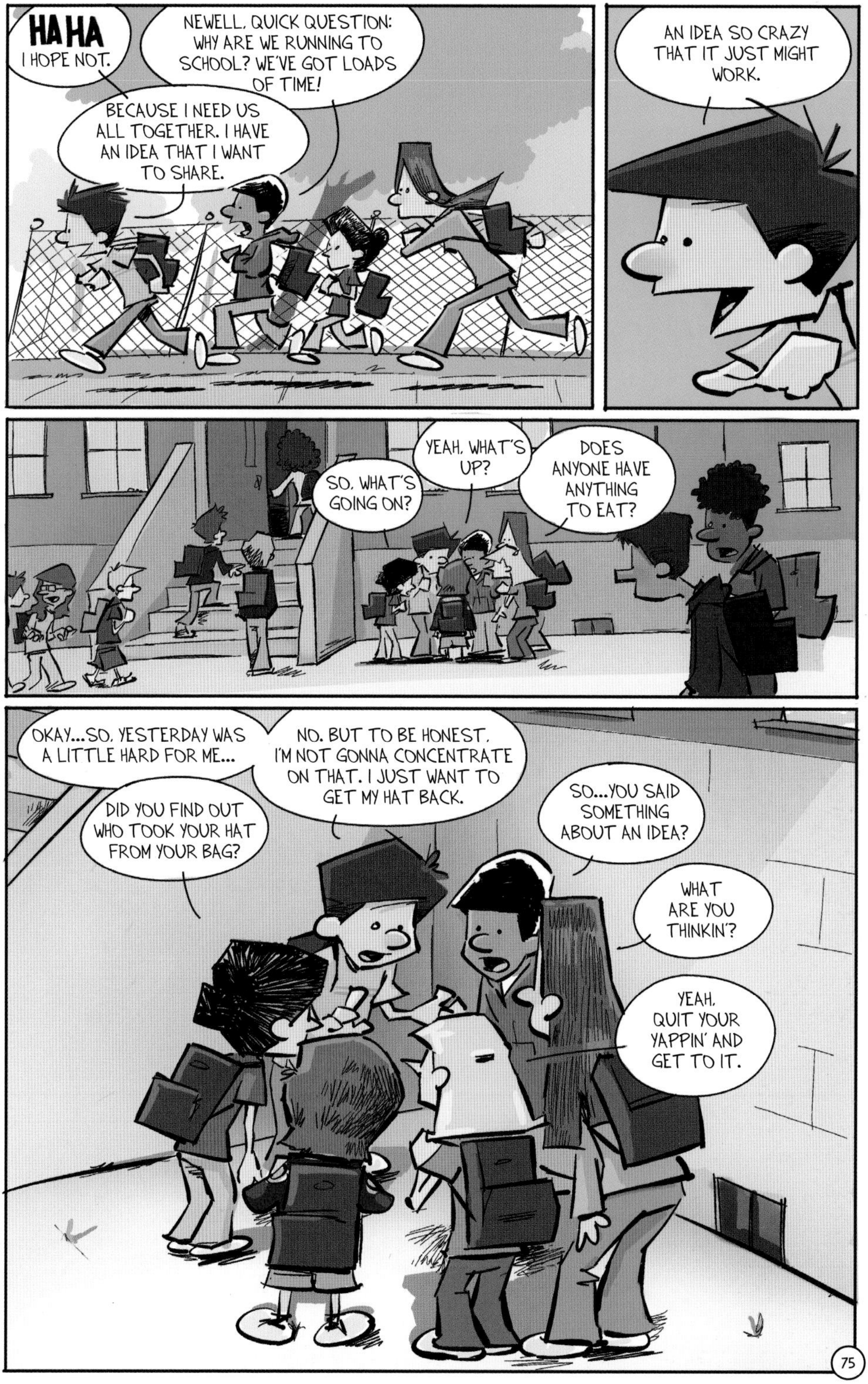
HA HA
I HOPE NOT.
NEWELL, QUICK QUESTION: WHY ARE WE RUNNING TO SCHOOL? WE'VE GOT LOADS OF TIME!
BECAUSE I NEED US ALL TOGETHER. I HAVE AN IDEA THAT I WANT TO SHARE.
AN IDEA SO CRAZY THAT IT JUST MIGHT WORK.
SO, WHAT'S GOING ON?
YEAH, WHAT'S UP?
DOES ANYONE HAVE ANYTHING TO EAT?
OKAY...SO, YESTERDAY WAS A LITTLE HARD FOR ME...
DID YOU FIND OUT WHO TOOK YOUR HAT FROM YOUR BAG?
NO. BUT TO BE HONEST, I'M NOT GONNA CONCENTRATE ON THAT. I JUST WANT TO GET MY HAT BACK.
SO...YOU SAID SOMETHING ABOUT AN IDEA?
WHAT ARE YOU THINKIN'?
YEAH, QUIT YOUR YAPPIN' AND GET TO IT.

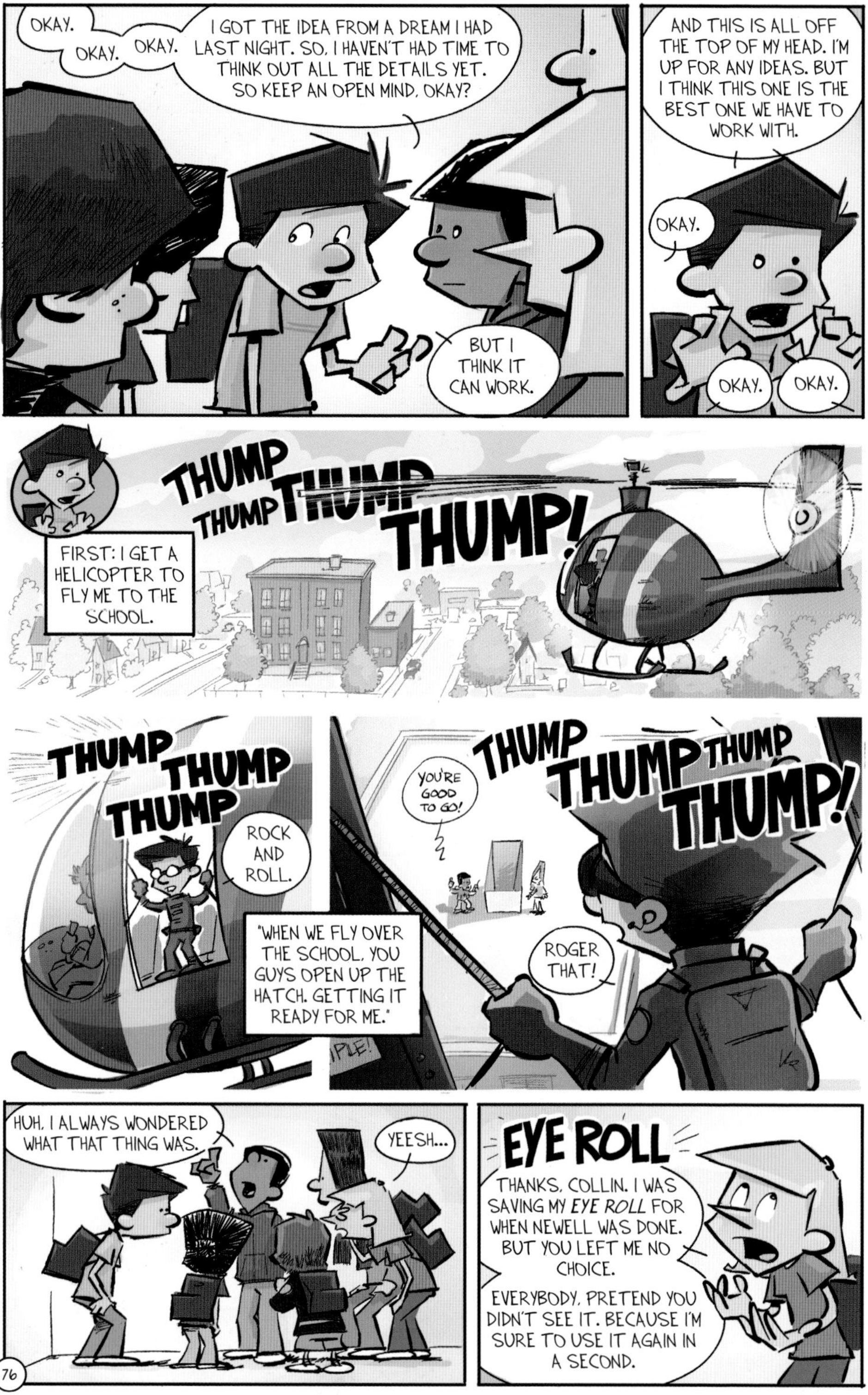
OKAY.
OKAY.
OKAY.
I GOT THE IDEA FROM A DREAM I HAD LAST NIGHT. SO, I HAVEN'T HAD TIME TO THINK OUT ALL THE DETAILS YET. SO KEEP AN OPEN MIND, OKAY?
BUT I THINK IT CAN WORK.
AND THIS IS ALL OFF THE TOP OF MY HEAD. I'M UP FOR ANY IDEAS. BUT I THINK THIS ONE IS THE BEST ONE WE HAVE TO WORK WITH.
OKAY.
OKAY.
OKAY.
THUMP THUMP THUMP THUMP!
FIRST: I GET A HELICOPTER TO FLY ME TO THE SCHOOL.
THUMP THUMP THUMP
ROCK AND ROLL.
"WHEN WE FLY OVER THE SCHOOL, YOU GUYS OPEN UP THE HATCH. GETTING IT READY FOR ME."
THUMP THUMP THUMP THUMP!
YOU'RE GOOD TO GO!
ROGER THAT!
HUH, I ALWAYS WONDERED WHAT THAT THING WAS.
YEESH...
EYE ROLL
THANKS, COLLIN. I WAS SAVING MY *EYE ROLL* FOR WHEN NEWELL WAS DONE. BUT YOU LEFT ME NO CHOICE.
EVERYBODY, PRETEND YOU DIDN'T SEE IT. BECAUSE I'M SURE TO USE IT AGAIN IN A SECOND.

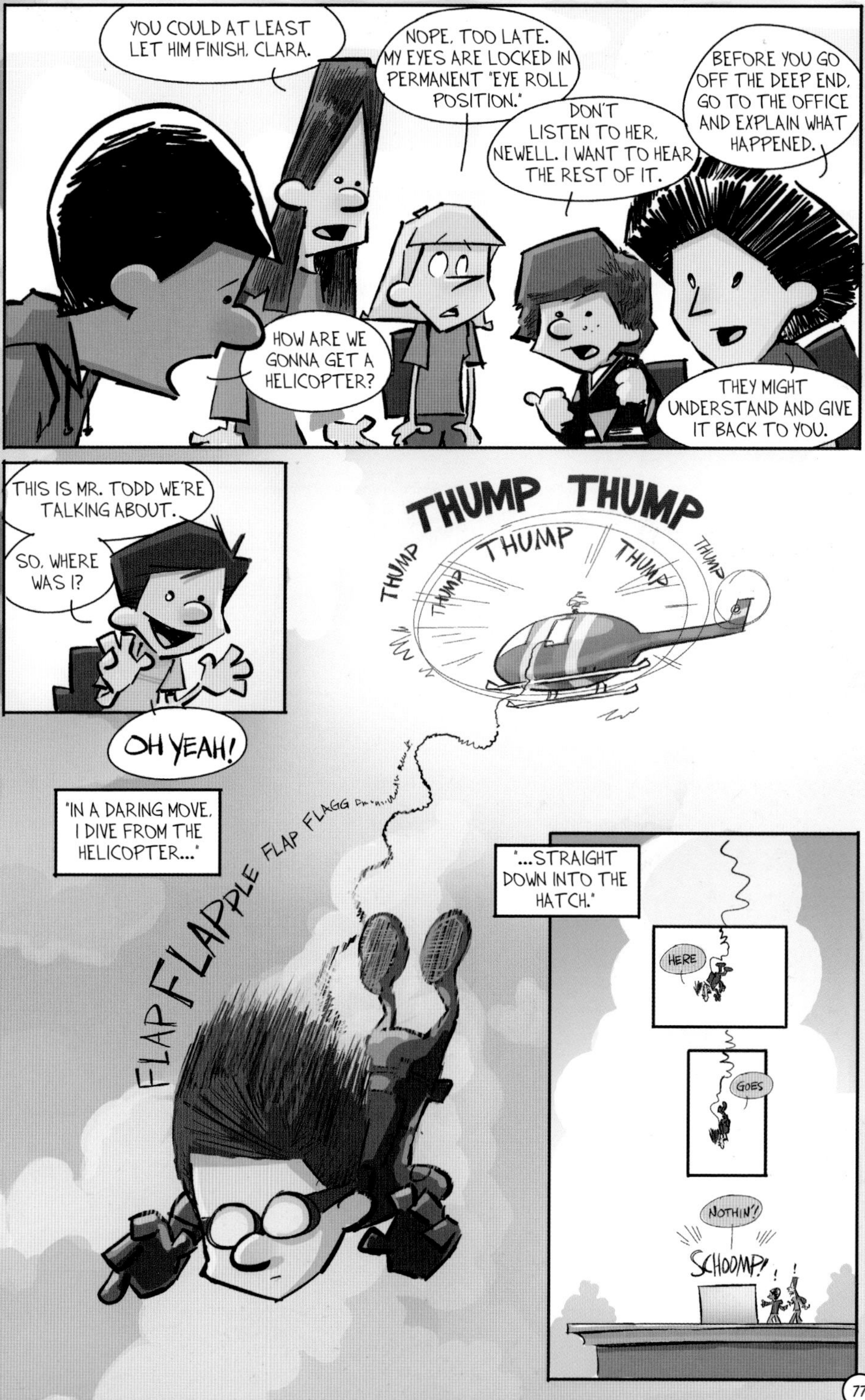
YOU COULD AT LEAST LET HIM FINISH, CLARA.
NOPE, TOO LATE. MY EYES ARE LOCKED IN PERMANENT "EYE ROLL POSITION."
DON'T LISTEN TO HER, NEWELL. I WANT TO HEAR THE REST OF IT.
BEFORE YOU GO OFF THE DEEP END, GO TO THE OFFICE AND EXPLAIN WHAT HAPPENED.
HOW ARE WE GONNA GET A HELICOPTER?
THEY MIGHT UNDERSTAND AND GIVE IT BACK TO YOU.
THIS IS MR. TODD WE'RE TALKING ABOUT.
SO, WHERE WAS I?
OH YEAH!
THUMP THUMP
THUMP THUMP THUMP THUMP THUMP THUMP
"IN A DARING MOVE, I DIVE FROM THE HELICOPTER..."
FLAP FLAPPLE FLAP FLAGG
"...STRAIGHT DOWN INTO THE HATCH."
HERE
GOES
NOTHIN'!
SCHOOMP!

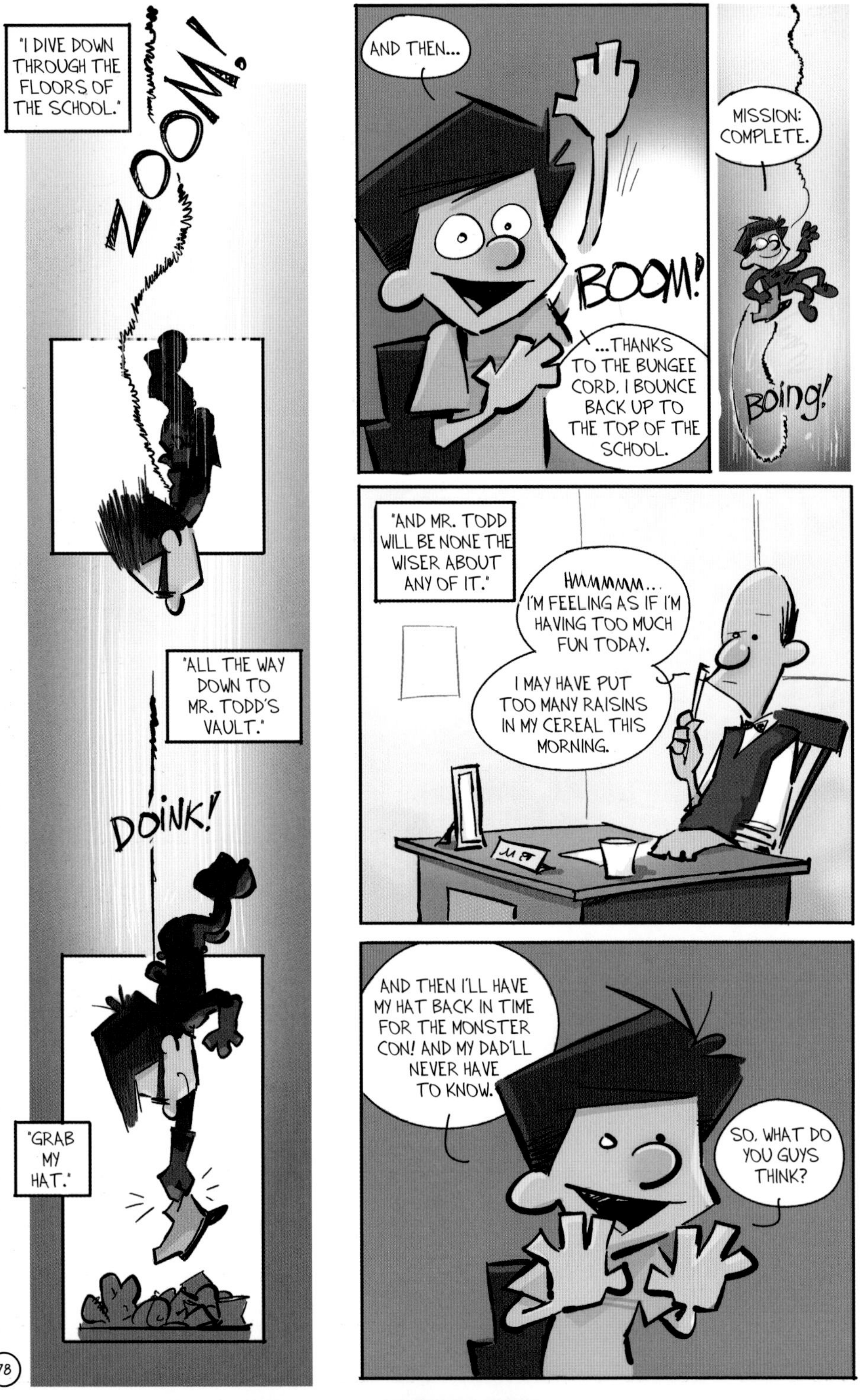

"I DIVE DOWN THROUGH THE FLOORS OF THE SCHOOL."
ZOOOM!
"ALL THE WAY DOWN TO MR. TODD'S VAULT."
DOINK!
"GRAB MY HAT."
AND THEN...
BOOM!
...THANKS TO THE BUNGEE CORD, I BOUNCE BACK UP TO THE TOP OF THE SCHOOL.
MISSION: COMPLETE.
BOING!
"AND MR. TODD WILL BE NONE THE WISER ABOUT ANY OF IT."
HMMMMM... I'M FEELING AS IF I'M HAVING TOO MUCH FUN TODAY.
I MAY HAVE PUT TOO MANY RAISINS IN MY CEREAL THIS MORNING.
AND THEN I'LL HAVE MY HAT BACK IN TIME FOR THE MONSTER CON! AND MY DAD'LL NEVER HAVE TO KNOW.
SO, WHAT DO YOU GUYS THINK?

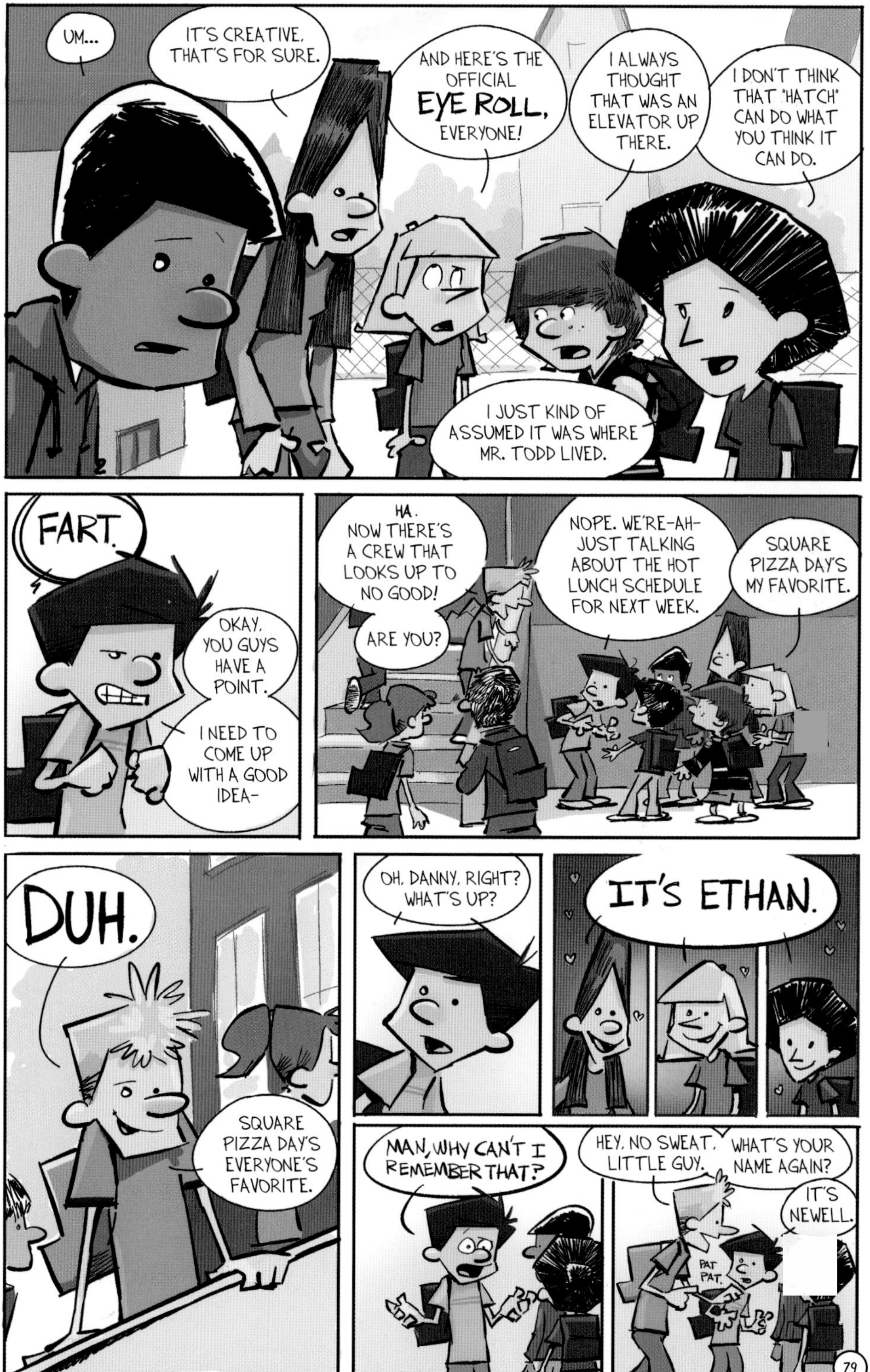
UM...
IT'S CREATIVE, THAT'S FOR SURE.
AND HERE'S THE OFFICIAL EYE ROLL, EVERYONE!
I ALWAYS THOUGHT THAT WAS AN ELEVATOR UP THERE.
I DON'T THINK THAT "HATCH" CAN DO WHAT YOU THINK IT CAN DO.
I JUST KIND OF ASSUMED IT WAS WHERE MR. TODD LIVED.
FART.
OKAY, YOU GUYS HAVE A POINT.
I NEED TO COME UP WITH A GOOD IDEA-
HA. NOW THERE'S A CREW THAT LOOKS UP TO NO GOOD!
ARE YOU?
NOPE. WE'RE-AH- JUST TALKING ABOUT THE HOT LUNCH SCHEDULE FOR NEXT WEEK.
SQUARE PIZZA DAY'S MY FAVORITE.
DUH.
SQUARE PIZZA DAY'S EVERYONE'S FAVORITE.
OH, DANNY, RIGHT? WHAT'S UP?
IT'S ETHAN.
MAN, WHY CAN'T I REMEMBER THAT?
HEY, NO SWEAT, LITTLE GUY.
WHAT'S YOUR NAME AGAIN?
IT'S NEWELL.
PAT PAT.

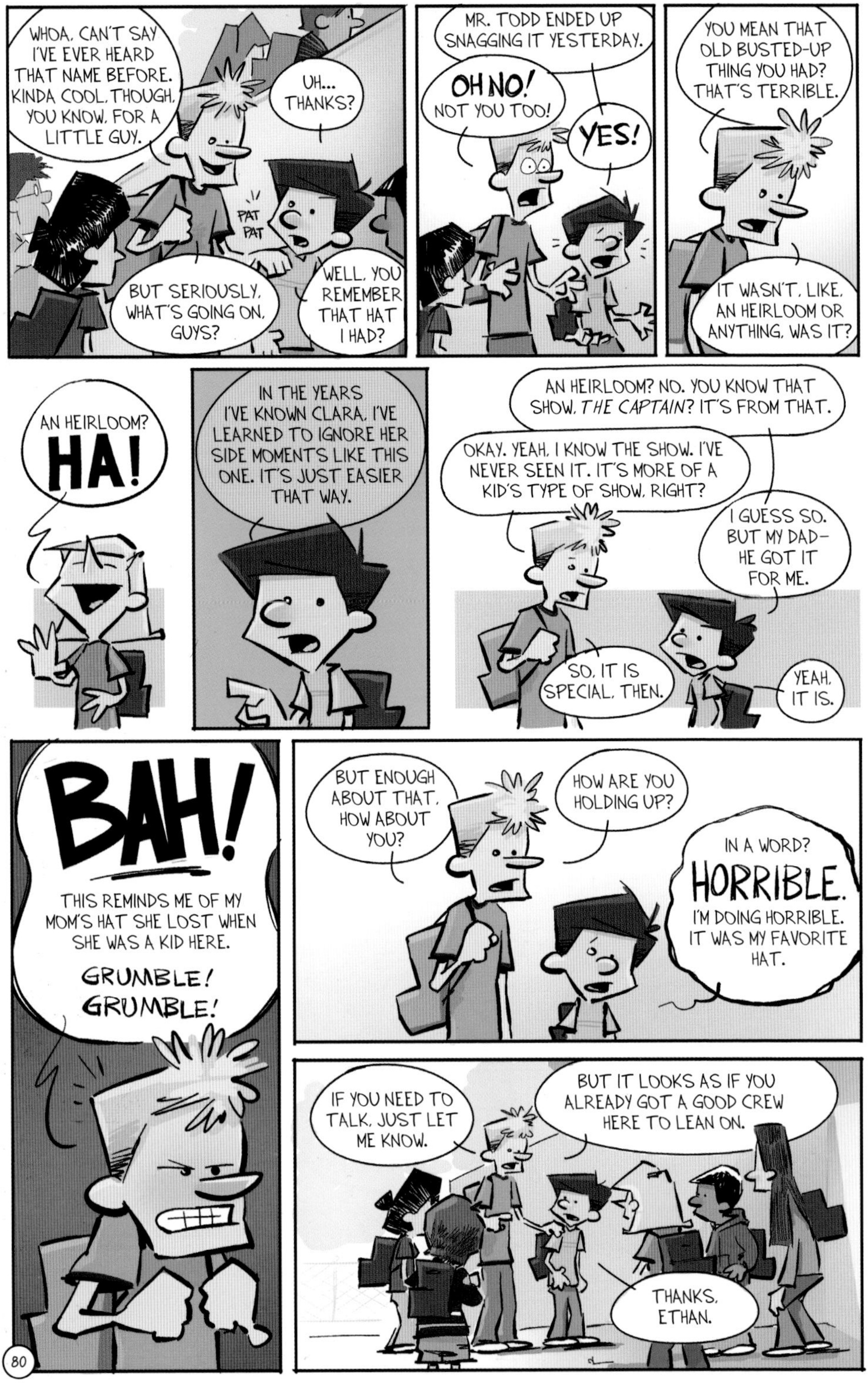

WHOA, CAN'T SAY I'VE EVER HEARD THAT NAME BEFORE. KINDA COOL, THOUGH, YOU KNOW, FOR A LITTLE GUY.
UH... THANKS?
PAT PAT
BUT SERIOUSLY, WHAT'S GOING ON, GUYS?
WELL, YOU REMEMBER THAT HAT I HAD?
MR. TODD ENDED UP SNAGGING IT YESTERDAY.
OH NO! NOT YOU TOO!
YES!
YOU MEAN THAT OLD BUSTED-UP THING YOU HAD? THAT'S TERRIBLE.
IT WASN'T, LIKE, AN HEIRLOOM OR ANYTHING, WAS IT?
AN HEIRLOOM? HA!
IN THE YEARS I'VE KNOWN CLARA, I'VE LEARNED TO IGNORE HER SIDE MOMENTS LIKE THIS ONE. IT'S JUST EASIER THAT WAY.
AN HEIRLOOM? NO. YOU KNOW THAT SHOW, *THE CAPTAIN*? IT'S FROM THAT.
OKAY. YEAH, I KNOW THE SHOW. I'VE NEVER SEEN IT. IT'S MORE OF A KID'S TYPE OF SHOW, RIGHT?
I GUESS SO. BUT MY DAD— HE GOT IT FOR ME.
SO, IT IS SPECIAL, THEN.
YEAH, IT IS.
BAH!
THIS REMINDS ME OF MY MOM'S HAT SHE LOST WHEN SHE WAS A KID HERE.
GRUMBLE! GRUMBLE!
BUT ENOUGH ABOUT THAT, HOW ABOUT YOU?
HOW ARE YOU HOLDING UP?
IN A WORD? HORRIBLE. I'M DOING HORRIBLE. IT WAS MY FAVORITE HAT.
IF YOU NEED TO TALK, JUST LET ME KNOW.
BUT IT LOOKS AS IF YOU ALREADY GOT A GOOD CREW HERE TO LEAN ON.
THANKS, ETHAN.

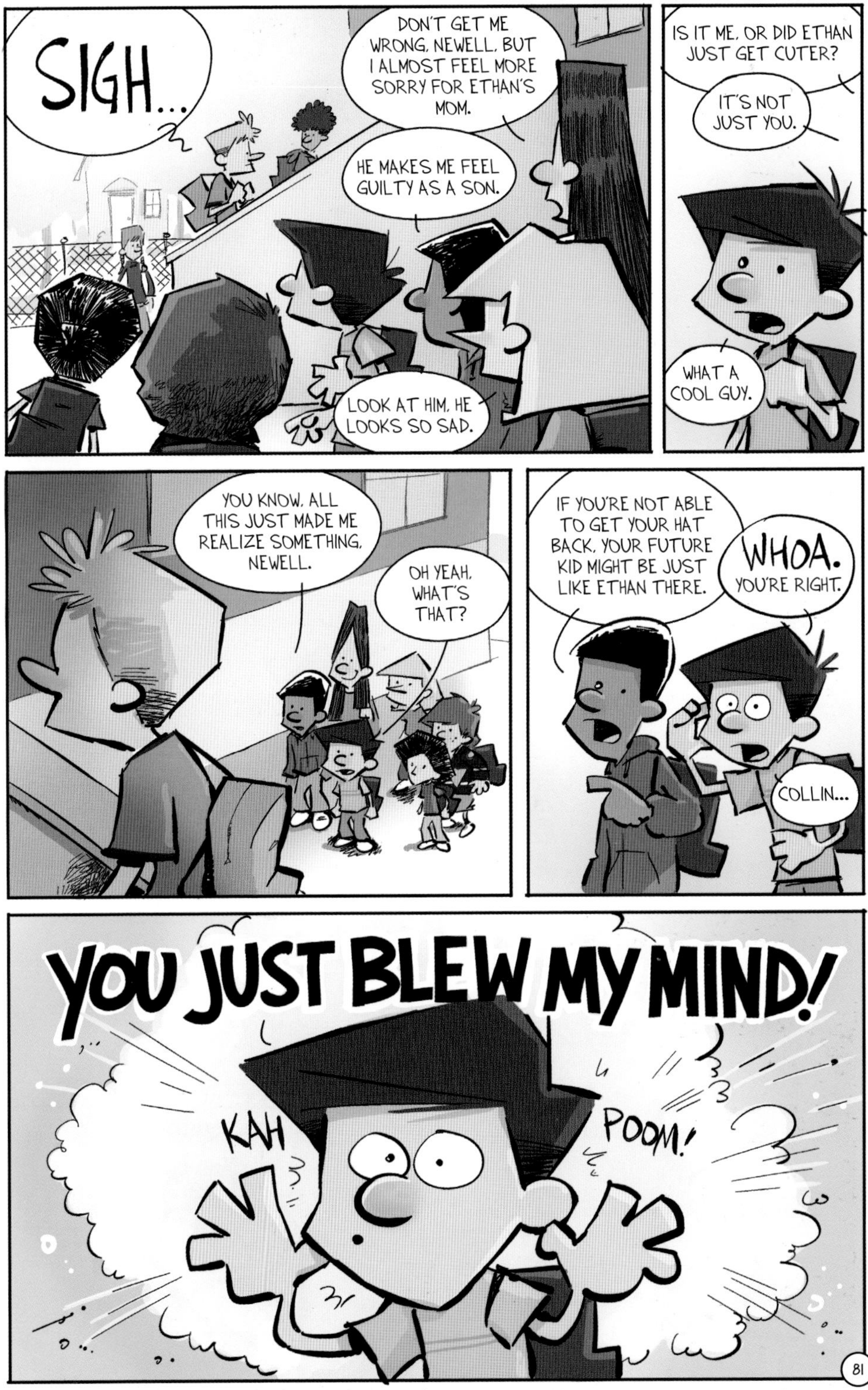
SIGH...
DON'T GET ME WRONG, NEWELL, BUT I ALMOST FEEL MORE SORRY FOR ETHAN'S MOM.
HE MAKES ME FEEL GUILTY AS A SON.
LOOK AT HIM, HE LOOKS SO SAD.
IS IT ME, OR DID ETHAN JUST GET CUTER?
IT'S NOT JUST YOU.
WHAT A COOL GUY.
YOU KNOW, ALL THIS JUST MADE ME REALIZE SOMETHING, NEWELL.
OH YEAH, WHAT'S THAT?
IF YOU'RE NOT ABLE TO GET YOUR HAT BACK, YOUR FUTURE KID MIGHT BE JUST LIKE ETHAN THERE.
WHOA. YOU'RE RIGHT.
COLLIN...
YOU JUST BLEW MY MIND!
KAH
POOM!

CHAPTER FIVE
THE SETUP

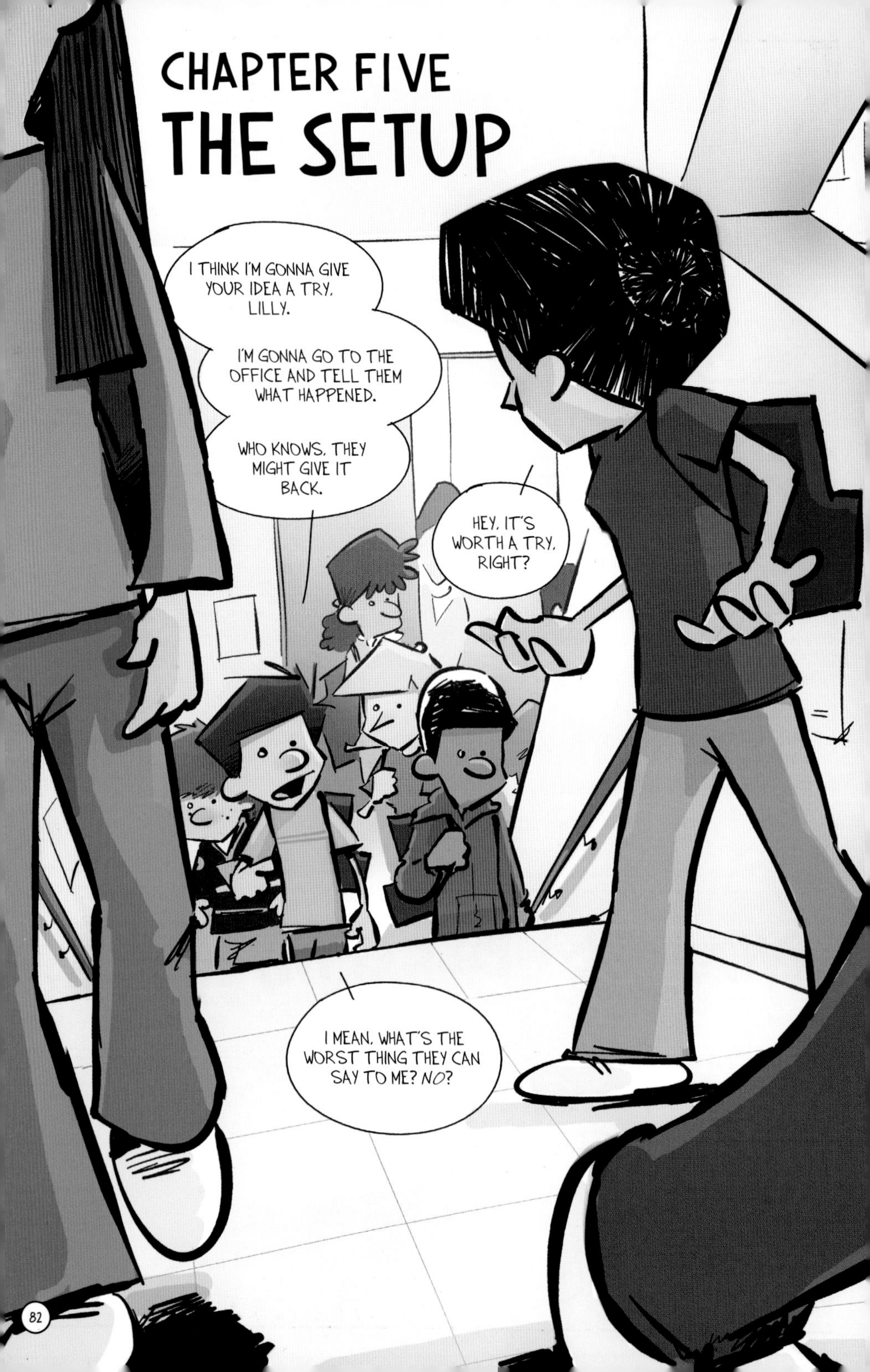
I THINK I'M GONNA GIVE YOUR IDEA A TRY, LILLY.
I'M GONNA GO TO THE OFFICE AND TELL THEM WHAT HAPPENED.
WHO KNOWS, THEY MIGHT GIVE IT BACK.
HEY, IT'S WORTH A TRY, RIGHT?
I MEAN, WHAT'S THE WORST THING THEY CAN SAY TO ME? *NO*?

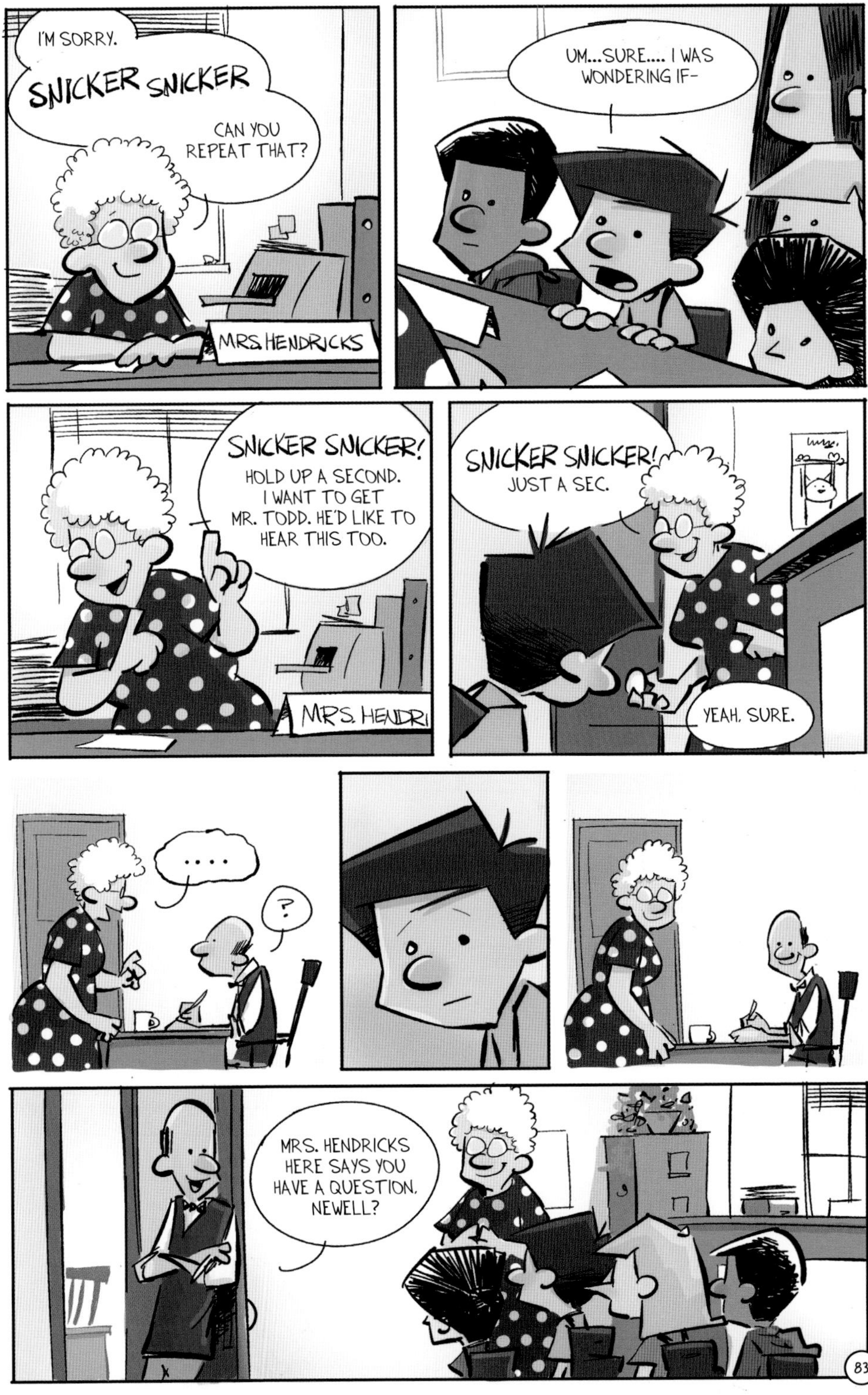
I'M SORRY.
SNICKER SNICKER
CAN YOU REPEAT THAT?
MRS. HENDRICKS
UM... SURE.... I WAS WONDERING IF-
SNICKER SNICKER!
HOLD UP A SECOND. I WANT TO GET MR. TODD. HE'D LIKE TO HEAR THIS TOO.
MRS. HENDRI
SNICKER SNICKER!
JUST A SEC.
YEAH. SURE.
....
?
MRS. HENDRICKS HERE SAYS YOU HAVE A QUESTION, NEWELL?

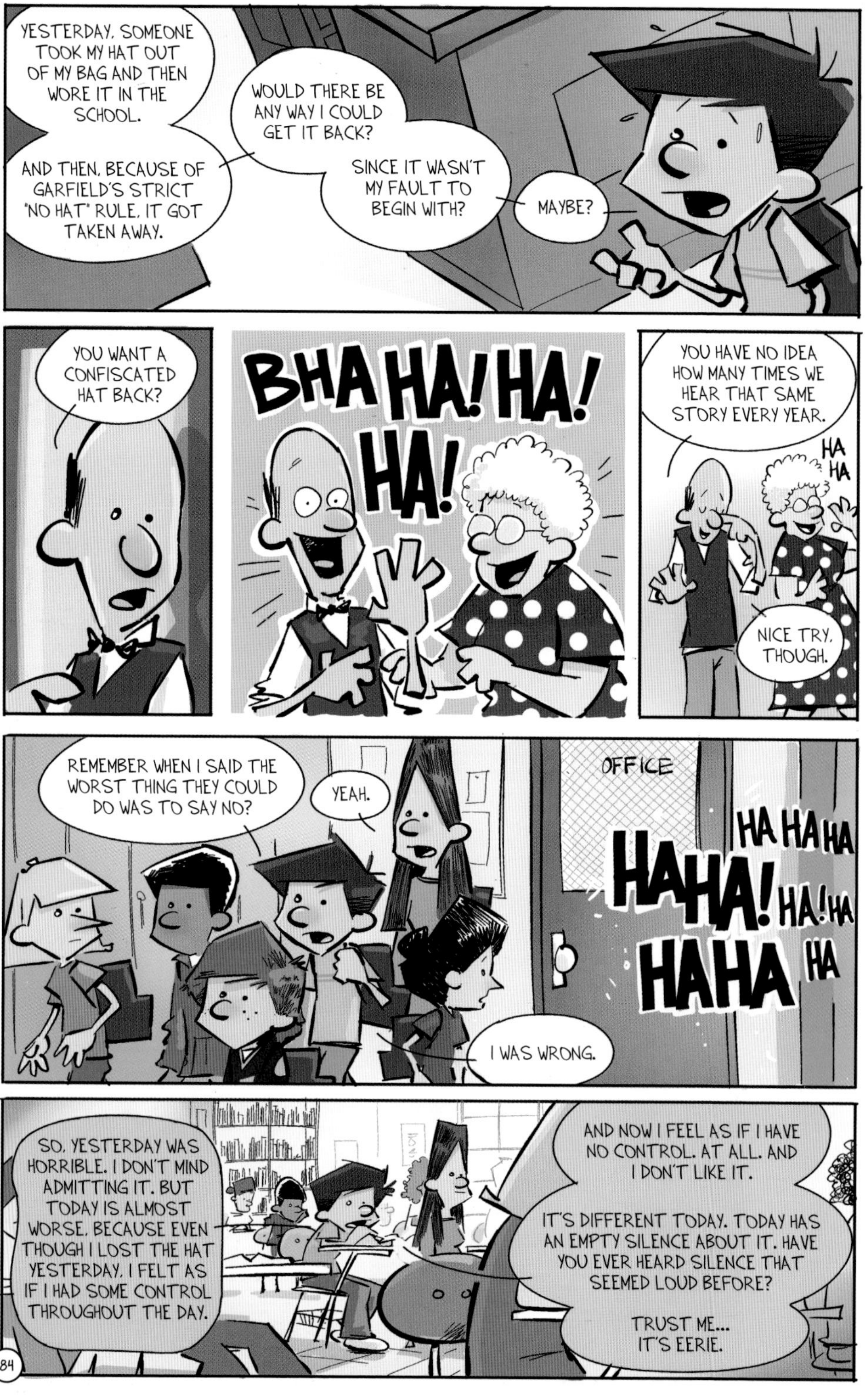
YESTERDAY, SOMEONE TOOK MY HAT OUT OF MY BAG AND THEN WORE IT IN THE SCHOOL.
AND THEN, BECAUSE OF GARFIELD'S STRICT "NO HAT" RULE, IT GOT TAKEN AWAY.
WOULD THERE BE ANY WAY I COULD GET IT BACK?
SINCE IT WASN'T MY FAULT TO BEGIN WITH?
MAYBE?
YOU WANT A CONFISCATED HAT BACK?
BHA HA! HA! HA!
YOU HAVE NO IDEA HOW MANY TIMES WE HEAR THAT SAME STORY EVERY YEAR.
HA HA
NICE TRY, THOUGH.
REMEMBER WHEN I SAID THE WORST THING THEY COULD DO WAS TO SAY NO?
YEAH.
OFFICE
HA HA HA
HAHA! HA! HA
HAHA HA
I WAS WRONG.
SO, YESTERDAY WAS HORRIBLE. I DON'T MIND ADMITTING IT. BUT TODAY IS ALMOST WORSE, BECAUSE EVEN THOUGH I LOST THE HAT YESTERDAY, I FELT AS IF I HAD SOME CONTROL THROUGHOUT THE DAY.
AND NOW I FEEL AS IF I HAVE NO CONTROL. AT ALL. AND I DON'T LIKE IT.
IT'S DIFFERENT TODAY. TODAY HAS AN EMPTY SILENCE ABOUT IT. HAVE YOU EVER HEARD SILENCE THAT SEEMED LOUD BEFORE?
TRUST ME... IT'S EERIE.

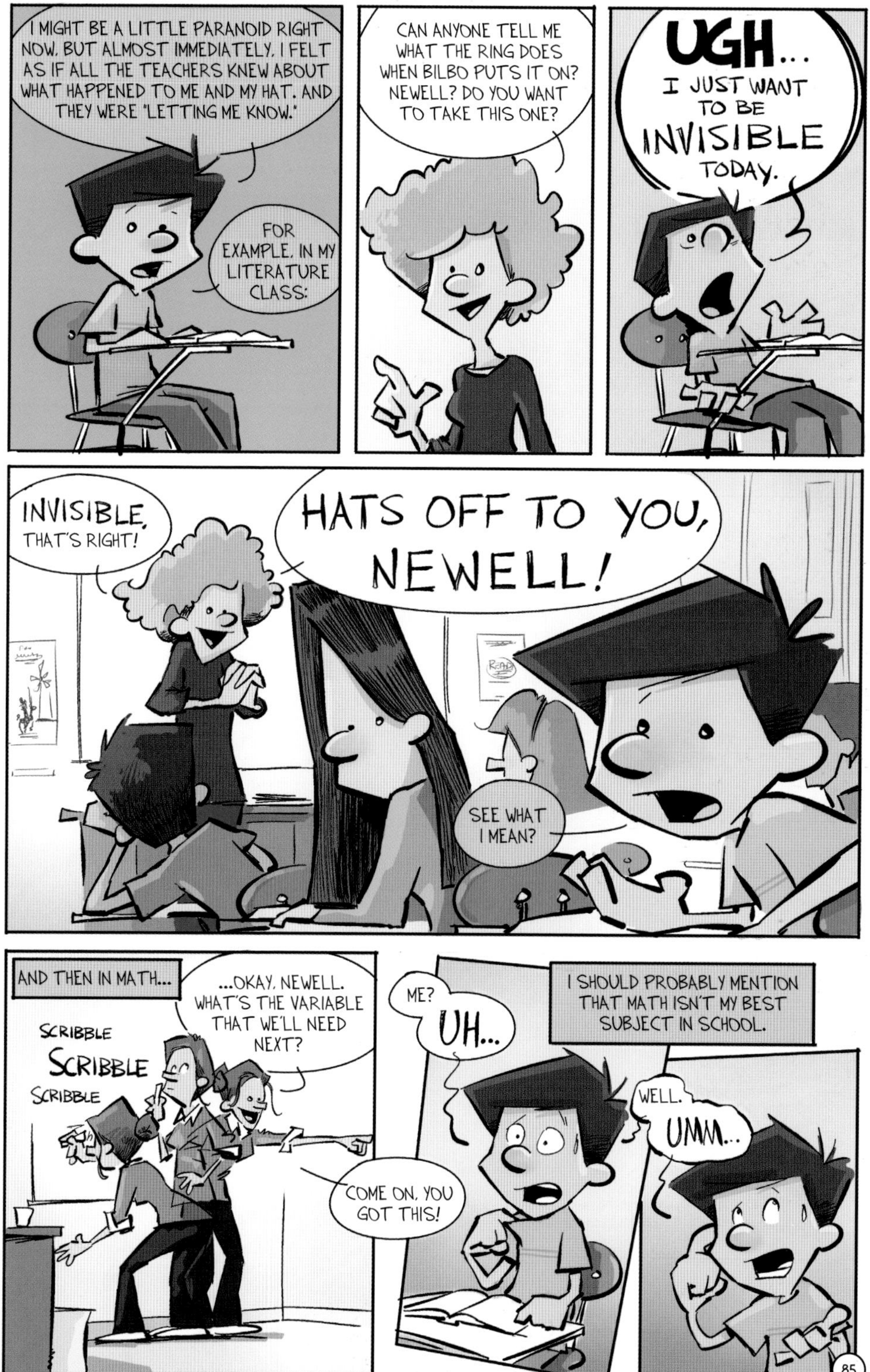
I MIGHT BE A LITTLE PARANOID RIGHT NOW, BUT ALMOST IMMEDIATELY, I FELT AS IF ALL THE TEACHERS KNEW ABOUT WHAT HAPPENED TO ME AND MY HAT. AND THEY WERE "LETTING ME KNOW."
FOR EXAMPLE, IN MY LITERATURE CLASS:
CAN ANYONE TELL ME WHAT THE RING DOES WHEN BILBO PUTS IT ON? NEWELL? DO YOU WANT TO TAKE THIS ONE?
UGH... I JUST WANT TO BE INVISIBLE TODAY.
INVISIBLE, THAT'S RIGHT!
HATS OFF TO YOU, NEWELL!
SEE WHAT I MEAN?
AND THEN IN MATH...
...OKAY, NEWELL. WHAT'S THE VARIABLE THAT WE'LL NEED NEXT?
SCRIBBLE
SCRIBBLE
SCRIBBLE
COME ON, YOU GOT THIS!
ME? UH...
I SHOULD PROBABLY MENTION THAT MATH ISN'T MY BEST SUBJECT IN SCHOOL.
WELL. UMM...

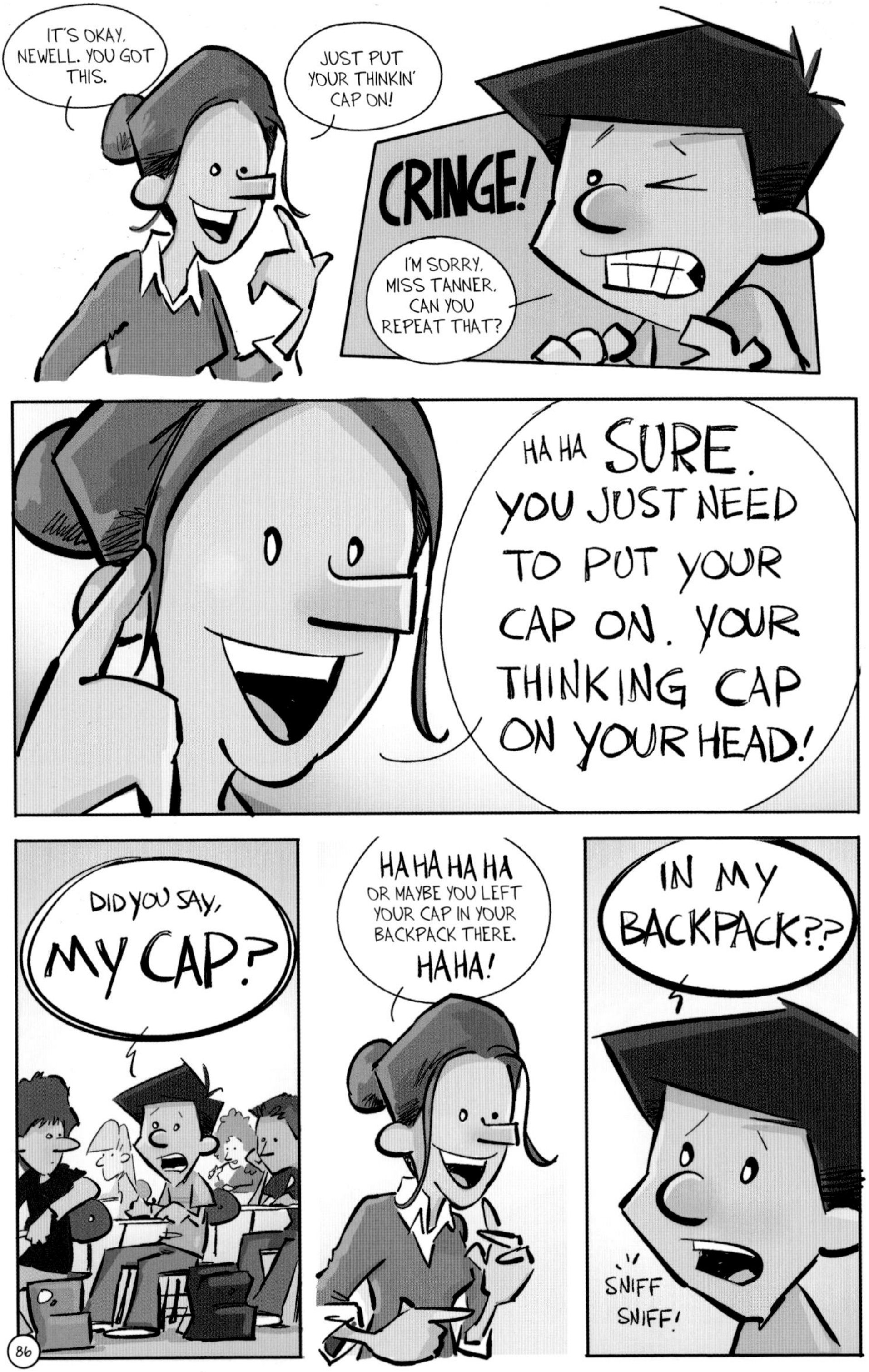

IT'S OKAY, NEWELL. YOU GOT THIS.
JUST PUT YOUR THINKIN' CAP ON!
CRINGE!
I'M SORRY, MISS TANNER, CAN YOU REPEAT THAT?
HA HA SURE. YOU JUST NEED TO PUT YOUR CAP ON. YOUR THINKING CAP ON YOUR HEAD!
DID YOU SAY, MY CAP?
HA HA HA HA OR MAYBE YOU LEFT YOUR CAP IN YOUR BACKPACK THERE. HA HA!
IN MY BACKPACK??
SNIFF SNIFF!

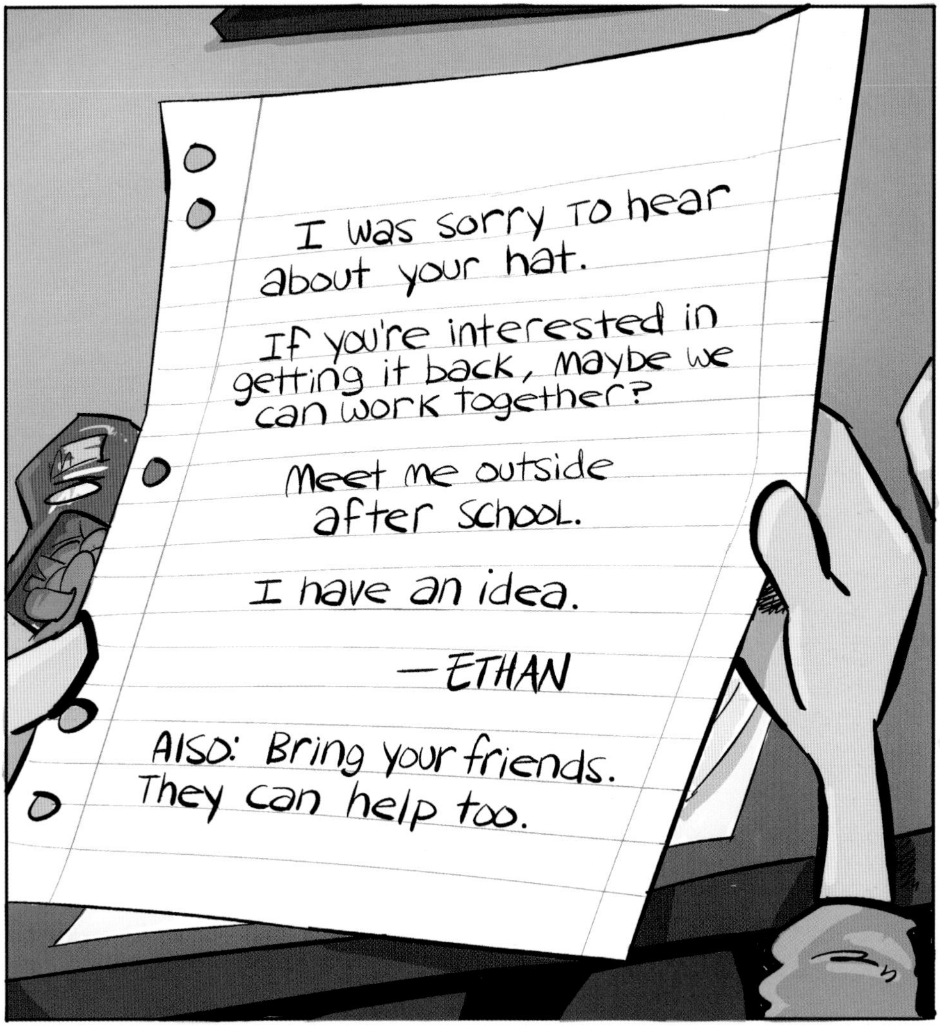
I was sorry to hear about your hat.
If you're interested in getting it back, maybe we can work together?
Meet me outside after school.
I have an idea.
—ETHAN
Also: Bring your friends. They can help too.

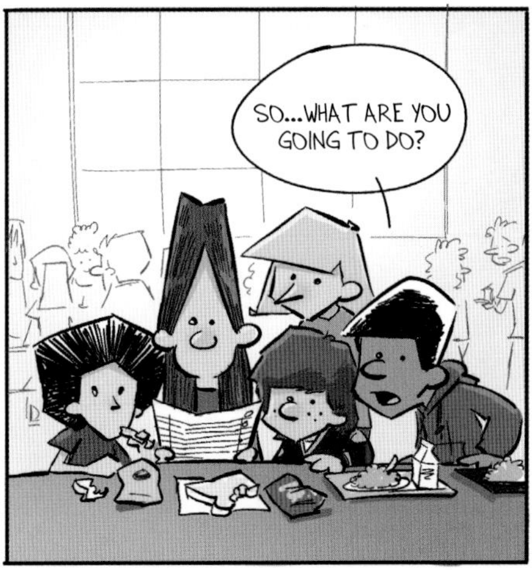
SO...WHAT ARE YOU GOING TO DO?

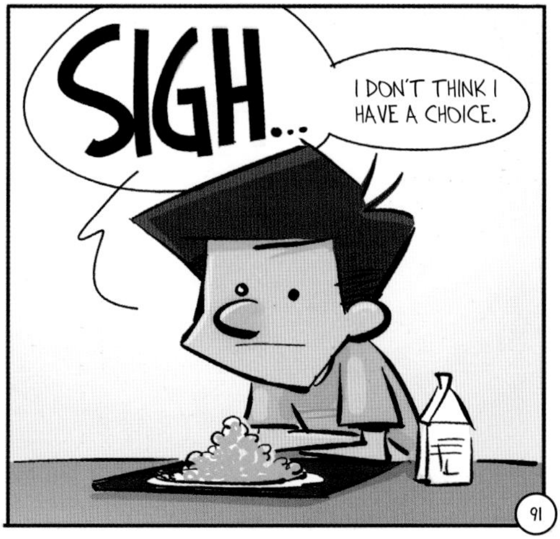
SIGH...
I DON'T THINK I HAVE A CHOICE.

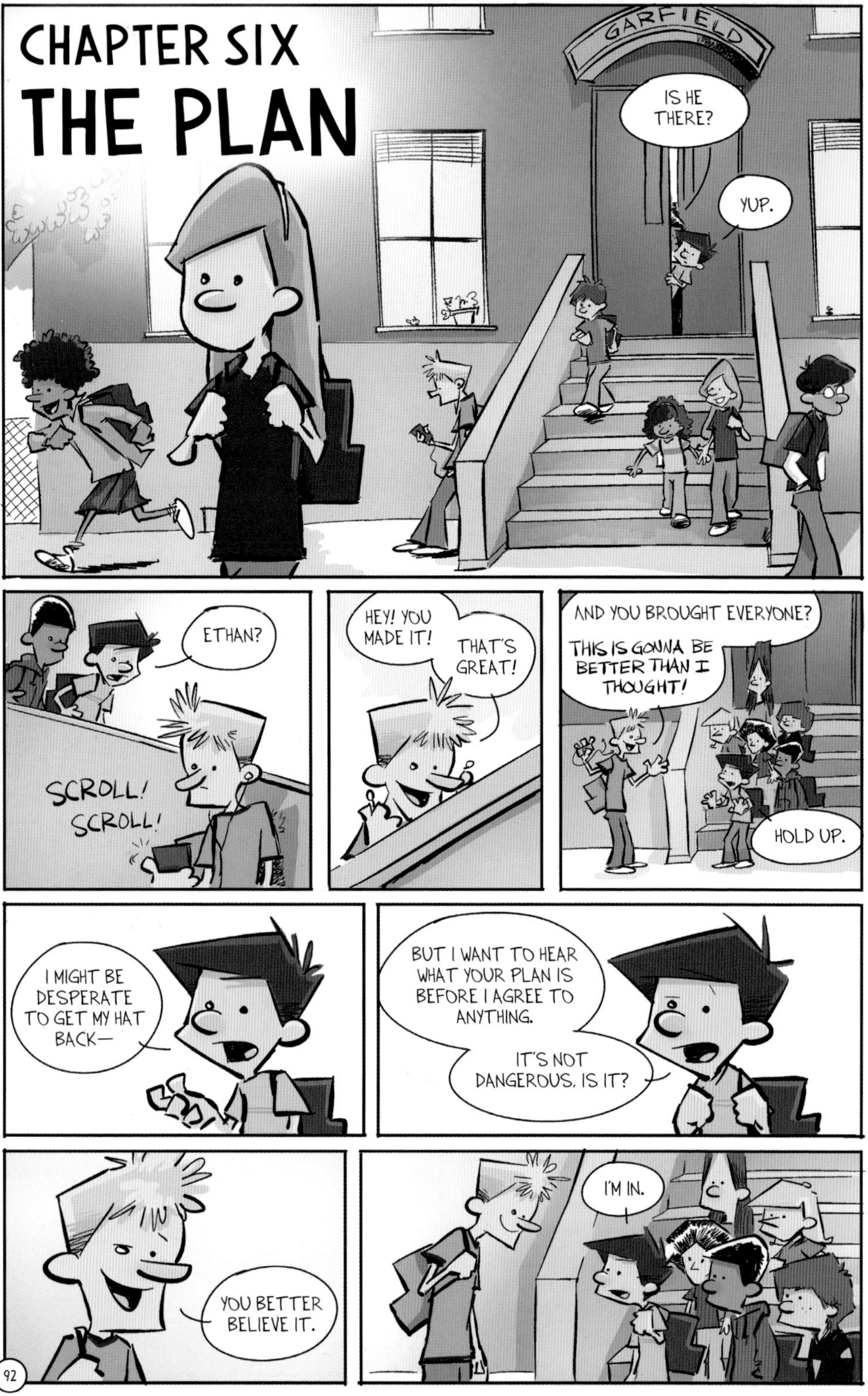
CHAPTER SIX
THE PLAN
GARFIELD
IS HE THERE?
YUP.
ETHAN?
SCROLL! SCROLL!
HEY! YOU MADE IT!
THAT'S GREAT!
AND YOU BROUGHT EVERYONE?
THIS IS GONNA BE BETTER THAN I THOUGHT!
HOLD UP.
I MIGHT BE DESPERATE TO GET MY HAT BACK—
BUT I WANT TO HEAR WHAT YOUR PLAN IS BEFORE I AGREE TO ANYTHING.
IT'S NOT DANGEROUS, IS IT?
YOU BETTER BELIEVE IT.
I'M IN.

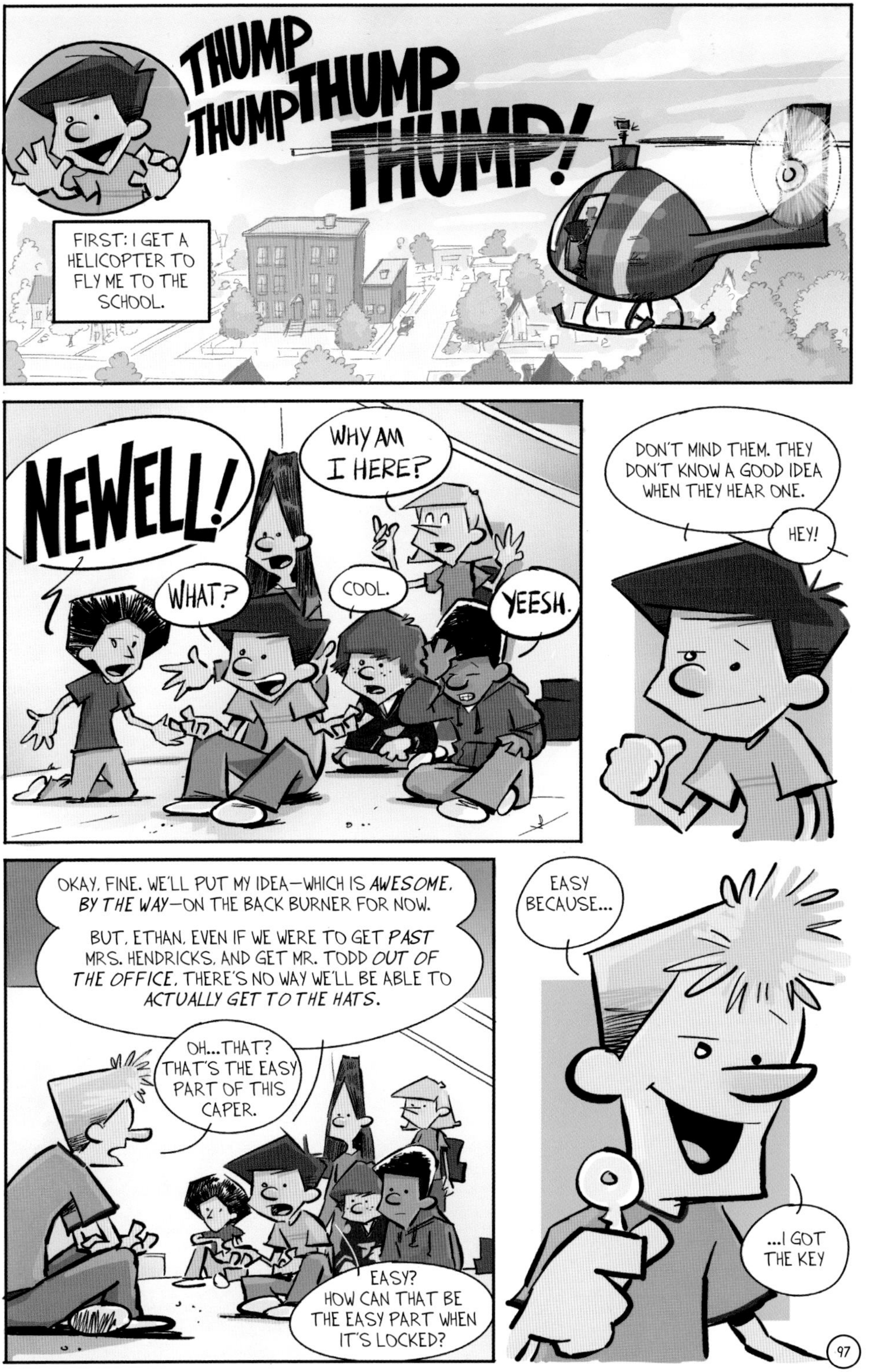
THUMP THUMP THUMP THUMP!
FIRST: I GET A HELICOPTER TO FLY ME TO THE SCHOOL.
NEWELL!
WHY AM I HERE?
WHAT?
COOL.
YEESH.
DON'T MIND THEM. THEY DON'T KNOW A GOOD IDEA WHEN THEY HEAR ONE.
HEY!
OKAY, FINE. WE'LL PUT MY IDEA—WHICH IS *AWESOME, BY THE WAY*—ON THE BACK BURNER FOR NOW.
BUT, ETHAN, EVEN IF WE WERE TO GET *PAST* MRS. HENDRICKS, AND GET MR. TODD *OUT OF THE OFFICE*, THERE'S NO WAY WE'LL BE ABLE TO *ACTUALLY GET TO THE HATS*.
OH...THAT? THAT'S THE EASY PART OF THIS CAPER.
EASY? HOW CAN THAT BE THE EASY PART WHEN IT'S LOCKED?
EASY BECAUSE...
...I GOT THE KEY

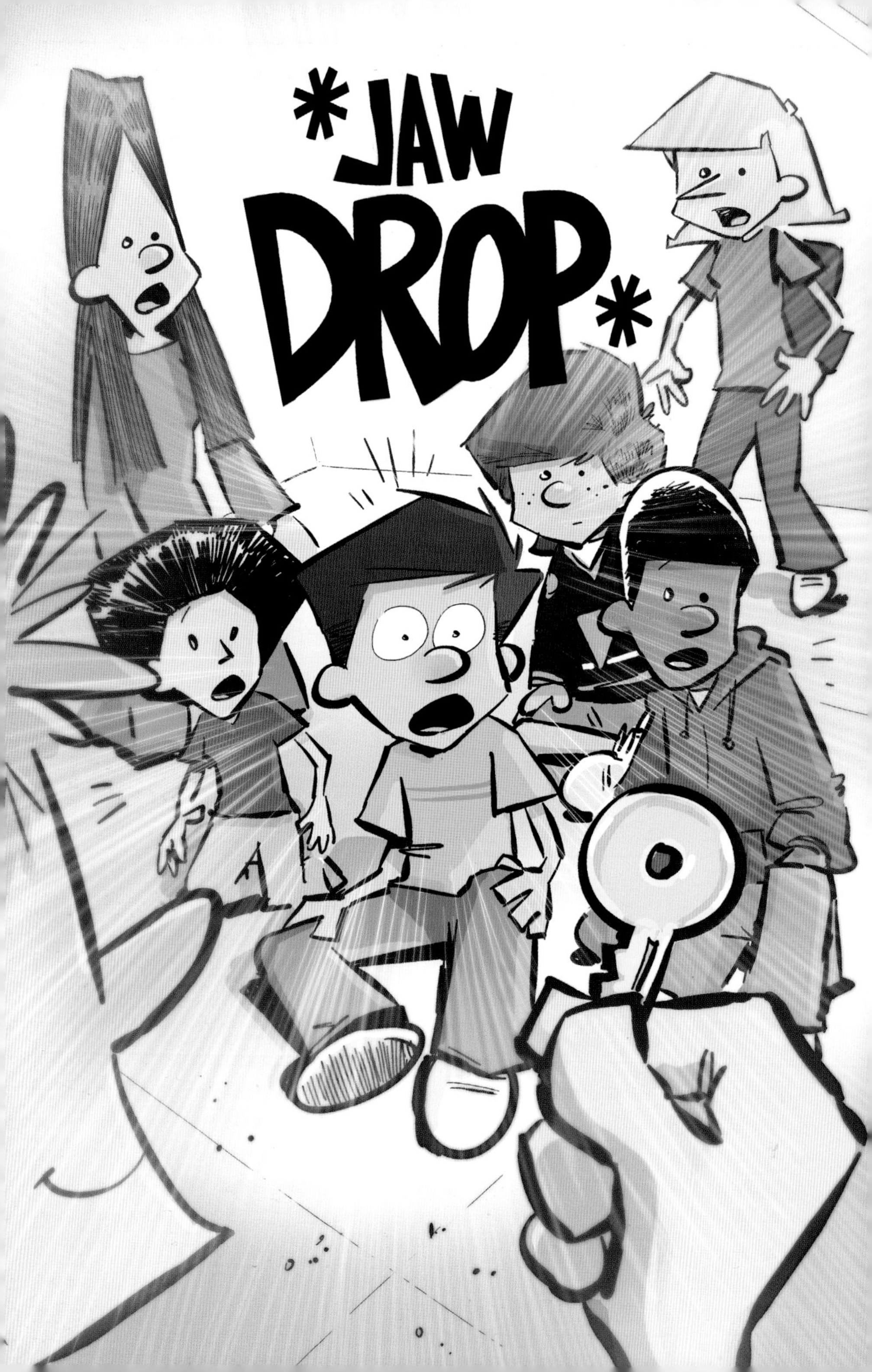
JAW DROP

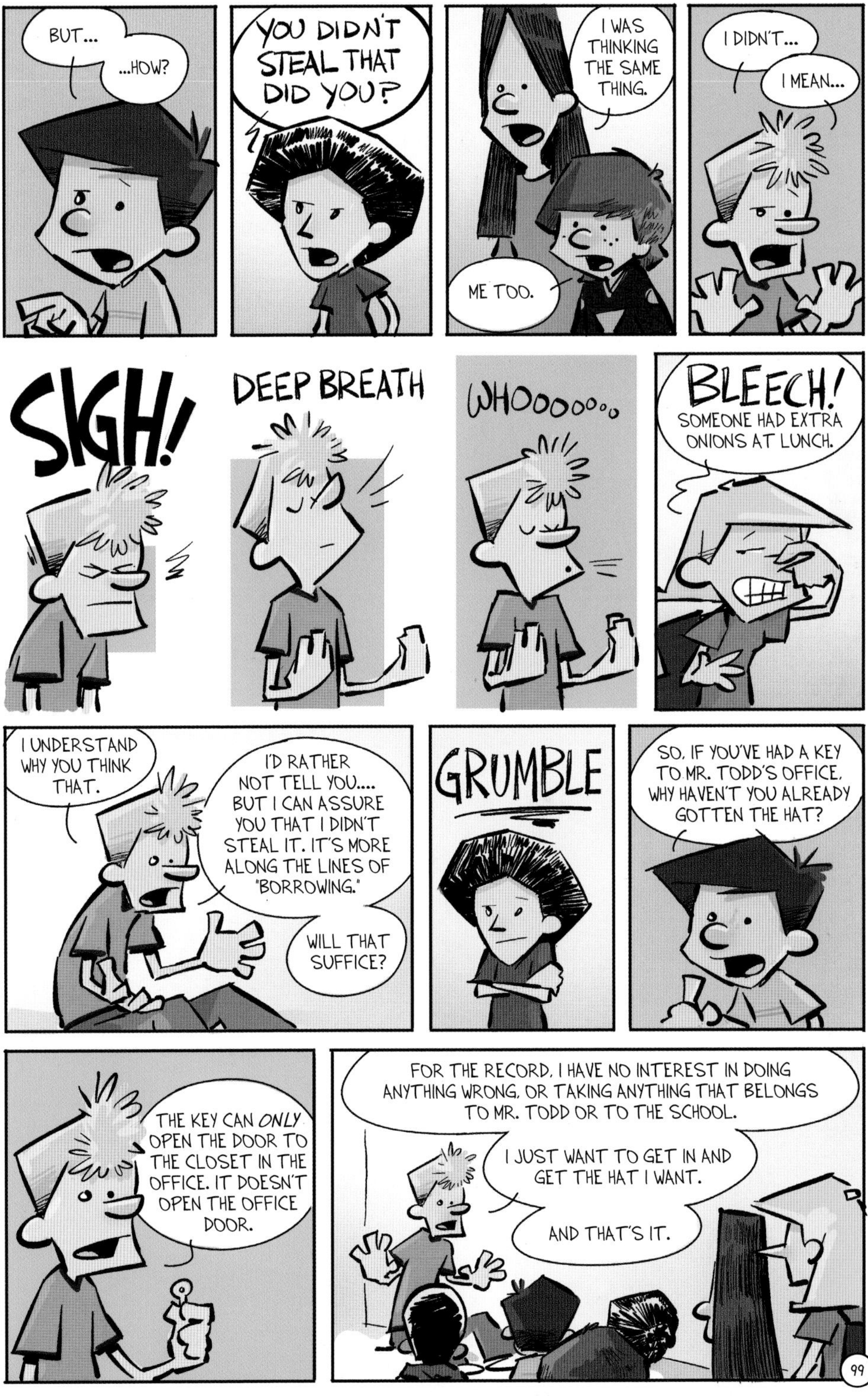
BUT...
...HOW?
YOU DIDN'T STEAL THAT DID YOU?
I WAS THINKING THE SAME THING.
ME TOO.
I DIDN'T...
I MEAN...
SIGH!
DEEP BREATH
WHOOOOOOO
BLEECH!
SOMEONE HAD EXTRA ONIONS AT LUNCH.
I UNDERSTAND WHY YOU THINK THAT.
I'D RATHER NOT TELL YOU.... BUT I CAN ASSURE YOU THAT I DIDN'T STEAL IT. IT'S MORE ALONG THE LINES OF "BORROWING."
WILL THAT SUFFICE?
GRUMBLE
SO, IF YOU'VE HAD A KEY TO MR. TODD'S OFFICE, WHY HAVEN'T YOU ALREADY GOTTEN THE HAT?
THE KEY CAN *ONLY* OPEN THE DOOR TO THE CLOSET IN THE OFFICE. IT DOESN'T OPEN THE OFFICE DOOR.
FOR THE RECORD, I HAVE NO INTEREST IN DOING ANYTHING WRONG, OR TAKING ANYTHING THAT BELONGS TO MR. TODD OR TO THE SCHOOL.
I JUST WANT TO GET IN AND GET THE HAT I WANT.
AND THAT'S IT.

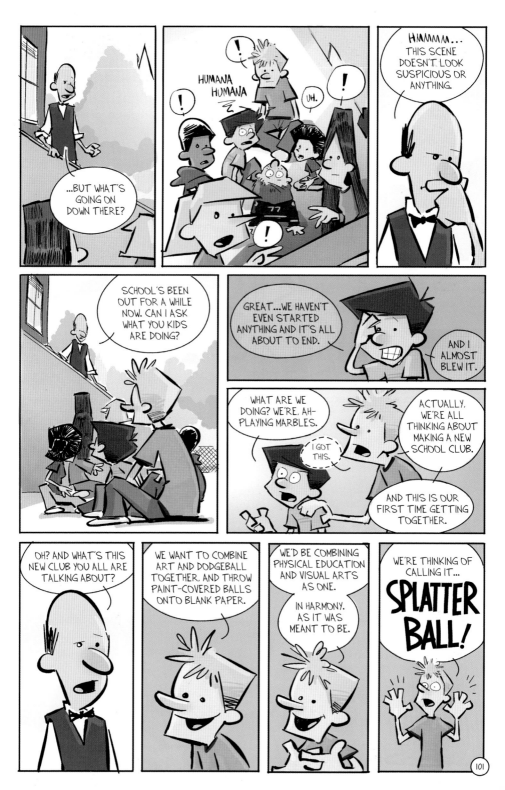

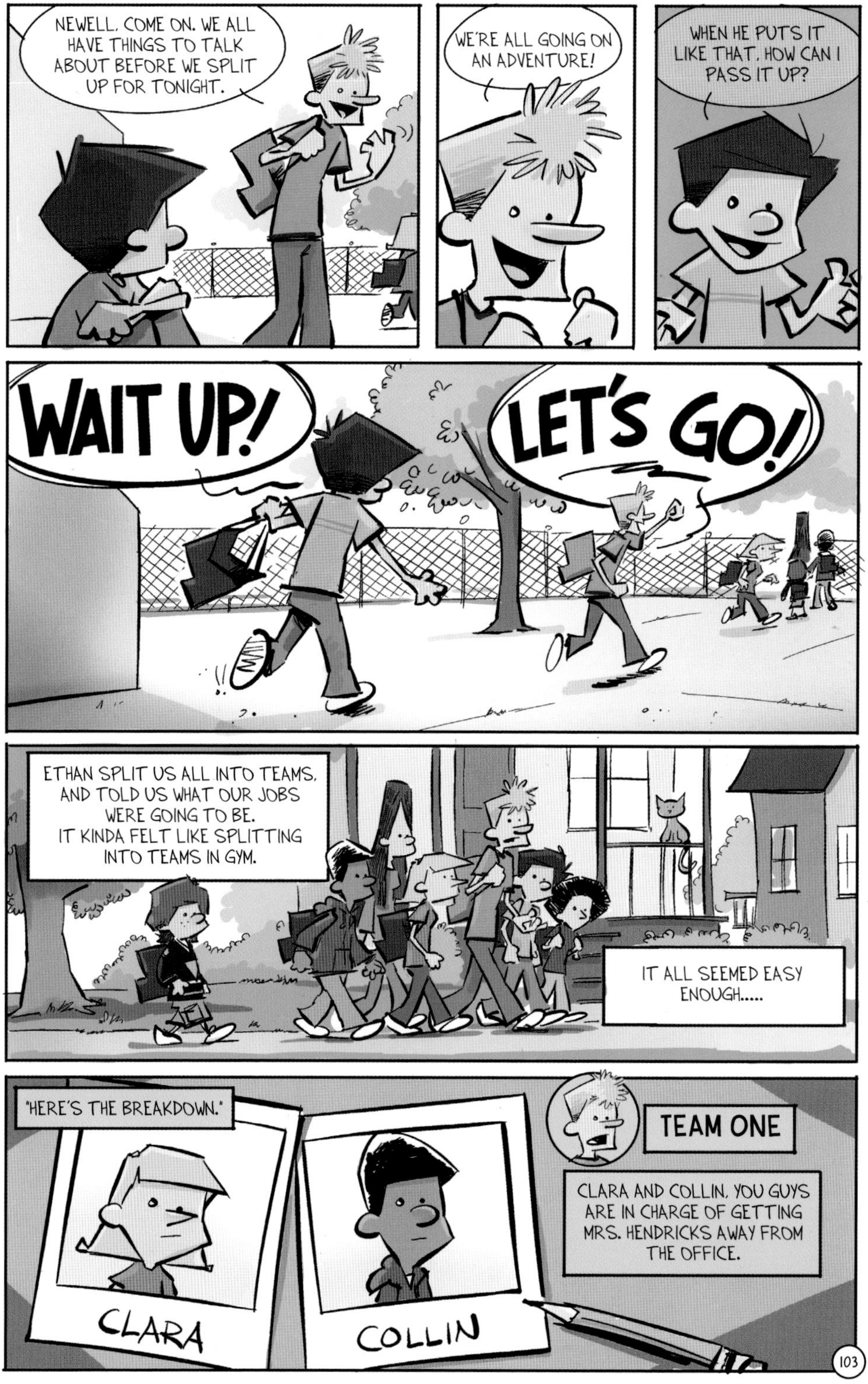
NEWELL, COME ON. WE ALL HAVE THINGS TO TALK ABOUT BEFORE WE SPLIT UP FOR TONIGHT.
WE'RE ALL GOING ON AN ADVENTURE!
WHEN HE PUTS IT LIKE THAT, HOW CAN I PASS IT UP?
WAIT UP!
LET'S GO!
ETHAN SPLIT US ALL INTO TEAMS, AND TOLD US WHAT OUR JOBS WERE GOING TO BE. IT KINDA FELT LIKE SPLITTING INTO TEAMS IN GYM.
IT ALL SEEMED EASY ENOUGH.....
"HERE'S THE BREAKDOWN."
CLARA
COLLIN
TEAM ONE
CLARA AND COLLIN, YOU GUYS ARE IN CHARGE OF GETTING MRS. HENDRICKS AWAY FROM THE OFFICE.

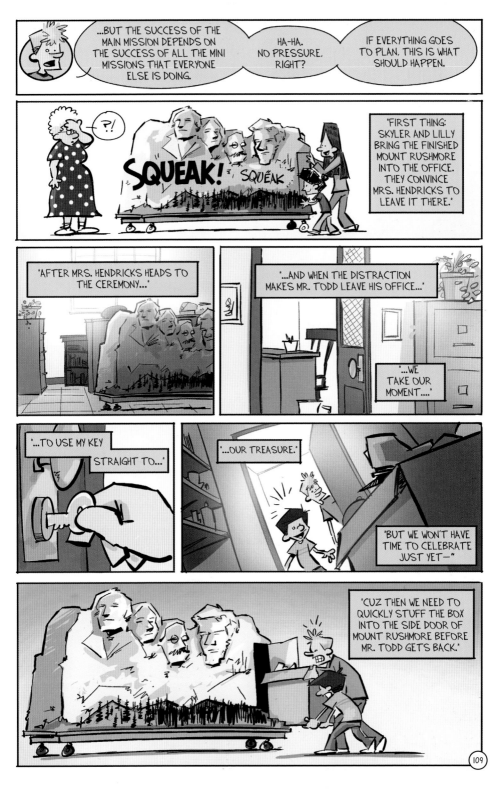

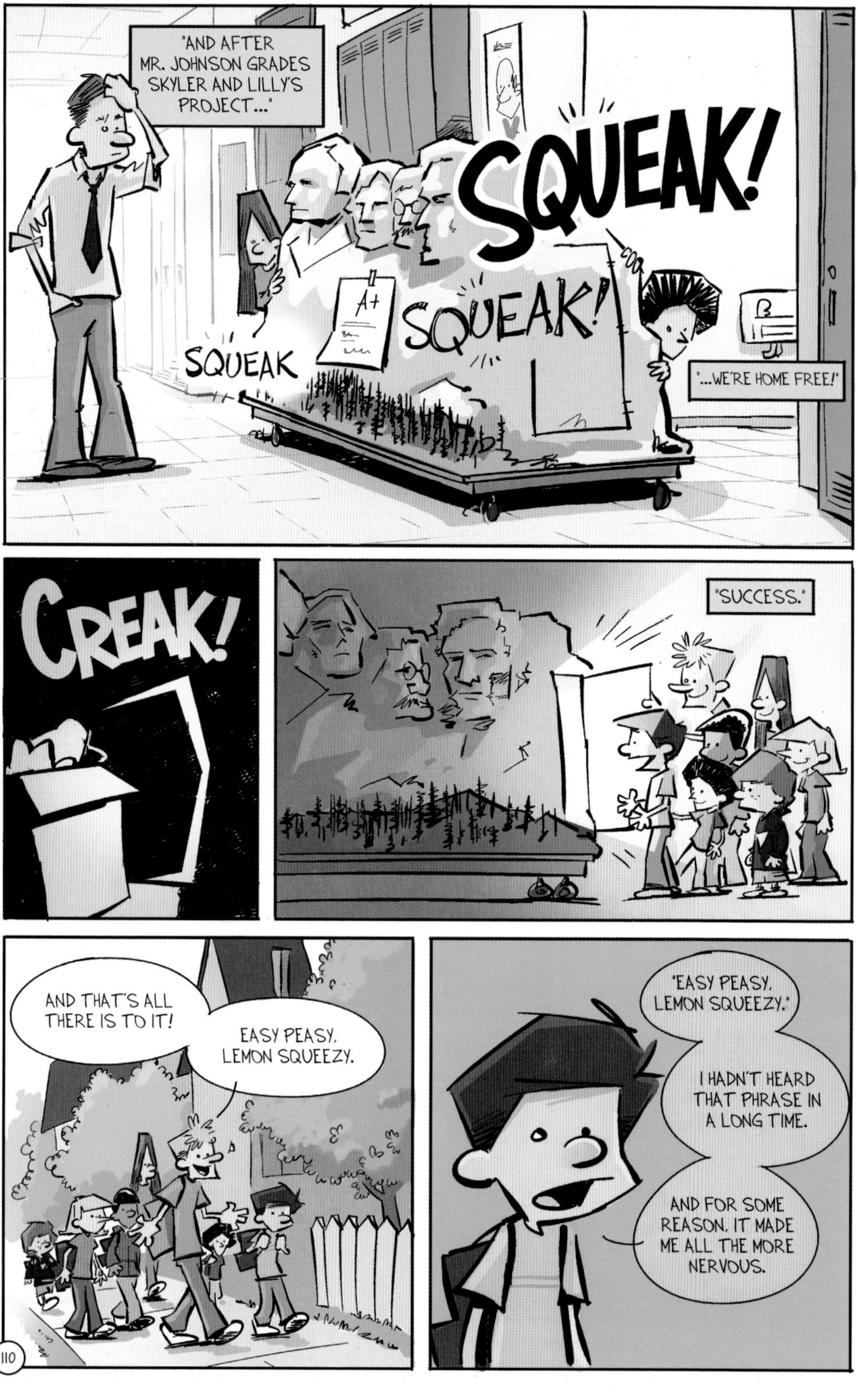
"AND AFTER MR. JOHNSON GRADES SKYLER AND LILLY'S PROJECT..."
SQUEAK!
SQUEAK!
SQUEAK
A+
"...WE'RE HOME FREE!"
CREAK!
"SUCCESS."
AND THAT'S ALL THERE IS TO IT!
EASY PEASY, LEMON SQUEEZY.
"EASY PEASY, LEMON SQUEEZY."
I HADN'T HEARD THAT PHRASE IN A LONG TIME.
AND FOR SOME REASON, IT MADE ME ALL THE MORE NERVOUS.

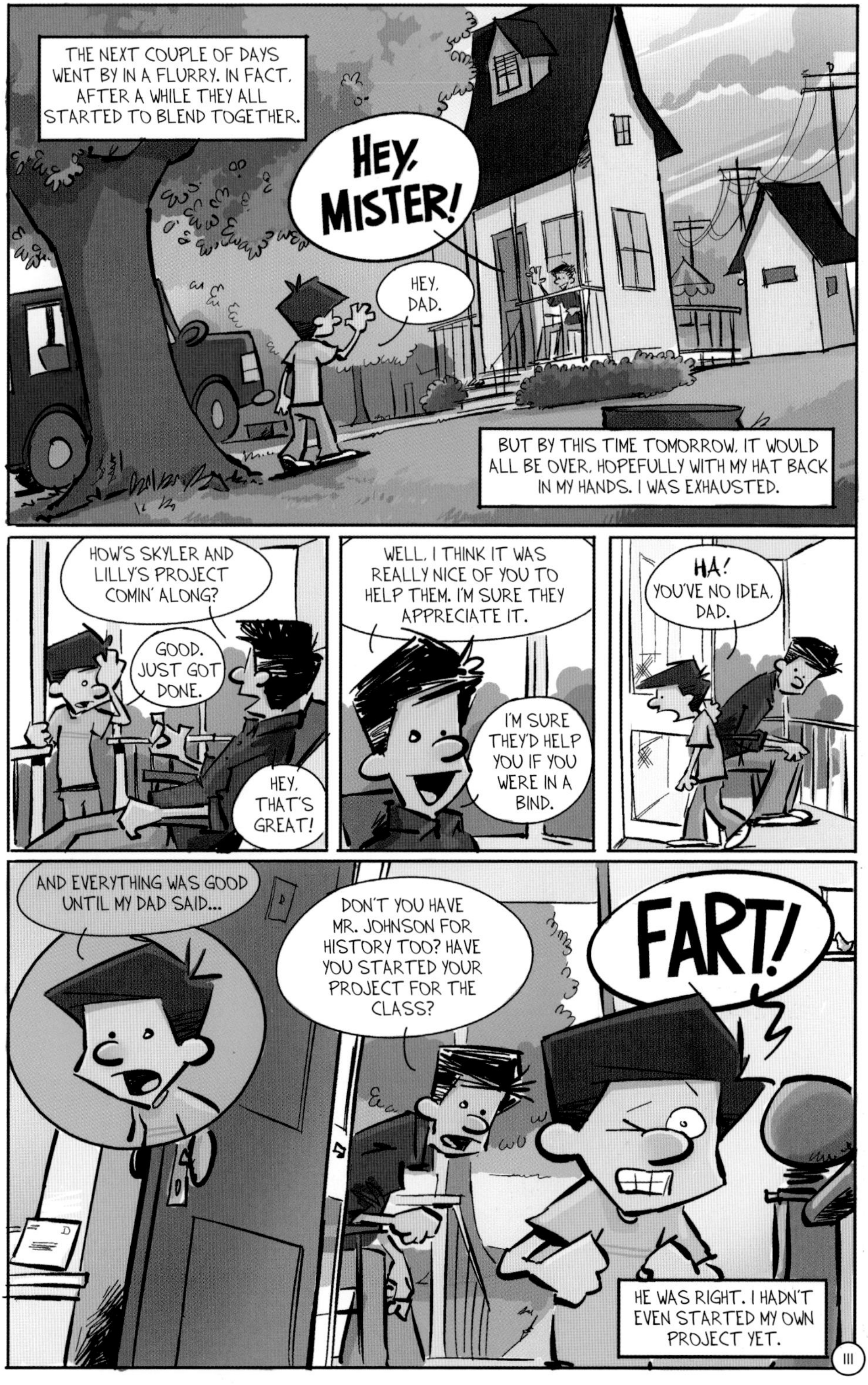
THE NEXT COUPLE OF DAYS WENT BY IN A FLURRY. IN FACT, AFTER A WHILE THEY ALL STARTED TO BLEND TOGETHER.
HEY, MISTER!
HEY, DAD.
BUT BY THIS TIME TOMORROW, IT WOULD ALL BE OVER, HOPEFULLY WITH MY HAT BACK IN MY HANDS. I WAS EXHAUSTED.
HOW'S SKYLER AND LILLY'S PROJECT COMIN' ALONG?
GOOD. JUST GOT DONE.
HEY, THAT'S GREAT!
WELL, I THINK IT WAS REALLY NICE OF YOU TO HELP THEM. I'M SURE THEY APPRECIATE IT.
I'M SURE THEY'D HELP YOU IF YOU WERE IN A BIND.
HA! YOU'VE NO IDEA, DAD.
AND EVERYTHING WAS GOOD UNTIL MY DAD SAID...
DON'T YOU HAVE MR. JOHNSON FOR HISTORY TOO? HAVE YOU STARTED YOUR PROJECT FOR THE CLASS?
FART!
HE WAS RIGHT. I HADN'T EVEN STARTED MY OWN PROJECT YET.

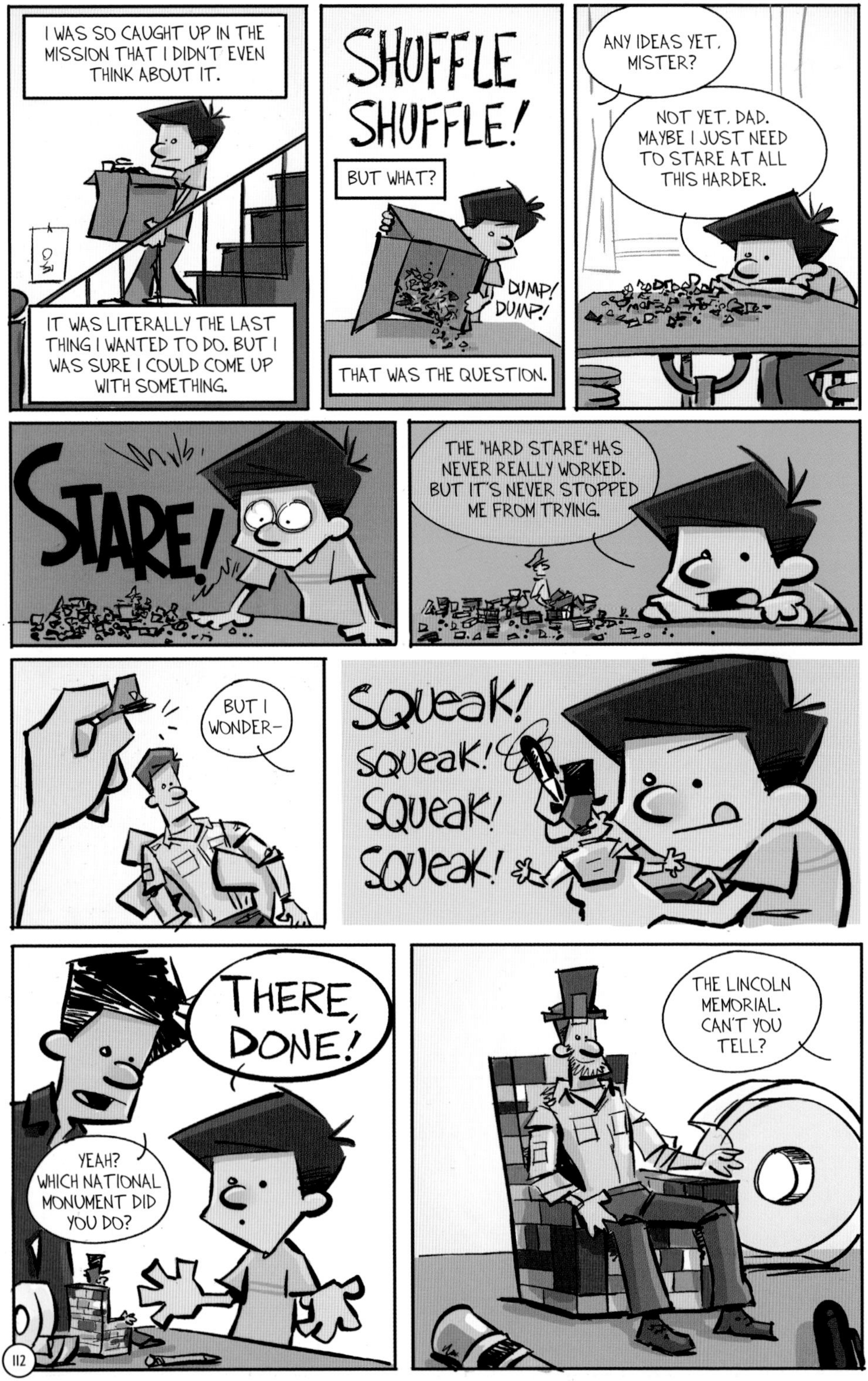

I WAS SO CAUGHT UP IN THE MISSION THAT I DIDN'T EVEN THINK ABOUT IT.
IT WAS LITERALLY THE LAST THING I WANTED TO DO. BUT I WAS SURE I COULD COME UP WITH SOMETHING.
SHUFFLE SHUFFLE!
BUT WHAT?
DUMP! DUMP!
THAT WAS THE QUESTION.
ANY IDEAS YET, MISTER?
NOT YET, DAD. MAYBE I JUST NEED TO STARE AT ALL THIS HARDER.
STARE!
THE "HARD STARE" HAS NEVER REALLY WORKED. BUT IT'S NEVER STOPPED ME FROM TRYING.
BUT I WONDER-
SQUEAK! SQUEAK! SQUEAK! SQUEAK!
THERE, DONE!
YEAH? WHICH NATIONAL MONUMENT DID YOU DO?
THE LINCOLN MEMORIAL. CAN'T YOU TELL?

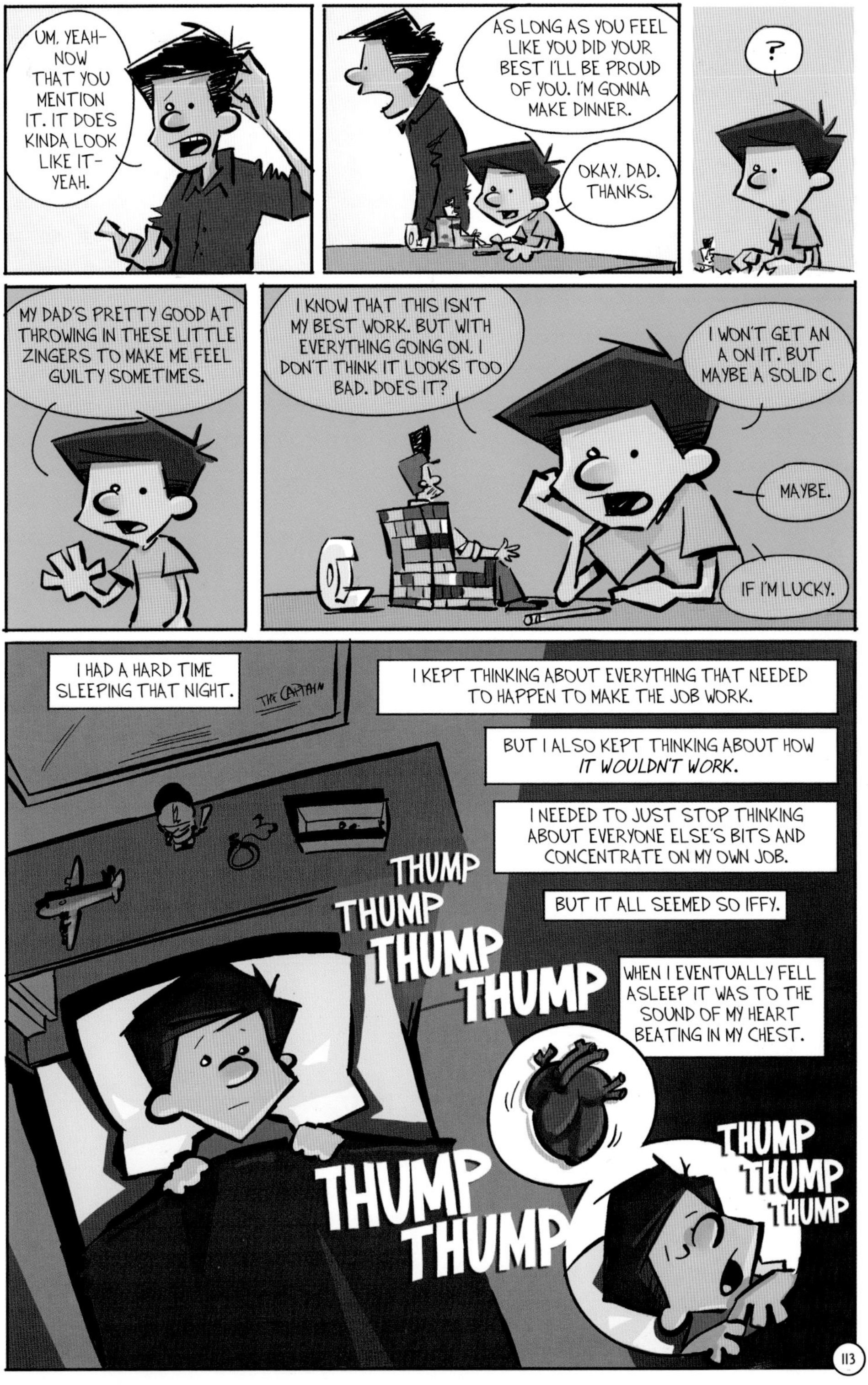

UM, YEAH-NOW THAT YOU MENTION IT. IT DOES KINDA LOOK LIKE IT-YEAH.
AS LONG AS YOU FEEL LIKE YOU DID YOUR BEST I'LL BE PROUD OF YOU. I'M GONNA MAKE DINNER.
OKAY, DAD. THANKS.
?
MY DAD'S PRETTY GOOD AT THROWING IN THESE LITTLE ZINGERS TO MAKE ME FEEL GUILTY SOMETIMES.
I KNOW THAT THIS ISN'T MY BEST WORK. BUT WITH EVERYTHING GOING ON, I DON'T THINK IT LOOKS TOO BAD. DOES IT?
I WON'T GET AN A ON IT. BUT MAYBE A SOLID C.
MAYBE.
IF I'M LUCKY.
I HAD A HARD TIME SLEEPING THAT NIGHT.
THE CAPTAIN
I KEPT THINKING ABOUT EVERYTHING THAT NEEDED TO HAPPEN TO MAKE THE JOB WORK.
BUT I ALSO KEPT THINKING ABOUT HOW *IT WOULDN'T WORK*.
I NEEDED TO JUST STOP THINKING ABOUT EVERYONE ELSE'S BITS AND CONCENTRATE ON MY OWN JOB.
BUT IT ALL SEEMED SO IFFY.
THUMP
THUMP
THUMP
THUMP
WHEN I EVENTUALLY FELL ASLEEP IT WAS TO THE SOUND OF MY HEART BEATING IN MY CHEST.
THUMP
THUMP
THUMP
THUMP
THUMP

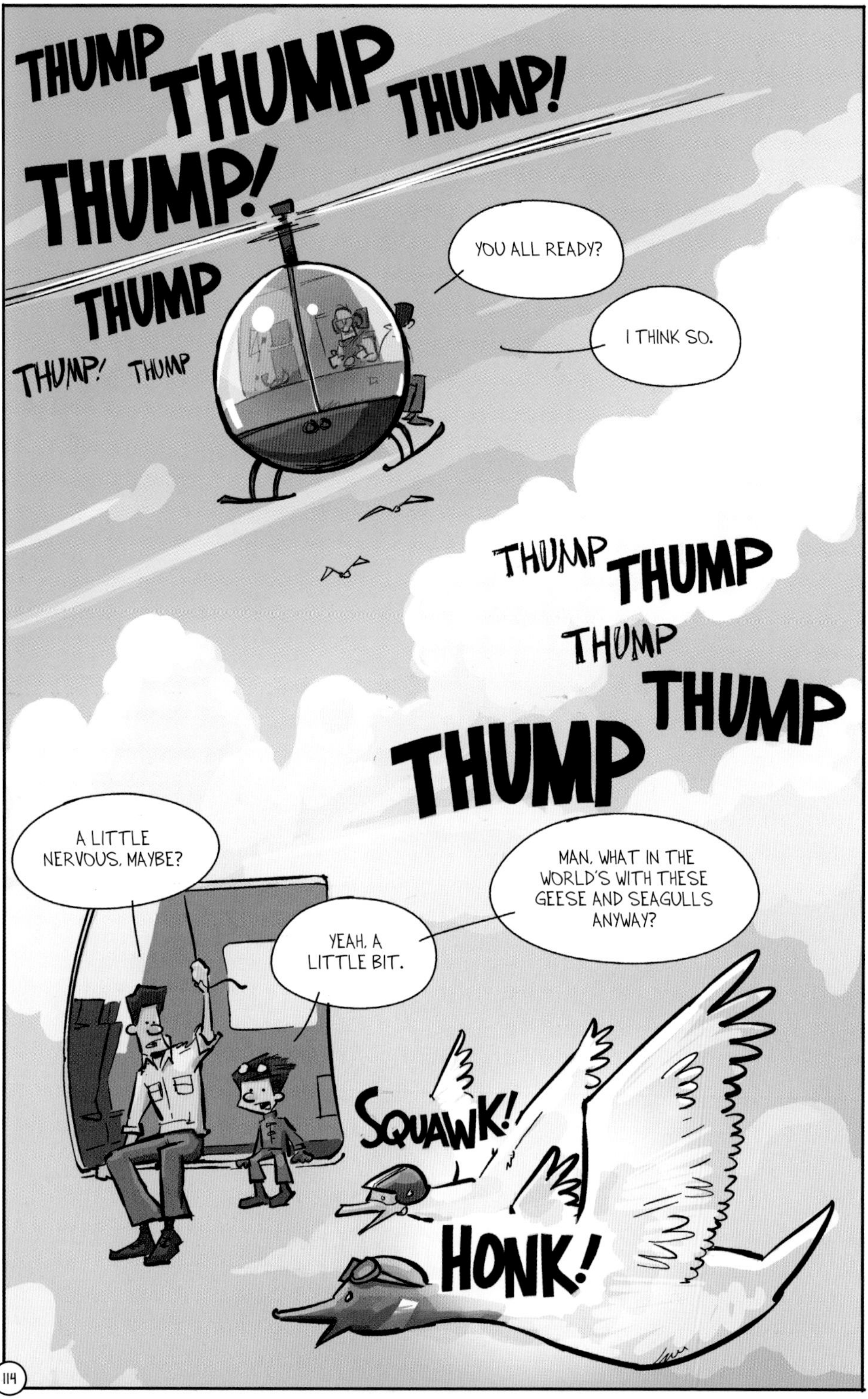
THUMP THUMP THUMP!
THUMP!
THUMP
THUMP! THUMP
YOU ALL READY?
I THINK SO.
THUMP THUMP
THUMP
THUMP
THUMP
A LITTLE NERVOUS, MAYBE?
YEAH, A LITTLE BIT.
MAN, WHAT IN THE WORLD'S WITH THESE GEESE AND SEAGULLS ANYWAY?
SQUAWK!
HONK!

CHAPTER SEVEN
THE HEIST

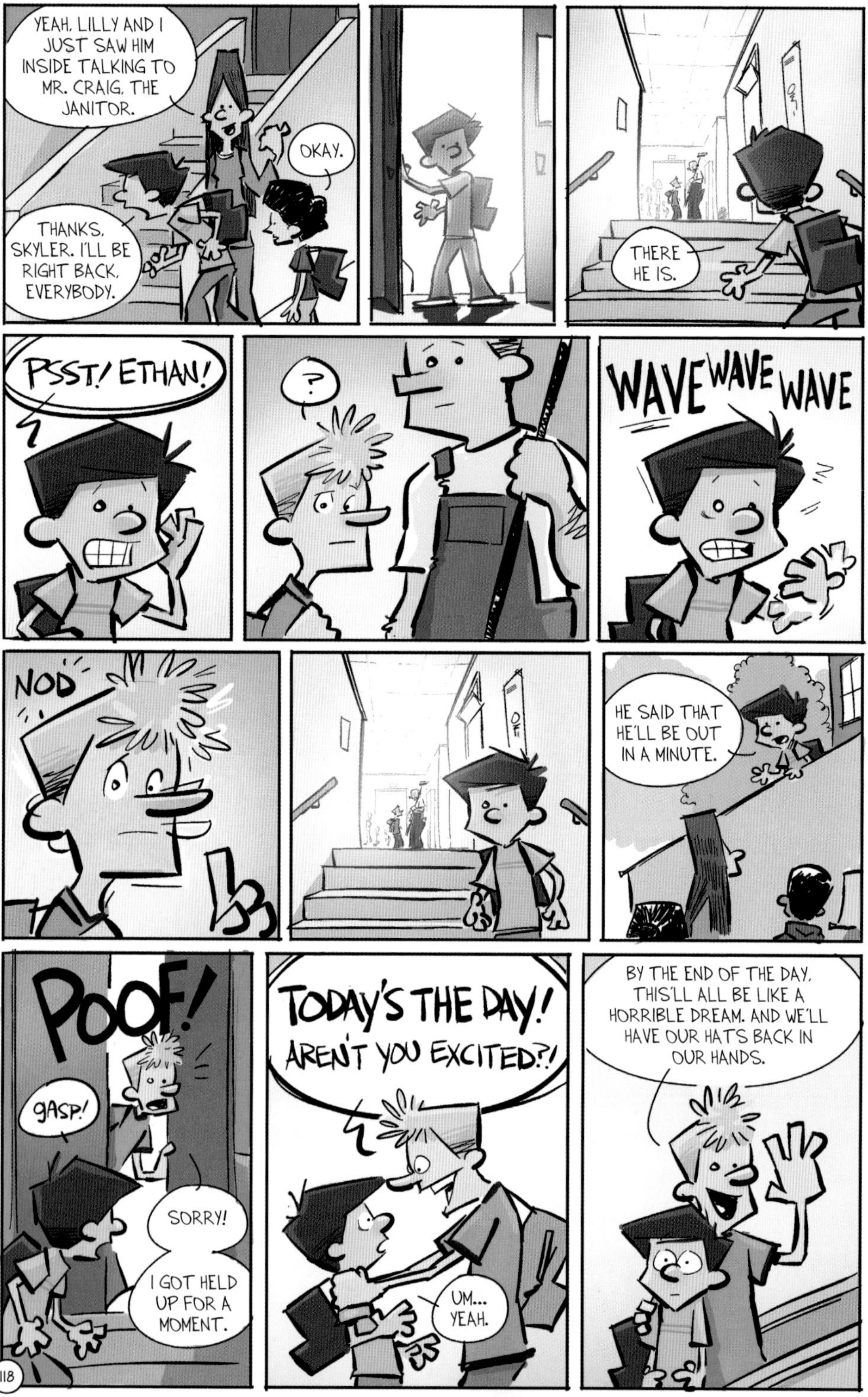

YEAH, LILLY AND I JUST SAW HIM INSIDE TALKING TO MR. CRAIG, THE JANITOR.
THANKS, SKYLER. I'LL BE RIGHT BACK, EVERYBODY.
OKAY.
THERE HE IS.
PSST! ETHAN!
?
WAVE WAVE WAVE
NOD
HE SAID THAT HE'LL BE OUT IN A MINUTE.
POOF!
GASP!
SORRY!
I GOT HELD UP FOR A MOMENT.
TODAY'S THE DAY! AREN'T YOU EXCITED?!
UM... YEAH.
BY THE END OF THE DAY, THIS'LL ALL BE LIKE A HORRIBLE DREAM. AND WE'LL HAVE OUR HATS BACK IN OUR HANDS.

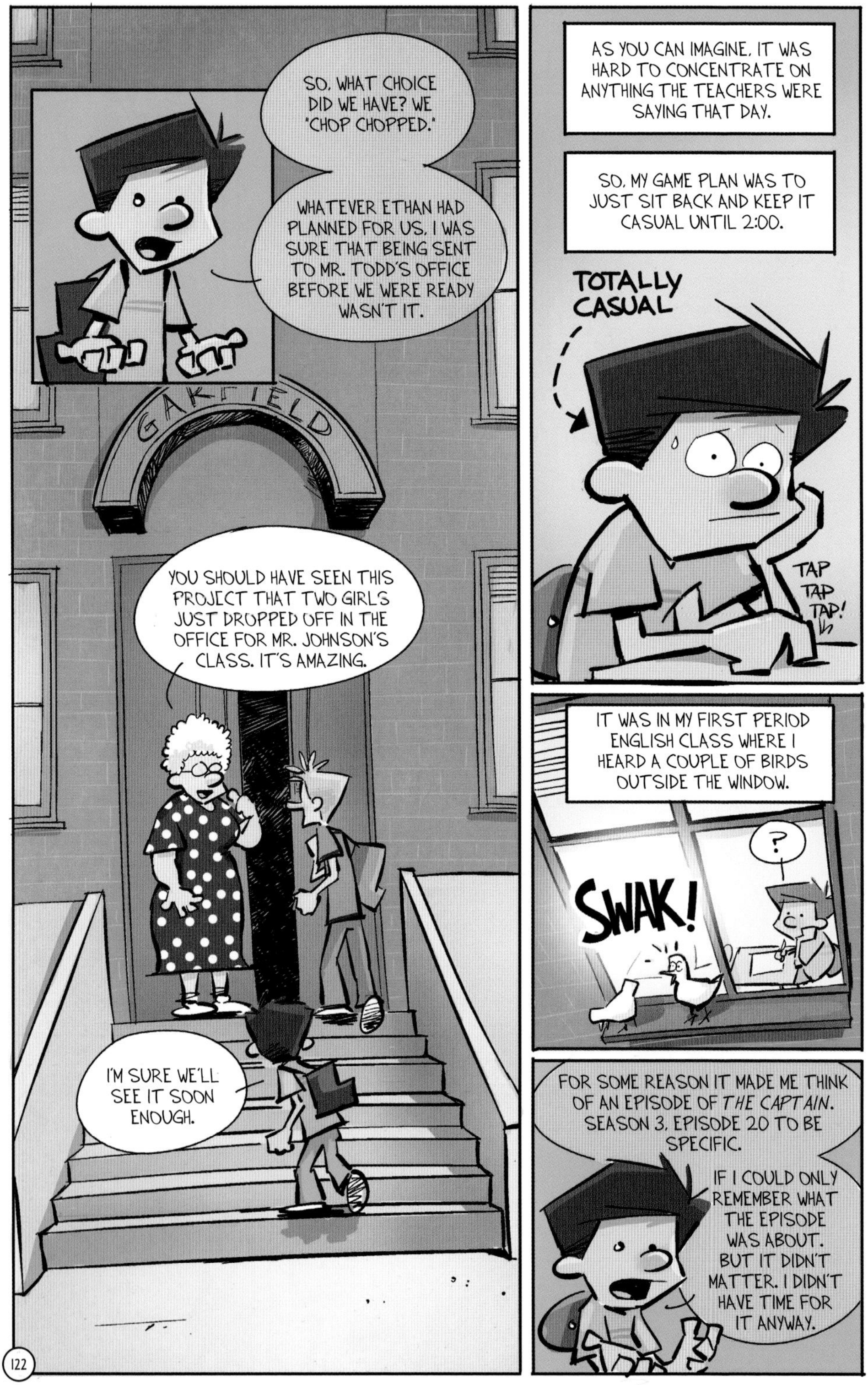
SO, WHAT CHOICE DID WE HAVE? WE "CHOP CHOPPED."
WHATEVER ETHAN HAD PLANNED FOR US, I WAS SURE THAT BEING SENT TO MR. TODD'S OFFICE BEFORE WE WERE READY WASN'T IT.
GARFIELD
YOU SHOULD HAVE SEEN THIS PROJECT THAT TWO GIRLS JUST DROPPED OFF IN THE OFFICE FOR MR. JOHNSON'S CLASS. IT'S AMAZING.
I'M SURE WE'LL SEE IT SOON ENOUGH.
AS YOU CAN IMAGINE, IT WAS HARD TO CONCENTRATE ON ANYTHING THE TEACHERS WERE SAYING THAT DAY.
SO, MY GAME PLAN WAS TO JUST SIT BACK AND KEEP IT CASUAL UNTIL 2:00.
TOTALLY CASUAL
TAP TAP TAP!
IT WAS IN MY FIRST PERIOD ENGLISH CLASS WHERE I HEARD A COUPLE OF BIRDS OUTSIDE THE WINDOW.
SWAK!
?
FOR SOME REASON IT MADE ME THINK OF AN EPISODE OF *THE CAPTAIN*. SEASON 3, EPISODE 20 TO BE SPECIFIC.
IF I COULD ONLY REMEMBER WHAT THE EPISODE WAS ABOUT. BUT IT DIDN'T MATTER. I DIDN'T HAVE TIME FOR IT ANYWAY.

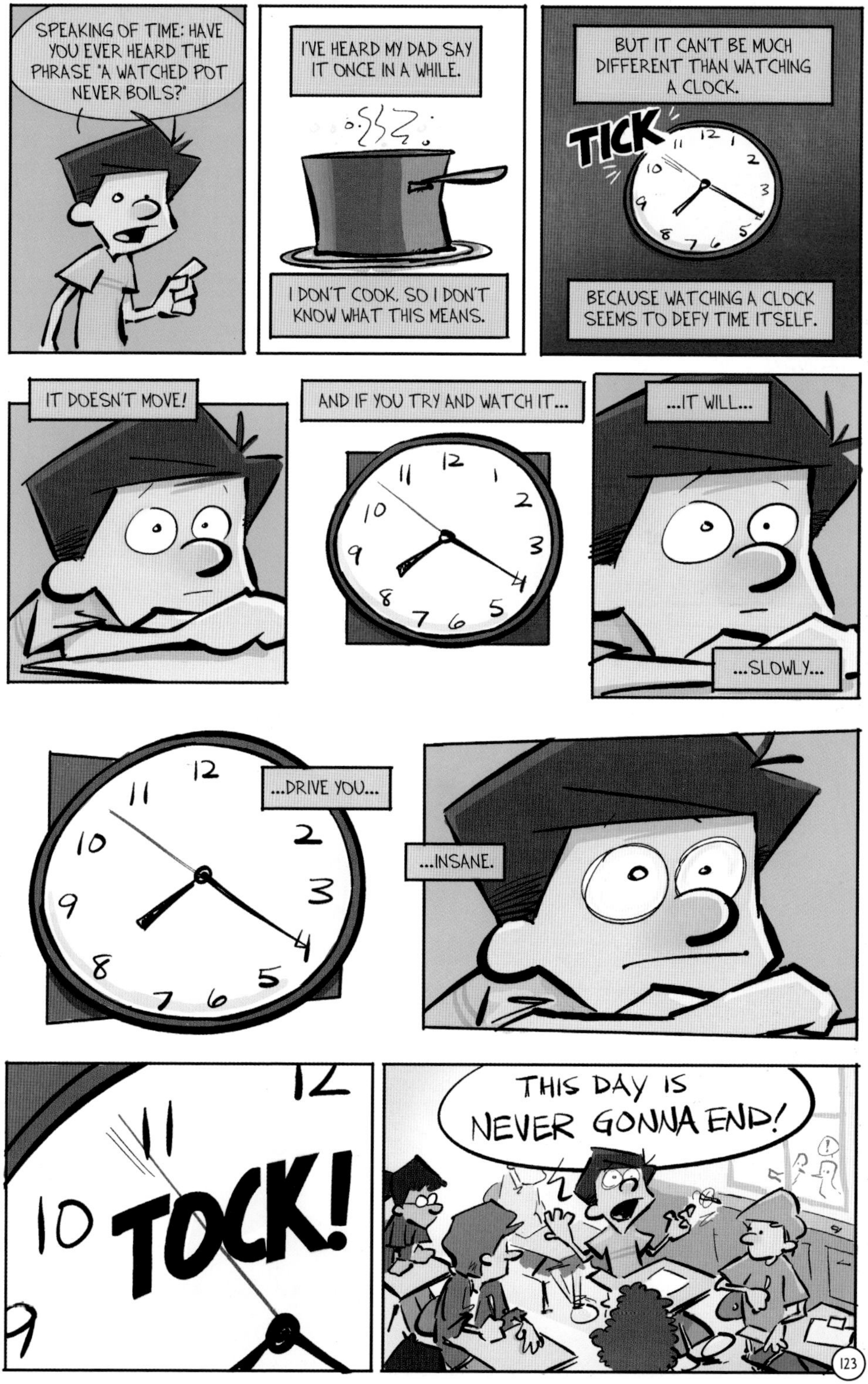
SPEAKING OF TIME: HAVE YOU EVER HEARD THE PHRASE "A WATCHED POT NEVER BOILS?"
I'VE HEARD MY DAD SAY IT ONCE IN A WHILE.
I DON'T COOK, SO I DON'T KNOW WHAT THIS MEANS.
BUT IT CAN'T BE MUCH DIFFERENT THAN WATCHING A CLOCK.
TICK
BECAUSE WATCHING A CLOCK SEEMS TO DEFY TIME ITSELF.
IT DOESN'T MOVE!
AND IF YOU TRY AND WATCH IT...
...IT WILL...
...SLOWLY...
...DRIVE YOU...
...INSANE.
TOCK!
THIS DAY IS NEVER GONNA END!

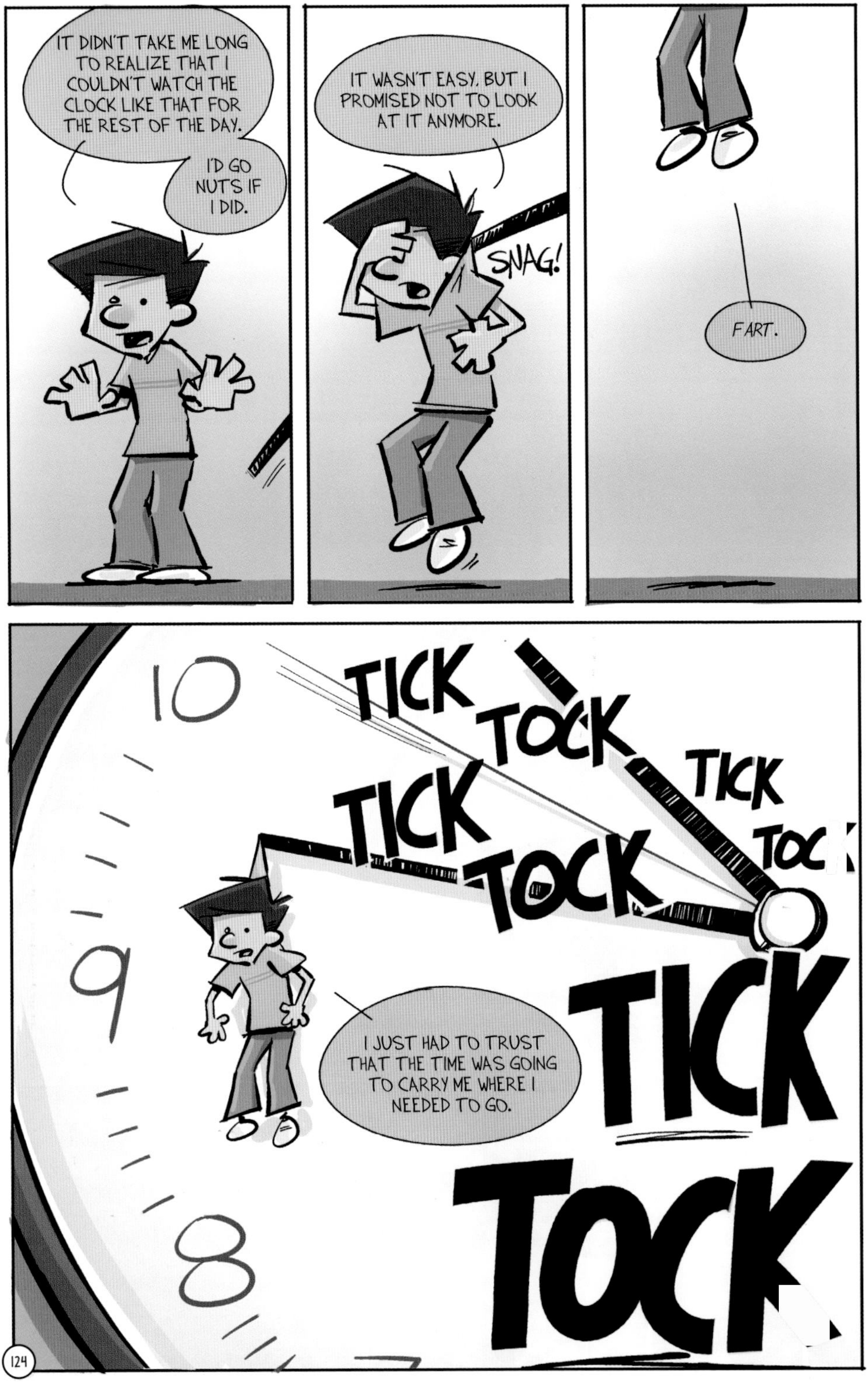
IT DIDN'T TAKE ME LONG TO REALIZE THAT I COULDN'T WATCH THE CLOCK LIKE THAT FOR THE REST OF THE DAY.
I'D GO NUTS IF I DID.
IT WASN'T EASY, BUT I PROMISED NOT TO LOOK AT IT ANYMORE.
SNAG!
FART.
10
TICK
TOCK
TICK
TICK
TOCK
TOCK
9
TICK
I JUST HAD TO TRUST THAT THE TIME WAS GOING TO CARRY ME WHERE I NEEDED TO GO.
TOCK
8

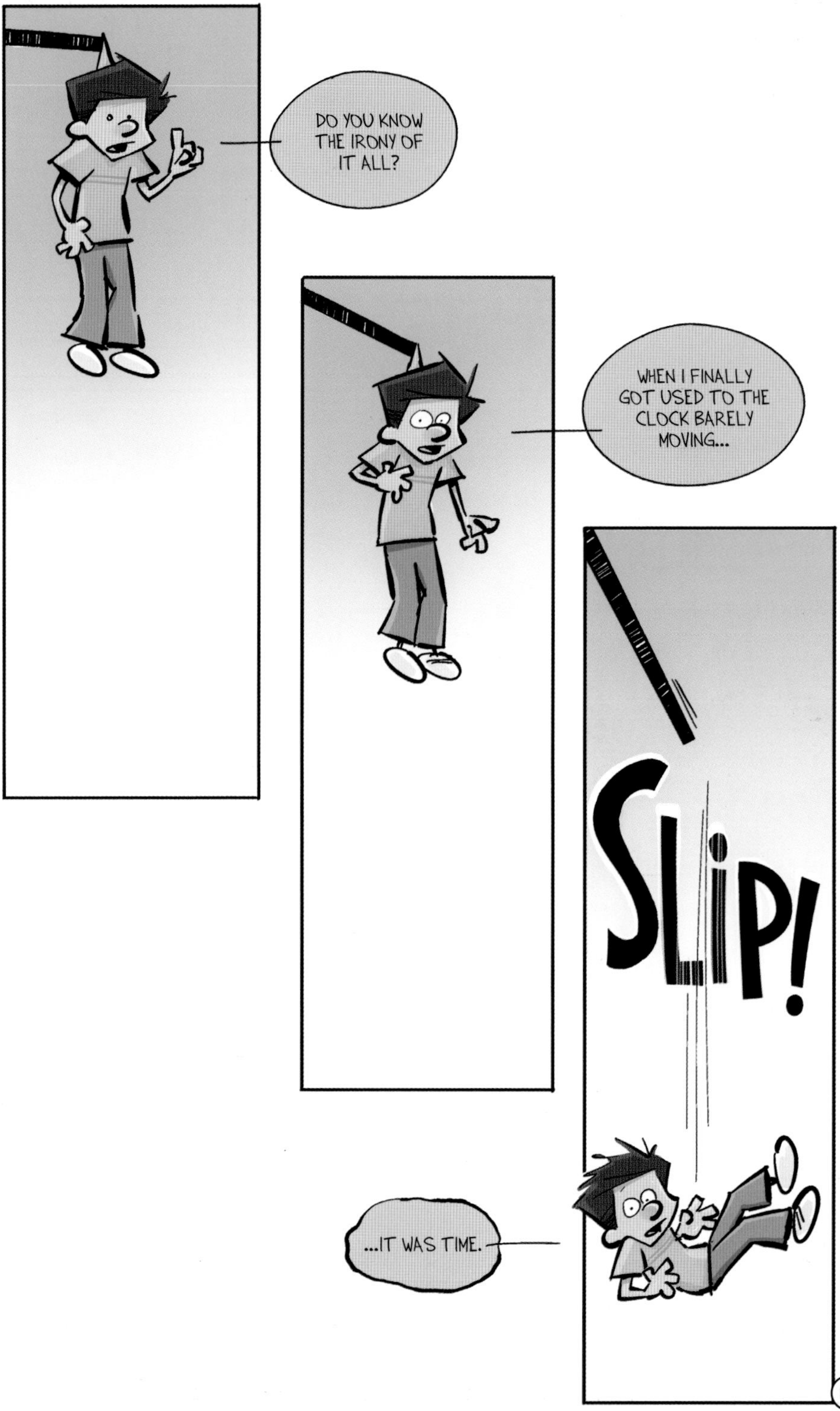
DO YOU KNOW THE IRONY OF IT ALL?
WHEN I FINALLY GOT USED TO THE CLOCK BARELY MOVING...
SLIP!
...IT WAS TIME.

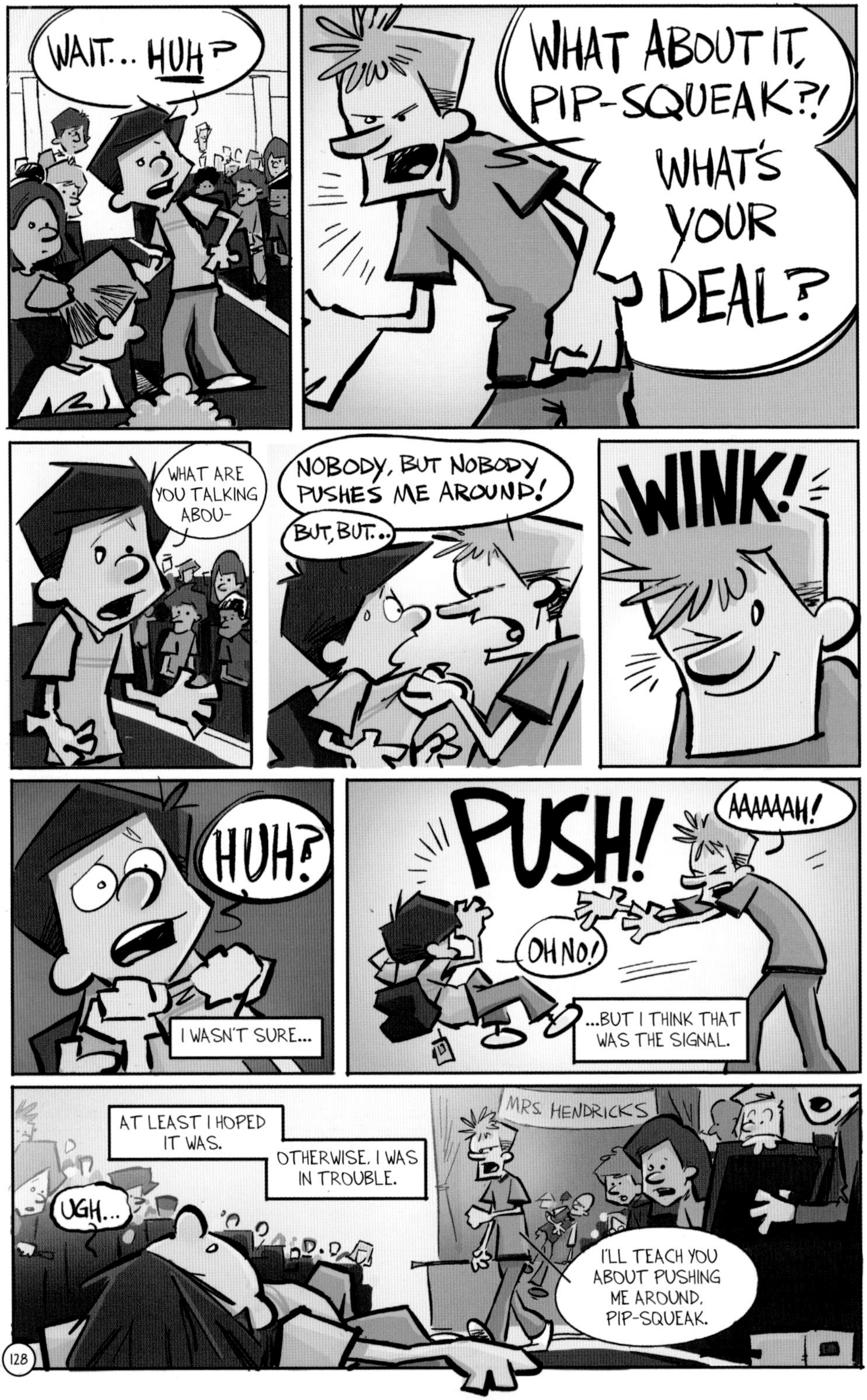

WAIT... HUH?
WHAT ABOUT IT, PIP-SQUEAK?!
WHAT'S YOUR DEAL?
WHAT ARE YOU TALKING ABOU-
NOBODY, BUT NOBODY PUSHES ME AROUND!
BUT, BUT...
WINK!
HUH?
I WASN'T SURE...
PUSH!
AAAAAAH!
OH NO!
...BUT I THINK THAT WAS THE SIGNAL.
AT LEAST I HOPED IT WAS.
OTHERWISE, I WAS IN TROUBLE.
MRS. HENDRICKS
UGH...
I'LL TEACH YOU ABOUT PUSHING ME AROUND, PIP-SQUEAK.

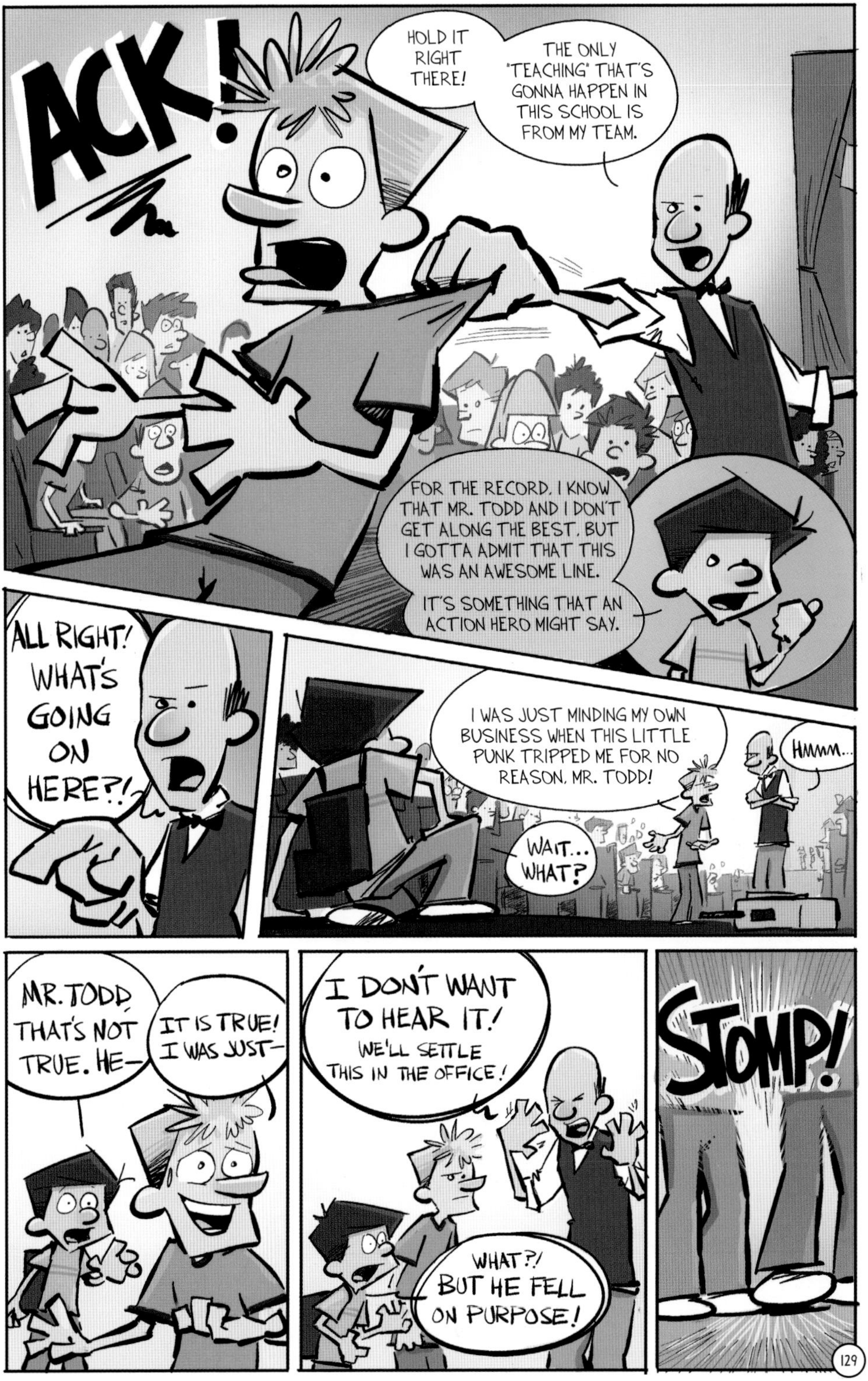
ACK!
HOLD IT RIGHT THERE!
THE ONLY "TEACHING" THAT'S GONNA HAPPEN IN THIS SCHOOL IS FROM MY TEAM.
FOR THE RECORD, I KNOW THAT MR. TODD AND I DON'T GET ALONG THE BEST, BUT I GOTTA ADMIT THAT THIS WAS AN AWESOME LINE.
IT'S SOMETHING THAT AN ACTION HERO MIGHT SAY.
ALL RIGHT! WHAT'S GOING ON HERE?!
I WAS JUST MINDING MY OWN BUSINESS WHEN THIS LITTLE PUNK TRIPPED ME FOR NO REASON, MR. TODD!
HMMM...
WAIT... WHAT?
MR. TODD, THAT'S NOT TRUE. HE—
IT IS TRUE! I WAS JUST—
I DON'T WANT TO HEAR IT! WE'LL SETTLE THIS IN THE OFFICE!
WHAT?! BUT HE FELL ON PURPOSE!
STOMP!

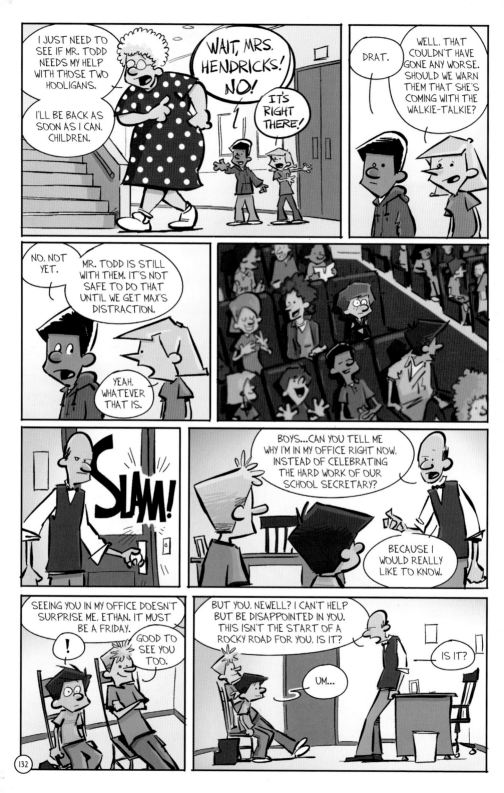

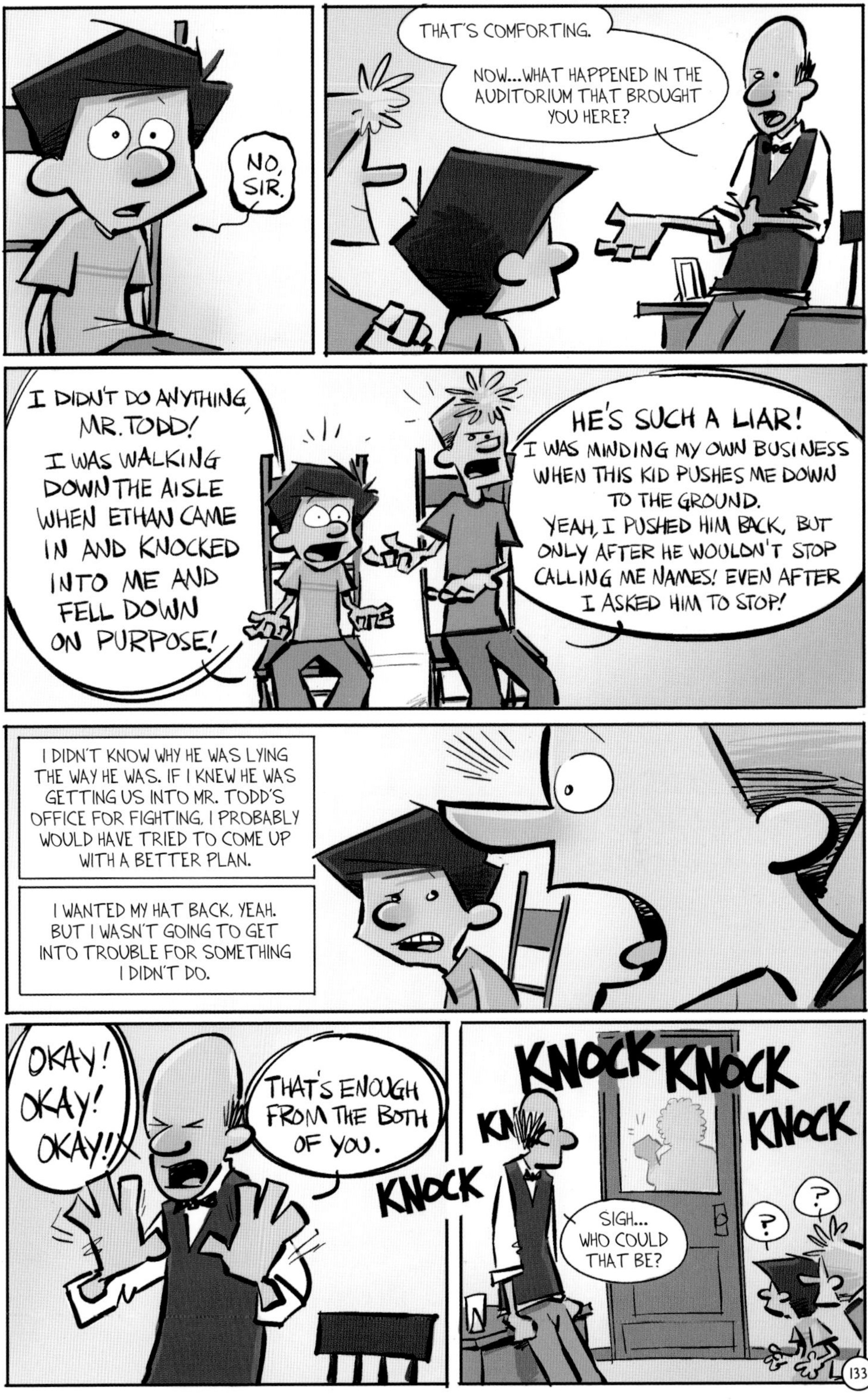
NO, SIR.
THAT'S COMFORTING.
NOW...WHAT HAPPENED IN THE AUDITORIUM THAT BROUGHT YOU HERE?
I DIDN'T DO ANYTHING, MR. TODD! I WAS WALKING DOWN THE AISLE WHEN ETHAN CAME IN AND KNOCKED INTO ME AND FELL DOWN ON PURPOSE!
HE'S SUCH A LIAR!
I WAS MINDING MY OWN BUSINESS WHEN THIS KID PUSHES ME DOWN TO THE GROUND. YEAH, I PUSHED HIM BACK, BUT ONLY AFTER HE WOULDN'T STOP CALLING ME NAMES! EVEN AFTER I ASKED HIM TO STOP!
I DIDN'T KNOW WHY HE WAS LYING THE WAY HE WAS. IF I KNEW HE WAS GETTING US INTO MR. TODD'S OFFICE FOR FIGHTING, I PROBABLY WOULD HAVE TRIED TO COME UP WITH A BETTER PLAN.
I WANTED MY HAT BACK, YEAH. BUT I WASN'T GOING TO GET INTO TROUBLE FOR SOMETHING I DIDN'T DO.
OKAY! OKAY! OKAY!!
THAT'S ENOUGH FROM THE BOTH OF YOU.
KNOCK KNOCK
KN
KNOCK
KNOCK
SIGH... WHO COULD THAT BE?
?
?

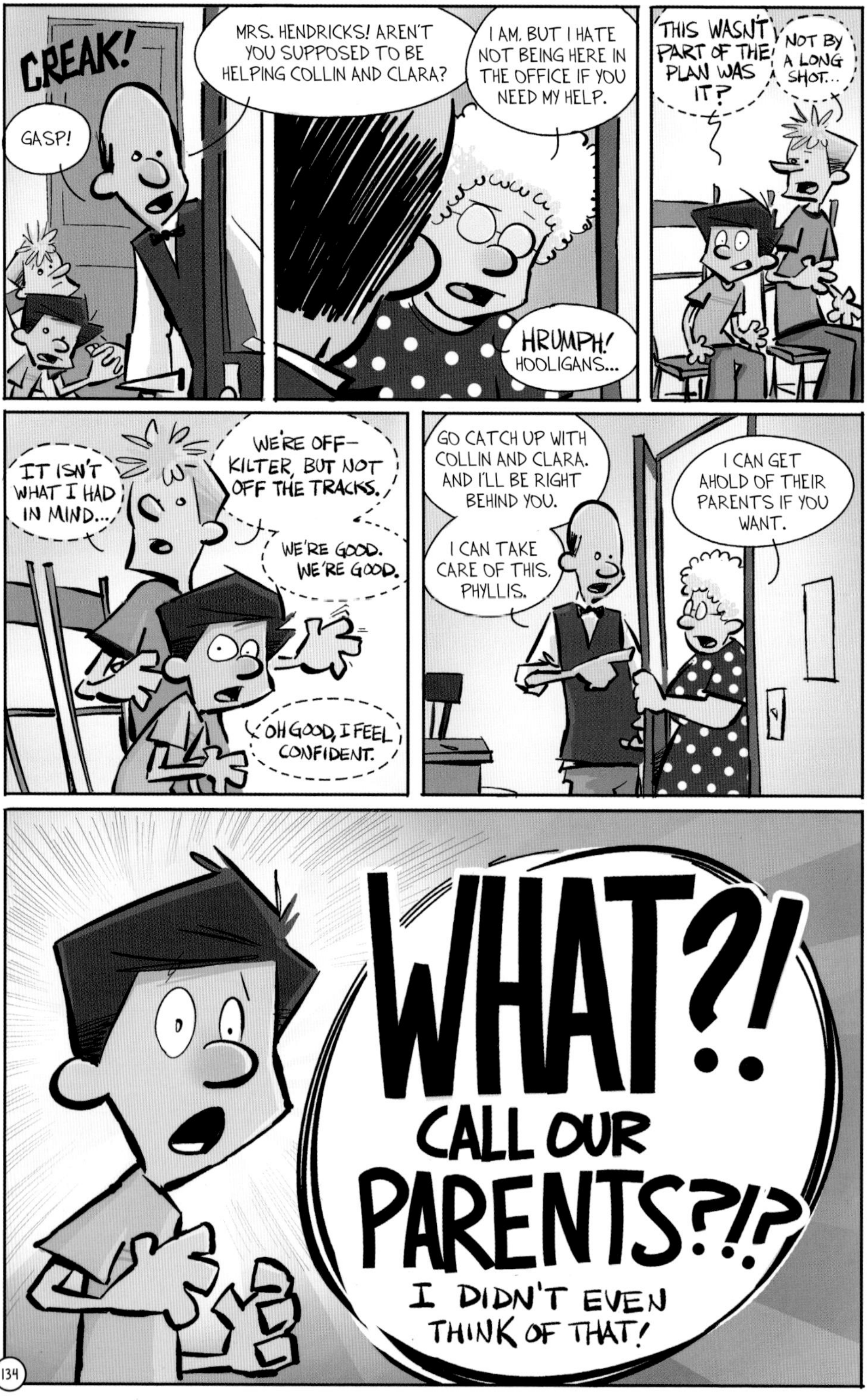
CREAK!
GASP!
MRS. HENDRICKS! AREN'T YOU SUPPOSED TO BE HELPING COLLIN AND CLARA?
I AM, BUT I HATE NOT BEING HERE IN THE OFFICE IF YOU NEED MY HELP.
HRUMPH! HOOLIGANS...
THIS WASN'T PART OF THE PLAN WAS IT?
NOT BY A LONG SHOT...
IT ISN'T WHAT I HAD IN MIND...
WE'RE OFF-KILTER, BUT NOT OFF THE TRACKS.
WE'RE GOOD. WE'RE GOOD.
OH GOOD, I FEEL CONFIDENT.
GO CATCH UP WITH COLLIN AND CLARA. AND I'LL BE RIGHT BEHIND YOU.
I CAN TAKE CARE OF THIS, PHYLLIS.
I CAN GET AHOLD OF THEIR PARENTS IF YOU WANT.
WHAT?! CALL OUR PARENTS?!? I DIDN'T EVEN THINK OF THAT!

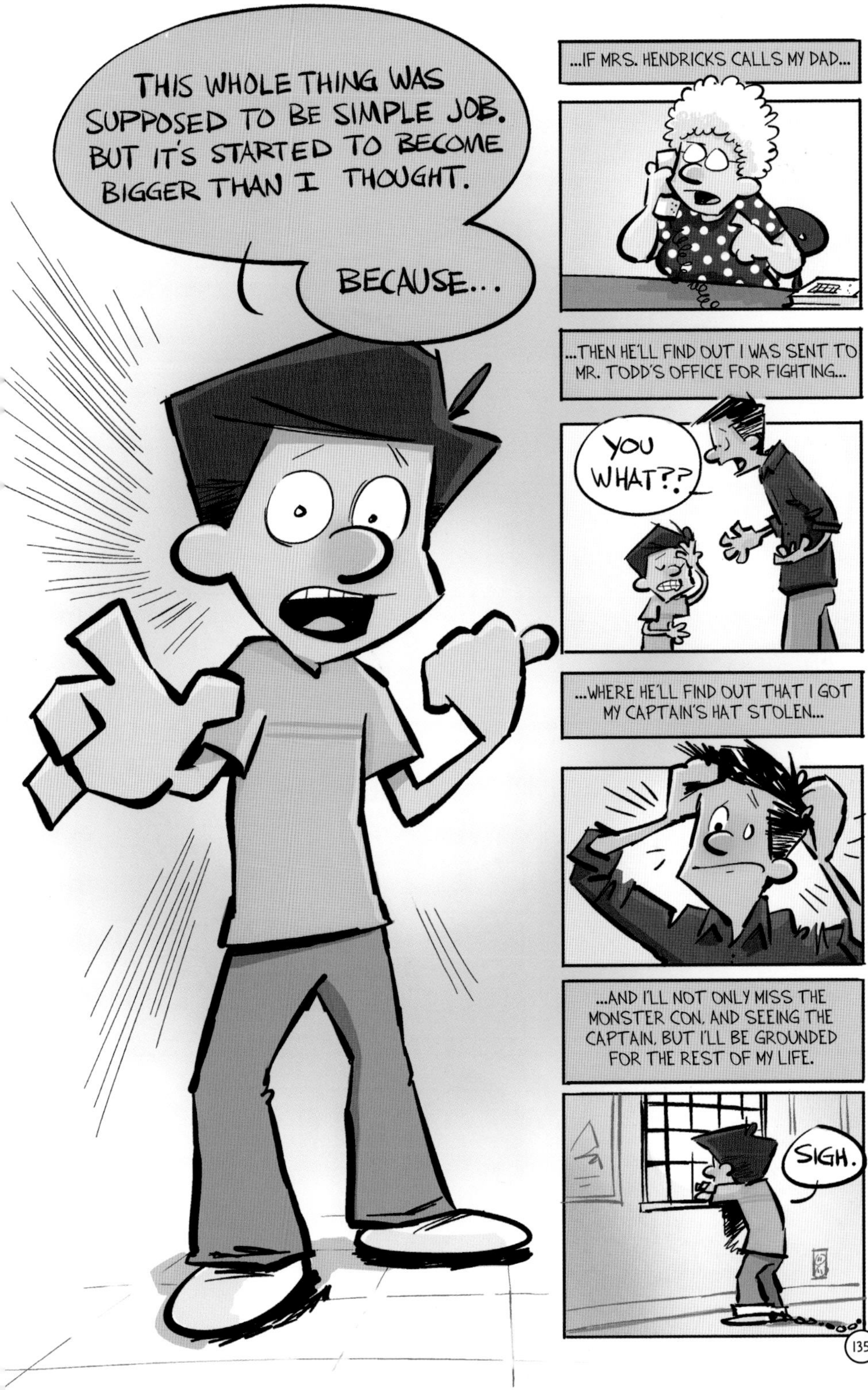
THIS WHOLE THING WAS SUPPOSED TO BE SIMPLE JOB. BUT IT'S STARTED TO BECOME BIGGER THAN I THOUGHT.
BECAUSE...
...IF MRS. HENDRICKS CALLS MY DAD...
...THEN HE'LL FIND OUT I WAS SENT TO MR. TODD'S OFFICE FOR FIGHTING...
YOU WHAT??
...WHERE HE'LL FIND OUT THAT I GOT MY CAPTAIN'S HAT STOLEN...
...AND I'LL NOT ONLY MISS THE MONSTER CON, AND SEEING THE CAPTAIN, BUT I'LL BE GROUNDED FOR THE REST OF MY LIFE.
SIGH.

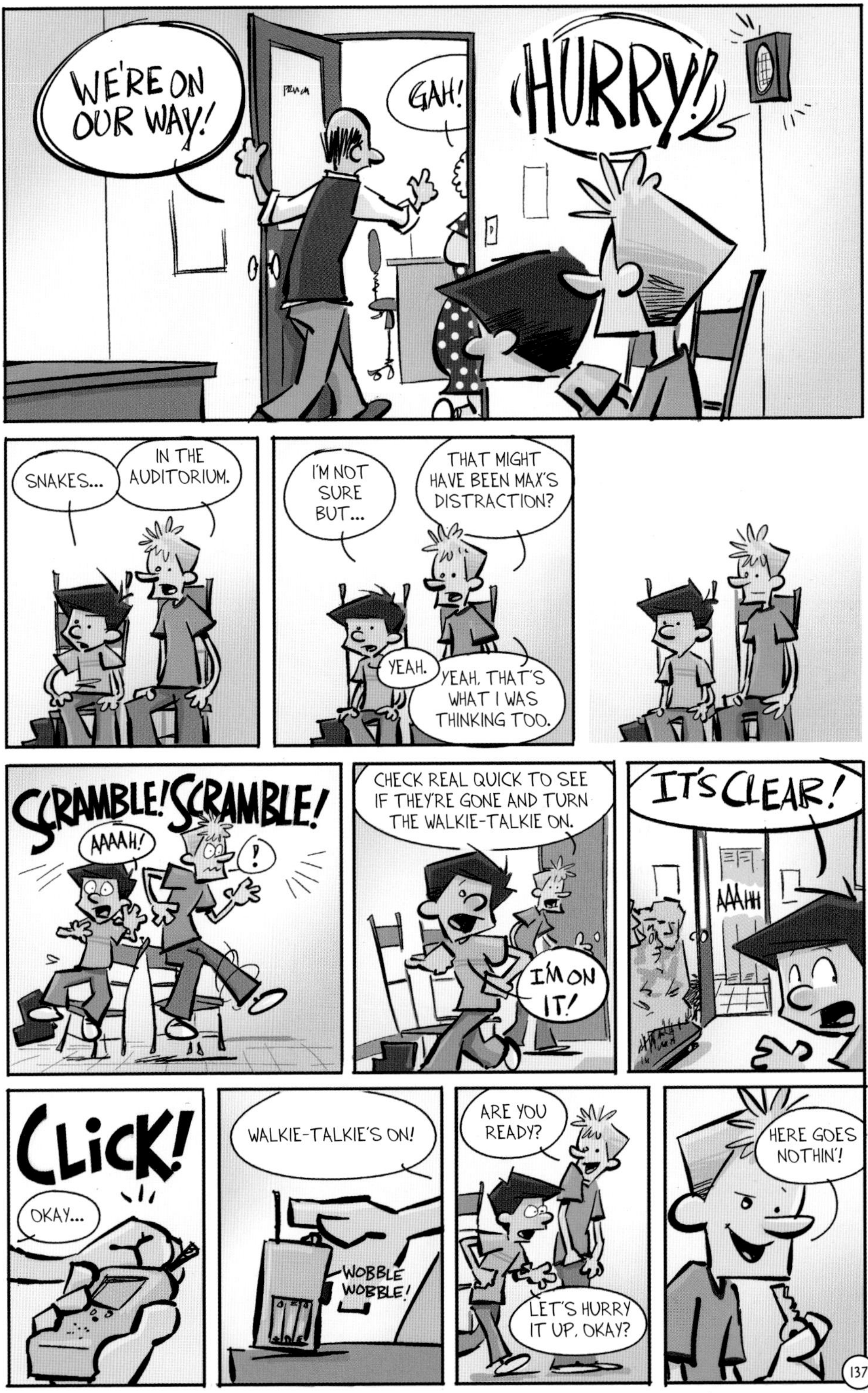
WE'RE ON OUR WAY!
GAH!
HURRY!
SNAKES...
IN THE AUDITORIUM.
I'M NOT SURE BUT...
THAT MIGHT HAVE BEEN MAX'S DISTRACTION?
YEAH.
YEAH, THAT'S WHAT I WAS THINKING TOO.
SCRAMBLE! SCRAMBLE!
AAAAH!
!
CHECK REAL QUICK TO SEE IF THEY'RE GONE AND TURN THE WALKIE-TALKIE ON.
I'M ON IT!
IT'S CLEAR!
AAAHH
CLICK!
OKAY...
WALKIE-TALKIE'S ON!
WOBBLE WOBBLE!
ARE YOU READY?
LET'S HURRY IT UP, OKAY?
HERE GOES NOTHIN'!

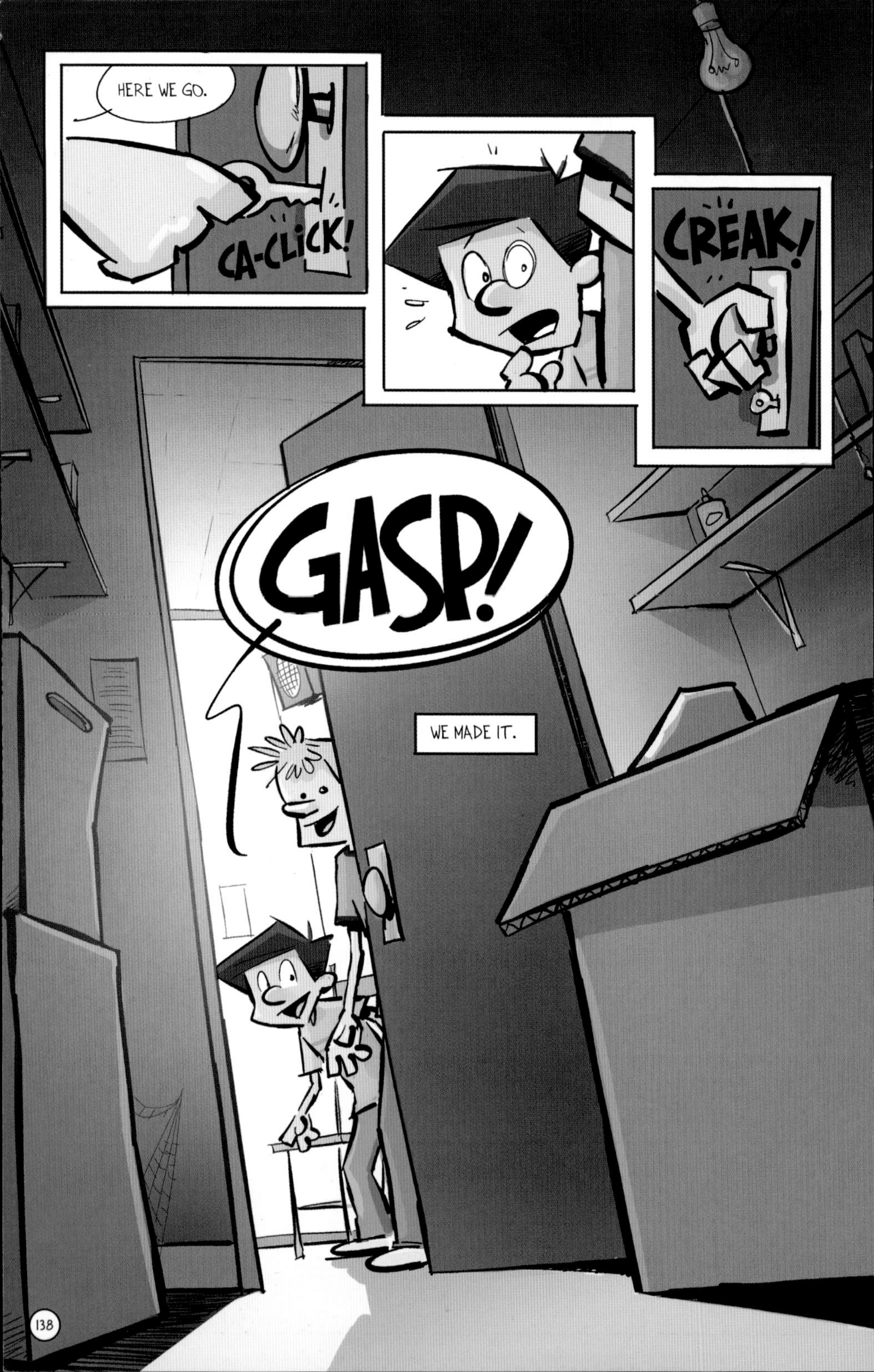
HERE WE GO.
CA-CLICK!
CREAK!
GASP!
WE MADE IT.

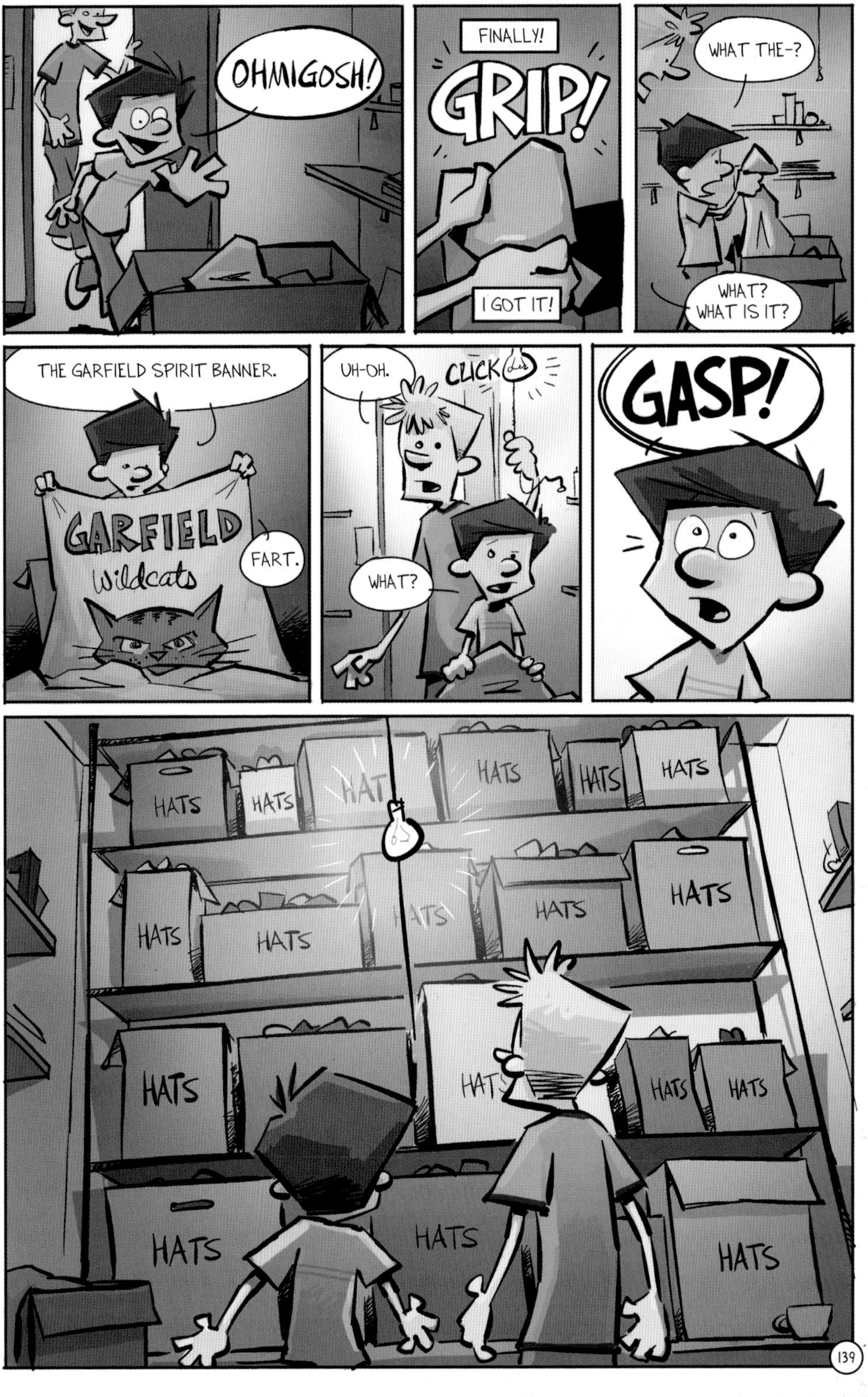
OHMIGOSH!
FINALLY!
GRIP!
I GOT IT!
WHAT THE-?
WHAT?
WHAT IS IT?
THE GARFIELD SPIRIT BANNER.
GARFIELD
Wildcats
FART.
UH-OH.
CLICK
WHAT?
GASP!
HATS
HATS
HATS
HATS
HATS
HATS
HATS
HATS
HATS
HATS
HATS
HATS
HATS
HATS
HATS
HATS

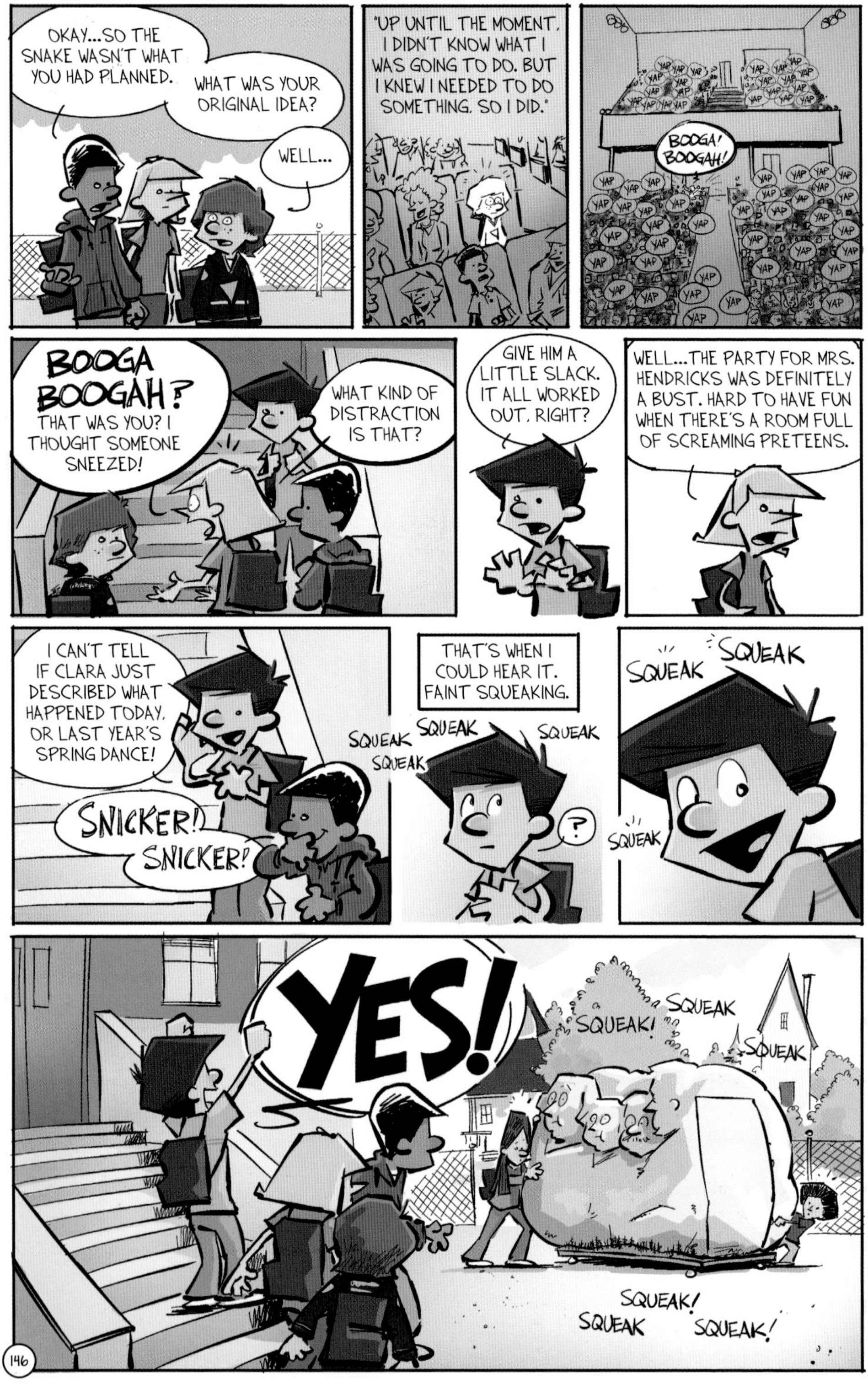
OKAY...SO THE SNAKE WASN'T WHAT YOU HAD PLANNED.
WHAT WAS YOUR ORIGINAL IDEA?
WELL...
"UP UNTIL THE MOMENT, I DIDN'T KNOW WHAT I WAS GOING TO DO. BUT I KNEW I NEEDED TO DO SOMETHING, SO I DID."
BOOGA! BOOGAH!
YAP
BOOGA BOOGAH? THAT WAS YOU? I THOUGHT SOMEONE SNEEZED!
WHAT KIND OF DISTRACTION IS THAT?
GIVE HIM A LITTLE SLACK. IT ALL WORKED OUT, RIGHT?
WELL...THE PARTY FOR MRS. HENDRICKS WAS DEFINITELY A BUST. HARD TO HAVE FUN WHEN THERE'S A ROOM FULL OF SCREAMING PRETEENS.
I CAN'T TELL IF CLARA JUST DESCRIBED WHAT HAPPENED TODAY, OR LAST YEAR'S SPRING DANCE!
SNICKER!
SNICKER!
THAT'S WHEN I COULD HEAR IT. FAINT SQUEAKING.
SQUEAK SQUEAK SQUEAK SQUEAK
?
SQUEAK SQUEAK SQUEAK
YES!
SQUEAK SQUEAK! SQUEAK
SQUEAK! SQUEAK SQUEAK!

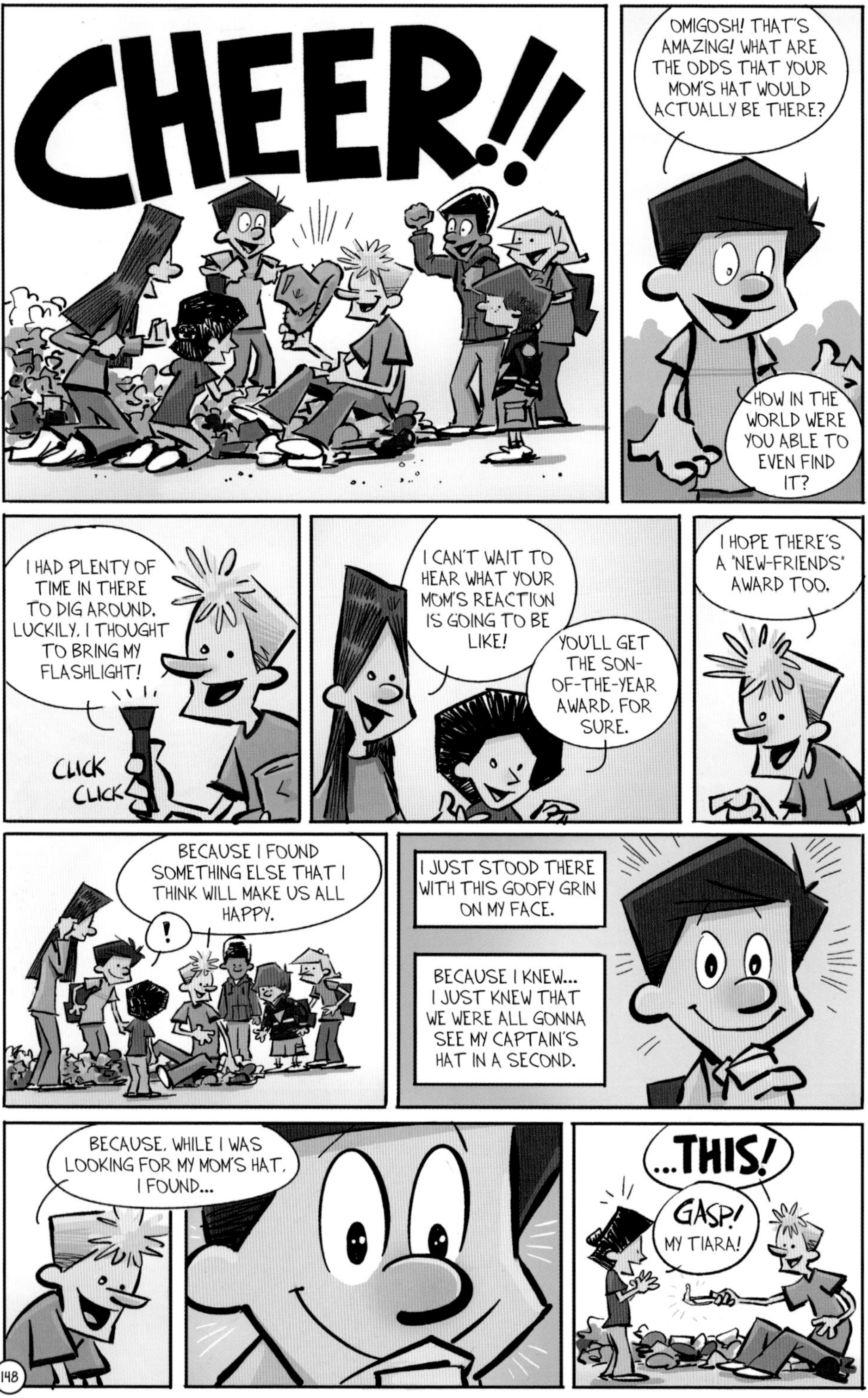
CHEER!!
OMIGOSH! THAT'S AMAZING! WHAT ARE THE ODDS THAT YOUR MOM'S HAT WOULD ACTUALLY BE THERE?
HOW IN THE WORLD WERE YOU ABLE TO EVEN FIND IT?
I HAD PLENTY OF TIME IN THERE TO DIG AROUND. LUCKILY, I THOUGHT TO BRING MY FLASHLIGHT!
CLICK CLICK
I CAN'T WAIT TO HEAR WHAT YOUR MOM'S REACTION IS GOING TO BE LIKE!
YOU'LL GET THE SON-OF-THE-YEAR AWARD, FOR SURE.
I HOPE THERE'S A "NEW-FRIENDS" AWARD TOO.
BECAUSE I FOUND SOMETHING ELSE THAT I THINK WILL MAKE US ALL HAPPY.
!
I JUST STOOD THERE WITH THIS GOOFY GRIN ON MY FACE.
BECAUSE I KNEW... I JUST KNEW THAT WE WERE ALL GONNA SEE MY CAPTAIN'S HAT IN A SECOND.
BECAUSE, WHILE I WAS LOOKING FOR MY MOM'S HAT, I FOUND...
...THIS!
GASP! MY TIARA!

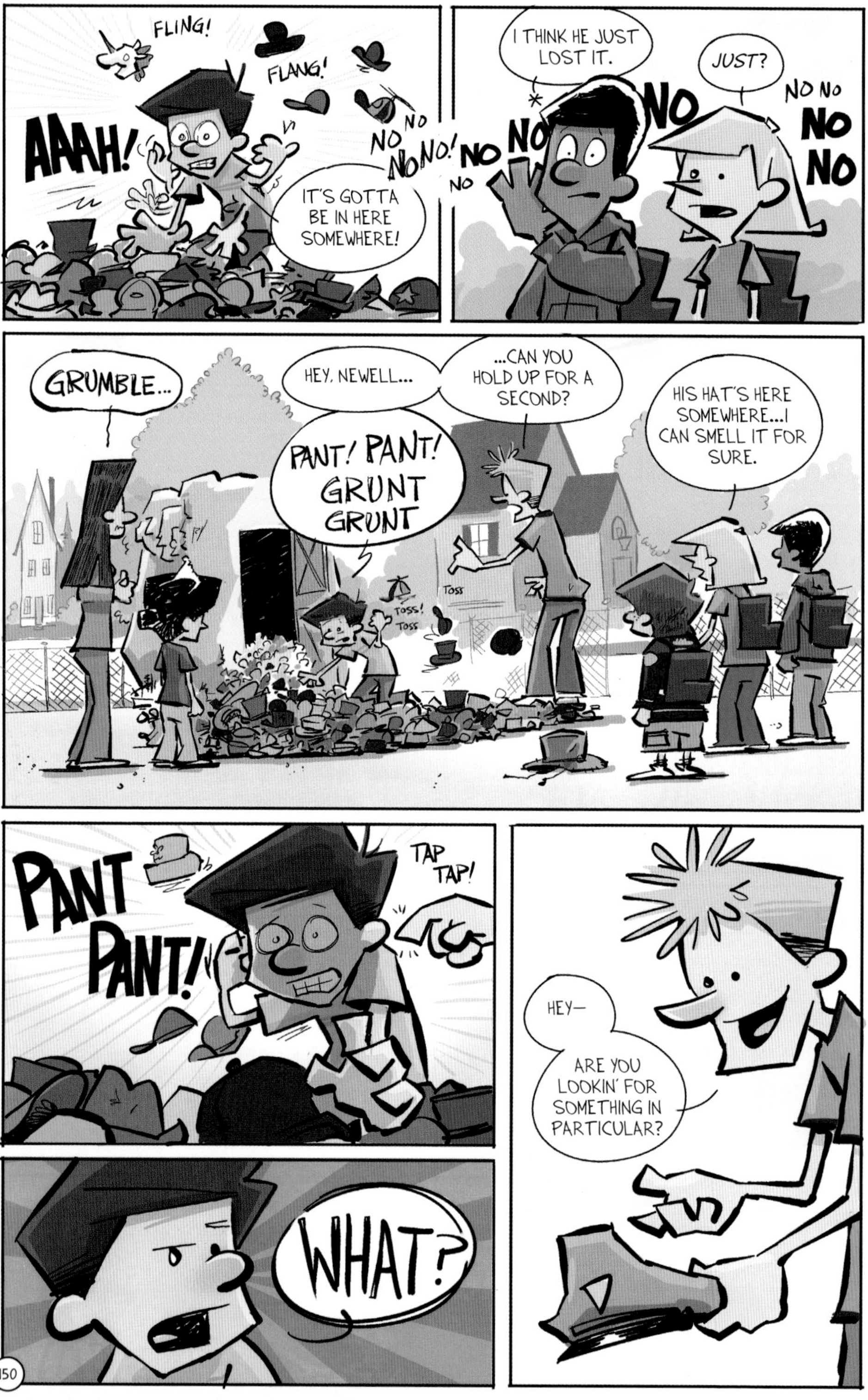
FLING!
FLANG!
AAAH!
NO NO NO NO!
IT'S GOTTA BE IN HERE SOMEWHERE!
I THINK HE JUST LOST IT.
JUST?
NO NO NO NO NO NO NO NO
GRUMBLE...
HEY, NEWELL...
...CAN YOU HOLD UP FOR A SECOND?
PANT! PANT! GRUNT GRUNT
HIS HAT'S HERE SOMEWHERE...I CAN SMELL IT FOR SURE.
TOSS
TOSS! TOSS
TOSS
PANT PANT!
TAP TAP!
HEY—
ARE YOU LOOKIN' FOR SOMETHING IN PARTICULAR?
WHAT?

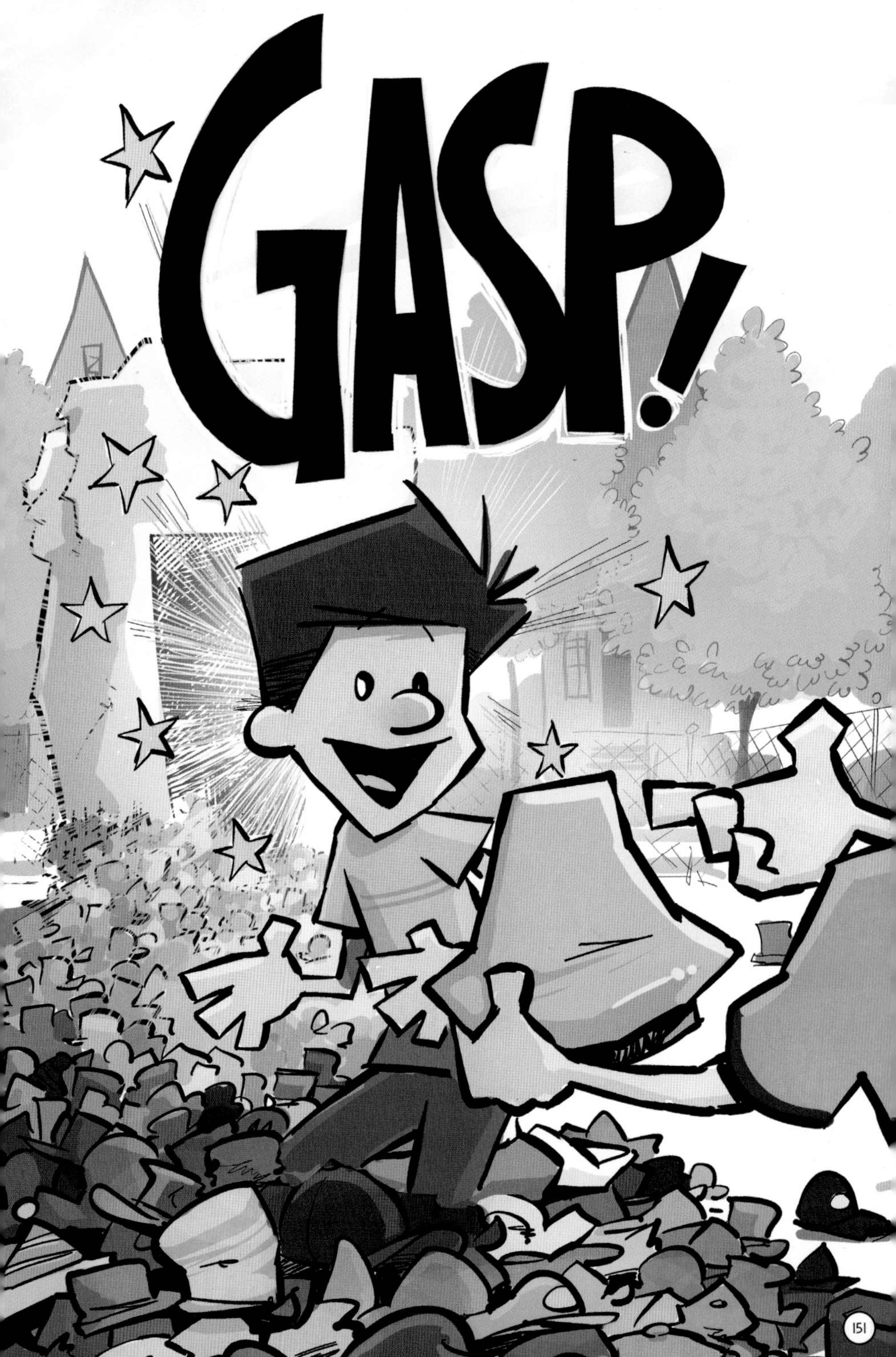
GASP!

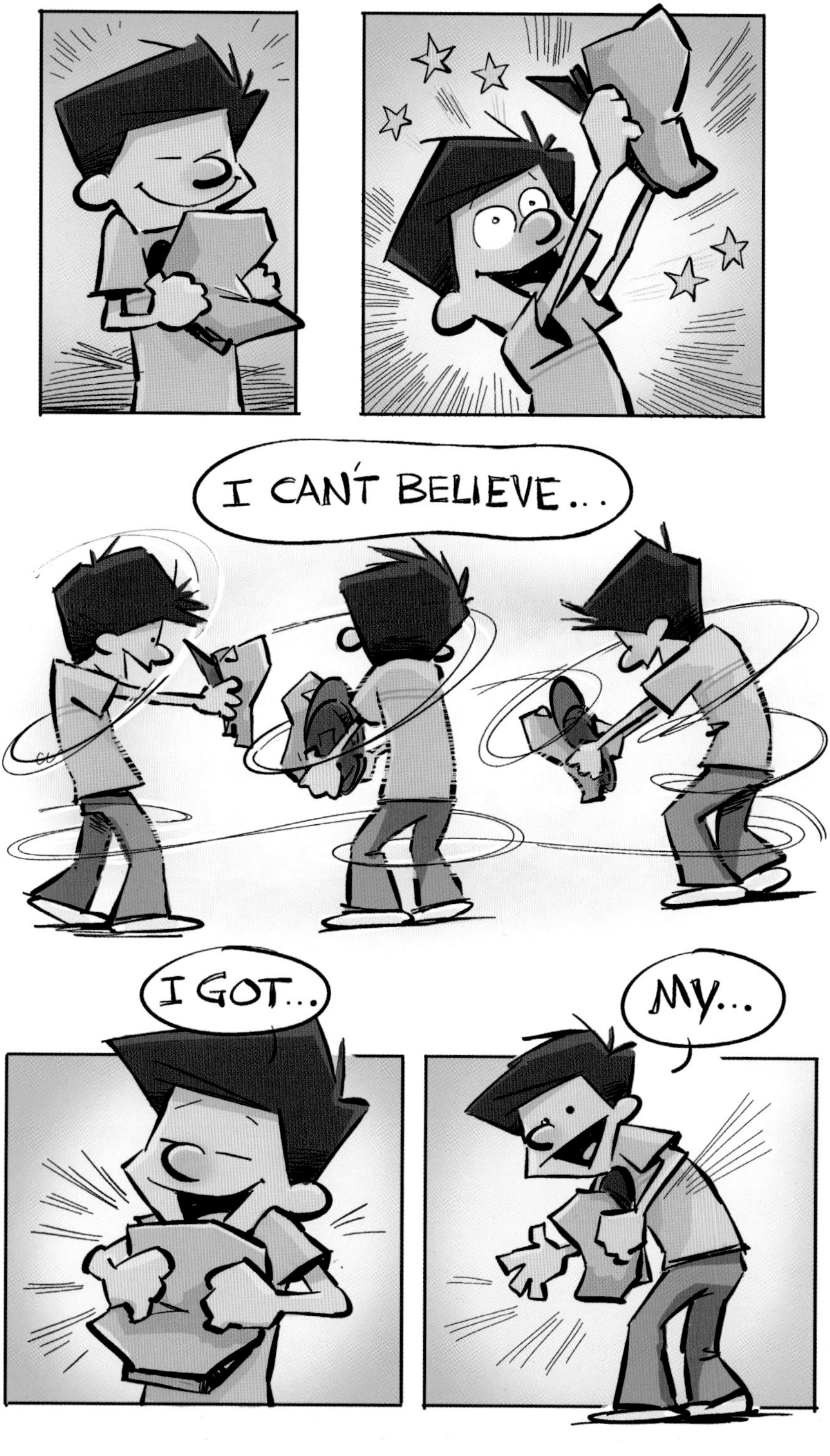
I CAN'T BELIEVE...
I GOT...
MY...

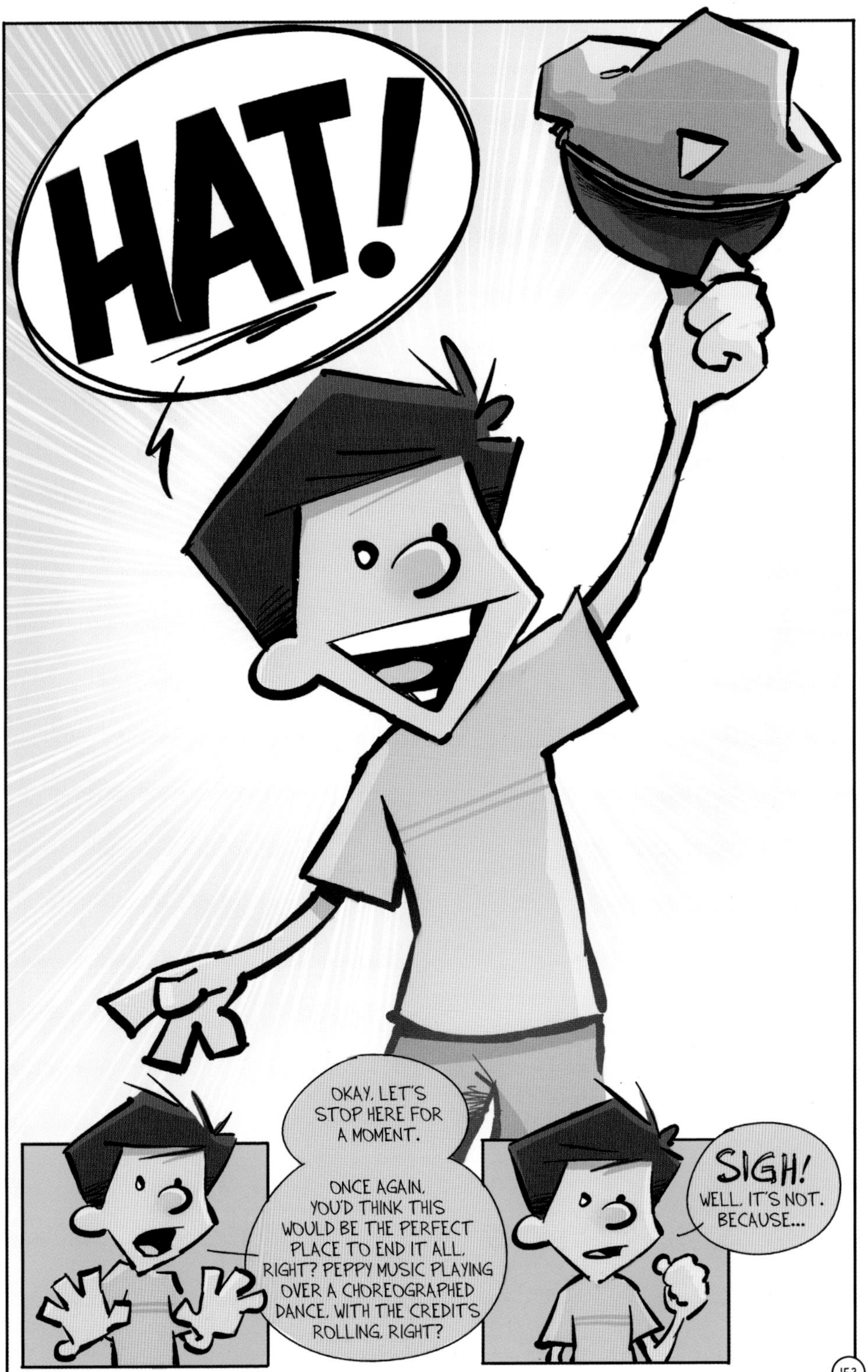
HAT!
OKAY, LET'S STOP HERE FOR A MOMENT.
ONCE AGAIN, YOU'D THINK THIS WOULD BE THE PERFECT PLACE TO END IT ALL, RIGHT? PEPPY MUSIC PLAYING OVER A CHOREOGRAPHED DANCE, WITH THE CREDITS ROLLING, RIGHT?
SIGH!
WELL, IT'S NOT. BECAUSE...

CHAPTER EIGHT
IT'S ONLY THE BEGINNING...AGAIN

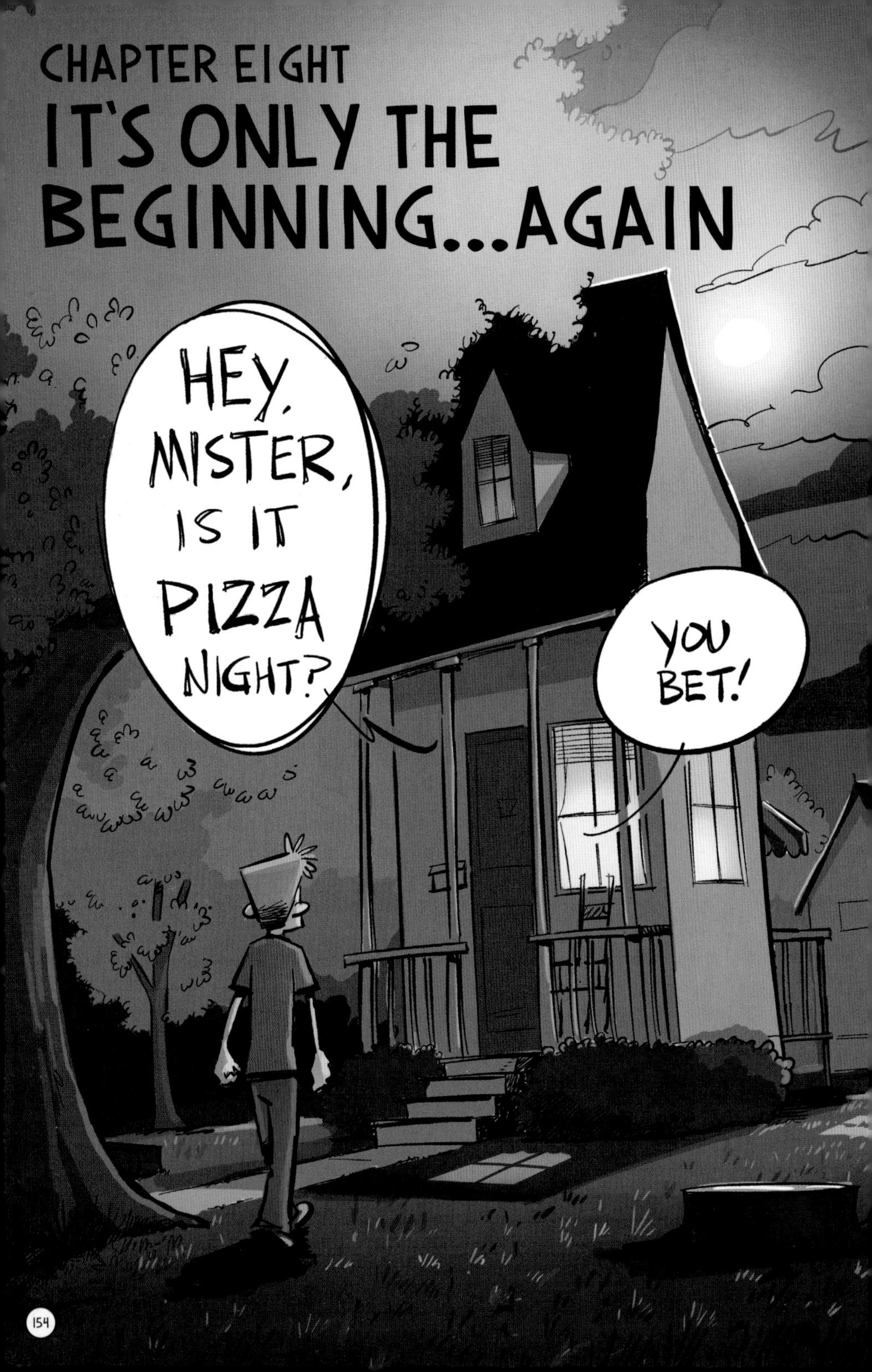
HEY, MISTER, IS IT PIZZA NIGHT?
YOU BET!

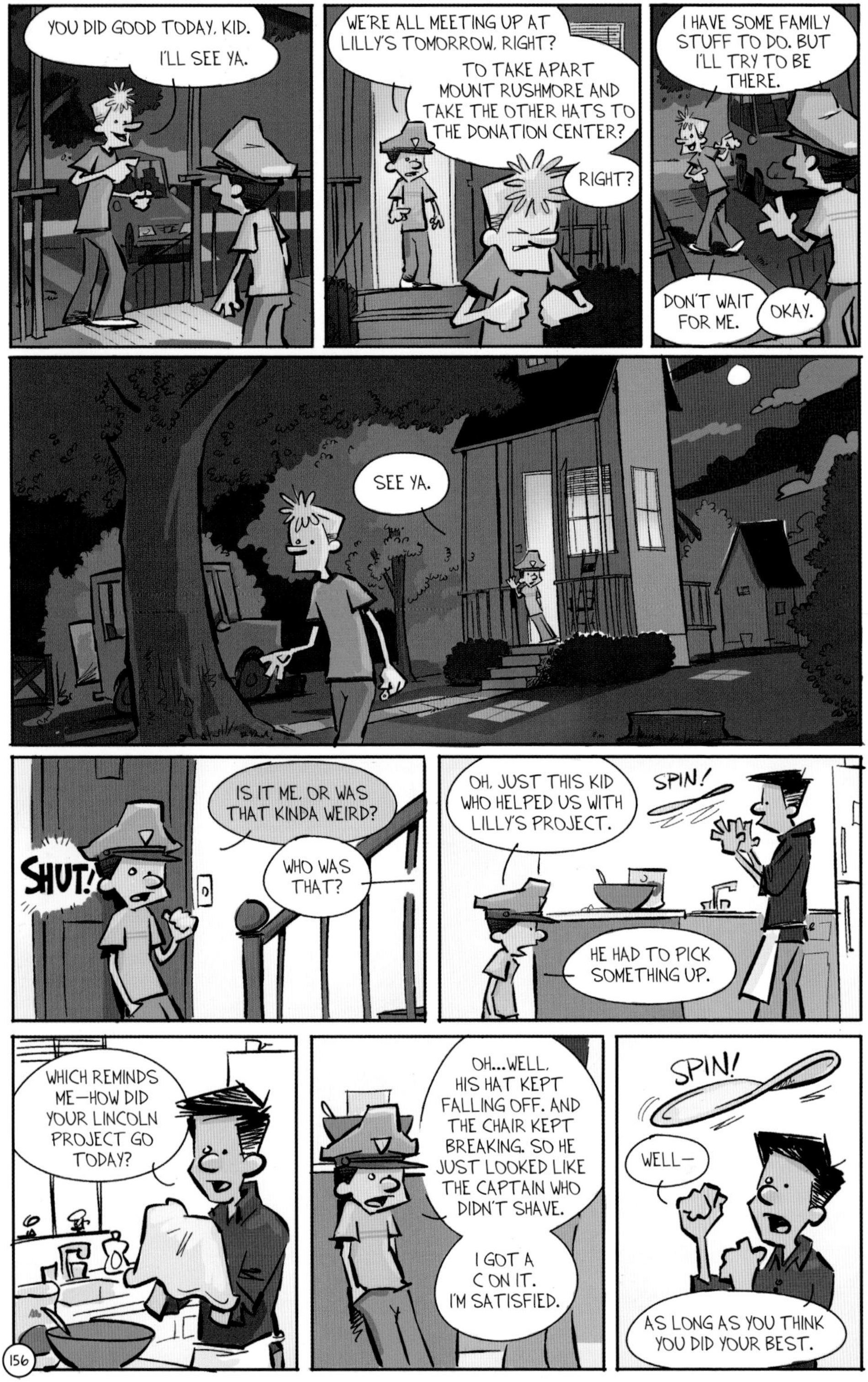
YOU DID GOOD TODAY, KID.
I'LL SEE YA.
WE'RE ALL MEETING UP AT LILLY'S TOMORROW, RIGHT?
TO TAKE APART MOUNT RUSHMORE AND TAKE THE OTHER HATS TO THE DONATION CENTER?
RIGHT?
I HAVE SOME FAMILY STUFF TO DO. BUT I'LL TRY TO BE THERE.
DON'T WAIT FOR ME.
OKAY.
SEE YA.
SHUT!
IS IT ME, OR WAS THAT KINDA WEIRD?
WHO WAS THAT?
OH, JUST THIS KID WHO HELPED US WITH LILLY'S PROJECT.
SPIN!
HE HAD TO PICK SOMETHING UP.
WHICH REMINDS ME—HOW DID YOUR LINCOLN PROJECT GO TODAY?
OH...WELL, HIS HAT KEPT FALLING OFF. AND THE CHAIR KEPT BREAKING. SO HE JUST LOOKED LIKE THE CAPTAIN WHO DIDN'T SHAVE.
I GOT A C ON IT. I'M SATISFIED.
SPIN!
WELL—
AS LONG AS YOU THINK YOU DID YOUR BEST.

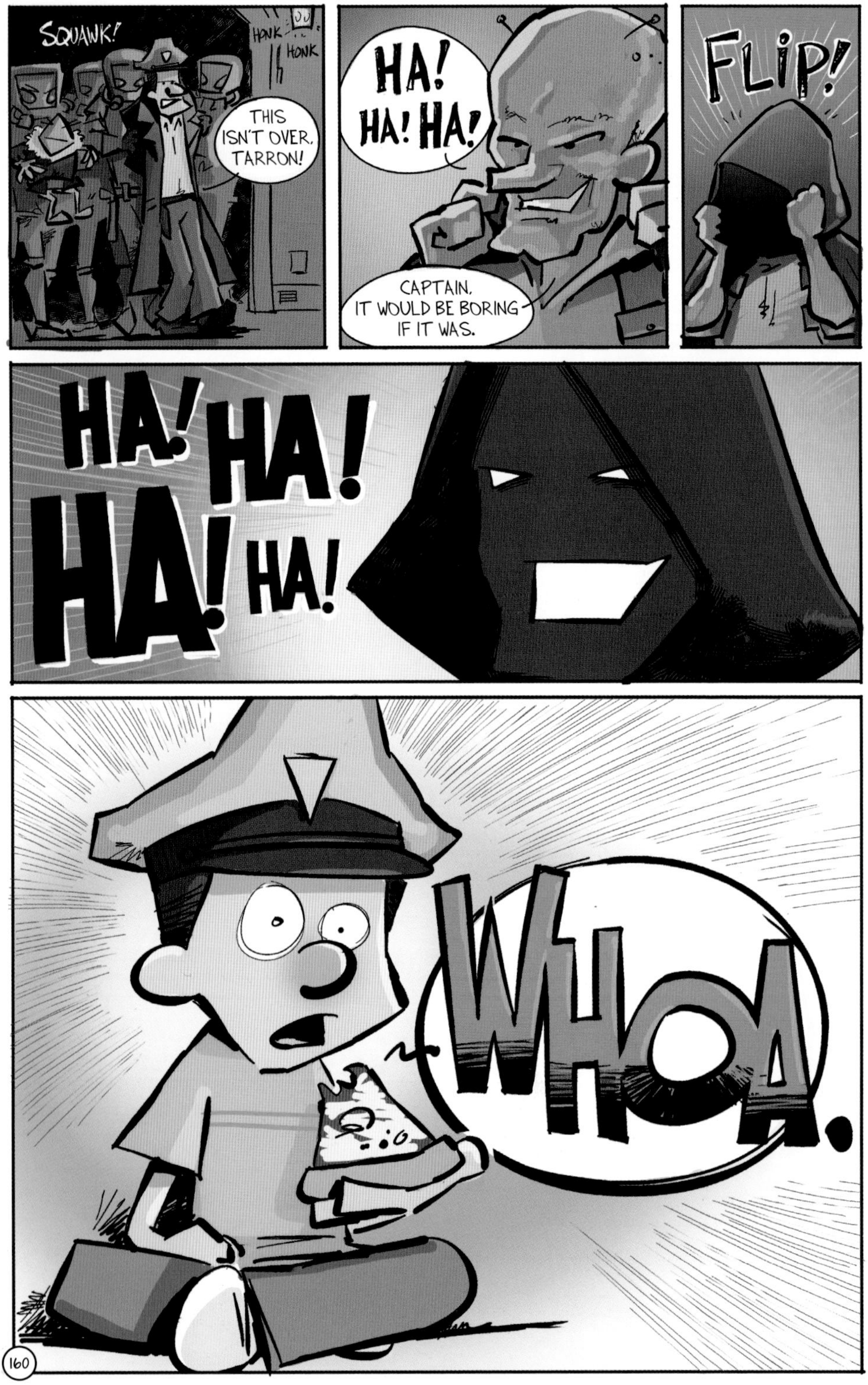
SQUAWK!
HONK
HONK
THIS ISN'T OVER, TARRON!
HA! HA! HA!
CAPTAIN, IT WOULD BE BORING IF IT WAS.
FLIP!
HA! HA! HA! HA!
WHOA.

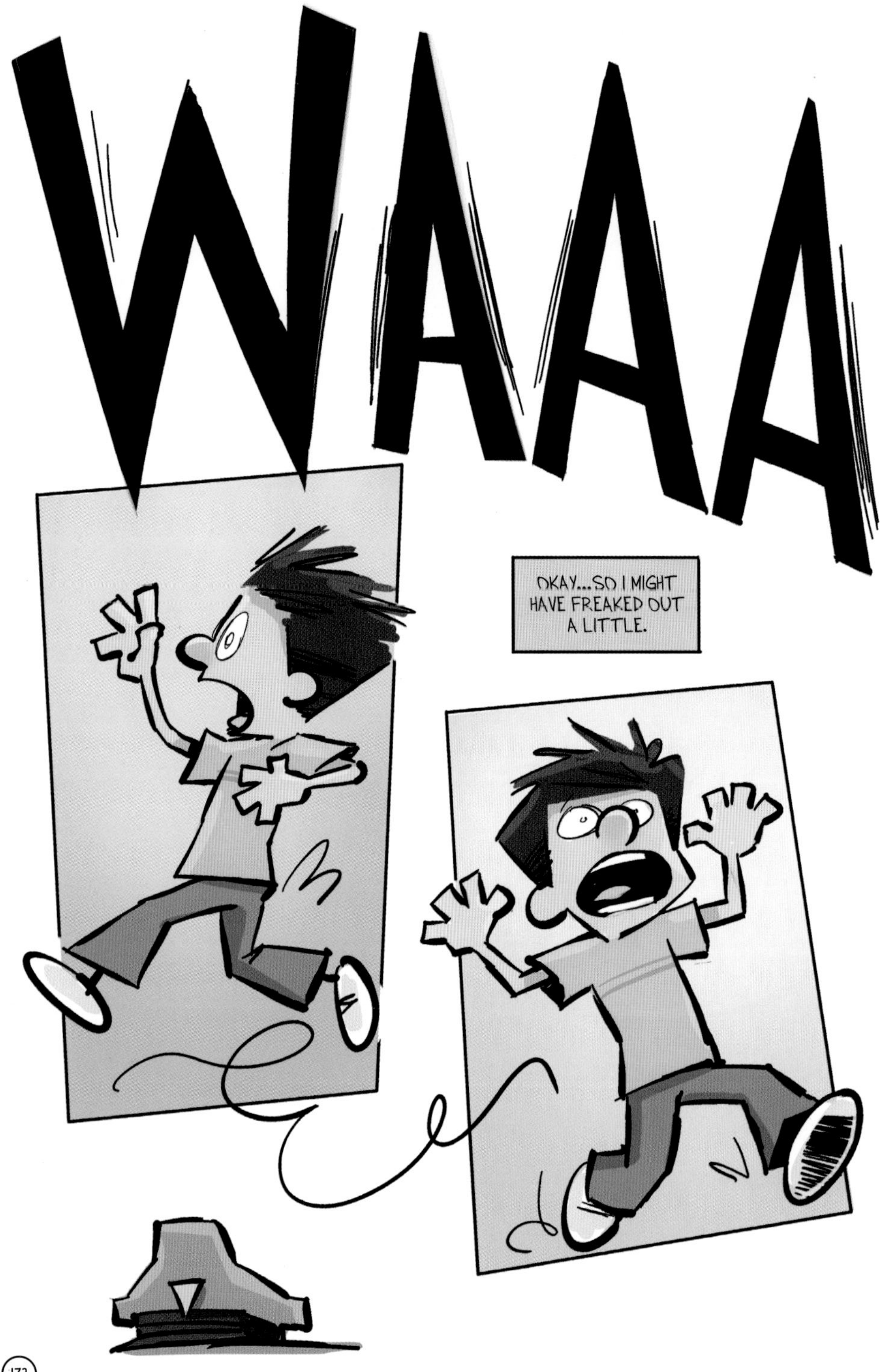
WAAA
OKAY...SO I MIGHT HAVE FREAKED OUT A LITTLE.

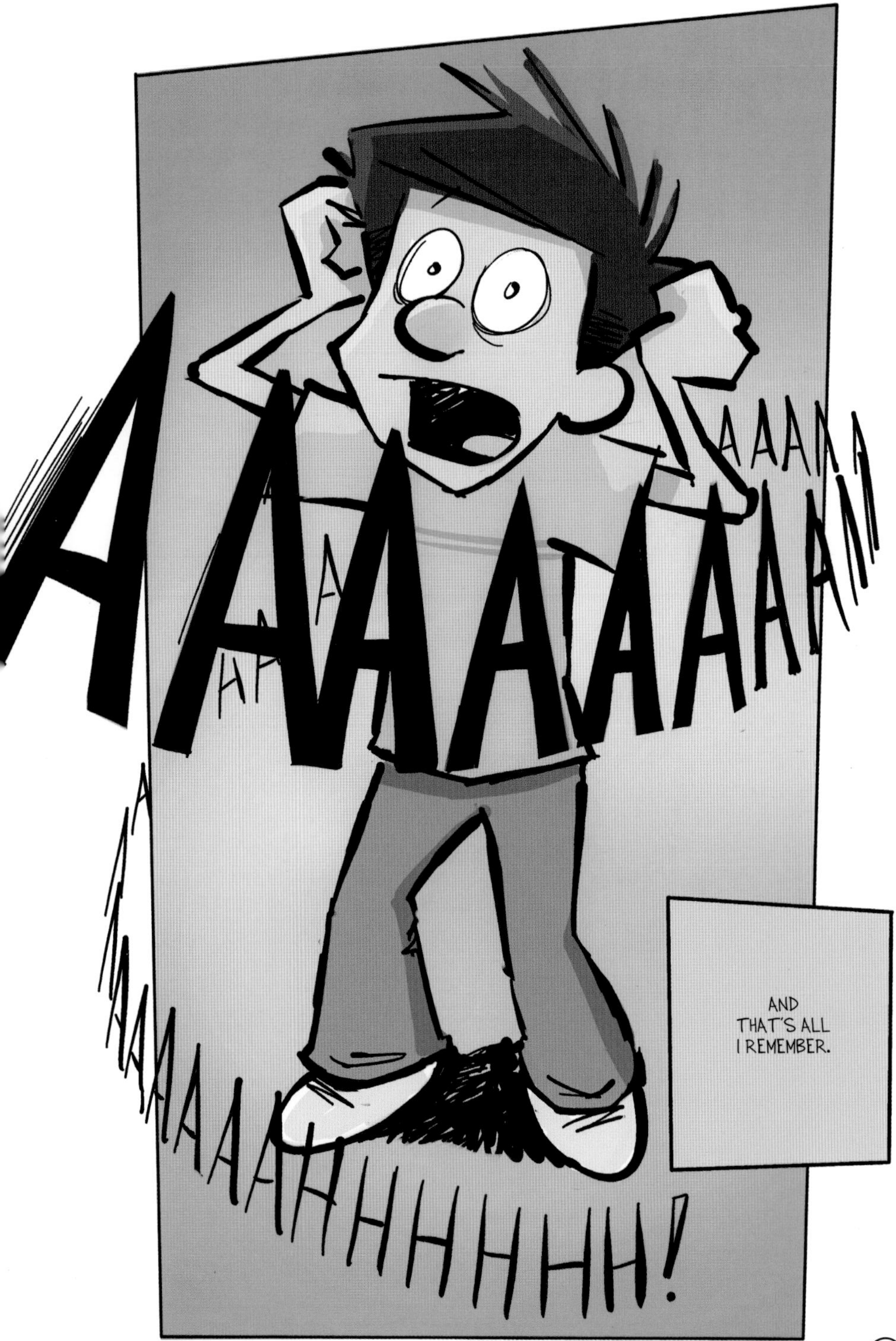
AND THAT'S ALL I REMEMBER.

CHAPTER NINE
THE DOUBLE TAKE

NEWELL?

* SHAKE
SHAKE
SHAKE *

DUDE?

NEWELL?

DANG, HE'S NOT DEAD, IS HE?

* SHAKE
SHAKE SHAKE *
SHAKE
SHAKE
SHAKE *

* SHAKE
SHAKE
SHAKE *

NO.
HE JUST FAINTED,
THAT'S ALL.

I DUNNO...
HE LOOKS DEAD
TO ME.

HE'S
NOT
DEAD!

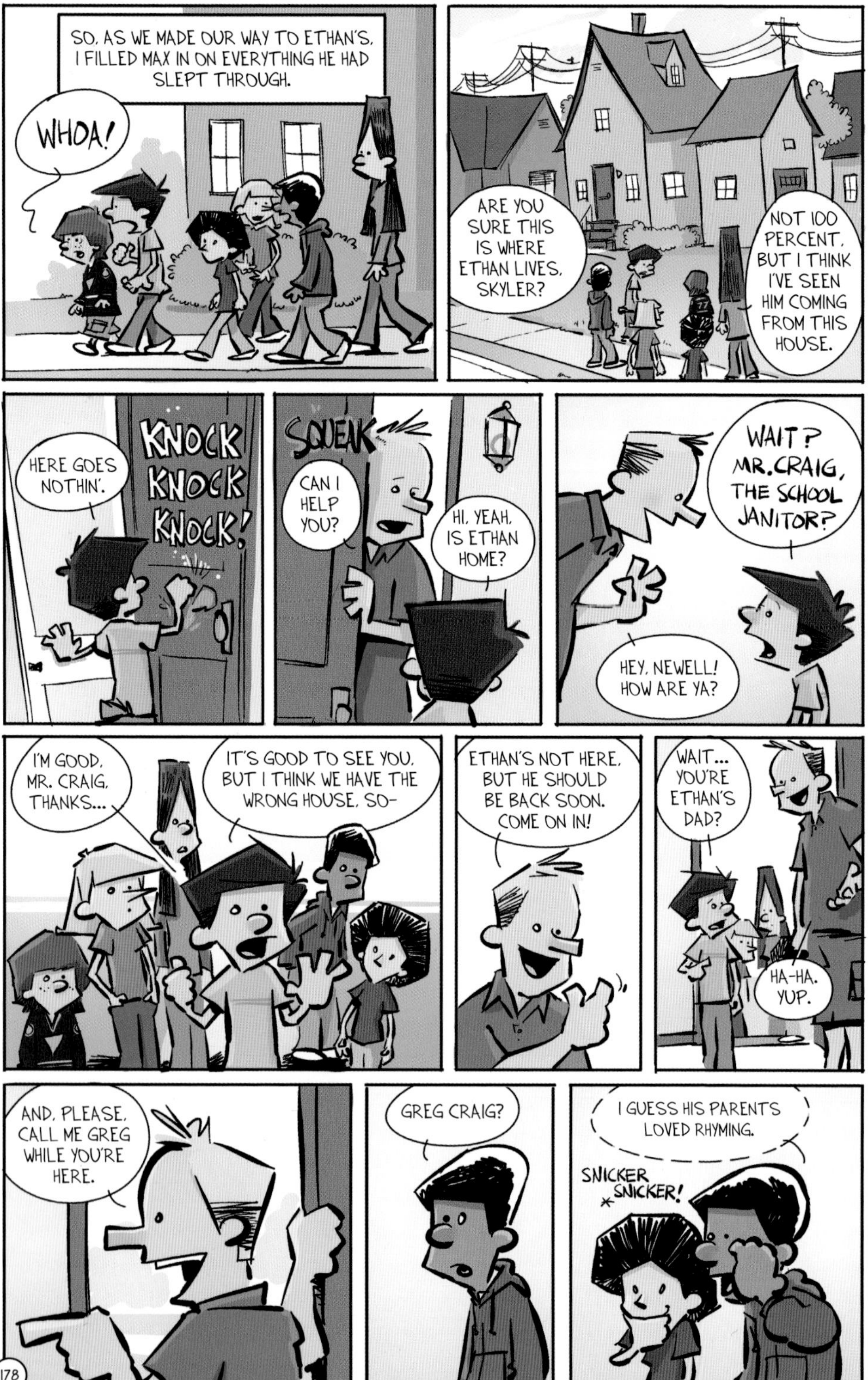
SO, AS WE MADE OUR WAY TO ETHAN'S, I FILLED MAX IN ON EVERYTHING HE HAD SLEPT THROUGH.
WHOA!
ARE YOU SURE THIS IS WHERE ETHAN LIVES, SKYLER?
NOT 100 PERCENT, BUT I THINK I'VE SEEN HIM COMING FROM THIS HOUSE.
HERE GOES NOTHIN'.
KNOCK KNOCK KNOCK!
SQUEAK
CAN I HELP YOU?
HI, YEAH, IS ETHAN HOME?
WAIT? MR. CRAIG, THE SCHOOL JANITOR?
HEY, NEWELL! HOW ARE YA?
I'M GOOD, MR. CRAIG, THANKS...
IT'S GOOD TO SEE YOU, BUT I THINK WE HAVE THE WRONG HOUSE, SO-
ETHAN'S NOT HERE, BUT HE SHOULD BE BACK SOON. COME ON IN!
WAIT... YOU'RE ETHAN'S DAD?
HA-HA. YUP.
AND, PLEASE, CALL ME GREG WHILE YOU'RE HERE.
GREG CRAIG?
I GUESS HIS PARENTS LOVED RHYMING.
SNICKER SNICKER!

179

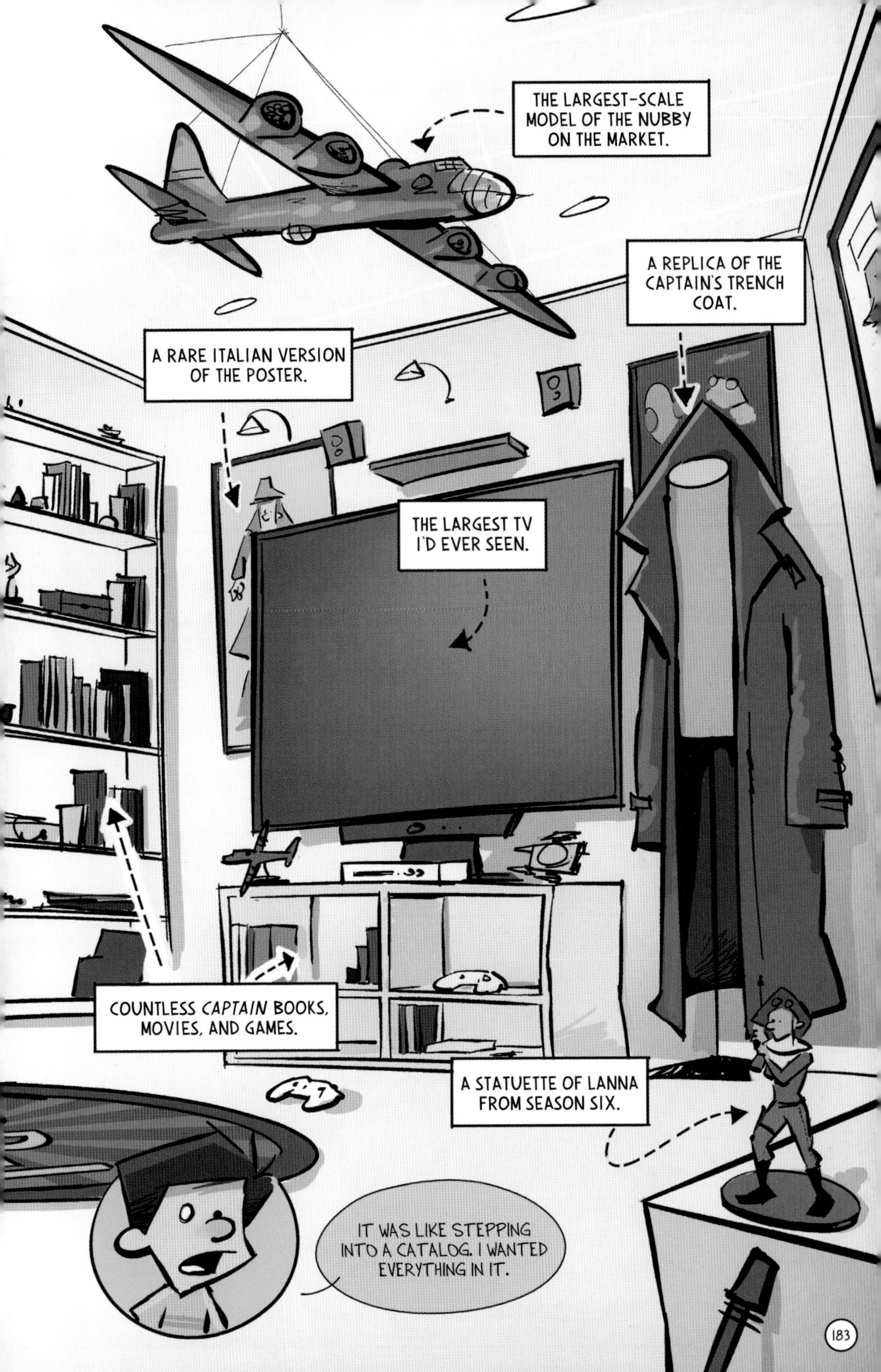
THE LARGEST-SCALE MODEL OF THE NUBBY ON THE MARKET.
A REPLICA OF THE CAPTAIN'S TRENCH COAT.
A RARE ITALIAN VERSION OF THE POSTER.
THE LARGEST TV I'D EVER SEEN.
COUNTLESS *CAPTAIN* BOOKS, MOVIES, AND GAMES.
A STATUETTE OF LANNA FROM SEASON SIX.
IT WAS LIKE STEPPING INTO A CATALOG. I WANTED EVERYTHING IN IT.

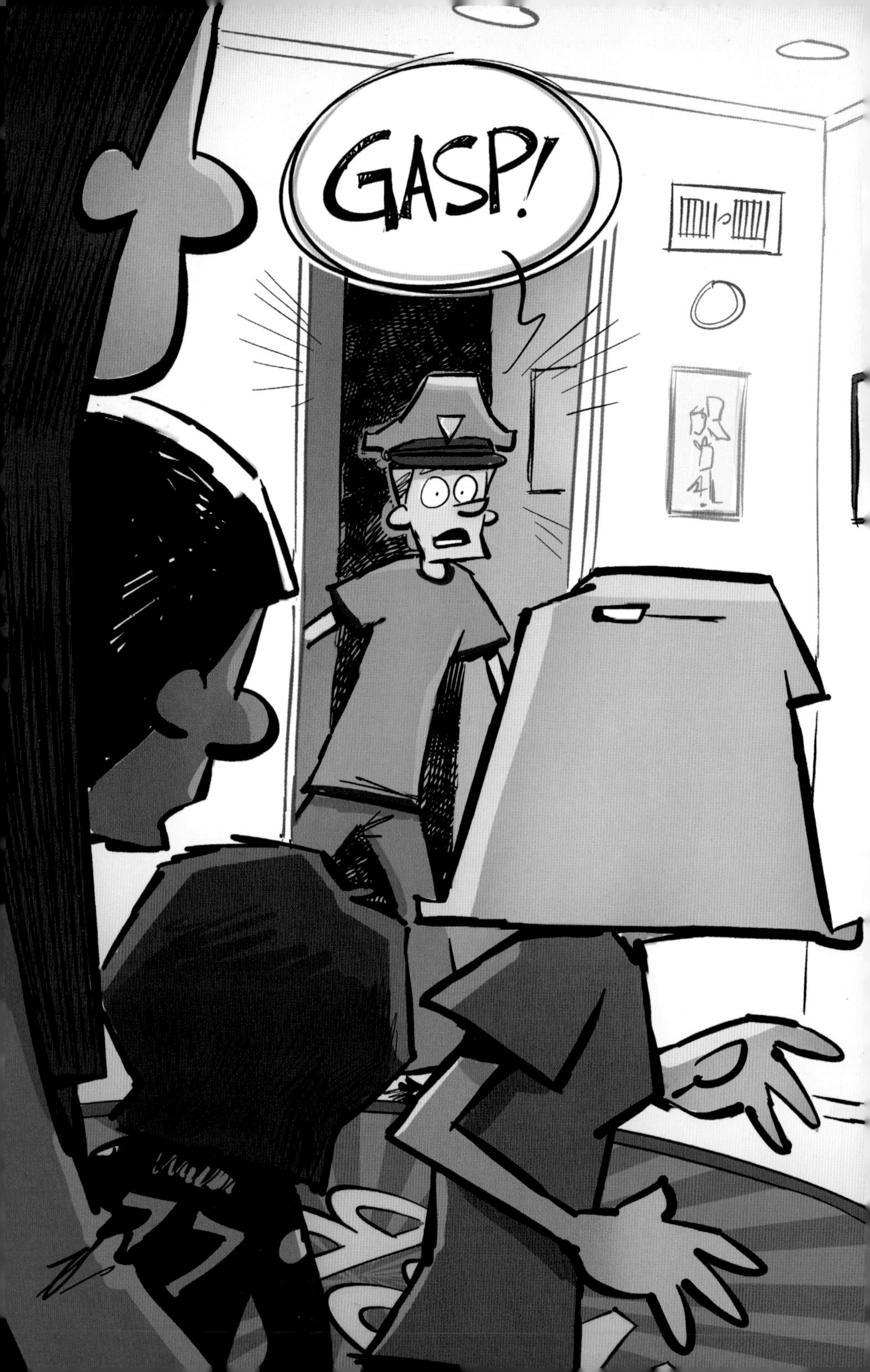
GASP!

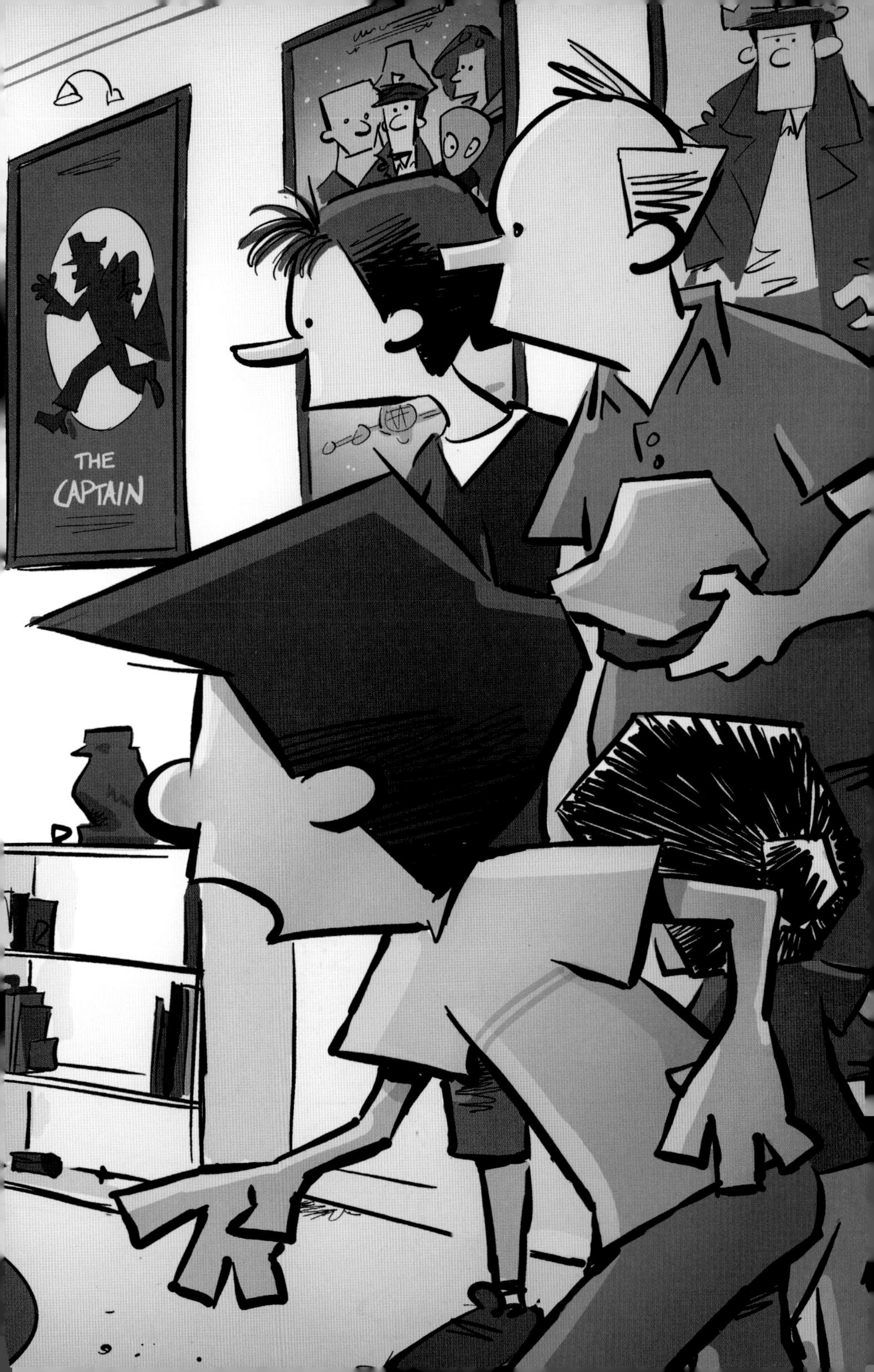
THE
CAPTAIN

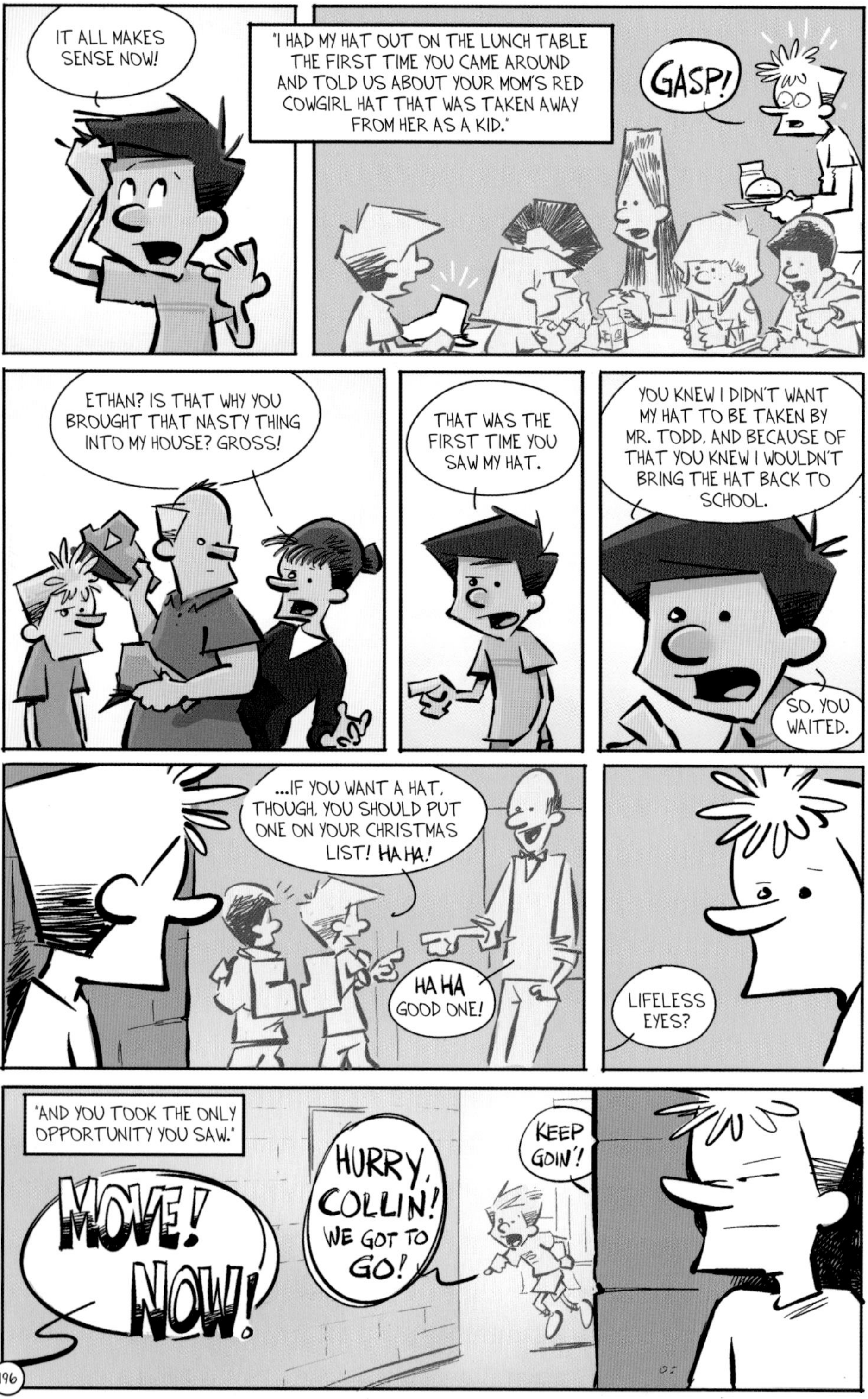

IT ALL MAKES SENSE NOW!
"I HAD MY HAT OUT ON THE LUNCH TABLE THE FIRST TIME YOU CAME AROUND AND TOLD US ABOUT YOUR MOM'S RED COWGIRL HAT THAT WAS TAKEN AWAY FROM HER AS A KID."
GASP!
ETHAN? IS THAT WHY YOU BROUGHT THAT NASTY THING INTO MY HOUSE? GROSS!
THAT WAS THE FIRST TIME YOU SAW MY HAT.
YOU KNEW I DIDN'T WANT MY HAT TO BE TAKEN BY MR. TODD, AND BECAUSE OF THAT YOU KNEW I WOULDN'T BRING THE HAT BACK TO SCHOOL.
SO, YOU WAITED.
...IF YOU WANT A HAT, THOUGH, YOU SHOULD PUT ONE ON YOUR CHRISTMAS LIST! HA HA!
HA HA GOOD ONE!
LIFELESS EYES?
"AND YOU TOOK THE ONLY OPPORTUNITY YOU SAW."
MOVE! NOW!
HURRY, COLLIN! WE GOT TO GO!
KEEP GOIN'!

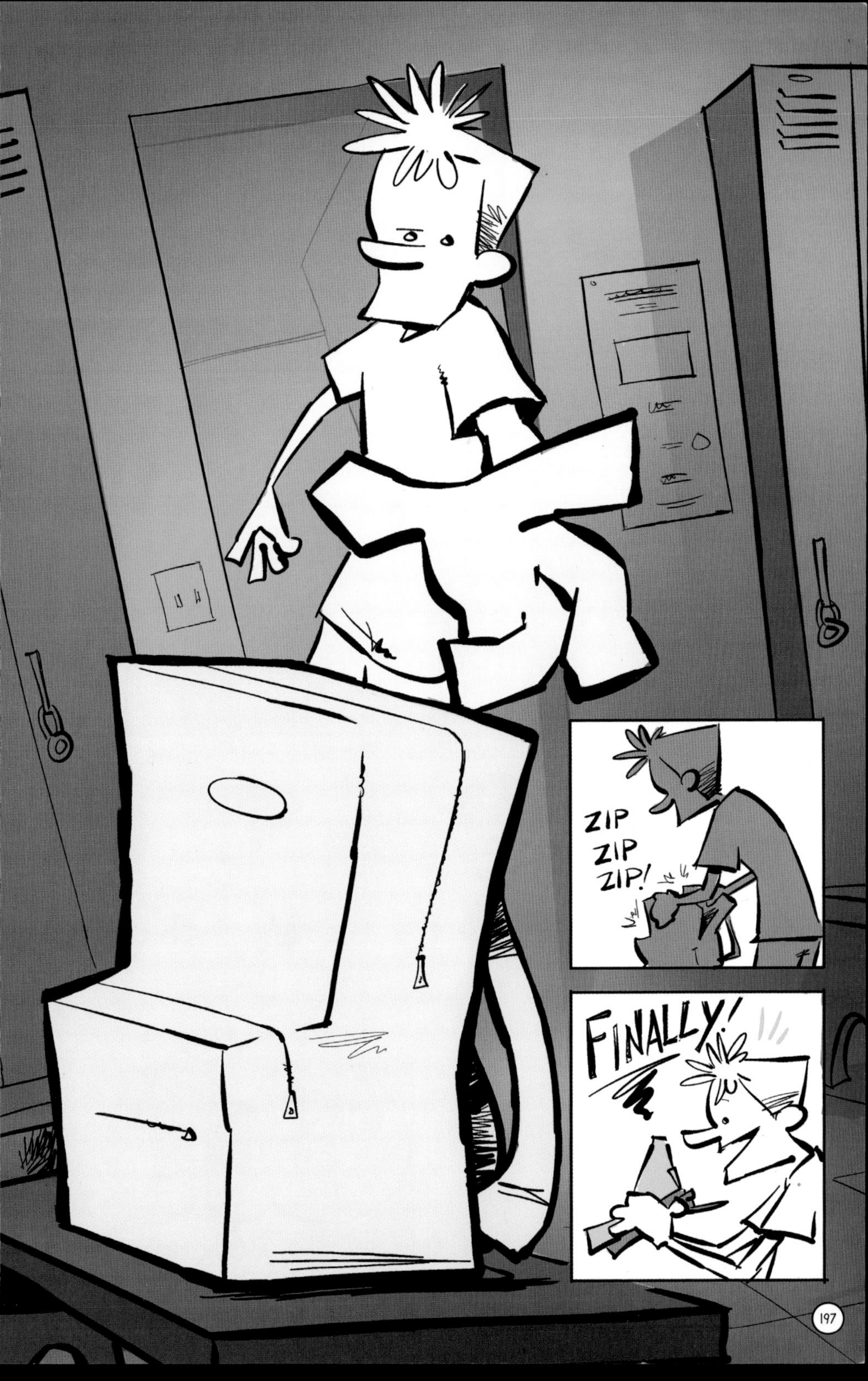
ZIP
ZIP
ZIP!
FINALLY!

199

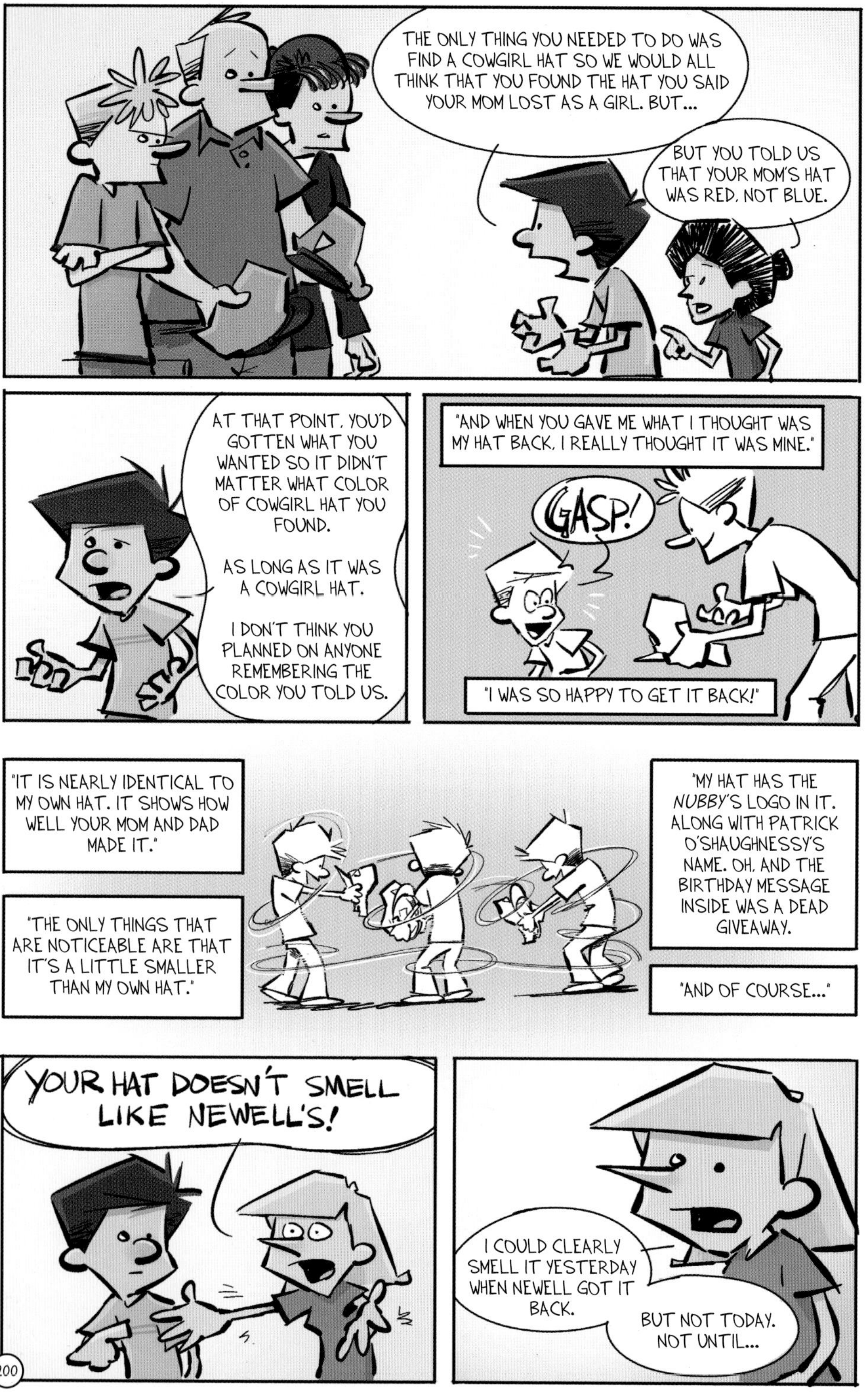
THE ONLY THING YOU NEEDED TO DO WAS FIND A COWGIRL HAT SO WE WOULD ALL THINK THAT YOU FOUND THE HAT YOU SAID YOUR MOM LOST AS A GIRL. BUT...
BUT YOU TOLD US THAT YOUR MOM'S HAT WAS RED, NOT BLUE.
AT THAT POINT, YOU'D GOTTEN WHAT YOU WANTED SO IT DIDN'T MATTER WHAT COLOR OF COWGIRL HAT YOU FOUND.
AS LONG AS IT WAS A COWGIRL HAT.
I DON'T THINK YOU PLANNED ON ANYONE REMEMBERING THE COLOR YOU TOLD US.
"AND WHEN YOU GAVE ME WHAT I THOUGHT WAS MY HAT BACK, I REALLY THOUGHT IT WAS MINE."
GASP!
"I WAS SO HAPPY TO GET IT BACK!"
"IT IS NEARLY IDENTICAL TO MY OWN HAT. IT SHOWS HOW WELL YOUR MOM AND DAD MADE IT."
"THE ONLY THINGS THAT ARE NOTICEABLE ARE THAT IT'S A LITTLE SMALLER THAN MY OWN HAT."
"MY HAT HAS THE *NUBBY*'S LOGO IN IT. ALONG WITH PATRICK O'SHAUGHNESSY'S NAME. OH, AND THE BIRTHDAY MESSAGE INSIDE WAS A DEAD GIVEAWAY.
"AND OF COURSE..."
YOUR HAT DOESN'T SMELL LIKE NEWELL'S!
I COULD CLEARLY SMELL IT YESTERDAY WHEN NEWELL GOT IT BACK.
BUT NOT TODAY. NOT UNTIL...

CHAPTER TEN
THE SHOWDOWN

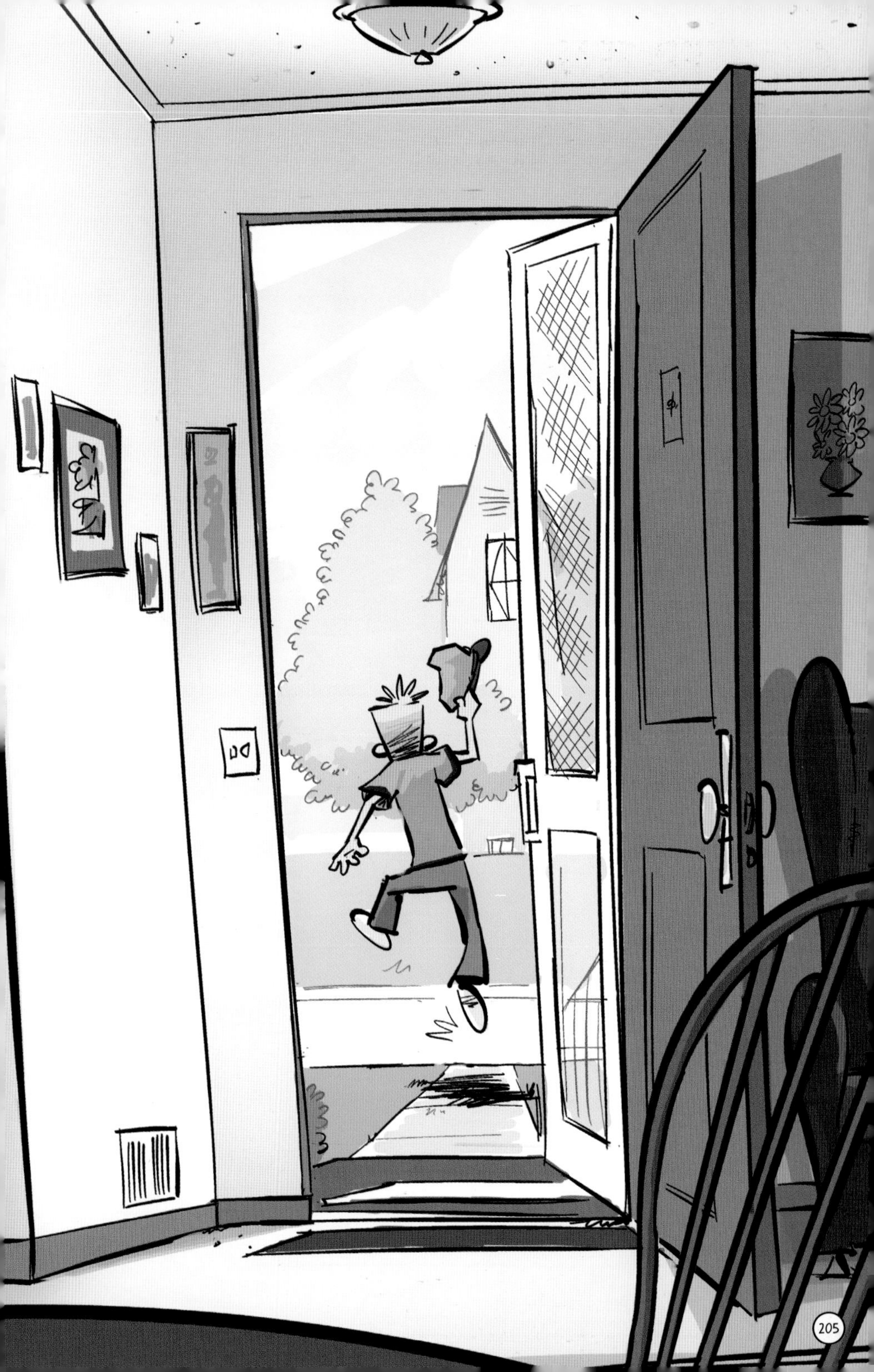

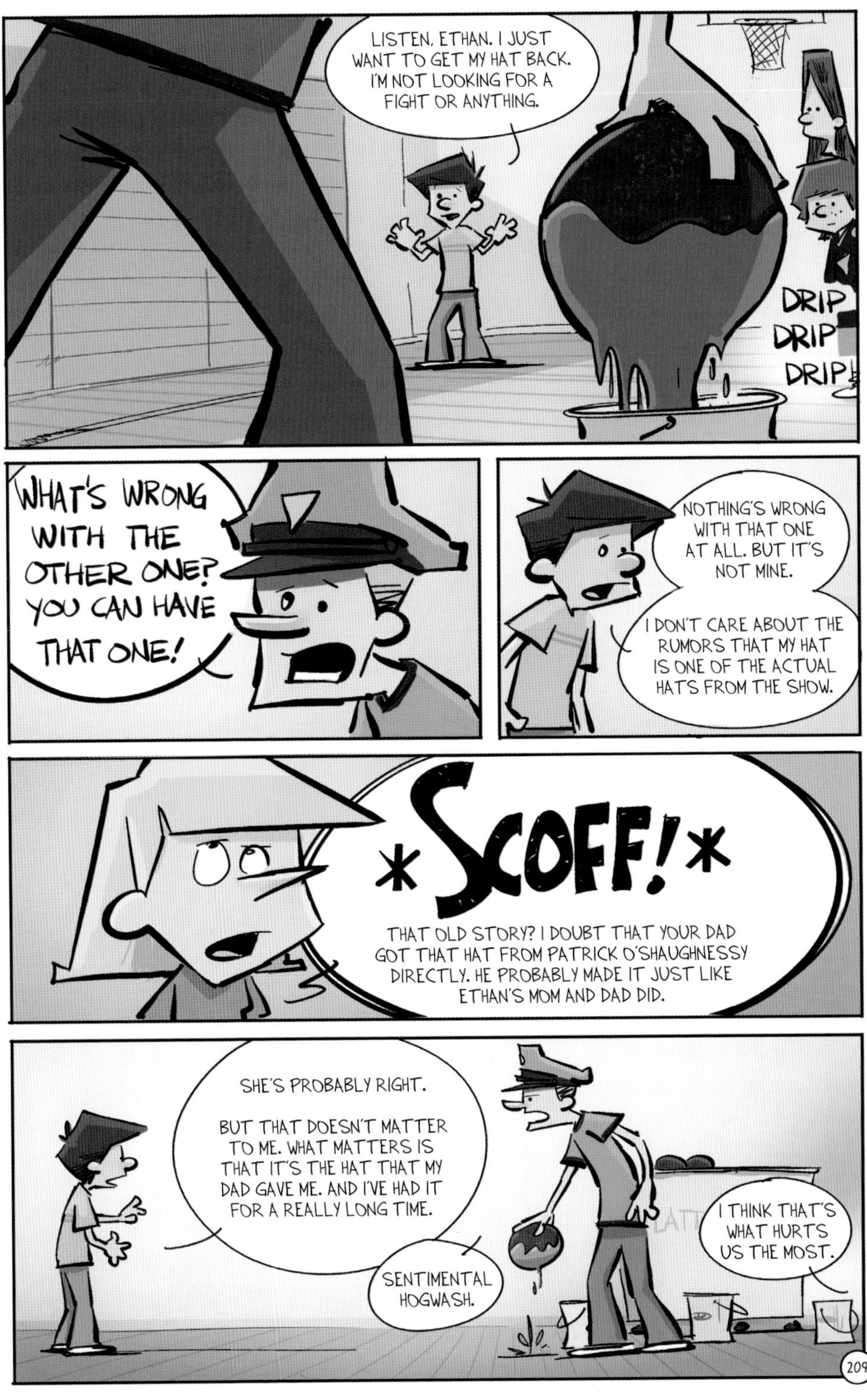

LISTEN, ETHAN. I JUST WANT TO GET MY HAT BACK. I'M NOT LOOKING FOR A FIGHT OR ANYTHING.
DRIP
DRIP
DRIP
WHAT'S WRONG WITH THE OTHER ONE? YOU CAN HAVE THAT ONE!
NOTHING'S WRONG WITH THAT ONE AT ALL. BUT IT'S NOT MINE.
I DON'T CARE ABOUT THE RUMORS THAT MY HAT IS ONE OF THE ACTUAL HATS FROM THE SHOW.
SCOFF!
THAT OLD STORY? I DOUBT THAT YOUR DAD GOT THAT HAT FROM PATRICK O'SHAUGHNESSY DIRECTLY. HE PROBABLY MADE IT JUST LIKE ETHAN'S MOM AND DAD DID.
SHE'S PROBABLY RIGHT.
BUT THAT DOESN'T MATTER TO ME. WHAT MATTERS IS THAT IT'S THE HAT THAT MY DAD GAVE ME. AND I'VE HAD IT FOR A REALLY LONG TIME.
SENTIMENTAL HOGWASH.
I THINK THAT'S WHAT HURTS US THE MOST.

221

ACKNOWLEDGMENTS

* * *

THANK YOU TO EVERYONE AT LITTLE, BROWN BOOKS FOR
YOUNG READERS WHO HELPED BRING THIS BOOK TO LIFE.
SPECIAL SHOUT-OUTS TO MY WONDERFUL EDITOR,
RACHEL POLOSKI; DESIGNER CHRISTINA QUINTERO (WHO
PATIENTLY WORKED WITH ALL THE PAGES I SENT ALONG);
AND DEIRDRE JONES. I COULDN'T HAVE DONE IT
WITHOUT YOU. YOU GUYS ROCK.

TO BOTH TIM TRAVAGLINI AND SAMANTHA HAYWOOD:
THANK YOU FOR ALL THE GUIDANCE YOU GAVE ME AT THE
BEGINNING OF THIS ADVENTURE.

AND TO BOTH J&J AND RUSS BUSSE, WHO ORIGINALLY
HELPED BRING MY FUNNY MISADVENTURES TO LIFE,
THANK YOU.

AND, OF COURSE, TO THE MAIN THREE. NO MISADVENTURE
IS WORTH HAVING IF YOU DON'T HAVE ANYONE TO SHARE IT
WITH. AND I GET TO SHARE MINE WITH THE BEST.
TO MY SON, WYETH; MY WIFE, ERIN; AND MY MOM, KATHY.
YOUR ENCOURAGEMENT HAS MEANT THE WORLD TO ME, AND
YOU HAVE MADE MY OWN MISADVENTURES ALL THE BETTER.
HOW ABOUT WE GO AND HAVE SOME MORE?!

JASON